VEILS
OF *Time*

VEILS OF Time

Lynn Kurland
Maggie Shayne
Angie Ray
Ingrid Weaver

BERKLEY BOOKS, NEW YORK

This is a work of fiction. Names, characters, places, and incidents are
either the product of the author's imagination or are used fictitiously,
and any resemblance to actual persons, living or dead, business
establishments, events, or locales is entirely coincidental.

VEILS OF TIME

A Berkley Book / published by arrangement with
the authors

PRINTING HISTORY
Berkley edition / July 1999

The Penguin Putnam Inc. World Wide Web site address is
http://www.penguinputnam.com

ISBN: 0-425-16970-7

BERKLEY®
Berkley Books are published by The Berkley Publishing Group,
a division of Penguin Putnam Inc.,
375 Hudson Street, New York, New York 10014.
BERKLEY and the "B" design
are trademarks belonging to Penguin Putnam Inc.

PRINTED IN THE UNITED STATES OF AMERICA

10 9 8 7 6 5

VEILS
OF *Time*

AND THE
GROOM WORE TULLE

Lynn Kurland

PROLOGUE

Scotland, 1313

Ian MacLeod lay in the Fergusson's dungeon and, not having much else to do, contemplated life's many mysteries.

How was it that the Fergusson could be so hopelessly inept at growing grain or raising aught but stringy cattle, yet have the knack of producing such a fine, healthy crop of rats? Ian would have been annoyed by this if he'd had the energy—especially given the fact that one of the rats was currently making a nest in his hair while the rodent's fellows sat in a half-circle around Ian, apparently waiting for the nest maker to finish and invite them to have a closer look at his building skills—but Ian didn't have the energy to even shake off the offender, much less muster up a good frothy head of irritation.

Secondly, he gave thought to the location of his sorry self. It wasn't often that a MacLeod found himself in a Fergusson hall, much less in his pit.

It wasn't as though his kinsmen hadn't made attempts to liberate him from their bitterest enemy's dungeon. They had and he had appreciated their efforts, even though they'd been to no avail. He would have liked to have forgotten about the entire affair, and the accompanying indignity of it, but he was, after all, the one sitting amongst the vermin, so thinking on it was almost unavoidable.

And then lastly, and by no means the least of any of the things clamoring for his attention, he thought he just might be dying.

That, however, was the only good thing to come of the past two months.

Ian settled back against the wall—or pretended to, as there wasn't much movement in his once finely fashioned form anymore—and gave thought to the whole business of dying. It was actually the only thought that had cheered him in days. His time in 1313 was obviously over and no one would miss him if he perhaps managed to elude death's sharp sickle and sneak off to the forest near the MacLeod keep. And if by some miracle he reached that forest and happened to find the exact spot that would carry a man hundreds of years into the Future, well, who would begrudge him that? What would one fine, manly addition to the Future hurt? It was either escape to there or toast his backside against the fires of Hell.

Unfortunately, Ian had no illusions about his sins. He'd spent too much time at the ale kegs, wenched more than any man should have without acquiring scores of bastards, killed with too much heat in his blood, and—surely the most grievous of all—wooed Roberta Fergusson to his bed and cheerfully robbed her of her virginity.

It was the last, of course, which had earned him a place in Roberta's father's dungeon.

It wouldn't have mattered so much had Roberta possessed any redeeming qualities besides her virginity. More was the pity for Ian that she sported a visage uglier than a pig's arse and the temper of an angry sow. Her guaranteed virtue had been her only desirable trait and she possessed that no longer.

Ian suspected that her new unmaidenly condition didn't trouble her overmuch. After all, he had taken great care with her and spared no effort to make the night memorable for her. 'Twas rumored, however, that her father had been less than enthusiastic upon learning of the evening's events. Ian had known there would be retribution. He also knew that 'twas almost a certainty that the Fergusson was in league with the Devil, which left him wondering what conversations the two had already had about him.

Best not to think on that overmuch.

He turned his mind quickly from the contemplation of Hell and settled back instead for speculation about where he would have gone had he had the choice.

The Future. Even the very word caused his pulse to quicken. He knew as much about the distant future as a man in Robert the Bruce's day should—likely more. He'd had a young kinsman travel to the Future and return briefly to tell of its wonders. And then another miracle had occurred and a traveler from the Future had arrived at the MacLeod keep. She had married the laird Jamie and carried him home to 1996 with her. Ian had grieved for Jamie's loss, for he was Ian's closest friend and most trusted ally, but he'd been afire with the idea that one day he too might travel to a time when men flew through the skies like birds and traveled great distances in carts without horses. At the time Jamie had forbidden him to come along with him to that unfathomable point so far ahead, telling Ian that his time in the fourteenth century would not be over unless he escaped certain death.

Ian was certainly facing death now.

Ach, but if that wasn't enough to make Ian ache for the chance to walk in the MacLeod forest, he didn't know what was. Ian dreamed of how it might have been had he managed to gain the future. He would have been dressed in his finest plaid, with his freshly sharpened sword at his side and a cap tilted jauntily atop his head. Future women would have swooned at the very sight of him and Future men would have envied him his fine form and ability to ingest vast quantities of ale yet still outsmart his shrewdest enemies—and all this, mind you, before even breaking his fast in the morn.

He would have searched for his kin soon after his arrival. Jamie would have been pleased to see him, and Ian would have been pleased to see Jamie. First he would have hugged Jamie fiercely, then planted his fist in Jamie's nose—repeatedly.

Jamie being, of course, the reason Ian found himself wallowing in the slime.

Ian found the energy to scowl. If he and Jamie just hadn't been in that one tiny skirmish together, Ian might have avoided having a rat fashioning a home upon his head. Jamie had caught William Fergusson's son scampering off to safety, boxed the lad's ears in annoyance, then filled them full of a message for the boy to take to his father. Of course, Jamie had informed the lad in the most impressive of details just how thoroughly Ian had bedded Roberta, then wished the family good fortune in finding a mate for her.

Ian's fate had been sealed.

Ian tried to shake the rat off the top of his head, but found that all he could do was sit in the muck and give a grim thought or two as to whether or not he should be repenting while he still could. Perhaps Saint Peter would have pity on him and let him squeak through the gates. Ian spared a thought as to whether those heavenly gates swung inward or outward, and the means of defending them if it were the latter, then he found that even that was too taxing a thought to ponder.

Death was very near.

Ian mustered up the energy to give one last fleeting thought to the Future. Perhaps if he vowed to leave off his wenching ways and settle down with one woman.

Aye, that he could surely do to earn himself a place in heaven. . . .

Suddenly a piercing light descended and blinded him. He closed his eyes against it, fearing the worst. Apparently not even his last-minute bargain was enough to save him. From behind his eyelids he could see that the light flickered wildly.

Damn. Hellfire, obviously.

Ian sighed in resignation and took one last deep breath.

And then he knew no more.

"Did ye get him?"

"Aye."

"Sword too?" the first asked.

"Aye," the second said, hefting his burden over his shoulder with one hand and holding onto the blade with the other. "Ye can see I've both."

"Is he dead, do ye think?"

"Dunno." The second would have taken a closer look, but his burden was heavier than he should have been after all that time in the pit. "Looks dead to me."

"Well, then," the first said, apparently satisfied, "take him and heave him onto MacLeod soil. Sword too. The laird wants it so."

The second didn't need to hear that more than once. Best to do what the laird asked. He had no desire to see the bottom of the Fergusson's pit up close. The riding would take all night, but 'twas best seen to quickly. He would return home just as quickly, for he had no desire to be nearby when the clan MacLeod discovered their dead kinsman.

"Was that a moan?" the first asked suspiciously.

"Didn't hear it," the second said, walking away. Dead, alive, he couldn't have cared less in what condition his burden found himself. He'd do the heaving of the man, then be on his way. If the MacLeod fool wasn't dead now, he would be in a matter of hours.

"Leave the sword near the body!" the first called.

"Aye," the second grumbled, tempted to filch it. But it was a MacLeod blade and he was a superstitious soul, so he turned away from thoughts of robbery and concentrated on the task before him. He'd return for his payment, then find a dry place to lay his head, hopefully with his belly full of decent fare and his arms wrapped around a fine wench. He'd do it in honor of the almost-dead man he prepared to strap to the back of his horse. The man might have been a MacLeod, but he was a Highlander after all, and deserved some kind of proper farewell.

The second man set off, his mind already on his supper.

1

Jane Fergusson sat with her chin on her fists, stared at the surroundings of her minuscule cubby at Miss Petronia Witherspoon's Elegant Eighteenth Century Wedding Fashions, and contemplated the ironies of life. There were a lot of them and her contemplating was taking up a lot of time. But that wasn't much of a problem, mainly because she had a long weekend stretching out in front of her and no beach house to retreat to. No, what she had was herself trapped in Miss Witherspoon's shop with only her imagination to keep her company.

What a waste that was. There she was in New York, city of designers, and she had the talent and ambition to design ultra funky clothes in a rainbow of colors. She had her health. She had pantyhose in her drawer without any nail polish stemming the tide of runaway runs. She even had an apartment she could afford. Surely with all those things in her favor, she should have been working at a fashionable house designing incredible things for only the long-legged and impossibly thin to wear.

But where did she find herself?

Trying to keep her head above the water line while drowning in vats of faux pearls and more lace than a Brussels seamstress could shake a seam ripper at—all for use in the design and construction of wedding gowns.

The problem was, Jane didn't particularly like bridal gowns.

In fact, Jane wasn't even sure she liked brides.

She sighed, closed her eyes, and let her mind drift back to how it had been in the beginning. She had come to New York with her head full of bold, energetic designs and her suitcase full of funky, short things in black. She'd heard that the truly chic of New York dressed all in black and she had cheerfully pitched every colored item she owned on the off chance that the rumor was true.

She had hoped for a place with someone big, really big; someone who was so ultrahip that even her stuff would look a little frumpy by comparison.

It was then that her course had taken a marked quirk to the left.

She'd been pawing through an upscale antique store's selection of vintage fashions, on the lookout for the elusive and the unusual and muttering to herself about how she would have designed the gowns differently, when she'd felt the imperious tap of a bony finger on her shoulder.

"Are you a seamstress, dear?"

The term alone should have sent up a red flag, but Jane had been so thrilled that someone might think her something akin to a designer that she'd bobbed her head obediently and waited breathlessly for some other gem of recognition. And when she'd been offered a place at Miss Witherspoon's salon, she'd leaped at the chance.

Little had she known that she would wind up designing wedding gowns for a woman who made *Oliver Twist*'s Fagan look like a philanthropist. And not only was she designing all those eighteenth-century wedding gowns, she was watching Miss Witherspoon's niece take credit for it. It was pitiful.

Jane planned to leave. She'd been planning to leave for almost three years, but what with one thing and another—mostly rent and food—she found herself staying. After all, she was actually doing a great deal of designing, and that wasn't something she could turn her back on lightly.

So she invested a lot of time trying to ignore the fact that she was basically an indentured servant. That invariably lead to questions about where her Prince Charming was hiding his white horse. Surely there was someone out there who would rescue her from the acres of tulle she'd gotten herself lost in.

She sighed and turned her mind away from the rainbow of colors she could be working with to more productive thoughts—such as if hari-kari were possible with dressmaker's pins. Before she could do any experimenting, the phone rang, making her jump. She was, of course, the only one left at the shop, having been assigned the task of closing up for the three-day weekend. She picked up the phone.

"Hello?"

"Jane, dear," Miss Witherspoon said, sounding rushed, "just a few last-minute things before we visit yet another royal residence. So many beautiful gowns preserved for the discriminating eye, you know. Remember that we'll be hopping back over the Pond on Tuesday."

Yeah, on the Concorde, Jane thought with a scowl.

"Europe has given Alexis such glorious design inspiration . . ."

Not even Europe will improve her stick figures, Jane thought with a grumble.

". . . Christy and Naomi will be in early next week, so you'll want to be sure to remain behind the scenes.

Alexis will do the showing of the gowns, of course, for we all know she has the beauty to compliment them while you do not!''

Jane had no reply for that, so she merely rested her chin on her fist and thought Gloomy Thoughts about her less-than-arresting face.

''Oh, and one last thing, dear. I want you to check in the workroom immediately. There was a rat heard frolicking about there this afternoon.''

Rats. What else? Jane put the receiver back in its cradle, her head down on her desk, and sighed. Miss Witherspoon never would have asked Alexis to check out a rat rumor. Alexis wouldn't have been any good at rat patrol anyway. Alexis was from California. If they had rats, which Jane doubted they did in Alexis's neck of the woods, they were no doubt tanned, relaxed, and unaggressive. Alexis was not up to the New York rat, a hearty, belligerent beast. Jane, however, was unafraid.

At least that's what she told herself as she picked up a yardstick and headed for the back room.

She opened the door, flicked on the light, and spared a brief moment to look at her creations hanging so perfectly on the long racks against the wall. Every pearl in place, every tuck just so, every drop of lace dripping as if it had been poured that way. Jane had to admit that even though she wasn't all that fond of bridal wear, the gowns were beautiful. She had taken the styles of the period and put as much of her personal stamp on them as she could get away with. It wasn't much more than an unexpected tuck here or an unusual bit of lace there, but at least it was something.

It was then that she was distracted by the sound of crunching.

She glanced down and saw a trail of junk food wrappers leading over to the corner.

And she muffled a squeak of fright.

Well, it was obvious that the rat wasn't dining on

satin, so what was the use of chasing him out right then? Jane let the benevolence of the moment wash over her as she quickly retreated from the room. She left the light on and shut the door. Maybe the light would convince the rat that he'd wandered into the wrong place and he would abandon his designs on the workroom.

That sounded much better than trying to convince him to leave by means of a flimsy stick.

She quickly packed up her bag, put on her sneakers with the rainbow shoelaces—not chic maybe, but definitely colorful—and hurried out into the Manhattan evening. The colors and smells of the twentieth century assaulted her, assuring her that she wasn't trapped in a Victorian sweatshop. She took a deep breath, slung her bag over her shoulder, and set off down the street to her sublet, thoughts of rats temporarily forgotten.

By the time she reached her building, she was sweating and cross. She trudged up three flights of stairs, stood outside her door until her breath caught back up with her, then shoved her key into the lock and welcomed herself home to her glorified attic apartment. She turned on the lights, then closed the door behind her and leaned back against it, letting her bag slide to the floor. A quick survey of her surroundings told her she was indeed in the black-and-white space she had created for herself upon her arrival in New York. She had been convinced a monochromatic scheme was perfectly in keeping with her chic, designer self and would do nothing but enhance her creativity.

Lately she had begun to have her doubts that this was good for her state of mind.

She pushed away from the door with a sigh and headed toward her bedroom to exchange her requisite working uniform of anything black—heaven forbid we should compete with the brides, dear!—to something at least in a comforting sweatsuity shade of gray. She usually found her bedroom, with all the purity of its white contents, soothing. Today it just felt sterile.

Jane quickly took stock of what she'd consumed that day, decided that the M&M's had pushed her over the edge, and vowed with a solemn crossing of her heart to stay away from the vending machine at some point in the very near future. Perhaps before she turned forty, in another decade or so.

There was one deviation from her color scheme and that was the hope chest her parents had insisted she take with her. It was a beautiful, rich cherry and it sat under her tiny window and beckoned to her with all the subtlety of a lighthouse beam at close range. Jane knew what was in the trunk.

She was tempted.

But she also knew where looking would lead, so she turned sharply away and rummaged in her dresser for something appropriate for her *aprez* work Friday night activity of watching an old movie.

Once she'd shed her Witherspoon image for something more comfortable, she made herself a snack and settled down with the remote. She couldn't afford cable, but the public broadcasting system always had something useful on Friday nights.

"Great," she groused, tuning in and getting ready to tune out. "Sheep."

Ah, but it was sheep in Scotland and that was enough to keep her thumb off the remote. Scotland and all those sheep who worked so hard to donate all that wool. Jane's fingers itched at the very thought of it. Truth be told—and it was something she didn't tell anyone at work lest it ruin her image as a user of already woven goods only—put a pair of knitting needles in her hands and she could work miracles.

And yarn came in such a rainbow of colors.

She watched until she knew more than she wanted to about sheep and their habits, then she turned off the TV and crawled into bed.

And she dreamed of Scottish sheep.

2

And back in the workroom . . .

Ian lifted his sword and plucked from the end another of the bags of food he had gathered. He broke open the outer coating and reached inside for some of the crunchy inner meat. While he ate, he looked at the words engraved upon the outside of the pouch. Cheetos. He nibbled, then looked with concern at the orange residue left upon his fingers. It only added to the acute alarm he felt. He continued to chew, certain he would need whatever nourishment he could have, and contemplated the direness of his situation. He was dead, obviously, for he was surely no longer in the Fergusson's pit. It concerned him, however, how much his mortal frame still pained him. He'd been certain he would have shed his body on his trip to the afterlife. But possess it he still did, and an uncomfortable thing it was indeed.

He looked about him. He was in a chamber full of white gowns. He hadn't seen them at first, as he had woken to complete darkness. Then a faint light had forced its way through a window, leaving him with the knowledge that he was no longer in the Fergusson's keep. He'd heaved himself to his feet in a desperate search for food and water.

It was then he'd espied the little box full of pouches. Drink he'd found there too, in little boxes and tasting of strange and exotic flavors. The drink he had enjoyed. The food, less so.

He'd staggered back to his corner and settled down for a rest when a light so bright it burned his eyes blazed to life before him. He'd been so stunned, he hadn't moved at first.

Heaven? he had wondered. Or perhaps a chamber assigned to those who awaited their journey to Hell. He couldn't be certain, but he strongly suspected that he had somehow, while being out of his head with weariness, escaped the Fergusson's guards and landed himself in a chamber containing gowns for future angels. There were, after all, all those garments in white to consider. And those little black machines on the tables. Ian hadn't dared touch them, but he'd read the words inscribed on them easily enough. Singer. If that didn't cause a body to think of singing angels, he surely didn't know what would.

But there had been no angels roaming about fingering the gowns so Ian had been left to ponder other alternatives. He'd eventually come to the conclusion that he wasn't in either Heaven or Hell, he was in Limbo, that horrible place between the two. The food alone should have told him as much. He looked about him at the remains of what he'd consumed. Cheetos, Milky Way, Life Savers—and aye, he could have used those in truth—all in colors he hardly recognized and tastes he'd never before set his tongue to. All in all, he couldn't help but wish heartily that he were back in Scotland braving the fare at his clan's table.

Then another more disturbing thought occurred to him. Perhaps the powers that were deciding his fate were still struggling to make up their minds about him.

He looked about him and frowned at the leavings scattered here and there. He'd had to remove the slippery outer coatings of the food—once he'd discovered those outer shells weren't fit to eat, that is. Perhaps 'twould make a better impression on Saint Peter's gate guards if Ian tidied up his surroundings. He struggled to his feet, using his sword to help him get there, then merely leaned upon his sword and caught his breath. Never mind where he was; what he needed was a decent meal and a fortnight's rest to recover from his stay in the Fergusson's keep.

Ian started to bend down to see to his clutter when a door at the far end of the chamber opened. He froze, afeared to draw attention to himself when he was looking less than his best.

A demon walked in. It could be nothing else. It was dressed all in black, its hair pulled up and pinned to its head with half a dozen sticks of wood. Ian spared a thought about what kind of pain that must have caused the beastie, then realized that it likely felt no pain. Dwelling in such a place as this would surely numb the senses.

The creature looked over the angels' gowns, thumbing through them with the air of one familiar with such things. The gowns hung on shiny poles in a most magical manner and Ian spared a bit of appreciation for such a finely wrought manner of hanging the clothing. Perhaps Limbo was a more advanced place than he'd thought at first.

The demon finished with its work, then turned his way. He watched its eyes roam over the chamber, then watched those eyes widen. The she-beastie, and he could now divine that it was a she and not a he, opened its mouth to speak—but no sound issued forth. Ian took the opportunity to assess his opponent before she spewed forth things he likely wouldn't care to hear.

Her face was unremarkable, but fair enough, though

Ian wasn't of a mind to examine her too closely. She was passing skinny. Perhaps she was only allowed to make a meal of her victims on an occasional basis. Ian was almost curious enough to ask her, but he was interrupted by the low whine that suddenly came from her. It started out softly enough, then increased in volume until it became a most ear-splitting shriek. Ian threw his Cheeto-encrusted fingers up over his ears until the beastie's mouth closed. Then he hesitantly took his hands down. The beastie blinked, shook her head, then blinked again.

"Only in New York," she said in a particularly garbled tone. "This could only happen in New York."

She repeated that as she turned and left the chamber by the door Ian hadn't dared open before.

New York? Was that what they called the place, then? Ian reached up to scratch his chin over that piece of news, then realized how unkempt he must have appeared to her. Then a more disturbing thought occurred to him. What if she had gone to tell the Deciders of His Fate about his less-than-pleasing appearance? By the saints, with the way he looked at present, the very last place they would think to send him was up the path to the Pearly Gates.

He looked about him frantically for aid. He had been strengthened somewhat by the ghoulish fare and felt certain that he had the vigor to make himself more presentable. Perhaps if he looked the part of an angel, they might mistake him for one and send him along on his way.

'Twas nothing short of a miracle what he was surrounded by.

Angel gowns.

He set his sword aside, peeled off his plaid and shirt, and set to work looking for something in his size.

•   •   •

Jane walked into her office, very proud of herself that she was still breathing normally. It wasn't every day that a woman saw a filthy, sword-bearing, bekilted man six inches taller than she loitering in her workroom. Her hand was very steady as she reached for the phone and dialed 91—

Her finger hovered over the last number. What was she going to tell the cops anyway—*hey, there's a grubby guy standing in the middle of junk food wrappers in the room down the hall?* For all she knew, they would come get *her* and haul her away. She slowly set down the receiver and took stock of the situation.

It was the Saturday before Memorial Day and given the fact that Miss Witherspoon had given the entire staff the long holiday off—except Jane, of course—it was a safe bet that she would be the only one in the salon until Tuesday.

Alone with a crusted-over Swamp Thing.

Jane looked around her for a weapon. Damn, nothing but a handful of dressmaker's pins—and she had already determined their lack of usefulness in inflicting fatal wounds. It looked as if her only option was to beat a hasty retreat and face the remains of the mess on Tuesday with everyone else.

Her hand hadn't gone halfway to her bag before she realized that wasn't an option either. The best gowns in that workroom were one-of-a-kind creations that she had put together herself. She had spent hours rummaging through estate sales, garage sales, and dusty antique shops to find the unique bits and pieces that went into making her additions to the salon truly special. Could she really allow those creations to be ruined because she'd been too cowardly to face the man nesting in the workroom? Besides, he really hadn't looked too steady on his feet. Maybe he needed help.

She squelched the Florence Nightingale thoughts before they could bedazzle her common sense, then gath-

ered up what she hoped was defense enough: a Bic pen
and a pair of very long, very sharp dressmaker shears.

"Here goes nothing," she muttered as she left her
office and tiptoed down the hallway to the workroom.

She stopped outside the door and put her ear to it.
Damned old metal things. Where was a good old-
fashioned hollow core wooden door when a girl needed
one? With one last deep breath, she flung open the door
and stepped inside.

Swamp Thing squeaked in surprise and spun around
to face her, his skirts rustling loudly in the sudden silence. Jane would have squeaked as well but she was
too dumbfounded by what she was seeing.

He was wearing the most modern of their gowns, a
nineteenth-century Southern Belle special. It was an off-
the-shoulder number with dozens of hand-placed pearls
and enough lace encrusting the bodice to turn the upper
half of the dress into the stiffest noncorseted creation
ever worn by anyone who'd ever said "y'all."

Well, at least he wasn't toting the matching parasol.

Jane felt her mouth working, but she found that all
sound refused to come out. There was a man in her
workroom wearing a bridal gown. It was too small by
several sizes, the hem hitting him midcalf. His relatively
hairy arms poked out at an awkward angle through the
sleeve holes and the neckline barely reached midster-
num. Jane decided right then that men with any amount
of body hair at all were not meant for shoulderless,
sleeveless bridal fashions.

And then Swamp Thing spoke.

"Would ye perrrchance be one of Saint Peterrr's ilk,"
he began, sounding rather nervous, "or are ye belonging
to the . . . errrr . . . Deevil's minions?"

His r's rolled so long and so hard, they almost
knocked her down. It occurred to her that he was a Scot,
which explained what had looked like a kilt before, but

it didn't explain what he was doing in Miss Witherspoon's shop.

And then it sunk in what he had asked her.

"Huh?" she said, blinking at him.

He took a deep breath. Then he put his shoulders
back—no mean feat given his attire. "Be ye angel," he
asked, "or demon?"

She was sure she'd heard him wrong. "Angel or demon?"

"Aye."

"Well," she said, wondering what planet he'd just
dropped down from, or, more to the point, what asylum
he'd escaped from, "neither, actually."

"Neitherrrr," he echoed.

That Scottish burr almost brought her to her knees.
Jane put her hand to her head to check for undue warmth
there. There was a lunatic standing ten feet away from
her and she was getting giddy over his accent.

He gave his bodice a hike up and scratched his matted
beard. "Limbo, then," he said with a sigh. "And here
I am, having taken such pains to look my best."

"Look your best," she said, watching him lean wearily against one of the worktables. "Is that why you put
on one of the dresses?" *Wacko,* she decided immediately. And one for the books.

He nodded, then explained, his r's rolling and all his
other vowels and consonants tumbling and lilting like
water rushing over rocks in a stream. Jane was so mesmerized by the sound of his speech, she hardly paid
attention to what he was saying.

'So, I was thinking that if you were indeed someone
keeping watch for Saint Peter that perhaps I'd make a
better impression if I wore something that would make
me seem more angelic"—and here he flashed her a
smile that just about finished off what his r's had done
to her knees—"and spare me a trip to Hell." He sighed
and rubbed his eyes. "But if you're trapped in Limbo

as well, I can see my efforts were for naught."

"Limbo," she repeated. "Why do you keep talking about Limbo?"

He looked at her as if she was the one who was seriously out of touch with reality. " 'Tis the place between Heaven and Hell, and you know nothing of it? 'Tis worse for you than I feared."

"Pal, we aren't in Limbo, we're in New York."

His expression of resignation turned to alarm. "New York? Is that closer to Hell, then?"

"It's actually closer to Jersey than Hell, but we try to forget that bit of geography, except when the wind's from the south, then it's an inescapable fact." She tucked the pen into her hair and loosened her grip on the shears. "Look, let's try to get you back to where you came from, okay? You tell me how you got here and I'll help you get home." That sounded reasonable enough.

He leaned more heavily against the table. "How can I go home? I'm dead." He shifted and a snootful of his aroma hit Jane square in the nose.

"Nope," she said definitively, "you're not dead. I told you, you're in New York. Different state of being entirely."

He looked very skeptical, but she pressed on.

"Do you have any family?"

"I've kin in the Highlands," he said. "I've also kin in the Future, but I daresay I've bypassed them to get to here."

A wacko with delusions of time traveling, she noted. She'd read those time-traveling romances and knew all about how it worked. Standing stones, faery rings, magical jewelry—those were all devices necessary for the time traveler. Since there were none of the above in the vicinity, it was a safe bet the guy was kidding himself. Jane wasn't familiar with any of the local sanitariums, so she decided to ignore that alternative for the moment. She took a different tack.

"You got family in the area?" she asked. "In Manhattan? Queens?"

"I'm first cousin to the laird of my clan," he said wearily. "But I fear there are no queens amongst our kin."

Jane opened her mouth to ask him what he meant, then shut it and shook her head. Better not to know.

"Okay," she said slowly, "how about your name instead."

"Ian MacLeod."

That was a start. "Birth date?"

"Allhallows Eve, 1279."

"Right," she said, starting to feel like Joe Friday. Maybe if she could get just the facts. "Whoa," she said, holding up her shears, "let's fix that. What year did you say?"

"The Year of Our Lord's Grace 1279," he repeated absently, looking around in something of a daze.

"All right," she said, putting that tidbit into the "Really Wacko" column. "Let's move on. What about your family?"

"All left behind in 1313," he said, plucking at his skirts with grimy fingers. "Save my cousin Jamie, of course, but he's in the Future."

Okay, we'll play it your way, she thought. "The Future? What year would that be?"

"1996," he said, leaving fingerprints behind on the antebellum gown. "That was the year he said they would hope for."

"Wrong," she said, shaking her head and hoping the motion would dislodge the rest of his words. The year they would hope for? What kind of babble was that? "1996 is the past, buster," she continued. "We're in 1999. Just a blink until the new . . . um . . ." she found her voice fading at the look on his face.

"1999?" he whispered.

"Yes."

"1999, not Limbo?"

She was sure she had never before seen such a look of dreadful hope on anyone's face. She nodded slowly.

"1999," she confirmed. "That's the year, New York is the place."

His eyes suddenly filled with tears. Before she could ask him why, he had fallen to his knees.

"Ach, merciful Saint Michael," he breathed, his hands clasped in front of him. "I escaped . . . I escaped in truth!"

Escape. Now there was a word she didn't really want to hear from him. It conjured up thoughts of bars and breakouts and maimed guards. But before she could tell him as much, he had begun to teeter on his knees.

"Um, Mr. MacLeod," she said, holding out her hand, "maybe you'd better . . ."

He looked up at her with a smile of such radiance, she almost flinched.

Then his eyes rolled back in his head, his eyelids came down, and he pitched forward, landing with his face on her toes.

She looked down, speechless.

A passed-out nutcase lying on her feet. What else could happen this weekend?

She was fairly sure she didn't want to know.

She stared down at the unconscious and very fragrant Ian MacLeod sprawled at her feet and wondered what in the world she was going to do with him now. And then she noticed the condition of his back revealed so conveniently by the zipper he hadn't been quite able to get up. She could have been mistaken, but those scabs looked an awful lot like Hollywood's rendition of healing whip marks.

Just what kind of trouble was he in?

And why was he so thrilled to be in New York in 1999?

Somehow, and she certainly couldn't have said why, she had the niggling suspicion that he was just as rational as she was and that he had never seen the inside of an asylum to escape from.

But that was a hunch she really didn't want to pursue. Instead, she turned her rampant thoughts to the matter at hand—namely getting Ian MacLeod out of Miss Witherspoon's workroom on the off chance that someone else was feeling exceptionally diligent and decided to come in for a little unpaid overtime.

Moving him without his help was out of the question. She wasn't a great judge of those kinds of things, but she hazarded a guess that he was several inches over six feet, certainly tall enough to get a kink in his neck while looking down at her. He was heavier than she was by far—even taking into account those last many pounds she hadn't managed to get off in time for bikini season. Dragging him out, even if she could manage it, would do nothing but leave grime on the carpet and ruin the gown. Short of dumping cold water on him, probably the best thing she could do was wait for him to wake up and hope he hadn't left too much of himself on the Scarlet O'Hara dress.

So she took a deep breath, sat down with her shears, and waited.

3

Ian woke with difficulty. It seemed to him as if he struggled up from his dreams like a man struggling to escape the embrace of a pond lest he drown. He knew there was a reason to wake, but he couldn't remember what it was. He only knew he had cause to open his eyes and soon, else he would lose what he desperately wanted.

He opened his eyes and realized he was still in the white room. He lifted his head to find the woman who had delivered the glad tidings sitting a few paces away from him, holding onto her strange weapon.

A Future weapon, by the look of it.

Ian smiled, a smile so fierce it hurt his face to do it. He had done it! He had escaped the past and landed himself precisely where he had dreamed of being for years.

By the saints, it was a miracle.

"How're you feeling?"

Ian looked at the woman and realized that he would have to do a great deal of work on his speech before he sounded as she did. He'd learned English, of course, being the laird's cousin and all and potentially in line for the chieftainship, and he'd practiced a bit with his cousin Jamie's wife while she was with them. Hopefully it would suffice him until he could master the new tongue.

"Well enough, mistress," he said, with as much dignity as he could muster, being facedown on the floor before her. "I fear I never asked your name."

"Jane," she said. "Jane Fergusson."

"Fergusson?" he croaked.

She waved her hand dismissively. "We've got a Scottish ancestor way up in the branches of the family tree."

"Well," Ian managed, "as long as he's not likely to drop from that tree upon me presently."

"He died a long time ago, I'm sure."

Ian decided on the spot to let the past stay in the past. No sense in punishing this girl for what her kin had done. For all he knew, she wasn't directly related to the Fergusson. As Ian's back twitched from a remembered flogging, he certainly hoped not.

Jane Fergusson rose to her feet. "We need to get you out of here."

Ian immediately felt her urgency become his. "Why? Is it a bad place?"

"You're in Miss Petronia Witherspoon's Elegant Eighteenth Century Wedding Fashions, and believe me when I tell you Miss Witherspoon would not be pleased to find you wearing one of her bridal gowns in your . . . um . . . present condition."

Ian heaved himself up. It took some doing, and he tangled himself soundly in his skirts before he managed to gain his feet. Even then he had to hold onto the table for a moment or two until the stars ceased to swim about his head. He looked sideways at Jane and tried to smile.

"I've been a bit . . . er, detained for the past pair of months."

"Detained?"

She looked less than eager to hear the entire tale, but Ian felt he owed it to her.

"I was in an enemy's dungeon. I fell asleep dreaming of Hell."

"And woke up just yards from Jersey," she said with a nod. "Makes sense."

Ian wasn't familiar with the place called Jersey, but he had the feeling he'd be well to avoid it. He continued, trying to piece together what must have happened. "I think they mistook me for dead and pulled me free," he said. "Perhaps they carried me to our land and left me there." He shrugged. "I've no idea, truly, but I'm grateful to be here." He smiled, to show her how grateful he was.

She looked less than convinced. Maybe she didn't believe his tale. Perhaps she would believe him when he found Jamie and Jamie could vouch for the truth of it.

"Dungeon?" she asked. "Here in New York?"

"Nay, in Scotland. In the Highlands. In 1313." He straightened and tried to look as trustworthy as possible. He truly didn't expect her to believe him immediately, but she would in time. Or perhaps she would merely take pity on him and help him find Jamie whether she believed him or not.

Assuming Jamie was in the Future. Ian had seen Jamie and his wife Elizabeth ride off into the forest. He'd even gone to the place where he knew the doorway into the Future to be and made certain they hadn't been overcome by beasties or brigands. There had been no sign of them. Ian had been convinced Jamie had found his way to 1996.

He most assuredly did not want to contemplate what a sorry state he would be in if he was wrong.

"Hmmm," she said, fingering her weapon. "1313?"

"I need to find my cousin, James MacLeod." There. Just saying the like made him feel more confident. Jamie had to be here. Ian would accept no other alternative.

He put all doubts from his mind and concentrated on the task at hand—mainly remaining upright.

"Maybe you'd better clean up first," she countered. "You really don't want to go around dressed like that now that you don't need to make an impression on Saint Peter anymore."

He looked down at the dress and frowned at the less-than-pristine condition of it.

"I fear I've ruined the frock," he said apologetically.

"Forget it. It wasn't one of my best anyway."

He looked up at her. "Yours?"

"I designed it." She looked around the chamber. "I designed all of these."

Somehow she didn't sound overly enthusiastic about it. Ian, however, was impressed. He'd fingered the majority of the gowns looking for something he could use. Jane was a fine seamstress indeed to have done so much work.

"They're passing fair," he offered. "Bonny, truly."

"For bridal gowns," she conceded. "Now," she continued briskly, "let's figure out what to do with you."

He made her as low a bow as he could manage without landing himself upon her toes again. "I am in your hands, my lady."

He looked out from under his eyebrows to see the effect his words had had on her. She was looking at him with pursed lips and he straightened with a sigh. So she was resistent to his charms. Ian remembered his hastily made vow that he would mend his ways and settle with one woman. Perhaps Jane was not the woman for him. After all, he had the entire Future to choose from. No sense in not looking them all over before he made his choice.

But that didn't mean that Jane didn't deserve his most gallant self. It was the least he could offer, given his current condition.

•   •   •

A short while later he found himself riding, trapped, in what Jane called an elevator. All he knew was that the floor was falling from beneath his feet and he thought he just might shame himself by crying out. To take his mind off the interminable ride, he fingered the buttons of the raincoat he'd been given to wear over the remains of his plaid. His feet were bare and his sword was wrapped in a sheath of white fabric. He'd seen the wisdom of not parading about with his weapon until he was more familiar with the conditions of the day.

He'd just prided himself on surviving the torture of the little descending box when he found himself outside Miss Petronia's dwelling, standing on strange ground that fair burned the soles of his feet. The heat rose in waves from the hardened ground and beat down upon his person so strongly, he thought he might expire on the spot.

"Are you certain this isn't Hell?" he asked Jane, wiping his grimy brow.

She put her fingers to her mouth and whistled so loudly, he clapped his hands over his ears.

"Nope," she said, when he pulled his hands away cautiously. "Welcome to New York in summer. It's hot as Hell, but still a different place entirely."

And then Ian noticed everything else. There were those little boxes on wheels—nay, those were the cars he'd heard tell of. He looked at them in astonishment, amazed at their speed and their braying calls as they surged by one another. Their drivers leaned out of them, shouting and swearing. He jumped as he heard one screech to a halt a mere finger's breadth from the back of another.

Then there were the people who hastened past him without marking him. He was pushed and jostled as more souls than he had ever seen in the whole of his life swelled around him.

The confusion, the noise, the heat and the mass of

humanity were almost enough to bring him to his knees weeping with uncertainty. He struggled to regain his courage—something he had never had trouble with in the past. But who could blame him? By the saints, this was a world he'd never expected, full of sights and sounds he could hardly digest. He clutched his hands together only to realize he was clutching Jane's hand between the both of his. He looked at her to find she was staring at him with something akin to pity in her eyes.

"I ... I fear ..." His voice cracked. "So many people," he managed.

She smiled, a gentle smile that almost had him kneeling at her feet in gratitude.

"We'll take a cab to my place," she said, giving his hand a squeeze. "You'll feel better once you've had a shower and something decent to eat."

Eat was the one thing he did understand at present, so he nodded over that and let her lead him into a little yellow car that suddenly stopped in front of them. He sat on the strange bench and closed his eyes as the car lurched forward, the driver swearing and bellowing his displeasure at those around him.

Ian began to pray.

It seemed to take forever until the car stopped at their destination. Jane handed the man pieces of paper that Ian surmised served as payment. Ian followed her from the car and into a tall, bricked keep. He sighed in relief at the sight of steps. At least there would be no more torture in the little box that went up and down.

"You'll probably want to eat first," Jane said after they had climbed the steps and she had led him through a doorway she had opened with a key. "Stand here and don't move."

Ian stood and he didn't move. He didn't dare. Her dwelling was a curious mixture of only black and white and he feared to soil anything he might touch. He watched as Jane came from another part of her house carrying a goodly bit of cloth. She spread it over a strangely cushioned bench, then motioned for him to sit.

"I'll bring you something to eat, then I'll go see if I can round up some clothes for you. You're not going to want to wear what you've got on much longer."

"Aye, it could bear a washing."

She looked skeptical that such a thing might suffice, but he didn't argue. His belly was nigh to burning a hole in his middle and he didn't want to distract her from her errand in the kitchen.

Within moments, Ian was holding a strange, round trencher with something called a BLT piled atop it. It was very edible and he ingested several, depleting Jane's loaf of bread, but unable to apologize for it. It had been a very long time since he'd had anything fit for a man to consume. After they had eaten, Jane took away their trenchers and headed toward a black box in the corner.

"Here's the television. You can change the channel if you want to. I'll be back in about an hour."

Ian started to say "fine," then gasped in surprise as Jane touched the box. It sprang to life, or rather the people trapped inside the contrivance sprang to life. Ian could only gape at the poor souls, unsure if he should try to rescue them or not.

"Ian? You okay?"

Ian looked up at her, still speechless.

"I know," she said with a sigh. "Saturday afternoon TV. It's pretty bad, but it'll keep you entertained. Here's the remote."

And with that, she left.

He was alone with the television.

By the saints, 'twas almost as frightening as contemplating another trip into the Fergusson's dungeon.

At the thought of that, he felt his eyes narrow of their own accord. Jane was a Fergusson, no matter how far removed she was. Had she turned on the beast to torment him?

He sat on the soft bench in her house and pondered that. Then he looked at the black sticklike thing she had placed into his hand. He pressed upon it and jumped at what happened inside the television. It was too horrifying to be believed. He pressed what he'd pressed before and, by the blessed saints, the group of players trapped inside changed yet again.

He wished somehow that Jane hadn't left him alone.

"Dolt," he muttered to himself. He was a score and fourteen, surely old enough to have lost his fear of things he didn't understand. This was a Future creation. There was no dark magic about it. It was just another marvel the men of the Future had invented to entertain themselves—the saints pity the poor fools they had shrunk and trapped inside the box to provide the amusement.

Could he rescue them? He gave that serious thought before deciding that perhaps that was what he needed to do. He leaned further up on the edge of the bench. The television paid him no heed. He rose slowly and approached as quietly as he could. His body was still battered, but he felt better than he had before. Another fortnight, and he would be fully himself again—if he survived an afternoon alone with the beast in front of him.

The television gave no sign of having marked his approach, so he moved even closer. Ian reached out to touch the smooth surface and jerked his hand back as the beast bit him with invisible teeth.

Ian sucked upon his fingers. As tempted as he was to do a bit of rescuing with his sword, he decided that perhaps patience was a virtue he could practice that afternoon. He retreated to his square of cloth and sat down again, eyeing the television with disfavor. Cheeky beast. Then he realized the players inside were speaking in

Jane's English and he saw the benefits of paying close attention to them.

But despite himself, he couldn't help but wish Jane would hurry with her errands.

4

Jane stood in her bedroom several hours later, leaned on her dresser and stared at herself in the mirror, and wondered if she would be better off to lock her door and forget what lay outside it. Somehow, though, she suspected locking it wasn't necessary to keep the non-native out. He didn't particularly seem up to turning the handle. Either he was a complete wacko, he was from a different planet, or he was from where he said he was.

Scotland, the Year of Our Lord 1313.

But she didn't want to think about how that could be possible.

Unfortunately it was a conclusion she was having a hard time avoiding, and that had everything to do with the afternoon and evening's events. She'd never considered herself a Sir Gallahad type, but she had done more rescuing in the past eight hours than Sir G. had likely done in his entire life.

Jane had initially—and with no small bit of trepidation—left Ian at home to watch television. She'd warned him under pain of death not to touch anything. She wouldn't have been surprised in the least to have returned and found her building belching smoke and fire into the afternoon air. She'd been relieved to find Ian in the same place she'd left him: gaping at the TV. He'd jumped half a foot when she'd touched his shoulder. She'd then found herself standing stock-still with a sword at her throat.

Whatever else she could say about Ian MacLeod, she had to admit he was apparently a helluva swordsman.

Once she'd been able to breathe again, she'd ushered Ian to the bathroom. She'd soon heard a serious clanking noise and had hurried to investigate only to find he had peed in the sink and was in the process of taking apart her plumbing. She'd saved him from being bonked over the head with her showerhead—by her. The last thing she needed was to have to call the super and ask him to come put her powder room back together. Deciding that perhaps Ian's next foray into the bathroom could wait, she'd taken him back to the kitchen for a second lunch.

That had precipitated his sudden love affair with the chrome toaster. Jane had barely managed to throw together a tuna casserole before she'd had to announce "stop" in a very loud voice to keep him from completing his investigation of the toaster insides with a sterling silver butter knife. He'd transferred his attentions to the outlet, necessitating a stern command that he park himself at the table with his hands empty and in plain sight.

He had subsequently looked at what had come out of the oven as if he'd never seen anything like it before in his life. She was the first to admit she was a lousy cook, but surely her offering hadn't merited such tentative pokes with a fork into the depths of the casserole dish. Apparently Ian's appetite was less threatened by her potato-chip crust than Ian was, because it induced him to wolf down the entire thing without missing a beat.

She'd headed him back into the bathroom again with grooming aids that hopefully wouldn't get him into too much trouble, and left him to it. Then she'd come into her room, leaned on her dresser, and looked at herself, wondering what had possessed her to bring Ian home.

And that brought her back to her initial problem of determining his origins: loony bin or fourteenth-century Scotland. She fervently hoped there was a difference.

Well, there was no sense in postponing the inevitable any longer. She would have to go out, find out the truth, and then figure out what to do about it. Maybe she could help him find his family and get him out of her life so she could get back to darts and gathers.

Somehow, though, after what she'd been through in the past eight hours, producing wedding gowns just didn't sound all that exciting anymore.

She took a deep breath and walked to her bedroom door. The apartment was minuscule, but it was hers alone. It had reminded her of drafty servants' quarters in some bad eighteenth-century penny novel and that had seemed so appropriate, she hadn't been able to pass it up. That and she could afford it. The down side was that there wasn't some long, elegant hallway separating her from the living room so she would have its length to get a good grip on herself.

She opened the door and stepped out into the living room/dining room/kitchen combination and for the second time that day found herself gaping at Ian MacLeod. Only this time terror had nothing at all to do with her speechless condition. He had risen to greet her and stood in front of her couch with his hands clasped behind him, a grave smile on his face. She was greatly tempted to swoon, a good, old-fashioned, antebellum kind of swoon. Instead, she shut her mouth and commanded her knees to remain steady.

He'd shaved. She noticed that right off. Amazingly enough, beneath that ratty beard lurked a granitelike jaw, chiseled cheekbones, and a full, pouty lower lip that had her biting hers in self-defense. She wondered if fanning herself would give the skyrocketing of her blood pressure away. And then there was his eyes, a vivid blue that made them seem as if they leaped from his face. They were eyes she could have lost herself in for centuries and not cared one bit about the passage of time.

His shoulders were impossibly broad and she was vaguely disappointed that she'd bought him an extra-large tee shirt. *Should have picked up that medium,* she thought with regret. It wouldn't have been as good as a wet tee shirt, but she wouldn't have quibbled. All in all, Ian MacLeod was the most handsome man she had ever laid eyes on in the whole of her twenty-nine years. Something nagged at her, but she shoved it aside in favor of more lusting. She looked lower and saw that his jeans hugged him most securely—and then it hit her what was so dreadfully wrong with the picture.

He was wearing boxer shorts.

On the outside of his jeans.

She looked up, startled, only to find that he'd turned himself around to look at a noise from the kitchen end of the living room and she got an eyeful of his long, glorious dark hair—tied back with a bright pink bow. The only relief she felt was knowing it was something he'd unearthed from one of her bathroom drawers.

But before she could say anything else, he'd turned back to her and given her another of his smiles, only this one wasn't grave. It was a heart stopper.

"My thanks for the clothing," he said, with a little bow. "Passing comfortable, these long-legged trews." He pulled at his jeans, then lovingly caressed the boxer shorts with the smiley faces on them. "Very cheerful and pleasing to the eye."

Jane didn't have the heart to tell him he had them on in the wrong order. Besides, it was New York. No one would look at him twice.

"Do you perchance have a map?" he asked, his lilt taking her for another roller-coaster ride. "I've a need to find my cousin as soon as may be and I'd best know where I am now. I'm not familiar with New York.''

"Sure," Jane said. She had an atlas. She'd bought it her first month at Miss Witherspoon's, based on her certainty that she'd be traveling to all the fashion hot spots soon and it would be best to know where she was headed.

It was, unsurprisingly, still in shrink-wrap. It had been, after all, a very expensive atlas.

But who better to use it on than a lunatic sporting a pink bow and wondering where New York found itself in the grander global scheme of things? Jane got the atlas and sat down next to Ian on the couch. She opened up to the world and then looked at Ian to see if anything was ringing a bell for him yet.

He was looking at it blankly.

Jane pointed carefully to the British Isles. "Scotland," she said. "I think the Highlands are up there."

Ian looked the faintest bit relieved to see something that was apparently familiar. "Aye," he said with a gulp. "And there's Inverness. Edinburgh. Those places I know. Now, where are we? Lower down?"

"A bit to the left," she said, sliding her finger across the Atlantic and stopping on Manhattan. "We're on a little island here."

Ian gaped. "Across the sea?"

"Across the sea."

"But," he spluttered, "how did I come across the sea?"

Jane looked at him carefully. "That's a very good question. How did you come across the sea?"

Ian closed his eyes and she watched him swallow very hard. It seemed to take him a moment or two to regain control of himself before he opened his eyes and looked at her.

"I live in Scotland," he managed. "How I came to be across that vast sea, I know not. But I must go home." He looked bleakly at the map. "I must go home."

There was a wealth of longing in those words and in spite of herself, Jane was moved. She recognized the feeling. She wanted to go home, wanted it more than anything, but home wasn't a return ticket to Indiana. She loved her family, but they were solid, dependable people with solid, dependable dreams. Jane, despite her solid, dependable name, had never been one of them, never shared in their dreams. They wanted accountants and bankers; Jane wanted a sheep farm, a spinning wheel, and dyes in vibrant, breath-stealing colors. Her dream home was a little house in the Scottish Highlands where she could weave in peace and never again look at a bridal gown, never again be bound by white and ecru, never again wear black unless someone had died.

Home. In a place she'd never dreamed of.

And with a person she'd never expected.

"I have to go home," Ian repeated.

She nodded. "I understand."

"Can you help me?"

She took a deep breath. "I can. In fact, let's start now. We'll call information and see if we can't get your cousin on the phone."

"The phone?"

She picked up the cordless and handed it to him. He was giving it the same look of intense interest he'd given the toaster, so she took it away from him.

And she couldn't help but wish he'd look at her that way. Maybe women hadn't changed enough since the Middle Ages for her to be all that much of a novelty.

She shook her head as she went to look for the phone book. "Maybe I'm the one who needs the asylum," she muttered under her breath. "I'm starting to believe him!"

Within moments, she was sitting next to him on the

couch, connecting with international information. She asked for a listing for James MacLeod in the Highlands.

"There are scores," the operator said with asperity. "Can you be a bit more specific?"

Jane put her hand over the mouthpiece. "Can you be more specific? A specific town?"

Ian peered at the map. "Well, 'tis a half se'nnight's journey from MacAllister's keep, but less from the Fergusson's. We've a forest nearby and the mountains are behind us."

He traced the map with his finger and as he did so, Jane made a decision.

"Thanks," she said to the operator and hung up the phone before she could change her mind. What she contemplated was possibly the stupidest thing she'd ever contemplated, but she was tired of her safe existence. Here she had the perfect opportunity to pick up and do something, well, colorful. There was every reason not to, but none of those reasons was appealing, so she ignored them. She looked at Ian. "We'll just fly over and you can get there by landmarks. You can do that, can't you?"

"Easily. But this flying . . ."

"In a plane. You'll love it."

"I will repay you—"

She held up her hand and cut him off. She didn't want to talk about money. It wasn't why she was doing it.

"I will," he insisted. "It isn't proper that you spend what you've earned on a stranger."

"We'll deal with that later."

He looked at her, then shook his head. "The journey will be very long. Your work—"

"I hate my work," she said, then shut her mouth when she realized what she'd said. Hate was a strong word. She took a deep breath. "It really won't take very long and I have some vacation time coming up anyway."

"I couldn't—"

"Please." She hadn't meant to say it, but it slipped out of her mouth just as surprisingly as had the other things. "I would very much like to see Scotland," she amended. "I hear it's beautiful."

Ian took her hand and squeezed it. "You're very kind, Jane Fergusson. You have my gratitude."

She would have rather had his unrestrained passion, but gratitude wasn't a bad start.

"How about a movie?" she asked, pulling her hand away before she did something stupid, like leave it in his. "We'll do popcorn, too."

"A Future tradition?"

With the way he said Future, she couldn't help but capitalize it in her mind. Whatever Ian's mental state, he certainly was enthusiastic about everything she suggested.

"Definitely," she answered him. "Maybe we'll do ice cream later." She'd already put her foot to the slippery slope of breaking out of her normal routine. Might as well go for the full trip.

Her only hope was that she had some heart left for beating in her chest once Ian was safely delivered home.

Three hours later, Jane huddled in her bed, wondering if she shouldn't have chosen a romantic comedy instead of an alien thriller. A tap on her door almost left her clinging to the ceiling.

"What?" she croaked.

The door opened a crack. "Jane, might I perchance sleep up here with you? On the floor, even."

More of Ian inched through her door, clad in boxers and dragging a blanket behind him.

"Well . . ." she began.

"I saw an alien in the garderobe."

She might have argued with him, but she was almost certain she'd seen the same thing in her closet.

"All right," she said slowly. *I am insane,* she thought. An unknown quality coming to sleep on the floor next to her bed. It would be just her luck to wake up throttled, or worse. She wasn't sure what anyone else might think would be worse than a throttling, but she could come up with a few things.

"A peaceful rest to you, my lady," came the deep whisper from beside her bed.

My lady. Well, how could you not feel just a little more relaxed with that kind of talk coming your way?

Jane closed her eyes, sighed, and then another thought occurred to her.

"Ian?"

"Aye."

"Do you have a passport?"

"Passporrrt?" he echoed in a sleepy burr.

"You know, papers to get you through customs and all?"

"Future customs," he murmured, smacking his lips a time or two. "Must learn those right away."

"Did you leave it at home?"

Her only answer was a snore. Besides, she thought, if he'd entered the country through the normal channels, surely he would have had it on him when he'd arrived in New York.

In Miss Witherspoon's salon, wearing filthy rags and spearing bags of munchies on the end of a sword.

She sighed. Wonderful. What she had was a wacko without the necessary documents to deposit him back on home soil. Why couldn't she have had a cousin in some illegal kind of import-export business?

Then again, there was Frank at Miss Whitherspoon's. He dressed like an aging urchin, bathed with the regularity of an eighteenth-century chimney sweep, and always had the faint hint of cannabis clinging to him. If anyone might know where to come up with a passport for Ian, Frank would. It was something to hope for. She closed her eyes and to her surprise, immediately and quite peacefully drifted off to sleep.

And she dreamed of Scotland.

5

Ian sat behind a strangely fashioned table in what Jane called her broom closet at Miss Whitherspoon's workplace and marveled at the fineness of the fabric surrounding him. It was all white, of course, but the variety and the beauty of it was truly a wonder. He picked up the Future weapon Jane had originally faced him with and saw that its jaws opened and closed with great precision. He reached for a swath of fabric to try it out upon. He hadn't but begun to close the teeth when he heard a screech that fair sent him scampering for cover.

"Stop!"

Ian stopped in mid-closing and looked up to find Jane teetering at the doorway.

"Don't cut that," she said, reaching out and taking the weapon from him. "Come with me. Frank wants to take your picture."

Ian followed her obediently through the empty hallways. Frank, he understood, would provide him with the necessary things he would need to return to Scotland. He wasn't exactly sure why he had come to New York in the first place, but he suspected there was something quite magical about the city that drew seekers of all kinds.

Or wackos, as he heard Jane occasionally mutter under her breath.

Within moments, courtesy of another claustrophobic ride in the elevator, Ian faced a small black box and was subsequently reeling from the shock of having a bright light explode in his eyes. He looked at Jane and blinked several times until his eyes cleared. He sincerely hoped whatever Frank intended to do for him was worth what he'd just faced.

"He can do this thing?" Ian asked her, rubbing his eyes.

"I know a guy," Frank said, busily attending to the torture device he'd just used on Ian.

"He knows a guy," Jane said, taking Ian by the arm and pulling him from the chamber. "Now to go beg for some vacation time," she said with a sigh. "This should be fun."

With the way she said it, Ian wasn't sure *fun* was something he wanted to be involved in. He put his shoulders back and tried to look his most confident. He didn't want to get in Jane's way as she negotiated for temporary freedom from her employer. It was more of a sacrifice than he was truly willing for her to make, but she seemed determined to come with him. And, if the truth were to be told, he wasn't sure he could get himself to Scotland of the Future without her.

Or, strangely enough, that he even wanted to.

He was almost certain it wasn't just misplaced gratitude, though he had enough of that and to spare. How he ever could have survived his arrival in the Future without Jane having been there, he surely didn't know. She had fed him, clothed him, and given him a place to lay his head. There was much to be said for that.

And then he quite suddenly lost track of all his thoughts as the elevator doors opened, he stepped into

the passageway, and his rather starved libido caught an
eyeful of the women who had suddenly filled Miss Witherspoon's place of commerce.

Too skinny by half, most of them, but passing beautiful. Tall, willowy, in all colors and shapes. Ian could
only gape at them, stunned mainly by the looks they
were giving him, looks that said they would be more
than willing to engage in whatever activity he might suggest. He knew the look. He'd seen it before and he'd
certainly taken advantage of it before.

"Models," Jane threw over her shoulder as she
plunged into the midst of them. "They wear the bridal
gowns for the customers."

Brides? He could hardly believe it, for none of them
looked nervous enough to be contemplating their first
night with a man. Just as well. Ian was acutely aware of
the last virgin he'd tutored and where that evening's instruction had landed him. It was far better to indulge in
one of these. Or several.

His conscience gave him a sharp poke, reminding him
that at one point in the Fergusson's dungeon he'd made
a last-minute plea for forbearance based on the promise
of pledging to one woman.

He looked at Jane as she parted the way before him.
She was dressed all in black again and Ian wondered if
that was so she would fade when compared to the other
creatures circling him like carrion birds dressed in white.
Her hair was confined the same way he'd seen it at first,
all bunched at the back of her head with a handful of
sticks poking from it. They were pencils he knew now,
but they still looked odd to him. She was almost as tall
as the other women but not nearly as slender, though
her shape was a fine one.

One woman.

Or the score he currently waded through.

Jane, or a variety of delicacies he thought he just
might want to sample.

He felt a smack on his backside and he yelped as the hand lingered. Ian couldn't tell who had done it, but there were several standing about him who looked capable of such an intimate gesture. Jane turned around and frowned at the lot of them.

"Down, girls. He's out of your league."

One of the women snorted. "As if he's in yours, Janey."

It was at that point that Ian began to suspect that beneath all the beauty and seductiveness might lie less-than-nice souls. He also cared not for the quickly hidden flinch he'd seen Jane display. These women knew nothing of her and yet she allowed them to wound her? Ian stepped up to Jane's side and took her hand.

"Let us be off," he said, casting the disparaging woman a look of disapproval. Jane didn't pull her hand away, but Ian felt her fingers fluttering nervously. It was as if he'd caught a butterfly. It was not the hand that would take liberties with an unknown man's backside.

"Models," Jane muttered with distaste. "They're very dangerous."

"So I see," Ian said, rubbing his abused backside with his free hand.

"And what we're going to face is even more dangerous. We're almost there." She looked up at him. "Try to look helpless and pathetic. We're going for the mercy vote."

As you will Ian had planned to say, but before he could get the words out, the door to Miss Witherspoon's office had been opened and he'd gotten a complete eyeful of Miss Witherspoon.

"Oh," Jane said, sounding less than pleased. She pulled Ian behind her into Miss Witherspoon's private chamber. "Where is she?"

"Out," the vision purred, coming to her feet from behind the impressively large table, revealing impressively large proportions herself.

Ian could only gape at the woman, speechless. This was obviously not the stern and unyielding employer Jane had told him about.

"And who do we have here?" the young woman continued.

"A friend of mine," Jane said. "Ian, this is Alexis, Miss Witherspoon's niece. Alexis, Ian."

Ian had never seen such lush curves. He suspected he'd never even dreamed of such a form, impeccably rounded in the proper places and impossibly slim everywhere else.

"Aahh," he attempted.

And then she held out her hand and he looked down to see blood dripping from all her fingers.

"Ach!" he cried, jumping back.

Alexis only stretched and smiled like a satisfied cat, practically clawing the air with her daggerlike hands. "Just nail polish, silly. They're my own nails, of course."

Ian could see that and he was afraid. He knew what kind of marks a Fergusson whip could leave. He could only imagine how a man's back might pain him after a night abed with those.

"Oh, Jane dear, I see you've finally arrived."

Ian found himself pushed aside by a solidly built woman well past the prime of her life. She cast him a practiced look of assessment before she turned her attentions back to Jane.

"Alexis drew some wonderful ideas on the way back. You'll see them mocked up as soon as possible."

"Well," Jane began.

Ian looked down to find that Alexis had sidled up to him and was placing her considerable charms beneath his nose for closer inspection.

"I design all the gowns, you know," she whispered, reaching up to tap his chin with one long nail. "No matter what you've heard. Jane just does the sewing."

She slid her finger down and began to toy with one of the buttons on his shirt. "I'm going to be a famous designer one day."

Ian vowed he would believe anything she said to him if she would just cease with her descent down the front of his chest.

"I need my vacation time," Jane said calmly. "Ian needs to get back to Scotland and I've volunteered to get him there."

"No."

Ian looked to Miss Witherspoon. She hadn't bothered to look up from what she was doing.

"I'll take him," Alexis offered. "I've always wanted to see Scotland."

"I've already offered," Jane said.

Miss Witherspoon shoved a handful of pages at Jane. "Get to work on these. I want mock-ups done before next week."

Ian watched Jane take the pages, then he caught sight of the drawing upon the topmost sheaf. And he suspected that even he might be more successful at creating a bridal gown than the woman who had done the depictions before him.

It was then that he began to understand.

"Get to work on my stuff," Alexis said, giving Jane a little push toward the door. "We'll take good care of Ian."

Ian watched Jane hold onto the pages and consider. And for a moment, he thought she just might do as she was bid. Then he watched her put her shoulders back.

"I have three years' worth of vacation time coming," she said firmly, "and this is something of an urgent situation. I'm sorry I can't give more notice, but it's imperative that Ian return to Scotland as soon as possible and he needs me to get there."

Alexis made a scornful sound, then looked up at Ian.

"I can take him places you couldn't even imagine in your wildest dreams."

Ian was afraid to ask where those places might be and what Alexis might do to him with her claws if he let her escort him there.

"I said no and I meant it," Miss Witherspoon said sternly. "Now, get to work on those, Jane. I don't have any more time for your foolishness."

Ian saw Jane begin to falter and he cleared his throat. "I beg your pardon, my lady Witherspoon, but I do indeed need her assistance. If you would be so kind—"

"Alexis can accompany you," Miss Witherspoon said with a curt nod. "I have no more time for either of you."

"Alexis is not accompanying Ian anywhere," Jane said. "I want to go to Scotland. I've wanted to go to Scotland for years."

"Have you?" Ian asked, surprised. He hadn't realized the desire was so firmly planted in her, though he could well understand the like.

"Lots of sheep there," Jane said shortly, then she turned her attentions back to Miss Witherspoon. "We're leaving on Wednesday. I'll be back—"

"You'll go nowhere," Miss Witherspoon said, the edge in her voice as cutting as any blade Ian had run his fingers across. "Those designs must be fleshed out."

"That's right," Alexis said, turning to glare at Jane as well. "You can't go."

"It's only a couple of weeks," Jane said firmly. "You'll survive that long without me finishing up your homework for you."

Alexis gasped as if she'd been struck and Miss Witherspoon looked as if she might reach out and slap Jane. Ian fumbled for his sword, then realized he'd left it at Jane's home.

"You'll stay," Miss Witherspoon commanded, "and you'll apologize to my niece!"

Jane laid the drawings on Miss Witherspoon's desk and stepped back. "I'll be back in two weeks."

"If you walk out that door," Miss Witherspoon said angrily, pointing at Jane with a trembling finger, "you're fired."

"Yeah," Alexis added enthusiastically. Then she blinked a time or two, turned, and looked at her aunt in dismay. "But then who will—"

"Fired," Miss Witherspoon repeated. "Do you hear me?"

Jane took a deep breath, then shrugged. "Have it your way. You owe me for six weeks' vacation. I expect to find the check in my mailbox when I get home. Come on, Ian. We've got to go pack."

And with that, he found himself being towed behind her out of Miss Witherspoon's presence and down the passageway back to the broom closet.

"Stupid job," Jane was muttering under her breath as she stomped down the hall. "Didn't like it anyway."

Before much time had passed, Ian found himself loaded down with all manner of odds and ends from Jane's little working chamber. He followed her out into the passageway only to find Alexis blocking his path.

"You can't take anything with you," Alexis said with a sneer. "Take nothing—which is what you came here with."

"These are my personal things," Jane said, brushing past her.

Ian gave Alexis's hands a wide berth and hastened down the passageway after Jane.

Once they reached her dwelling, Jane obtained by messenger a foodstuff called pizza. She hardly partook, though, before she excused herself and shut herself into her private chamber. Ian couldn't see letting the food go to waste, so he finished off what was left and felt himself as full and satisfied as he ever had after a meal at Jamie's table. He placed the pizza container in the kitchen then paused in the television chamber, wondering what he should do. It was then that he heard the sound of weeping.

He went to press his ear to Jane's door. The sounds were muffled, but he hazarded a guess that the weeping was not of the joyous kind. He tapped on the door and the snuffling abruptly stopped.

"What?"

"How do you fare?" Ian asked through the wood.

"Nothing's wrong," came the answer. "Really."

The last was accompanied by a mighty sniff. Ian knew enough about women to know that such a sound could only mean more tears to follow. He didn't wait for permission to enter, he merely turned the knob on the door and poked his head in the chamber. And what he saw took his breath away.

There was color everywhere. Balls and skeins of yarn in every imaginable color littered the floor where Jane sat. She had obviously unearthed these things from some hidden trunk. Ian walked over to her and knelt down amidst the riot of color. He picked up a ball of particularly vibrant purple, then looked at Jane in surprise.

"I had no inkling," he began.

"I pull them out to make myself feel better," she said, dragging her sleeve across her eyes. "But not very often, because it never makes me feel better."

"I had no idea you cared for such color."

"Yeah, well, I've got plenty of time to do all I like with it now." She looked at him bleakly. "I can't believe I lost my job. It wasn't a great job, but at least it allowed me to eat."

Ian gestured to the yarn. "Have you made aught with these things?"

She nodded, then pointed to the trunk Ian hadn't noticed before. He reached over and drew out a heavy tunic woven of thick, deep red yarn. It was something that would keep any man warm even in the hard winters of the Highlands. Then he pulled out a blanket woven of so many strands of differing colors that it almost hurt his eyes to look at it. It too was made of heavy wool.

"Beautiful," he said, stunned by the sight of the rich colors.

"The yarn was imported from Scotland." She fingered the blanket absently. "Lots of sheep there, you know."

"Aye, I do," he said, fingering the wool.

"I could see myself in a little cottage on the side of a hill, spinning and weaving to keep myself busy."

To his surprise, so could he. He looked at her with her slender hands and could easily picture those hands spinning and weaving.

And tending the small joys and sorrows of a handful of children as well.

He didn't know where it had come from, that thought, but he knew it was a good one. He reached over and pulled the sharp sticks from her hair, watching as the wavy strands fell about her shoulders. Even still wearing her black clothing, she looked much more at peace, much freer than he'd seen her before.

Aye, he thought, here was a woman who could share a hearth with him and not mind the keeping of it.

She began to put her things away and Ian stopped her by taking her hand.

"'Tis a pity to waste your gift only on white," he said.

She shrugged. "It's what bridal gowns are made from."

"In my time, a bride wore the colors she found near her home."

"Then your brides were a lot more fun to design for than mine," she said with another sigh. She looked around her at the remaining piles of yarn. "Maybe I can start over again in Scotland."

"Aye—"

She interrupted him with a half laugh that contained no humor whatsoever. "Who am I kidding? I don't have the money to start over. I don't even have the money to go back home to Indiana."

Yet Ian had heard her talking into that magical telephone contrivance, promising to pay for both her and his travel to Scotland. Was that the last of her funds? He couldn't allow her to spend all upon him.

On the other hand, he had to get home.

He picked up a ball of yarn and handed it to her. "I'll find a way to repay you," he pledged. "Or perhaps you can remain with us for a time until Miss Witherspoon regains her senses and takes you back."

"Hrumph," she said with a scowl. "Poverty or indentured servitude. I don't know what's worse."

Ian looked again at the fragments of her dreams laying in lumps around her feet and thought perhaps that returning to Miss Witherspoon's was the very last thing Jane should be doing.

A little cottage was starting to sound better by the moment. Hopefully they would travel to Scotland and find Jamie there. There was no guarantee Jamie would have returned to their clan home, but Ian couldn't imagine him doing anything else. What other place on earth would call to Jamie but their keep in the Highlands?

Nay, Jamie had to be there and Ian would find him.

And then he would find some way to make Jane's dream come true.

6

Jane stumbled off the plane wishing she had somehow managed to acquire a Valium or two before embarking. She looked at Ian who walked beside her, his eyes burning with a feverish light.

"Ach," he purred like a satisfied cat, "now *that* was a proper rrrush."

"Too much television," she chided, ignoring those blasted r's of his.

"We must do it again. I'll pay for the privilege next time."

I'd rather go by boat, she almost said, then realized that was likely what half of the *Titanic*'s passengers had said.

"Sure," she said aloud, "only next time let's go first class."

"First class?"

"Bigger seats. Better food."

As those had been his two complaints about that ride, Ian only nodded in agreement. Jane didn't let herself think about the fact that the odds of her ever traveling again with Ian MacLeod were practically nil. He would find his cousin and be merrily off on his way while she was left to return to the States and face her nonlife.

Maybe she could beg Miss Witherspoon for her job back.

She almost pursued that thought when she realized it was out of the question. She'd spent half a night fondling skeins of vibrantly colored wool and fantasizing about what she would make from it. She could knit. She could weave. Surely she could make a living doing that. Or maybe she would take those colors, have cloth dyed to match, and design her own clothes. That was what she'd started out to do anyway, before money for rent and food had gotten in the way.

Jane would have given that more thought, but she suddenly found herself facing the rental car and realized that there was no wheel on the driver's side where it was supposed to be. She looked at Ian, but he was too busy peering into the outside mirrors to give any indication that he found the wheel placement unusual.

"Well, here goes nothing," she said, going around to the right side and sliding in under the wheel. She pulled down the sun visor and was greeted with bold letters reminding her to Drive On The Left. "When in Rome," she said, waiting until Ian had clambered into the passenger seat before she turned the car on. She looked at him. "You don't know anything about this driving on the left business, do you?"

He looked at her blankly. "We were accustomed to letting our mounts go where they willed."

"That's what I was afraid of."

The next three days were an endless, relentless exercise in trying to remember which side of the wheel the turn signals were on and spending most of her time turning on the windshield wipers instead. By the time they reached Inverness, Ian had familiarized himself with all the workings of the dashboard doodahs and had apparently decided that bagpipes were much preferable to top forty on the radio. He seemed to have no trouble understanding the unintelligible news reports she couldn't decipher. He spent a great deal of time grunting, as if he couldn't believe what he was hearing.

They left Inverness and headed north. Jane did the best she could with the roads available to follow Ian's homing beacon. By the time they reached roads that had continually shrunk in width and increased in incline, she was convinced they were hopelessly lost. She stopped in a little town and found the first bed and breakfast—which wasn't hard, as it was a very small town indeed—and pulled in.

"Enough," she said, turning the car off and putting her head down on the steering wheel. "I can't drive anymore today."

"I could drive."

She turned her head and looked at him out of one eye. The light of intense desire was visible even in the twilight.

"Not a chance," she said, resuming her position. "We'll get going first thing in the morning. I need dinner and some sleep."

She heard Ian get out of the car, then felt a brush of cool air as he opened her door. He unbuckled her seat belt, then took her arm and gently pulled her out. Before she knew it, she was enveloped in a warm embrace.

"I have driven you hard," he said, running his hand over her back, "and I beg pardon for it. I am anxious to see my home and know if there is aught left of it."

And to see his cousin, no doubt. Though she hadn't heard him say as much since they'd left the States, she knew he was worried that he wouldn't find what he was looking for. That she was even considering the ramifications of him missing his family because they had landed in different centuries only indicated how very tired she was.

"It's okay," she said with a yawn. "I can understand the feeling." She would have pulled away, on the off

chance that such a thing might have gotten her dinner
sooner, but she found that she just couldn't move. It was
the strangest thing, but for the first time in her life she
was content. Content in spite of a blinding headache
from too much concentrating on the road, too little sleep,
and continually doing her best to ignore what she was
going to do when she returned to the States and faced
the shambles that was her life.

"Food," Ian announced, "then a bed if they have
one. I'll find some means of working for our keep this
eve. Surely they have a handful of odd things needing
to be done. Perhaps wood to be gathered for the fire or
animals to be tended."

The thought of Ian manhandling a chainsaw sent shivers down Jane's spine. She pulled back to look up at
him.

"I can pay for it."

"Nay, you cannot."

"I have enough left on my credit card."

His lips compressed into a tight line. "This does not
sit well with me. Already you have done more than you
should have."

"And if the shoe had been on the other foot?"

"How was that?"

"If I had been popped back to the"—and she had to
take a deep breath to keep from stumbling over the very
words—"fourteenth century, what would you have
done?"

He sighed. "Given you food and shelter, then seen
you home."

"What's the difference, then?"

"The difference, sweet Jane," he said as he smoothed
his hand over her hair and smiled down at her, "is that
being unable to provide for such needs wounds my
manly pride."

Jane wasn't sure about the condition of his manly
pride, but she was sure about the condition of her knees,

and that was completely unstable. She had never considered herself anything but fiercely independent. The thought of anyone, her family or a man, doing anything remotely akin to taking care of her was something she had avoided at all costs.

But somehow, standing in the Scottish twilight in a tiny town on the edge of the sea with Ian MacLeod's arms securely around her, the thought of allowing someone else to provide for her for a change wasn't so hard to stomach.

She savored the moment as long as she could, then pulled away.

"I am starving," she admitted reluctantly. "For all we know, they won't even take a credit card or traveler's checks and we may very well be relying on your ability to chop wood."

Ian kissed her gently on the forehead, then pulled back and took her by the hand. "Perhaps I will have the chance to repay you."

"Perhaps you will. We could head back to the fourteenth century," she offered.

He laughed. "You would find it a very primitive place indeed. No airplanes, no automobiles, and no MTV."

"Ugly," she agreed, and she tried not to enjoy overly the feeling of her hand in his. It was more delicious than she would have suspected and she could hardly keep herself from wishing such hand-holding might continue far into the future—say for the next fifty or sixty years. Or maybe for the rest of forever.

She put her free hand to her forehead. No fever. Maybe insanity didn't begin with an overheated brain. Just a gradual slip into believing things that couldn't possibly come to pass—such as sharing a life with a man who claimed to be from the year 1313.

The B and B did take credit cards and they also didn't pass up Ian's offer to do a few chores as the proprietress was very pregnant and her husband had been laid up for several weeks with a back injury. Jane figured it was the perfect situation. She got to eat and watch Ian strip off his shirt all in the same twenty-four hours. Life just didn't get much better than that.

Late the next morning, after a pair of hours watching Ian soothe his manly pride, Jane crawled behind the wheel of the car again and suppressed a groan. If she'd even suspected Ian might have the wherewithal to negotiate a stick shift, she would have turned the keys over to him happily. He'd tried to convince her he was capable, but he'd come close to plowing over half a dozen flowerpots on his way out of the driveway when he'd offered to demonstrate his skill. She'd taken the keys away and promised him a driving lesson somewhere less dangerous.

"Direction?" she asked, turning on the car.

"North."

North, north, and evermore north. Jane drove without hurrying and she wasn't sure exactly about her reasons for her leisurely pace. She told herself she was just meandering so she could enjoy the scenery. It was true that the mountains and forests were breathtaking. And every time they passed a little hamlet that deserved to be immortalized on some postcard, she couldn't help but imagine how life would be if she lived there.

And she sure as heck didn't imagine living there alone.

The drive was, needless to say, very hard on her heart.

Hours had passed and Jane's imagination, and her bladder, had taken just about all they could take. Espying a choice place to pull off, she did so before Ian could protest. She shut off the car and sighed.

"I don't think this map is accurate," she began. "Maybe it's all this driving on the wrong side of the road, but I don't see anything familiar. . . ."

"I do."

The tone of his voice sent shivers down her spine. She looked at him.

"You do?"

He nodded and pointed out the window. "There's the loch. We're a day's ride southeast. By horse," he added.

"Shouldn't be far in a car, then," she said slowly.

"Shouldn't be."

She pulled back out onto the little two-lane A road and continued slowly. They passed through a good-sized village and Jane slowed to a crawl.

"Recognize this?" she asked, then realized the answer was written in Ian's astonished expression. "I take it this wasn't here the last time you rode through."

He looked visibly shaken. "Nay, it wasn't."

She decided that any lightness was completely inappropriate, so she managed a bathroom stop before they continued through the village. The road then took a sharp turn west.

"Wait," Ian said, pointing to a very sketchy-looking road leading more northward still. "Take that."

"But it doesn't look—"

"It's the right direction."

"Whatever you say," she said, following the one-lane road away from the village. She could only hope no one would come flying down it the other way without honking first.

And then suddenly and without any warning at all, the road stopped in what could have been termed a cul-de-sac if one had been feeling generous terminology-wise. Jane hadn't taken the car out of gear before Ian was reaching over to pull the keys from the ignition.

"Come with me," he said, heaving himself out of the car.

"Bags?" she asked, following him.

"We'll come back for them. 'Tisn't far."

Never mind what kind of shape he'd been in when she'd first met him. A week of rest and her cooking, pathetic as it was, combined with the substantial meals they'd had in Scottish pubs, had restored him to a walking form she could barely keep up with. She just held onto his hand and ran to keep up with him as he strode first over a field and then plunged into a forest. It was perfectly quiet in amongst the trees and profoundly chilly despite the time of year. Ian continued to hurry until they were both almost running.

And then, without warning, the forest ended and they practically fell forward into a meadow. Jane hunched over with her hands on her knees and sucked in air until she thought she might be able to stand upright. Then she looked up, and felt her jaw go slack. She held out her arm and pointed.

"That," she spluttered, "that . . . is a castle." She'd seen plenty of them on their way, but this one was so . . . well . . . perfect.

Ian looked down at her, a smile of satisfaction on his face.

"Home," he said simply. He took her hand, hauled her into his arms, and kissed her full on the mouth before he threw back his head and laughed. "By the saints, Jane, we're home!"

Before she could decide how she felt either about a medieval-looking castle being given such a cozy moniker, or about being kissed by someone who had a sword strapped to his back, she found herself being pulled once again into a flat-out run.

Ian skidded to a halt some two hundred yards farther. "The village," he said in astonishment. " 'Tis gone."

"Well," she panted, "at least the castle is still there."

Ian looked at it suspiciously as well. " 'Tis in a far better state of repair than it was the last time I saw it."

Jane knew that had been something to concern him. They had seen enough ruins along the way to make Jane wonder how any medieval castle survived its trip through the ages.

" 'Tis a mystery we'll solve later," he announced, continuing on the way up the meadow. "Jamie will know the answer to this."

"Think your cousin's here?" she asked with a little wheeze.

"I hope so," Ian said somewhat grimly.

And then he seemed to find just getting to the castle to be taxing enough on his verbosity, because he said nothing else as they trudged toward a dwelling that was starting to give Jane the willies. She'd never seen a castle that looked that authentic and that lived-in. Admittedly, her experience in the British Isles was limited to their drive from Edinburgh, but this was still spooky.

"New gate," Ian remarked as he pulled her through it and across the small courtyard to the castle itself.

Jane didn't have a chance to say anything before he'd marched them up the steps and was pushing on the door. It didn't open, so Ian took his sword and banged on the portal with the hilt. Jane started to say that maybe he shouldn't, then she decided that arguing with a large man with a sword in his hands wasn't a very good idea.

The door finally opened and a young man looked out.

"Yeah?" he asked.

Jane judged him to be in his mid-twenties, exceptionally fine-looking, and obviously home alone based on the carton of milk he held. Bachelor, she deduced by the lack of glass in his hand.

"I am Ian MacLeod," Ian announced, as if that should have clarified everything for the guy.

Apparently it did, because his jaw went slack. "Jamie's cousin Ian?" he asked, looking with wide eyes at Ian's sword.

Ian threw Jane a look of supreme relief, then turned back to the young man. "And you are . . . ?" he demanded.

"Elizabeth's youngest brother," Elizabeth's youngest brother managed. "Zachary."

"Ah, Zach the Brat," Ian said, thrusting forward his hand. "I heard many tales of your escapades from your sister."

"I'll bet you did," Zachary said, stepping back a pace. "You may as well come in. Jamie and Elizabeth aren't here right now, which means there's nothing in the fridge, but you can make yourselves as at home as you can." He looked at them as if he'd just noticed them. "You guys are traveling light. Don't you have any bags?" He looked at Jane. "Are you fourteenth-century too?"

Jane shook her head with a smile. "Nineteen seventies vintage."

Zachary frowned. "How did you find Ian?"

"He showed up in my bridal salon."

"Figures," Zachary said.

Jane looked at Ian, then looked at Zachary. "You believe all this time-traveling business?"

Zachary gave her a world-weary yawn. "You live long enough in this place, you see it all. I believe just about anything anymore," he continued, turning and heading off to what Jane could only assume was the kitchen.

Ian shut the door, then looked down at her. "Do you believe me now?"

"I think I believed you from the start."

" 'Tis a miracle."

"You don't know the half of it," she said as he took her hand and pulled her through a large gathering room of some sort. Too much more holding hands with the guy and she'd start to believe in all sorts of miracles.

No, she decided as she walked across the huge room, it was already too late. She'd begun to believe the moment she'd seen Ian in an antebellum gown in Miss Witherspoon's workroom.

Now, she was completely lost—in Scotland, in a

medieval-looking castle, holding onto a man from a century far in the past.

A miracle?

Maybe they were possible after all.

7

Ian stood on the steps leading up to the great hall, stared out into the morning light of his first full day back at the MacLeod keep, and sighed a sigh of pure contentment. He was home, in an entirely different century, but home nonetheless. It was nothing short of amazing.

He had a chamber that had been reserved for him. He'd been surprised when Zachary had told him the like, but apparently Jamie had been either suffering from a serious bout of sentimentality, or he'd known Ian would somehow find his way forward in time. Ian hadn't even used the bed. He'd given it up to Jane for the night and slept in Jamie's thinking chamber. There was one of those strangely padded benches there for his pleasure and he'd found it comfortable enough. Saints, he would have slept in marshy rushes for the pleasure of being home again, except this time with a toaster nearby.

He heard a light footfall behind him and turned to see Jane in the doorway. The sight was so arresting, he had to turn fully to better appreciate it.

She was wearing jeans and a black sweater—he reminded himself to do something about the latter as quickly as he could—and her hair was flowing freely about her shoulders. He wasn't sure what had happened to her since arriving at the castle the day before, but it had been a happy transformation. Perhaps she would never possess the kind of beauty that caused a man to stop in his tracks and gape. Hers was a loveliness of a rarer kind, one that only showed itself upon closer examination. Ian had had the luxury of closer examination over the past se'nnight and he suspected he saw what others might miss. And today, not only was she lovely, but she looked perfectly content, as if she had found the peace she'd been seeking. Unbidden, the vision of her sharing hearth and home with him came to him.

By the saints, this was not what he'd expected to find so soon.

Was it too soon? Was it just the shock of the past se'nnight? Should he wait to see what other souls he might encounter?

Then she smiled.

And he thought he just might be lost.

"You have beautiful mornings here," she said.

"Oh, aye," he managed, jamming his hands into the pockets of jeans before they did something foolish, like grab her and never release her. He cleared his throat. "Would you care for a ride?"

"In the car?"

He smiled. "On a horse, actually. I understand Jamie's mount is going to fat in the stables from lack of activity. We could filch something from the kitchens and roam for the day."

"Sounds heavenly."

"If I see to the horse, will you forage for food? I fear I don't recognize most of what's available."

"Neither do I," she said with a laugh. "Zachary's diet isn't exactly stellar, but I'll see what I can do."

Ian nodded, smiled, then turned away and whistled as he headed toward the stables. He had the feeling it might turn out to be quite a wonderful day indeed.

• • •

Not two hours had passed that he wasn't congratulating himself on being such a successful seer. Astronaut, Jamie's horse, was as well behaved as he had been the last time Ian had borrowed him for a quick getaway. The weather was perfect, sunny with a bit of a chill wind from the north. The food was actually better than he had hoped.

'Twas the company, however, that gave him the most pleasure. Who would have thought that showing a woman from the Future all the places he had roamed in his youth and fought in the years of his early manhood would have given him such pleasure and puffed his chest out so far?

They spent the middle of the day at the flat top of Jamie's meadow, looking down over the castle and the forests flanking it. Ian told Jane of battles won, cattle lifted, enemies routed and sent home in shame. It was passing odd to see places he'd tramped over in his youth and realize how many years had passed since then. The landscape had changed, but not so much that he couldn't recognize his favorite retreats.

Then he rolled over onto his belly and watched Jane as she told him of her dreams. He'd expected to hear of grand schemes to see her designs made all over the world. Surely she had a gift for it.

But she told him instead of her wish for a little cottage on the side of a hill and a spinning wheel by the hearth. He watched a faraway look come into her eye when she spoke of the colors she would use and the objects she would make with her hands.

It was then he began to wonder if Fate hadn't had a hand in his delivery to the Future. Surely he could provide her with her wishes. They were modest things surely, but he had the feeling that in her hands, they would be grand things indeed.

Once she was finished, he looked down the way and saw a place where such a thing could be built perfectly.

"Care you for that spot over there?" he asked casually, pointing to a little clearing above the western forest. The remains of a crofter's hut sat on the face of the land in the place he gestured to. It wouldn't make much of a house, but it could be used to build something else.

He looked at her from under his eyelashes as she contemplated the location. He didn't want to assume too much, but he could have sworn he saw a bit of longing sweep over her face.

"It's very beautiful," she said softly.

"Is it?" he mused. "Aye, 'tis pleasing enough, but yours is the beauty that holds my gaze."

She looked at him as if he'd lost his mind. Then she looked away, apparently dismissing his words.

"I'm in earnest," he insisted.

"No models around for competition," she said lightly.

Ian shuddered. "I care not for that kind of beauty. Rather, give me a woman whose loveliness runs true to her bones."

"Hmmm," she said, but she looked unconvinced.

So it would take him a while to persuade her. Fortunate he was then, to have the rest of the Future in which to do it.

He reached for her hand. "Stay here in Scotland for a bit," he said. *Stay forever,* he added silently, realizing as he thought it that it was indeed something he wanted very much.

She looked at him, then looked around her. It took no great powers to divine that she wanted to remain.

"Well," she said slowly, "the scenery *is* beautiful."

He smiled. "Thank you," he said modestly.

She laughed. "I suppose you are part of the package." She paused and sighed. "Well, my rent is paid up through next month. I guess I could get Miss Witherspoon to send my check here. Do we have an address to send it to besides 'Jamie's castle'?"

"I'm sure Zachary will know."

She paused again. "Will your cousin mind if I stay?"

" 'Tis as much my home as his," Ian said.

"Really."

" 'Tis our family home. One more addition, and such a fetching one at that, will not trouble him."

That earned him a bit of a blush from her and he was relieved to see that she wasn't entirely immune to his charms.

"All right," she conceded.

"Good," Ian said. He stretched out on the blanket and held open his arms. "I'm in need of a small rest after all that sentiment. Will you join me?"

She did. Ian closed his eyes, wrapped his arm around Jane Fergusson, and felt more at peace than he had the whole of his previous life.

He fell asleep with the sun shining down on his face.

Jane awoke, chilled. Obviously the sun had just gone behind a cloud because she found herself in shadows.

Then she realized it was only a single shadow and it came from a man looming over them. She sat up with a shriek.

And then everything happened too fast for her to do anything. Before she'd finished with her shriek, she found herself behind Ian, who was now on his feet with his sword drawn. There was, she decided, something to be said for having a medieval clansman as a boyfriend.

Boyfriend? She shook her head, deciding to give that more thought later. Now her time was probably better used wondering if she was going to die in the next three minutes.

Well, no blood was being spilt, so Jane took a good look at their attacker so she'd know who to finger in the lineup.

He was tall, perhaps even a bit taller than Ian, and definitely broader. She had to give Ian the benefit of the doubt, given what he'd been through in the past couple of months, but the guy facing him was in very good shape. He had dark hair, a commandingly noble face, and the most piercing pair of green eyes she had ever seen. These she noticed only because he had turned a bit to face Ian more squarely and the sun was shining down on him. And it was as she saw him fully illuminated that she realized what seemed wrong with the picture.

He was dressed—and she could only surmise this to be the case—in full pirate gear. His black boots gleamed. A long saber hung down alongside a leg that, along with the other leg, wore black-as-sin pants that poofed a little as they tucked themselves into the boots. A snowy white shirt, along with a red bandanna draped around his head in true pirate fashion, completed the picture. The only thing that seemed out of place were all the ruffles on his shirt, ruffles completely incongruous with the man's formidable frown.

And it was then that she thought Ian just might get them both shot with the gun the other man was toting so casually on his hip.

Ian reached out with his sword and flicked up a bit of lace.

"Lace?" he drawled. "Have you enough of it, or might there yet be a scrap of your shirt that isn't adorned with it?"

"Ian," Jane whispered fiercely, "shut up!"

The other man only folded his arms over his chest and frowned. " 'Tis pirate clothing, you fool."

"You look like a woman."

"But I still fight like a man. Would you care to test it?"

Then Ian, to Jane's consternation, tossed aside his sword. Well, if he was going to be that stupid, she would have to make up for it. She hauled herself to her feet and made a grab for the blade. It wasn't as heavy as she feared, but it wasn't exactly a pair of pinking shears, either. She managed to get it and herself upright only to find that instead of killing each other, the two men were exchanging a gruff embrace complemented by a great deal of hefty backslapping. It went on for a few minutes, then suddenly the two pulled apart and began to punch each other in the arms and pummel each other on the chest.

Jane rolled her eyes. Men.

"Ian, you randy whoreson!"

"Jamie, you bejeweled peacock!"

Jane let the point of the blade slip down. Jamie? This, then, was Ian's cousin? Dressed like a pirate, no less. She wondered if it was too late to hop in the car and drive off. She was beginning to have serious doubts about the rest of Ian's family and their taste in clothes.

Jamie pulled away and grinned. "Took you long enough to get out of the Fergusson's dungeon."

Ian gave him a healthy shove. "I wouldn't have found myself *in* his dungeon if it hadn't been for your wagging tongue."

Jamie rubbed his hands together gleefully. "Ah, but what a tale it had been to tell. How could I have resisted?"

"You could have clamped your lips together and remained silent, that's what!"

Jane found herself suddenly being scrutinized and she suppressed the urge to check to see if her clothes were on straight. After all, it wasn't as if she and Ian had been doing anything besides sleeping. Jamie made her a low bow.

"James MacLeod, your servant," he said. "If I might have the pleasure of your name, mistress?"

"Jane F—"

"She's from New York," Ian interrupted. "A very fine designer of bridal wear."

Jamie slapped Ian on the back again. "You didn't waste any time finding yourself a woman, cousin." Jamie winked at Jane. "Never lacked for a handsome wench did this one."

Jane found herself with the distinct urge to use Ian's sword. On Ian. Apparently Ian could see what she was thinking because he flinched visibly, then turned and gave this cousin another healthy shove.

"I've mended my ways."

"When hell freezes over!" Jamie laughed.

"It fair did to get me here and I tell you, I've changed."

"A last-minute bargain with Saint Peter?" Jamie asked in a conspiratorial whisper. "I can only imagine how the discourse proceeded. You always did have an excess of fair speech frothing from your head."

"The difference between you and me is," Ian said tightly, "that I know when to cease babbling and you do not!"

"I never babble."

"You do! That's what landed me in the Fergusson's dungeon, you babbling fool!"

"Fergusson?" Jane echoed. "What's this?"

"William Fergusson," Jamie said, scowling at Ian. "Our bitterest enemy. Ian helped himself to Roberta's—"

"Never mind what I helped myself to," Ian interrupted. He looked at Jane. " 'Tis in the past."

"But, Ian," she said slowly, "I'm a—"

"It matters not."

Jane found herself under Jamie's scrutiny again. She put her shoulders back. "My last name is Fergusson. I'm probably related to that William."

"And you've more than made up for William's lack of hospitality," Ian said, taking his sword away from her.

"Ian, I don't think . . . " Jamie began.

"Aye, generally you don't," Ian said, then he firmly

planted his fist in Jamie's face. "That's for the last time you babbled without thinking. Try not to do it again this time and foul up my future."

Jane would have checked to see if Jamie planned to get up off the ground from where he'd been knocked, but she found that she was being dragged by the hand down the meadow toward the castle. She had to run to keep up with Ian's furious strides.

"Hey, slow down," she panted.

Ian sighed and stopped. Then he stared off into the distance for several minutes while she caught her breath and he apparently worked every tangle possible out of his hair. At least that's what she thought he was doing, dragging his hands through it that way. Then he cleared his throat.

"I should likely tell you," he said, looking down, "of why I found myself in that dungeon."

She shook her head. "I'm getting pieces of it, and I don't know that I want to know any more."

"Jamie will tell you if I do not." He sighed again and looked heavenward. "I robbed a woman of her virtue."

Jane felt a chill come over her. "Forcefully?"

Ian looked so shocked, she immediately relaxed. "Saints, nay," he said, with feeling. "I did it cheerfully, for it made her father's life very difficult, but I wouldn't have done it had she not been willing." He smiled a little smile. "Willing is perhaps not a strong enough word. She knew who she stood to wed with and I daresay she considered me a more pleasant prospect for her deflowering."

"Was she very beautiful?" Jane asked wistfully.

Ian laughed. "Saints, nay. She was passing unpleasant, both of face and humor. And she threatened to unman me should I not do my work well."

"I take it you did your work well."

"Well enough," he said briskly. He looked very uncomfortable all of a sudden. "Now, must we discuss this further?"

She shrugged. "You brought it up."

"Aye, well, I did and I'm sorry for it. I daresay you don't want the details."

"Don't I?"

"You do not."

"Why not?"

"Because you and I . . . well . . ."

"Yes?"

"You and . . . er . . . I . . ."

From out of the blue an unexpected warmth began in her heart. Jane had the most ridiculous idea creep up on her that Ian might actually be talking about her and him. Together. As a . . . well . . . couple. She found herself beginning to smile. "Yes?"

He frowned at her. "The past is dead and buried—"

"Yeah, I'll say it is. About seven hundred years buried."

"—and I'd prefer it stay that way," he finished with a darker frown. "I've mended my ways, though Jamie will likely never let me forget them. One does not discuss his past lovers with his future . . . er . . ."

"Yes?" She could hardly believe she was indulging in this word game, because she could hardly believe he might truly be interested in her, but there was that warmth in her heart. And he was definitely frowning. That could mean any number of things, but still . . .

Ian looked at her with narrowed eyes, then took her by the hand and pulled her along behind him to the castle. "I'm finished with this discourse."

"I'll just bet you are," she said, but she was very tempted to smile. His future what? Could he have been prepared to use the word *friend*? *Bride* would have been the expression she would have chosen, but it was still early yet. Maybe she would spend a few more days with Ian and decide that she really didn't like him. Maybe she would decide that Scotland wasn't really the place for her and she would scurry back to New York and throw herself on Miss Witherspoon's mercy.

Or maybe she would take Ian up on his offer and stay in Scotland for a little while. Who knew what might happen if she did?

8

Two weeks later, Jane found herself sitting on a bench with her back against the castle wall waiting for Ian and Jamie to indulge in a little swordplay.

"And he clouted me in the nose!" Jamie was saying to his wife Elizabeth as they came onto the field. "Just reared back as casually as you please and took his fist to my sweet visage!"

Elizabeth only sighed lightly. "Yes, Jamie, we've heard all about it for the past two weeks. Go use Ian up in the lists to soothe yourself."

"Never should have named my bairn after him," Jamie grumbled, as he kissed his wife and walked away. "What possessed me to do the like?"

Jane had watched Ian's face when he'd first been introduced to his little cousin Ian, and watched the emotions that had crossed that face when he realized how he'd been honored. It had resulted in a more backslapping with Jamie, but no apology for the condition of Jamie's nose. Jane suspected Ian was still suffering from very vivid memories of his time in the Fergusson's dungeon.

That she had begun to accept the time-travel story as fact had ceased to surprise her. Maybe it was the Scottish

air. Maybe it was the countless walks and rides she'd
been on with Ian where he spoke so easily of events in
the past. It also could have been watching Jamie and
Elizabeth together and hearing them talk so easily of
events that they claimed had happened hundreds of years
ago.

Or maybe it was just watching Ian, who was no slouch
in the sword department, practice against the supposed
former laird of the clan MacLeod, who was even less of
a slouch when it came to swordplay.

"Ian's still getting his strength back."

Jane looked at Elizabeth who had sat down on the
bench next to her. Jane had come to like Jamie's wife
in the short time she'd known her. Elizabeth somehow
managed to keep equilibrium in her life despite a very
strong-willed husband and a rambunctious toddler. She
managed the two quite well, seemingly kept up a writing
career, and remained a hopeless romantic all without
breaking a sweat.

"I think that couple of months took more out of him
than he wants to admit," Elizabeth continued. "Especially to you."

Jane paused, considered the far-fetchedness of that,
then shook her head. "Ian couldn't care less about my
opinion."

Elizabeth looked at her so appraisingly that Jane felt
herself begin to squirm.

"Well," Jane began defensively, "he really couldn't."

"I think," Elizabeth said slowly, "that you give yourself too little credit. And you give Ian even less. He
wouldn't lead you on. That makes him sound shallow,
and that's the last thing I would call him."

Jane felt her cheeks begin to burn and for the first
time in a long time, she felt ashamed. "I know he's not
shallow. I didn't mean that."

"Then why don't you trust him to know his own
heart?" Elizabeth asked with a gentle smile. "He's old

enough to have figured out what he wants.''

"He hasn't seen what's available this century."

Elizabeth laughed. "Well, he saw more than his share in the past, so don't feel too sorry for him. Ian was something of a—"

"Free spirit?"

"Lothario was more what I was going for," Elizabeth said with a grin, "but how could he help himself? He was a MacLeod minus the grumbles. Women were always throwing themselves at him."

"And he rarely resisted," Jane finished.

"No cable TV," Elizabeth said, as if that should have proven beyond doubt that there was little else to do besides give in. "And it was a hard life. Men died young. It wouldn't have made sense to them to refuse a willing woman."

"Why didn't Ian ever marry?"

"Well, you were here and he was still there," Elizabeth said slowly. "What else could he do?"

Jane leaned her head back against the cold stone. It was so very tempting to believe such a thing when one was surrounded by Scottish countryside. Almost anything seemed possible there. "Hope is a terrible thing," she said with a sigh.

"I think Ian's gone way past hope. He was haggling with Jamie last night over his share of the MacLeod fortune, and that's no small sum."

"Really," Jane said.

Elizabeth nodded. "Jamie unloaded some family treasure he found in the fireplace. I think Ian wants to have a house built before winter. I suspect he doesn't intend to live there alone."

"You're one of those happy ending kind of girls, aren't you?"

Elizabeth only laughed. "Guilty." She smiled at Jane. "Don't you believe in fate?"

"Ian asked me the same thing."

"Did you ever wonder why?"

Jane didn't know how to answer that, so she turned to watch the spectacle in front of her. She suspected that even once Ian got his complete strength back that he might still never be exactly the same kind of swordsman that Jamie was, though she had no doubts he could protect her quite nicely if the need arose. Ian was just, well, less intense than Jamie seemed to be. She couldn't see Jamie loitering by a fire with his feet up and a book in his hands while Elizabeth spun wool into thread. Then again, she couldn't imagine Elizabeth spinning, so maybe it was a good match there.

But she was a weaver herself.

And Ian enjoyed a hot fire and a good book.

"It's all true," Jane said softly. She turned to Elizabeth. "Isn't it?"

"Oh, yes," Elizabeth said, just as quietly. "All of it."

"You lived in the fourteenth century and married Jamie there."

Elizabeth nodded.

"And Ian was there, too."

Elizabeth nodded again.

Jane rubbed her eyes. "The funny thing is, I'm starting to believe it's true, too. Not that I'd want to go back in time and see for myself," she said quickly. "I'll opt for the cable TV, thanks."

"And you know Ian isn't about to give up the possibility of more plane rides."

Jane nodded, trying to put that thought out of her mind. If Ian had his way, they would be flying from one corner of the world to the other on a regular basis, just for the fun of it. She'd been heartily disappointed to find that Jamie had a private jet. Jane had the feeling that if she did intertwine her life with Ian's, she would be flying the friendly skies more often than she wanted to.

But if she had Ian's hand to hold, what was a little turbulence now and then?

She folded her arms over her chest, then looked down at the sweater she was wearing and felt herself smile. It was the most colorful of the sweaters in the local woolen shop and Ian had made her change into it the minute after he'd bought it for her. He'd also bought her a pair of boots for hiking and spent half an hour diligently threading her rainbow-colored shoelaces through the eyes.

If she hadn't loved him before, she thought she just might have begun to then.

"Uh-oh," Elizabeth said, shaking her head. "They're reverting to the native tongue for insults now. Once the Gaelic begins, it's all downhill from there." She looked at Jane as she rose. "Going to stick it out?"

Jane nodded happily. "Wouldn't miss it."

Elizabeth smiled a half smile. "It's easier to watch when you know it's just them keeping in shape, not them preparing for battle."

She invited Jane to come in later for cookies, then walked back around the corner to the front door. Jane turned the thought of Ian going off into battle over in her head for a while as she watched him and Jamie go at each other with their swords. She'd spent ample time studying the two and had come to recognize when Jamie was pushing his cousin and when he wasn't. Ian had long since stripped off his shirt and his back was a patchwork of healing stripes.

It was a chilling sight.

"Bad ancestor," she muttered under her breath, wishing she could give William Fergusson a piece of her mind. "Bad, bad ancestor."

But despite Jamie's well-rested self and Ian's back, Ian was indeed something amazing to watch. She had no doubts that every one of his boasts about his successes in battle was true. She was only relieved that she hadn't known him then to worry over him. Talk about turbulence!

And then talk about turbulence.

"Where is she? Where is that girl?"

The imperious tone that had the power to etch glass cut clearly through the midday summer air. Jane felt her teeth begin to grind of their own accord. And then her jaw went slack as she realized she was hearing Miss Petronia Witherspoon in person. Well, maybe that was what she deserved for even alerting Miss Witherspoon to her whereabouts.

Even the two combatants in the yard turned to look as Miss Witherspoon rounded the corner of the castle like a battleship in full regalia, all sails unfurled. Alexis, clad in a painted-on leopard-print catsuit, came trotting behind her in her wake, loaded down with a couple of bolts of fabric and a pair of dressmaker's shears in her arms. Miss Witherspoon clutched a rolled-up drawing in her hand and brandished it like a sword.

This was not good.

Jane watched Alexis come to a dead stop when she saw both Ian and Jamie in skirts, wielding swords. Jane was used to the sight of them fighting in their plaids. She couldn't decide if Alexis was more shocked by the sight of bare knees or bare chests. Then she took a look at the men and decided it was the latter—definitely the latter.

Miss Witherspoon, however, seemed unmoved by the sensational view in front of her. She gave Jamie a cursory glance, did the same to Ian, then turned and fixed Jane with what Jane always called her eighteenth-century bring-your-sorry-indentured-servant-butt-over-here-this-instant look.

"Jane! Jane!" Miss Witherspoon said this with an imperiousness that even Queen Elizabeth likely couldn't have mustered on her best day. "Jane!"

Jane looked at Ian to see how he was taking all the name-calling. He'd impaled the dirt in front of him with his sword and was resting his hands on the hilt, all the while watching with a smile playing around his mouth. She'd become very familiar with the look. It meant he found something vastly amusing but didn't want to spoil the fun by sticking his oar in where it might not be wanted. That was the thing about Ian. He always seemed to find something delightful about what was going on around him. Jane liked that about him. She especially liked that about him now that Miss Witherspoon was waving a bony finger in her direction and screeching her name. After having spent many days in Ian's company, she too could appreciate the absurdity of what to her had been life or death—read rent and food money—to her but a short three weeks ago. Ian had been talking to Jamie about his share of the MacLeod inheritance. Who needed Miss Witherspoon's paltry offerings?

Assuming he intended to see to the care and feeding of the both of them with that inheritance.

Well, if Elizabeth was worth her salt as a romantic, Ian intended to do something along those lines. In honor of that, Jane slouched back against the wall and propped an ankle up on the opposite knee in a very uneighteenth-century pose.

"Miss P.," she said with a little wave, "what's shakin'?"

"You disrespectful chit!" Miss Witherspoon said shrilly. "Without me you would be wallowing in the gutter!"

She had a point there, but Jane wasn't ready to concede the match. She went so far as to put both feet on the ground and stand up. She nodded her head in proper servant like fashion, but refused to curtsey.

"You're right," Jane said with another nod. "You took a chance on me. I wouldn't be where I am if it hadn't been for you." *And I never would have found Ian.* That alone had been worth three years of slavery.

"I should say not!"

"Your showroom wouldn't be where it is without me,

either,'' Jane said pointedly, ''as you cannot help but admit.''

Miss Witherspoon, surprisingly enough, was silent, but Jane could hear her teeth grinding from twenty paces.

''Alexis as well has benefitted from my skills,'' Jane continued.

''Alexis is a brilliant designer,'' Miss Witherspoon said stubbornly.

''Then why are you here?'' Jane asked.

''She needs a wedding gown,'' Miss Witherspoon said briskly. ''You'll sew it. She wants, and I cannot understand this for he certainly is not the man I would choose for her,'' and she drew in a large breath and released a heavy, disappointed sigh that almost blew Jane over, ''but she wants *him*.''

The bony finger lifted, spun around like a needle on a compass, and pointed straight at Ian.

Ian's smile disappeared abruptly. His glance dropped to Alexis's red fingernails and he emitted a little squeak.

''I like him,'' Alexis said, raking her claws down the bolt of tulle. She fixed Ian with a look that made him back up a pace. ''Do you always carry that sword?'' she purred.

''By the saints,'' Ian said, backing up again. ''I want nothing to do with this one.''

''Of course you do,'' Miss Witherspoon said briskly. ''Jane, come here and take the materials. Get started right away.''

Jane walked past Miss Witherspoon, pushed Alexis out of the way, and stood in front of Ian.

''Get lost,'' she said. ''The both of you. I found him first and I'm keeping him.''

''I want him,'' Alexis protested. ''Auntie said I could have him.''

''Auntie was wrong,'' Jane said, pointing toward the gate. ''Beat it.''

"Wait," Ian said, putting a hand on Jane's shoulder and pulling her to one side.

Jane looked at him in astonishment. "Wait?" she echoed.

"Aye," he said, looking in Alexis's direction with what could have been mistaken for enthusiasm. "Wait."

"But you just said you didn't want anything to do with her," Jane said. She shut her mouth abruptly, amazed that the words had come out of it. As if she should point out to Ian where she thought his eyes should and shouldn't be roaming!

"Aye, well, let us not be so hasty," Ian said, continuing to study Alexis closely.

Jane felt her face go up in flames, taking her heart with it. She couldn't believe she'd misread Ian so fully, but apparently she had. He wouldn't look at her, which convinced her all the more that somehow she had overlooked the fact that he was a rat.

A rat. Hadn't it all started that way? She should have known.

"Let me see the design," Ian said, holding out his hand to Miss Witherspoon.

He unrolled it and looked it over. Jane didn't want to look, but her curiosity got the better of her. She snorted at the sight. One of her designs, of course, and one Alexis had no doubt swiped from her office. It wasn't Miss Witherspoon's normal fare. It was gauzy and flowing and like nothing Miss Witherspoon or Alexis had ever imagined up in either of their worst nightmares.

Ian held up the drawing and compared it with Alexis, as if he tried to envision how it would look on her. Then he looked over the materials she'd brought with her. He fingered, rubbed a bit against his cheek, then fingered some more. Alexis had begun to salivate. Jane wanted to barf and she was on the verge of saying as much when Ian spoke.

To her.

"Make this," he said, gesturing toward the drawing.

Jane was speechless. She could only gape at him, wondering where she was going to find air to breathe again since he'd stolen it all with his heartless words. It was bad enough he was dumping her for Alexis. To demand that she make the wedding dress was just too much to take.

"I have my measurements written down for you," Alexis said, baring her teeth in a ferocious smile. She shoved the material at Jane.

Jane had just gotten that balanced when Ian placed the drawing on top. It was the killing blow. Jane felt the sting of tears begin to blind her.

"If you think for one moment," she choked, "that I'm going to do any of this—"

"Of course you'll do it," Ian said. "The gown is perrrfect."

Jane had the distinct urge to suggest he take his damned r's and wallow in them until he drowned.

"But," he added, reaching over and placing the point of his sword down in the dirt between Alexis and her, " 'tis the wrong color entirely, that fabric."

"Huh?" Alexis said.

"Huh?" Jane echoed, looking up at him. Damn him if that little smile wasn't back.

"White isn't your color," he said, the smile taking over more of his face, "but I suspect you'll look stunning in blue. A deep blue, perhaps. We'll find the dye for the cloth and then you'll make up the gown."

Alexis stamped her feet, setting up a small dust storm. "Blue is *not* my color!"

"Aye," Ian said with a full-blown grin, "I daresay it isn't. But 'twill suit Jane well enough."

"But . . . but . . ." Miss Witherspoon was spluttering like a teakettle that couldn't find its spout to vent its steam.

Ian waved his sword in their direction and sent both

Miss Witherspoon and Alexis backing up in consternation.

"Off with ye, ye harpies," he said, herding them off toward the gate with the efficiency of a border collie. "Ye've made my Janey frrrown and I'll not have any morre of it."

Jane stood in the middle of James MacLeod's training field, her arms full of her future and could only stare, speechless, as Ian threw her tormentors off the castle grounds. Then she looked at Jamie who was rubbing his chin thoughtfully. He made her a little bow.

"I'll see to a priest," he said, then he walked away.

Jane watched him go, then continued to stand where she was, finding herself quite alone.

It had to be something in the air. Or the water.

"I think," she said to no one in particular, "that I've just been proposed to."

No one answered. The clouds drifted lazily by. Bees hummed. Birds sang. The wind blew chill from the north, stirring her hair and the material in her arms. The castle stood to her right, a silent observer of the morning's events. It seemed disinclined to offer its opinion on what it all meant.

And then Ian peeked around the corner, startling her.

"Well?" he asked.

Jane looked at him, noted the grin that was firmly plastered to his face, and considered the possibilities of this turn of events.

She tilted her head and looked at her potential groom.

"Will my little stone house have indoor plumbing?"

"For you, my lady, aye, I'll see it done."

"Electricity?"

"If it suits you."

Well, Ian had lived most of his life without it. It was a certainty that he'd probably live a lot longer if he didn't have any outlets to stick metal implements in.

"I'll give it some thought," she allowed. "How about cable TV?"

That brought him around the side of the castle and over to where she stood. Before she could find out how he felt about television in general, he'd put his hand behind her head, bent his head, and kissed her.

And then before Jane could suggest that perhaps it might be more comfortable if she put the material and sundry down, Ian had wrapped his arms around all of her and her gear and pulled her gently to him. He smiled down at her before he kissed her again, a sweet, lingering kiss that stole her breath and her heart.

By the time he let her up for air, she was convinced he intended that her heart be permanently softened and her knees nothing but mush. If she hadn't been such a good designer, she probably would have lost her grip on the material. As it was, she was sure she'd lost her grip on her sanity because she was seriously considering marrying a medieval clansman who kissed like nobody's business. Heaven help her through anything else he might choose to do.

"Wow," she gasped, when he finally let her breathe again.

He smiled down at her smugly. "We won't need TV."

"I guess not."

His blue eyes were full of merriment and love and dreams for the future. "A spinning wheel, though," he said. "And a hearth large enough for us to warm ourselves by in the evenings."

"And to gather the children around to hear glorious stories of their father's conquests in battle?" she asked, feeling her heart break a little at the thought.

"Aye, that too," he said gently, then he kissed her again. "That too, my Jane, if it pleases you."

She would have told him what pleased her, but he kissed her again and the sensation of having her toes curling in her boots was just too distracting to remember what it was she'd meant to tell him.

Then he put his arm around her and led her back to the castle. He was already planning their future out loud and she suspected she wouldn't get a word in edgewise until he was finished. But since his dreams included her, she wouldn't begrudge him his plans. She was a weaver and he was a storyteller. She would weave her strands in and out of his dreams and he would tell everyone who would listen how it had been done.

And somehow, she suspected they would live out their lives in bliss, quite likely by candlelight.

When you had a fourteenth-century husband, things were much safer that way.

EPILOGUE

Ian MacLeod sat in a comfortable chair in front of a large hearth, toasting his toes against the warmth of the fire, and contemplated life's mysteries. They were many, but the evening stretched out pleasantly before him, so he had the time to examine them at length.

The first thing that caught his attention and qualified for an item of true irony was that he warmed his toes against a fire in a little stone hut when he had a perfectly good manor house up the way with all the modern amenities a goodly portion of his money could buy. His toes could also have been enjoying a fine Abyssinian carpet and his backside a well-worn leather club chair. Even more distressing was the thought of the stew simmering in the black kettle in front of him when there was a shiny red Aga stove sitting in the kitchen waiting for him to pit his skill against it.

By the saints, he might as well have still been in the Middle Ages for all the advances he'd made in his living conditions.

The sound of a spinning wheel distracted him and he found himself smiling in spite of his longing to test out a few new electrical gadgets. He looked to his left and saw the most wonderful of life's great mysteries.

There she sat, the woman of his dreams, the woman he had searched for all his life and never would have found had it not been for a twist of time. She was born and bred in an age far removed from his, yet she was at her most peaceful when they retreated to a place that could have found itself existing comfortably several centuries ago.

Jane's spinning was soothing with its rhythmic sounds and Ian found himself relaxing as he watched her be about her work. Firelight fell softly upon her sweet visage and caressed her long, slender fingers as she fashioned her strands of wool. They were tasks belonging to another age. There were times during the evenings they spent at the cottage when Ian would have to go to the door occasionally to assure himself that his shiny red Jaguar still sat in front of the door.

Ian had discovered that he liked red.

He had also discovered that he liked going very fast.

He leaned his head against the back of the chair and looked at his wife, noting the changes. Her long skirt was a riot of colors. Her sweater was a rich, vibrant red that brought out the strands of flame in her hair and the fine porcelain of her skin. Whatever wildness had resided under her constrained hair and black clothes had found full freedom in the Highlands. Ian found himself smiling. How changed Miss Witherspoon would have found her.

"You're smirking."

Ian looked at Jane, startled by her voice. "How can you tell?" he asked, moving his feet closer to the fire.

She didn't look up, but instead continued with her work. "I can feel it."

"You're guessing," he countered.

She looked at him then and smiled. The sight of it smote him straight in the heart. Aye, this was where she belonged and he praised every saint he could think of with his few poor wits that he'd had the good sense to wind up in Miss Witherspoon's shop on Jane's watch.

"What were you thinking?" she asked with another smile.

"I was just wondering what Miss Witherspoon would say at the changes in your appearance."

Jane laughed. "She'd have heart failure on the spot. I think color makes her nervous."

"We could go to New York and show your colors to other designers," he said, for surely what had been the hundredth time in the past year. "The apple is a large place."

"That's the Big Apple, Ian. And no," she said, holding up her hand, "I'm not all that interested in going back right now." She looked around the hut with satisfaction, then smiled happily at him. "I like it here."

Ian couldn't blame her, for he felt the same way. It had taken them a year to see their two dwellings built and furnished to their satisfaction. Fall was already hard upon them and perhaps it wasn't the best of times to travel. And what need had they to venture forth when so many things came to their door? Ian had come to look forward to the afternoons when he managed to snatch the mail away before Jane could retrieve it first and hide all the catalogs from him. Shopping by Her Majesty's postal service was another of the Future's great inventions that Ian had discovered he enjoyed very much.

"I can sell enough of my work in the village to keep me happy for now," she continued. "And you have a new batch of students coming in before January."

"Aye, there is that," he agreed. His students were souls who came to him for lessons in swordplay. Through the connections of various kin and partly due to fool's luck, he'd managed to meet a pair of men of the Hollywood ilk who needed a swordmaster for their filming in Scotland. Ian had taken on the task and found himself with a new and goodly work to do. Perhaps it wasn't as exhilarating as battle, but 'twas a great deal less hazardous to his health.

"Perhaps in the summer, then," he said. "A journey to the States."

She shook her head. "You'll be busy in the summer."

He frowned. "I've no students then."

"You'll be helping take care of a baby."

"Elizabeth is with child?" Jamie would be pleased, but Ian suspected Elizabeth's days of traveling would be over for the foreseeable future.

Jane stopped her spinning and looked at him. "No, Elizabeth is not pregnant."

"But who . . . else . . ." He stopped and looked at his wife who had turned a bright shade of red. Ian liked red very much. Indeed, the color had begun to swim before his vision, along with a chamber full of stars.

And then he found himself with his head suddenly between his knees.

"Breathe," Jane commanded, with her hand on his neck.

Ian did as she bid until he thought he might manage to get to his feet and remain there successfully. He stood, gathered his lady wife into his arms, and looked down at her, feeling a great sense of awe.

"You didn't tell me," he whispered.

"I wanted to be certain before I did."

"A son," he said reverently.

"It could be a girl," she pointed out.

"A wee lass," he said, petrified. By the saints, the young men he would have to slay to keep her safe from their clutches!

And then another thought occurred to him. He looked at Jane sternly.

" 'Tis too cold here for you," he said firmly.

"In Scotland?" she asked incredulously.

"In this cottage," he clarified, feeling the thrill of electricity rush through him. Finally he would investigate the mysteries of man's inventions to his heart's content. ''We'll repair immediately to the house where it's warm.''

''I'm suspicious of your motives,'' she said, but she smiled as she said it.

''Be suspicious after you've warmed up. I'll return later for supper and the spinning wheel.''

He pulled the door firmly shut behind him and herded his wife efficiently toward the marvels of the Future that awaited him at home.

It was very much later that Ian lay in his exceedingly comfortable feather bed with his lady sleeping sweetly in his arms, and gave thought not to the ironies of life, but to the sweet mysteries. There were no angry clansmen who stood to break down his door any time in the foreseeable future. He wouldn't find himself woken from a deep sleep with the necessity of being on his feet with his sword in his hand prepared to fight in any future he could envision. His greatest danger would likely come from machines that wouldn't stop merely when he said ''whoa'' in a loud voice. That he could live with, especially when the reward for it was the finding of his love and—the saints aid him to be equal to the task of fatherhood!—a bairn.

He surely had no desire to thank William Fergusson for the hospitality of his pit, but Ian couldn't deny that it had certainly been a path to his future and he couldn't help but be grateful for it.

He closed his eyes, sighed, and fell asleep to the comforting click of the radiator.

And he dreamed, for a change, of the Present.

THE CON AND THE CRUSADER

Maggie Shayne

PROLOGUE

Jack McCain pulled the last weed in his grandma's vegetable patch and wiped the dirt off his hands on the seat of his pants.

"Good job, young man," Grandma said from her perch on the front porch. "Now you can have that ice cream I promised you."

Jack sighed. "I don't see why I couldn't have had it before."

"Because you hadn't earned it before. Now you have. It's what I keep telling you, boy. Hard work pays off. A lazy man will never get ahead in life."

"Ahh, phooey." Jack climbed up the front steps. His back ached and he thought he might wind up with blisters on his fingers by morning. "I'm never gonna do hard work when I grow up. I'm gonna use my brains, and make a fortune, and never pull a weed again."

Grandma got to her feet with an effort, and held the screen door open. Jack went inside and headed to the kitchen to wash his hands while Grandma dished up the ice cream.

"You'll find," she said as she set two dishes on the table, "that hard work can be its own reward. Why, when you see those vegetables growing, don't you feel awfully good about yourself? Knowing you had a hand in them? When we pick a fresh tomato off the vine, don't you feel—''

"All I feel is that it would've been a heck of a lot easier to buy a tomato at the A&P.'' Jack dried his hands on a towel and sat down at the table, almost too tired to enjoy the ice cream now, he thought glumly.

"Oh, you have so much to learn, boy,'' Grandma said. "Just how do you plan to get ahead in life if you aren't willing to work for it? Hmm?''

Jack shrugged, shoveled a spoonful of ice cream into his mouth, and decided he wasn't too tired to enjoy it after all. "I don't know. If I could find that wishin' well you're always talkin' about, I'd wish myself a million dollars and then I'd pay someone to do the weeding.''

His grandma clicked her tongue and shook her head. "That well only appears to people when they truly need its magic . . . people who are deserving. So the legend goes, anyway.''

"Well, I need it,'' Jack moaned. "Look at my hands!'' He held one palm up for his grandma's inspection, while scooping up another bite with his free hand.

"But even so,'' Grandma went on, "the wishes aren't free. You have to earn them just like anything else in life. There's a stone beside that well. My grandmother saw it once, and she memorized the words that were engraved there, and told them to me, and I've told them to you.''

"Yeah, yeah,'' Jack said, rolling his eyes and knowing Grandma was about to recite the old poem yet again. She never got sick of telling her crazy wishing-well stories.

And sure enough, she did. In her singsong voice that was reserved only for reading bedtime stories or poems.

"Make a wish upon this well, but wishes don't come free.

Make a promise here, as well, and your wish you will
   see.
A voyage will you take then, your promise to fulfill.
And when you've kept your vow, I shall appear here
   on this hill.
With one more wish to grant you, one more gift to
   bestow.
Any wish you care to make; to stay, perhaps, or go.''

Grandma got a sappy look in her eye as she recited
the verse. Jack just finished his ice cream and shook his
head. He didn't even think that well was real. He'd
looked for it time and time again, but he'd never found
it. Well, it didn't matter. He was smart. He had the gift
of gab, his grandma said. He could talk anyone into
doing just about anything. Why, just last week he'd
conned Mary Ellen McMadden into doing his math
homework for him.

Nope, Jack McCain wasn't going to spend his life
pulling weeds or getting dirty. He vowed it. Wishing
well or no wishing well, he'd make his fortune, and he'd
make it without working his tail off for it, too!

1

It wouldn't have been all that uncomfortable without the handcuffs. Jack had no doubt whatsoever they were little more than a prop being used for effect. To drive home a point.

"So really, guys, who put you up to this?" he said, smiling his most winning smile at the backs of their crew cuts. The two cops in the front seat didn't seem to notice. "I mean, it's obviously a joke, right?"

"Sam, did you tell this clown he had the right to remain silent?" one crew cut said to the other.

"Sure did."

"Hmph. Wouldn't know it, would you?"

"Nope."

"Aw, come on, guys, gimme a break." His spotless Armani suit was picking up lint from the seat, and he shuddered to think where that lint might have come from.

"You've had all the breaks you're getting, pal. You've run your last con."

"That's bull! For cryin' out loud, guys, I gave up conning the upstanding citizens of Hillcrest a long time ago. I've gone straight, and you know it."

"Right." One of the cops turned in his seat. "Now you only con drug lords."

"Yeah," said the other. "And organized crime bosses, right?"

He shrugged and tried not to look too sheepish. It was true, he'd turned the confidence game into an art form, and he'd swindled some major bucks out of some big-time criminals. But it wasn't like they couldn't afford it.

"Beats digging ditches for a living," he said, admitting nothing.

"You never were one to want to get your hands dirty."

The cops exchanged a glance, a nod, and all of a sudden the cruiser slowed and pulled off to the shoulder. The two cops turned in the seat to look back at him. And he would have loosened his collar if his hands hadn't been cuffed behind his back. It was getting damned warm in this car. And they were basically in the middle of nowhere. Not a house for a mile in either direction, and he knew that, because he'd grown up in one of them. His grandmother's run-down farm house, abandoned now. He hadn't been back there since she'd died and the government had taken it for back taxes. Dear old Grandma. She used to say there was a wishing well around here somewhere. One that really granted wishes.

A fairy tale to give a lonely kid hope, that's all her stories were. You didn't get what you wanted by wishing for it, or by working your fingers to the bone for it the way she had, either. You got it by using your brains, and going out, and taking it from those who had it in spades.

"What's this," he asked, and he tried not to sound nervous. "You gonna rough me up now? Should I be hoping for a passerby with a camcorder?"

The cop named Sam smiled, shaking his head. "We have you cold, Jack. You know that, right? That swampland you sold to Arturo, the phony stock sales, all of it. We can make this bust stick."

Jack only shrugged. "I can't imagine a judge and jury feeling too vindictive against me for picking on poor, defenseless kingpins like Arturo," he said. "Not that I'm saying I did."

"Like I said, we can make it stick. But we don't have to."

Jack's attention was caught and he looked up slowly.

"We can help each other out," the cop went on. "You give us a hand with our little problem, and uh, we'll see what we can do about yours."

"You want to make a deal with me," he said slowly, finally understanding what this little bust was all about. "But what do I have that you could possibly want—"

"Oh, come on Jack. You know damn well what you have. We've been trying to bust Arturo for months, but he's slicker than Satan. Slicker than *you,* even."

"You can give us names," said the other cop. "Dates, places, times. Where he's been, who he's been talking to."

"Yeah," Jack said. "Right. And get my head blown off an hour later. No thanks, guys. I think I'll just take my chances with whatever trumped-up charges you can think up to try to pin on me."

Sam shrugged, shaking his head slowly. "Thing is, Jackie, my boy, that's liable to happen either way."

"Huh?"

"Well . . . we got leaks. I mean, we do what we can, but it happens, you know? So chances are, Arturo already knows you've been picked up. And my guess is he knows why."

Jack was silent for a long moment. Then he said simply, "Shit."

"You cooperate with us, we'll keep you in protective custody until he's safely behind bars, my friend. You don't . . . well, we'll take you downtown, spend a couple

of hours questioning you, and then turn you loose."

"In full view of anyone who cares to be watching."
Jack could fill it all in pretty easily. "Anyone being
Arturo, who'll figure I spilled everything I knew, and
pop me at the first opportunity."

"Gee, do you really think he'd do that?"

"Sarcasm doesn't become you, Sam."

"So? You gonna tell us what you know?"

Jack sighed, shook his head, and glanced behind him
for about the fifth time. "I don't think I'm going to get
the chance to, fellas." He said it calmly. He was noted
for keeping a cool demeanor under any circumstances—
wise-cracking his way through life-and-death struggles,
interrogations, death threats. He was also known for
making a lot of money without lifting a finger. It had
been his goal for as long as he could remember to get
rich without working for it. Grandma always told him
he'd have to pay the piper some day. Looked like that
day had arrived.

The dark sedan which had been a discreet distance
behind them sped up, closing the gap.

"Shit," Sam said. "We've got a tail."

"Gee, do you think?" Jack asked, just as another car
suddenly pulled across the road in front of them. The
two cops drew their guns, and Sam grabbed the mike
with his free hand and started yelling for backup. Four
goons in very nice suits and very dark glasses got out
of their vehicles with automatic weapons.

"Jesus, forget the damn radio and gimme the keys to
these cuffs!" For once, Jack's coolness deserted him.
Sam tossed a set of keys into the backseat. By the time
Jack turned ass backwards to snag them in his cuffed
hands, the bullets had started flying, and he ducked low.
He heard glass shatter, a dull grunt, constant blasting,
but none coming from within the car. He lifted his head
just long enough to see what he wished he hadn't. The
two cops in the front were full of more holes than Swiss

cheese, and the bad guys were approaching from the driver's side of the car. He ducked again. There was no time to unlock himself. Just to stuff the keys into a back pocket, wrench open the passenger-side door at his back, and roll through it into the ditch at the roadside.

He hit the ground, got up, and dug in. Running for all he was worth, hoping the maniacs didn't see him, he ducked into the nearby woods.

Shouts, gunshots, and running footsteps followed.

Shit. They'd seen him, all right. And they were thundering after him, even now.

His grandma had been right. Crime didn't pay, and dammit, this was a fine time for him to realize it. These guys meant *business*. Deadly business.

They were gaining on him. Tough to run very fast with your hands trussed up behind your back, and roots leaping up to trip you every few feet. A bullet whirred past his ear, and he spotted what looked like a curving stone wall just ahead, mostly overgrown with vines and brambles. Cover. It wasn't much, but if he dove beyond it, it might block a few bullets. Buy him another second or two of life.

He ran full tilt, reached the little wall, and dove head-first over it.

Only, it wasn't a wall. He figured that out when he didn't hit the ground on the other side. It was a well. And he was plummeting down into inky darkness, and no bottom in sight.

If the landing didn't kill him, the bad guys would. No way out. "God, don't let me end up like this. If I had one more chance, I'd work for a living. I swear I would. Get me out of this one and I'll prove it. I'll work harder than I ever have in my life! Honest, I will!"

His only answer was a powerful thud when he hit the bottom.

2

Emily Hawkins wiped the sweat from her brow, and eyed the unplowed ground that stretched out in front of her. She'd been driving the damn mule all morning, and had little more to show for it than an aching back and a few crooked furrows.

So far, her experiment was failing. But failure was not something she could tolerate easily. Nor would she. If it killed her she would raise a crop, sell the grain, and make the final mortgage payment on time. She would. Oh, no one else believed it. Everyone in this town had urged her to sell the farm before her husband was even buried. And when she'd told them all that she intended to keep it, to run it herself, and make that payment rather than sell it for the criminally low offers her neighbors and local banker had made on the place, they'd laughed at her.

Laughed! At *her*!

"Well, we'll just see who's laughing when I've finished!" she huffed, and yelled again at the mule. "Come on, Molly! We've work to do!"

"Aunt Emily?"

She stopped what she was doing and turned to see her precious ones, Sarah Jane and Matthew, staring up at her. Beyond them, one hand on either shoulder, stood Mary Brightwater, the local schoolteacher.

"Your children are wanting their lunch, Mrs. Hawkins."

Emily bit her tongue before she could tell the schoolmarm to mind her own business. "I was just on my way."

Mary was clean and shiny, yellow hair spilling from beneath her pretty bonnet. Young, fresh. She made Emily feel like a dirt-covered crone.

"I'll be happy to help," Mary said with a youthful smile, sunlight glinting in her hair.

"I can manage just fine," Emily replied, taking a small hand in each of hers. Then, remembering her manners, "But you're welcome to join us, if you like."

"I would, thank you. I've been wanting a word with you, you know."

Emily crooked a brow, certain she was about to be on the receiving end of yet another lecture on a woman's place, and the futility of her efforts. As a foursome, they trekked across the wide-open expanse, down the slight incline to the pretty white clapboard farmhouse beyond. There was a well in front, its pump handle freshly painted. And a small barn off to the left, in need of a new coat itself. But there were only so many hours in the day. The wide front porch was swept clean and the house was in order, though. Sarah Jane and Matthew raced ahead. Emily watched Sarah's auburn braids flying behind her, and thought again that she would do anything, *anything,* to keep this place for the children. They'd lost so much already....

The children played outdoors while Emily prepared lunch, and despite her insistence that she needed no help, Mary pitched in anyway.

"Mrs. Hawkins ... Emily," Mary began as they sliced cheese and bread that wasn't quite as light as it should have been. Oh, how Emily missed the days when she'd had time enough to cook a proper meal. "May I call you that? I hope you don't mind my speaking plainly to you. I know it's not my place to advise you, but I feel I must."

Emily closed her eyes and sighed. "Say what you will. But know that I will not be swayed."

"I'll say it then. You simply cannot continue trying to run this farm and raise these children on your own."

Emily met Mary's eyes straight on. "I shall tell you what I've told everyone else. I have no choice." She went to the window and looked out at the children playing in the yard. "Look at them, Mary. They lost their mother when they were almost too young to know her."

"Your sister was a fine woman," Mary said. "Everyone thought so."

"Yes, and no one thought I could ever fill her shoes. But I have. I came here and cared for those two as if they were my own. I married my sister's husband to halt the town gossips pecking about how improper it was for us to be living together as we were. I love them. And I would do anything for them."

"You've more than proven that."

"Now that Clem is gone, I'll take his place as well. I can do this, I know I can."

"It's too much for one woman. Any woman, even you."

The words sounded almost like a compliment, but Emily thought her ears must be deceiving her.

"Look at you, Emily. You've grown thin, you have dark circles under your eyes, no doubt from lack of sleep. And your hands." As she spoke she gripped Emily's wrist and turned her palm up. "Lordy, when these blisters break you'll be unable to grip a wooden spoon, much less the reins of that mule."

Emily pulled her hand free, turning away. She could not admit defeat. She *would not*. "So what do you suggest? That I give up? That I let this place go to the bank for lack of one final payment?''

''No. I don't suggest that at all.''

Emily turned around to stare at the young woman. ''You don't?''

Mary shook her head. ''I am aware that's what everyone else has been telling you to do, Emily, but I've seen enough of you to know you're not the type to do things the easy way. Nor to give up easily. And moreover, if there is any woman who could achieve this, you are she. In fact, I *want* to see you succeed.''

''You do?'' Emily was bewildered.

Mary nodded. ''I've never known a woman as strong as you are, Emily. And I'd dearly love to see you prove once and for all that the men of this town are wrong. I simply have a suggestion for you. One which I think would make things a good deal easier.''

''My goodness.'' Emily had to blink away her shock. ''I . . . I'm surprised.''

''Sit,'' Mary said. ''And try to keep an open mind.''

Emily sat, and Mary poured coffee into two tin cups, then brought them to the table and took a seat of her own. ''Emily,'' she said, ''what you need to enable you to bring in the crop and keep this farm, is a man.''

Emily's shoulders slumped. ''I had so hoped you would have a *plausible* suggestion.'' She sighed. ''I've no time for courtship, nor flirting, nor fixing my hair in hopes of enticing some man into wedlock. I vow, Mary, I'm not the sort of woman a man would want anyway.''

''You're joking, surely. Why, Emily, I can name a dozen men who would break their legs racing to the altar for you!''

Emily met her eyes. ''For my land, you mean. For this farm.''

Mary's eyes widened. ''Is that what you truly believe?''

''It's what I know. I am a thirty-five-year-old widow

with two children to raise. I've carrot-hued hair that refuses to be tamed, and since I've begun running this farm I've become hard in all the places a woman should be soft. My hands are callused, my face is sunburned. Please, need I go on?"

Mary only shook her head as if in disbelief. Very polite of her. "And I cannot afford to hire help just now."

"No, of course you can't. But . . ." Mary paused, licked her lips. "What if there were a way you could get a man to do the work around here without hiring one . . . or courting?"

Frowning over her cup, Emily looked up. "Whatever do you mean?"

"Emily, there is a statute still in effect in this town. I came upon it while teaching my class about local government and how it's run. The mayor gave us a look at the town's statutes. And that's when I saw it. It dates back fifteen years, to a time when Hillcrest seems to have had a severe shortage of . . . men."

"A man shortage?"

"Um-hmm. And with the prison nearby, men were being transported through here all the time. So the law was written and passed by the town council, and then signed by the governor. Any single woman or widow who owns property may choose a prisoner to marry. The man goes right back to jail if he mistreats, displeases, or tries to leave his bride. He has to agree to the terms she sets beforehand."

Emily felt her eyes widen; felt hope spring to life for the first time in months. But then she sighed and lowered her head. "It . . . it would be impossible. He'd expect . . . certain . . . things . . ." She met Mary's eyes again. "With Clem, it was different. We were Anna's sister and Anna's husband, bound together for the sake of Anna's children. We were friends, and helpmates, but never . . . never husband and wife. Not . . . not *really*."

"I see."

"Of course . . . I suppose if I could find a prisoner who could never possibly be interested in . . . in such things . . ."

Mary sighed. "All men are interested in . . . such things."

"I mean with me. Suppose I were to get one older than me?"

"Men love younger women."

"A lot older, I mean."

Mary tilted her head. "You want him to be strong enough to work, don't you?"

"Mmm, that's true. Younger, then. Yes, that's it! I'll find one so young he wouldn't dream of . . . of *such things* . . . with a woman of my age."

"Oh, now we're getting there! It will positively scandalize the entire town!" Mary said this as if it were a good thing.

"And it isn't as if it would be impossible. I'm hardly attractive."

"Oh, Emily, this will drive Mr. Sheldon absolutely mad!"

Emily lowered her eyes to hide the flash of anger in them. "Sometimes I think he only holds that mortgage over my head to force me into accepting his marriage proposal. I hate to be so suspicious of him, but . . . well, he *is* a banker."

"Never mind him. Go fix yourself up, Emily! There's a whole group of prisoners due in this afternoon. I'll finish the children's lunch. Go on now. Go!"

"I hardly see why I need fix myself up at all."

Mary eyed her, then shook her head. "The prisoner has to agree to this too, you know. You mustn't scare him so badly he'd prefer serving his sentence to marrying you."

"Oh," Emily said, glancing down at her dirt-streaked dress. "All right, then. I suppose . . ." She turned to go to the well for water, and as she went, she asked herself just what she was thinking. But then, this might be the only way. "I can do this," she muttered, bolstering herself, raising her chin. "I can. I must. For the children."

Jack shook himself, lifted his head, and realized that he was still alive. Then he realized something else, as well. He wasn't at the bottom of any well. In fact there was no well in sight. He thought he'd glimpsed it when he'd first opened his eyes, but when he looked again, there was nothing there.

And for just an instant his grandmother's wishing well fairy tale had whispered through his mind. But that was ridiculous.

At any rate, there was no one shooting at him now. He was on a dusty road. A group of men were shuffling past him, all looking like extras from a cheap Western: unshaven and dusty, wearing faded jeans and tattered hats. Some wore leg-irons, some handcuffs, some both. At the front and rear some guys in antiquated prison guard uniforms strode along with rifles.

"What the hell . . . ?"

"Get up, fellow." A booted foot nudged him in the rib cage. "Come on, now. It ain't that long a walk."

"No, look, I'm not one of these—"

"I *said* get up." This time the fellow moved his rifle, just a little, enough to remind Jack it was there.

Jack got up. "Look, you're making a mistake. I'm not—"

"Back in line."

"But I don't belong in line. I just—"

Thud. The rifle butt drove into his belly hard enough to send the wind gusting out of him. He dragged in a breath when he could, and took his place in line, doubled over, but at least he was in line. Damn, but this was weird. Where the hell was he?

Up ahead a town came into view. Only it was more

like a handful of buildings in the middle of nowhere.
Little Town on the Prairie or something. The dirt track
led to it, through it, and vanished. He'd freaking landed
in nowhere land. "What the hell is this place?" he
asked.

"Hillcrest. Prison's just up yonder."

"Hillcrest my ass." He looked, then looked again.
There was nothing, no camera crew, not a vehicle in
sight, but he could still swear he'd fallen into the middle
of a movie set. He'd see Eastwood toting a six-shooter
any minute, he was sure of it.

"Now, look'ere, Mr. Fancy-duds, I've had just about
enough of your lip."

"Mr. Fancy-duds? Gee, you oughtta be on stage with
witty lines like that, pal."

"I ain't yer pal." The guy spit on the ground. "But
these other fellas in line will be, once you're all in prison
together. Gee, you think they'll like you?"

Jack took a look at the filthy, smelly, oversized,
dangerous-looking bunch of convicts around him, and
wished for Arturo's gangsters again. "Listen, mister, I
don't know what the hell this is, but there's been some
kind of mistake. I don't belong here."

"Then how'd you git here? Fall down outta the sky?"

"I don't know." Jack felt dizzy and disoriented. He
tried to go back over the last few minutes as he remembered them but they made no sense. Maybe he'd been
shot after all, or hit his head when he fell into the well
and this was just . . .

Wait a minute. The well. Grandma's *wishing well*?

Nah. Couldn't be. . . .

Maybe. He *had* sort of made a wish. *And* a promise.
Hadn't he?

"Hold up there!" someone called.

Jack glanced ahead, saw a pair of horses galloping
toward him, one pulling a . . . a buggy. With a fringe on

top. Jesus H. . . . The other horse carried a rider wearing a badge.

"Look, I think I must have banged my head. *Hard.* Could you check?" he asked the ugly guard.

"You don't shaddup and *I'm* gonna bang your head." The guard looked toward the rider. "What is it, Sheriff?"

The sheriff dismounted and walked over to the now-halted buggy, leaned inside to talk to someone Jack couldn't see, and came back out with some papers. "I uh . . ." The sheriff pushed his hat back and scratched his head. "Hillcrest has an arrangement with the prison. It uh . . . it goes back a ways, but it's still on the books and . . . well, I know this is highly irregular, but . . ." Shaking his head, he thrust a sheaf of papers into the guard's hand. The guard surprised Jack by being capable of reading them, then he looked up at the sheriff.

"You have *got* to be kiddin', Sheriff."

"It's the law," the sheriff said. "And she qualifies, and she's *insisting.*"

Frowning, the guard sighed. "Well, the law's the law, I suppose. Is she *sure* about this?"

"There's no talking her out of it, I'm afraid," the sheriff replied.

The guard shook his head again. "So, uh . . . which one does she want?"

The sheriff went to the buggy, and came back again. "Ahem . . . er . . . which one is the youngest?"

The guard looked the prisoners over, rubbing his chin. "That would be Johnny over there. Twenty-one. Killed a family of seven and burned their house 'cause their wagon splashed mud on him one day."

The sheriff paled. Shaking his head, he walked to the buggy again. Then turned back. "How old's the odd-lookin' one?"

"Hey!" Jack said when they both looked at him. But they just waited. "Twenty-eight," he finally answered.

"And I'm not odd-looking, and furthermore, I'd like to know just what the hell is—"

"She'll take him," the sheriff said.

"Now wait a minute! Who'll take me, and where, for Pete's sake, and—"

The guard shook out the papers. "Says here he has the right to refuse the offer."

"He'd have to be a raving fool. I mean, hell, man, look at the alternative." And with that the sheriff gazed up at a distant hillside, where the most grim-looking place on the planet loomed; gray stone, high walls, barbed wire, and armed guards in towers.

"That there is Hillcrest Prison, Mr. Fancy-duds," the ugly card said almost in Jack's ear. "And that's where yer headin' if you turn the lady down. Frankly, I hope you do. I'd like to see just how long a tenderfoot like you would last up there."

Jack shivered. "Look, guys, if you'd just tell me what the hell is going on here . . ."

"Town statute," the sheriff said. "Any land-owning female who is either single or widowed may, at her discretion, choose a prison-bound male to marry her—"

"Marry?"

"Yeah." The guard elbowed him in the ribs. "Trade one prison for another, eh pal?" Then he laughed so loud Jack could smell his breath.

"You can refuse, of course," the sheriff said. "But if you agree, you have to play by the rules. No beating her . . ."

"Beating her?"

". . . no consorting with lewd women, no drinkin', no gamblin', and you can't leave her, 'cause if you do, you go right back to prison. Got it?"

"Uh . . . yeah. Sure. But as I've been trying to tell this gentleman here, I'm not on my way to prison. I'm . . . I'm sort of lost, and I just stumbled onto this group of . . . er . . ."

"Right. In handcuffs."

Jack tugged, remembered, and felt the first stirrings of panic take hold. "But this isn't fair. Look, I really don't . . . I mean I wasn't . . ."

"I know it's an arcane law, son," the sheriff said. "Hell, it's fifteen years old, written back in seventy-five when the town was founded."

Jack pulled out of his panic long enough to note, "You can't even add, and they made you sheriff?"

"I can too add. Eighteen seventy-five plus fifteen is ninety, and that's exactly right. Eighteen ninety."

Jack blinked. Then he looked around him at all the others. "This is a joke. You guys are all in on it, and this is some kind of a—"

"Come 'ere and meet the widow Hawkins, son." The sheriff gripped his arm and tugged him over to the buggy. Then he rapped on the door. "Come on out, Miss Emily. Might as well get a good look at him and make sure about this. I mean, hell, he's not only way too young for you, he's slightly insane to boot. You sure about this?"

She was old? They wanted him to marry some old lady named Miss Emily? The widow Hawkins? Good God!

She peered out the window, but had a big bonnet on and a fan in front of her face. All he could see were a pair of eyes. Green eyes. And they didn't look like the eyes of an old lady, either. A few reddish wisps of hair had escaped the bonnet. Not gray, but a pretty color. Like a sunset.

She met his eyes, and her gaze locked with his for just a minute. She looked scared, nervous, and maybe a little embarrassed. And then she spoke in a deep, rich voice that sounded the way melting butter would sound if it could speak, he thought.

"I know this is very odd, sir. But I assure you, it's perfectly legal. And . . . and necessary. All I will expect from you is honest work," she said. "Nothing more."

And her eyes met his once again, a quick glance, filled with meaning. "Nothing more," he repeated, getting the message loud and clear. "You sure you want a husband, lady? Sounds more like you need a hired hand."

"If I could afford a hand, sir, do you think I would be opening my home to a criminal?"

"I am *not* a—"

"It's either me, or prison, sir. So are you going to get into this buggy or continue walking with your . . . companions?"

He glanced back at the guys he'd be rooming with at the prison, then at the ugly guard who seemed to have it in for him. Nobody was listening when he said this was a mistake. And he might have stood a chance of making them listen if he could explain any of this. But he couldn't. At least with the lady, he might have a chance to figure things out. From behind those prison walls, he didn't think he ever would. Drawing a deep breath, he met those green eyes again and said, "I'm getting in."

He thought she sighed very softly . . . , in relief? "Good."

The sheriff opened the buggy's door. But the lady . . . Miss Emily . . . stopped him. "Take off those hand shackles, Sheriff."

The sheriff glanced down and then frowned. He gripped the cuffs, shaking his head. "Dang. I don't know who put these on you, pal, but I've never seen their like around here. I doubt my keys will—"

"That's okay. The keys are in my back pocket."

At that the sheriff frowned.

"I told you, Sheriff, I'm not a criminal. I was arrested because the cops thought I could give them some information. They intended to let me go, even gave me the keys and then all hell broke loose and I wound up here, and I still don't know how. . . ."

"Ah, hell," the sheriff said, pulling out the key and unlocking the cuffs. "Shut up, already."

"I gotta warn you, Miss Emily," the ugly guard put in, "this guy talks a blue streak. Crazy talk, too. Why, he'll talk till your ears bleed, if you let him."

Jack glanced up at the woman in the buggy and thought he detected a smile in her eyes, but she looked away before he could be sure. He rubbed his wrists where the cuffs had chafed him and finally climbed into the buggy, taking the seat across from her.

The sheriff got back aboard his horse. "Just so you don't get any ideas, mister, I'll be escortin' you back to Miss Emily's place. And the preacher will be there waiting. There won't be any chance to go running off, so forget it if that's what you're thinking. And if you want to change your mind, now's the time to do it."

He sat there, hearing the sheriff, but looking at the lady. Curiosity made him lift his hand, touch the fan she held, and gently push it aside so he could see her face. And when he did, he wondered why the hell any woman as beautiful as this one would have to resort to such an odd method of getting herself a husband. His eyes slowly traced over high cheekbones, lean features, full pink lips. And more curling strands of cinnamon hair framing the rest.

"I'm uh . . . I'm not gonna change my mind, Sheriff," he said.

She blushed a pretty shade of pink, but there was just a hint of alarm in her wide green eyes.

3

"It . . . doesn't look as if you've been well treated," Emily said. Anything to break the strained silence that filled the buggy. He was, she noticed, a handsome man. Though his suit was very odd. She'd never seen one like it. He must be from back East. He had dark brown hair, tousled now. A hard, strong face, though it was scratched in several places, and there was a bruise along the side of his temple.

She hadn't thought this through quite thoroughly, then, had she? She should have chosen an ugly man. Though the others she'd glimpsed would have likely frightened the children. And she certainly didn't want that.

He reached up to touch the bruise. "Oh, they didn't do this. I was . . . it uh . . . happened before."

"I see." She didn't. Not really. "I . . . um . . . I don't even know your name." She smiled uneasily.

"It's Jack," he said. "Jack McCain." He held out a hand.

Emily took it, hesitantly, but the warmth and strength that surrounded hers when she did made her even more uneasy. His grip was firm, tight. She pulled her hand away, averting her eyes. This was not going to be as easy as Mary had made it sound.

"Well, Mr. McCain—"

"I kind of think it's safe for you to call me Jack," he said, interrupting her. "If we're going to . . . you know . . . get married." He lowered his head, shook it slowly. "I can't even believe all this."

Tilting her head, Emily studied him. He looked upset. Confused. "What were you arrested for, Mr. . . . er . . . Jack?"

His head came up, eyes meeting hers. He had blue eyes. Very blue . . . and very piercing. When he looked at her it was as if he were looking more deeply than anyone ever had before. "It's a long story. And you wouldn't believe me if I told you." He frowned, searching her eyes. "It is *really* eighteen ninety?"

Blinking rapidly, she caught her breath. Lordy, but what if he *was* slightly insane, as the guard had suggested? "I . . . yes. Why does that surprise you?"

"Because I . . ." He lowered his gaze and shrugged. "Never mind. It sounds crazy even to me, and I'm the one living it. Tell me something, Emily, is there a wishing well around here?"

Again she frowned and searched his face for signs of lunacy. But he had the look of a normal man asking a perfectly normal question. "There is a story about a well, not far from where you just were, with the prisoners. It . . . well, there are tales about it. I don't know of anyone who's ever seen it." But she had seen it. She'd seen it herself one day. But it had been gone the next. "Some say it truly can grant wishes." She shrugged. "I've never been much for believing in such things myself."

His lips thinned. "You ever try it?"

"Making a wish at a well?" She hesitated. "I'm embarrassed to admit it, but . . . yes."

"What did you wish for, Emily?"

His voice was soft . . . but she felt it brushing against her nerves like a touch. He was disturbingly intense, this man. "That is personal."

"Did it come true?"

She drew a breath. Did it? She'd wished for a means to keep the farm, give the children a wonderful, happy upbringing, and perhaps . . . find some kernel of happiness for herself in the process, though that part of her wish was the least important of all. "I suppose," she finally answered, "that it is still too soon to tell. Tell me, Jack, do you like children?"

His eyes widened, and it seemed she'd succeeded in distracting him from this odd talk of wishes and wells. "Why? Do you *have* children?"

Smiling at his distress, she nodded. "Two of them. Sarah Jane and Matthew. Of course, they're actually my sister's children, but she . . . she died when they were just babies. So naturally I came here to care for them."

"Naturally." He was staring at her even harder now. "How old are they?"

"Sarah Jane is five, and Matthew is seven," she said.

"And uh . . . where is their father?"

He seemed truly interested in her situation. Of course, he would be. It was soon to become *his* situation as well. "I suppose I may as well tell you the whole of it. I married their father shortly after arriving here. Clem was a good man, and my sister loved him dearly. He was well respected in Hillcrest, but that didn't stop the townsfolk from gossiping about an unmarried woman living under the same roof with a widowed man and raising his children. So we married, and that ended the gossip."

Jack's brows bent until they touched. "How very . . . practical."

"It was best for the children."

"Uh-huh."

Emily didn't like the speculative look in his eyes, so

she went on with her story. "Clem died two months ago, leaving me with the farm, and one rather large mortgage payment due in the fall. If I can't raise a crop, I will lose the children's home to the bank, and that is unacceptable. But though I've tried, I fear I cannot do it alone."

"And that's where I come in," he said slowly.

She nodded, trying to look bright and hopeful. "Yes. And Mr. McCain—"

"Jack."

"Jack. When this payment is made, and the farm is safe, I will let you out of our . . . arrangement."

His brows went up. "You can do that?"

She nodded hard. "I've checked this statute thoroughly, and while you are forbidden from leaving me, I remain free to end our . . . marriage . . . at any time. So long as the decision is mine, you'll have fulfilled your obligation, and will be considered a free man."

"So . . . I'm sort of a summer rental?"

"Don't you see how perfectly this works out? I'll get to keep the children's home, you'll get your freedom. All in exchange for a few months of hard work."

"Hard work," he repeated, and for a moment he seemed to be thinking. But then he nodded. "It is . . . a pretty fair deal," he said. "But maybe it would've been better if you'd chosen somebody else. Emily, uh, you had no way of knowing this, but I . . . I don't know the first thing about farming."

The glimmer of hope vanished. "You don't?"

"I'm sorry. Maybe you should send me back with the sheriff and wait for someone else. I don't belong here. I'm . . . I'm kind of lost and . . . hell, I don't even know how I *got* here." He shook his head. "I need to figure this out, find out how I'm supposed to get back where I belong, and what all this means, and . . ." He ended with a deep sigh.

Emily's heart contracted just a little in her chest. The

maternal side of her, she supposed. He did indeed look lost. Alone and confused, though she didn't know why.

"Perhaps . . . I can help you find those answers."

He looked up slowly.

"It is the least I can do. I'm asking a great deal from you, Jack. You can learn farming. I can teach you that. But what I can't do is bring in a crop on my own." She lowered her head. "I need your help, Jack. And if you'll give it, wholeheartedly, I'll do everything I can to help you get back to . . . to wherever it is you call home. You have my word on that." She smiled, very slightly. "Do we have a bargain?"

She had him the minute she said she needed him. Jack didn't think anyone had *ever* needed him for a damn thing. Not once. But she seemed to be in a bind, and he seemed to be in a position to help her out of it.

And despite all the other unbelievably odd things that were happening to him, he found he wanted to.

There was a suspicion rattling around in his brain. One almost too absurd to even bear considering. But he was considering it anyway. Suppose that well he'd fallen into *had* been the one from his grandma's tales. He remembered begging for another chance, promising to work harder than he ever had in exchange for it. And he remembered his grandma reciting that verse. Something about the well appearing again once a person had fulfilled his end of the bargain. Well, crazy as it sounded, he didn't know how else to explain all of this. So maybe if he worked hard enough, he'd find that well again and he could wish himself right back to good ol' 1999.

Either that or he'd suffered a massive concussion when he'd fallen, and this was all one big hallucination. Yeah. Maybe that was it. It seemed more likely.

The buggy rattled to a halt, and Jack glanced out to see another woman, a young blonde, holding the hands of two of the cutest kids he'd ever laid eyes on. Red-haired, freckle-faced cherubs with green eyes like their aunt. Beyond them a guy in black stood with a book in his hand. The promised preacher, no doubt. And again he wondered just what would drive a woman like Emily to do something so drastic.

He eyed her, and found he really wanted to know. God, she looked nervous. "Emily, I want you to tell me one thing before we go through with this," he said, thinking back to when she'd chosen him from the crowd. "Why me? I mean, there were a lot of men there. So why did you pick me?"

She looked away, shrugging, not answering him.

"When you first arrived out there, you asked the sheriff for the youngest. And you asked my age before you chose me. That has something to do with it, doesn't it?"

To his surprise, her face turned crimson and she looked away. "I . . . I . . . thought choosing a younger man would simply help to avoid . . . complications."

"I don't think I follow."

Lifting her chin, she met his eyes. "I'll be blunt, then. I wanted a man young enough so there would be no danger of him . . . wanting to be . . . intimate with me. This is a business arrangement. Nothing more."

He absorbed that bit of information, failing to see any logic in it. "How old are you, Emily?"

She bit her lip and, lowered her head. "Thirty-five."

He nodded. "So you figured no twenty-eight-year-old man could possibly be attracted to a woman so ancient." For some reason it bothered him a great deal to have her thinking that way.

She looked up fast, a little flare in her eyes. "I'm *hardly* ancient, Mr. McCain."

"Exactly, Miss Hawkins."

Her eyes widened, and she looked away. "It's Mrs. Hawkins."

"If I'm reading you right, and I think I am, then I'd

say for all intents and purposes, it's Miss.''

Her saw her throat move as she swallowed convulsively. ''This is a business arrangement between us,'' she reminded him. ''That's all.'' Then she met his eyes, but it seemed as if she had to force herself to. ''I've told you my situation, set forth my terms. Do you agree or not?''

He glanced out again, saw the sheriff dismounting, gun in his holster at his side. It didn't look like he had much of a choice in the matter. For now. At least until he could figure out what the hell had happened to him, and whether or not this was all some kind of delusional episode caused by a bullet would or a concussion.

And being married to a woman like this one for the summer didn't seem like such a terrible chore. Even if she had made it pretty clear that it was a hands-off sort of proposal. He was a professional confidence man. And he was beginning to see her as a challenge.

''I agree to your terms, Miss Hawkins. And I'll abide by them until you change your mind.''

The look in those green eyes told him she knew exactly what he meant. ''I won't be changing my mind,'' she said.

He nodded and gave her one of his winning smiles. ''If you say so.'' Then he got out of the buggy and reached up to take her hand and help her down, just the way he'd seen gentleman cowboys do in the movies.

She took his hand, stepped down into the brilliant sunshine, and looked up at him. On the surface, she looked strong, determined, and stubborn to Jack. But he'd made a life out of reading people. And he could see beyond the surface of hers.

Miss Emily Hawkins was just a little bit attracted to him. And the feeling scared her to death.

4

Emily shifted nervously from one foot to the other when Reverend Waterman asked, "Are we ready to proceed, then?"

She looked at the stranger standing beside her, and for just a moment, panic fluttered in her belly as if she'd swallowed a hummingbird.

"If you have any doubts, Miss Emily, then now's the time to say so," Sheriff Stonewall said slowly. "We can take him right on up to the prison while you give this thing some more thought."

She sensed the man beside her stiffen, and almost gasped aloud when his hand curled protectively around hers. "Emily and I have made a bargain, Sheriff," he said. "She's not going to back down now."

Mary Brightwater quickly nodded. "You're doing the right thing, Emily," she said.

"Am I?" Emily bit her lip, but her doubts fled when she felt a small tug at her skirts and looked down at Sarah Jane.

Innocent green eyes stared up at her, darting every few seconds to the stranger, Jack McCain. "Is he gonna be our new uncle, Aunt Emily?"

Emily swallowed the dryness in her throat. But before

she could answer, Jack was hunkered down, eye to eye
with her precious niece. Little Matthew crept closer, nervous but protective of his sister in spite of that. "You
must be Sarah Jane," Jack said. Then he glanced at the
boy beside her. "And you're Matt, right?"

"That's right," Matthew said, straightening to his full
height.

"Well, you can call me Jack. I'd tell you to call me
Uncle Jack, but I figure that's a title I'm gonna have to
earn. Can't just waltz in and claim it, now can I?"

The children glanced at each other, then back at Jack
once more, nodding their agreement. "Now I'm gonna
need an awful lot of help from you two. Your Aunt Em
needs a hand running this farm, and there's a whole lot
about farming I don't know. But I'll bet you can teach
me most of it."

Matt's chin rose a notch. "I sure can," he said.

"Me too," Sarah Jane put in. "*I* can even show you
how to milk the cow."

Emily thought Jack's face pulled into an almost grim-
ace, but if it did, he covered it fast. "That's great," he
said. "But right now I need your help with something
else." He turned to little Matthew, his face very serious.
"I'd like to marry your Aunt Em, today, Matt. But you
being the man of the house, I figure I can't do that until
I get your permission. What do you think?"

Matt glanced up at Emily. "Do you want to marry
him, Aunt Emily?"

She found she couldn't speak. For some reason her
airways seemed choked off, so she simply nodded.

Matthew returned Jack's gaze. "You have to promise
to be nice to her," he said. Then Sarah Jane whispered
something to him, and he nodded. "And nice to us,
too."

"And take us fishin'!" Sarah Jane put in. "Like Pa
used to do."

"Yeah," Matthew said. "And . . . you gotta kiss her sometimes."

Emily felt her face heat. *"Matthew . . ."*

"He does, Aunt Em. Pa never did. Never once, that I saw, and all the married folks in town are always doin' it. I think you're supposed to when you're married."

She could feel Jack's eyes on her, but she couldn't look back at him to save her life.

"I'll do that," Jack said, and she knew his eyes were still on her. "But only if she wants me to."

"Okay then. I guess it's okay if you marry her."

Jack nodded and offered Matthew his hand. Matthew took it and shook in a very grown-up manner. "Now," Jack went on. "I'm gonna be needing a best man for this wedding. And your Aunt Emily needs a maid of honor. You two think you'd like the jobs?"

Emily couldn't remember the last time she'd seen those two little angels light up the way they did then. Sarah Jane smiled so hard her eyes crinkled at the corners. And Matthew just beamed.

Truly this man couldn't be so bad. No man who treated children so kindly could possibly be. But a new worry began creeping into Emily's mind. The children could easily fall in love with a man like Jack McCain. What would it do to them when he left again in the fall? Goodness knows they'd lost so much already: their mother, their father.

But not their home. She'd see to that. And she'd simply have a talk with Jack about trying not to get too close to them. This would work. It had to work. For the children.

Lifting her chin and facing the preacher, she nodded once. "I suppose we're ready to proceed, Reverend Waterman."

"Very well." He opened his Bible and began to read. The sheriff looked on in unveiled disapproval while Mary watched with a dreamy expression in her eyes.

And when the ceremony ended and the preacher intoned, "You may kiss the bride," Jack turned to Emily, and for just a second she thought he might be every bit as nervous as she was. She didn't want to be dragged into those powerful arms, kissed by this handsome man. Not now, not this way, in front of all these people. She was terrified all at once, not of him . . . but of what her own reactions to such an experience might be.

Jack stared into her eyes for one long moment, and then he reached out, took her hand very gently in his much larger one, and lifted it to his lips. She felt his breath, his heat, as he brushed a soft kiss across the back of her hand. And she tingled all the way to her toes. Oh, my! She'd never felt such a tingle before.

Trembling all over, she whispered, "Thank you," for his ears alone. For she was certain he'd seen her fear, and deliberately spared her the embarrassment of being kissed full on the mouth in public.

"No," he said softly. "Thank *you.*" And then he smiled, and it took her breath away.

What have I just done, she wondered. *And what in the world do I do next?*

Damn, I'm good. Jack smiled to himself after the ceremony was over. For just a second there, it had looked as if Miss Emily was going to change her mind. And he knew right then that anything—even a sham marriage—was preferable to doing time in that prison on the hill beyond town. So he'd put his talents to work. You want to win a woman's trust, you be good to her kids. And conning a couple of kids was easy. Treat them like adults, show them some respect, and they'd respond every time. Kids liked that kind of crap. As for the lady, she'd be a little tougher. But he was getting the feeling that the mere suggestion of sex scared the hell out of her, and the fear in her eyes at the thought of kissing him had pretty well verified that theory. So he'd turned on the schoolboy charm, and kissed her hand.

She'd been relieved. And *grateful*. And that would go a long way toward getting things off to a good start here. Hell, he only had to convince her to put up with him until he figured out what the hell had happened to land him in this place and how to get back where he belonged. It would be the easiest con he'd ever played, and it would keep him out of prison in the meantime. Nothing to it.

Jack had pretty much determined that this was not a delusion or a dream. Or a joke. Somebody would have slipped up by now and given it away. No, it was lasting too long, and had too much detail to it, to be anything other than real. Somehow, something had happened when he'd fallen into that well. And he was pretty sure he'd truly landed in Hillcrest, Oklahoma, in the year 1890. It sounded crazy. It *was* crazy, but here he was, and there was pretty much no denying it.

So while he was here, he might as well make the best of it. And the best of it was not going to be found in any nineteenth-century prison.

So he'd just bide his time here. And sure, he'd have to do some farm work to earn his keep, but hell, how hard could it be?

He turned to his pseudo-bride, wearing his best smile. The sheriff and the minister were already walking away, shaking their heads in disapproval. What did he care if they didn't want to stay for the party? He was starving, and looking forward to a big celebratory meal, and maybe even a slice of pseudo–wedding cake.

"You'd best come on inside," Emily said to him. "You can't get any work done in those clothes."

Wait a minute. Work? Already?

"Clem's things ought to fit you fine. We might still get that north field plowed before dark if we get busy."

• • •

The man didn't seem to know anything. Lordy, but she ought to have listened to him when he'd said as much, but she couldn't quite believe any grown man could be so completely ignorant about simple farm work.

But she'd been wrong. He was worse at driving the mule than she was, for heaven's sake. And by the time she'd shown him how to do it three times over, they'd wasted a solid hour of the afternoon.

Still, any help was better than none at all, she supposed. At least she was able to return to the house and get the other chores done at a decent hour for a change. And she couldn't remember the last time she'd managed to have a suitable supper ready before the children started complaining that they were hungry.

Jack hauled himself through the front door at dark, and he looked for all the world as if he'd been dragged through the dirt by a runaway horse and beaten with a sizable club. His face bore so much dirt that his eyes seemed to be peering at her from a dark hole.

"My goodness," she said, hurrying forward and easing him into a chair. "What happened?"

The children looked at him with wide eyes. He only shrugged. "I *plowed*." Then with a sigh, he shook his head. "I didn't get the whole field done. Three-quarters of it, though."

Closing her eyes, Emily sighed. "It was half done when you started," she said.

"Yeah. And I'm having trouble swallowing that you did all that by yourself and lived to tell the tale."

Sarah Jane giggled behind her hand. Matthew looked puzzled. "My dad used to plow the north field in one afternoon, Jack," he said.

"Then your dad must have been one heck of a man," Jack replied, apparently taking no offense.

Matthew smiled. "You'll get the hang of it in no time."

Emily had her doubts. "I kept your dinner warm,"

she said, bending to the oven to remove the steaming plate. Jack's stomach growled noisily, and Sarah Jane giggled again.

Jack sent her a playful scowl and got to his feet with a groan, eyeing the heaping plate. "Man, that smells good."

Emily shrugged, and tried not to feel the rush of pleasure. "It's nothing special. Roast beef and vegetables, biscuits and gravy. There's blueberry pie for dessert."

His wide eyes went from the plate to Emily's face. "You *made* all that? On that thing?" He glanced at the wood stove that took up most of the space in one corner of the kitchen. And as she nodded, he leaned over, inhaling the steam and closing his eyes. Then he opened them again. "And there's pie, too?"

She couldn't help but smile as she nodded again. That he should be so impressed before he'd even tasted a bite . . . and she *had* gone to more trouble than usual, though she'd told herself again and again not to.

"I'll go wash up," he said quickly. "Where's the . . . uh . . ."

"The well is right out front. Didn't you see it there?"

"Oh. Right, the well." He shook his head and turned to limp back outside.

Emily set his plate on the table, and wiping her hands on her apron, followed him. She found him by the well, pumping water into a pail. As she approached, he plunged his hands into the cool water, tipped his head back, and sucked air through his teeth.

She walked up to him. "Let me see them."

"What?" he asked, turning quickly.

"Your hands, Jack. Let me see them." When he didn't move, she reached out and took his hands, pulling them from the water and turning his palms up. "Mercy!"

"That bad, huh?" He glanced down at his hands and made a face.

"Jack, you should have stopped. Lord, you won't even be able to hold onto the plow tomorrow. Look at you!"

"Well, this isn't exactly the kind of work I'm used to."

Emily frowned at him as she quickly untied her apron, took it off, and dipped an end into the water. "Just what sort of work *are* you used to, Jack?" As she spoke she gently washed the dirt from his red, blistered palms.

Jack had gone still. He just stood there, silent, as she dipped and washed, dipped and washed. His hands, his forearms, his neck. Running the cool cloth over his face, she stopped suddenly. "Jack?"

"What?"

"I asked what kind of work you usually do. Did you fall asleep on your feet?"

"I . . . no . . . it's just . . . I'm not used to being . . ." His eyes met hers.

Emily lowered her head. "Oh."

"You must be pretty disappointed in me so far, huh?"

Lifting her head again, she shook it. "No, Jack. You're trying your best, and that's all I can ask."

"It's not gonna be enough, though. Emily, we're gonna need some more help around here if we have any shot at getting that crop of . . . of whatever it is you plan to plant—"

"Sorghum," she interrupted.

"Right."

"But I have no money to pay for hands, Jack. I've explained that to you."

"Yeah, well, how about you just leave that part to me?"

She tilted her head. "I don't understand."

"I have an idea. Tomorrow, I'll go into town. And if I can't con . . . er, convince . . . two or three plowboys to come back with me and help get that crop in, then my name isn't Jack McCain."

She shook her head slowly. "Don't you think I've tried? It won't work, Jack. Nobody works for nothing."

"Hey. Trust me. Okay?"

She looked up at him. Shook her head. "We'll lose a day's work if you spend it in town."

"Then we'll gain a week's work when I get back. I promise."

She sighed, certain he had no hope of getting anyone to come here and help him. But then his hands came to her hair, stroking a path from the top of her head to the back of it, and gently tipping it up. And every bit of common sense fled her mind like geese flying south for the winter. "You're one pretty woman, Emily McCain. Especially out here, like this, with the stars twinkling behind you and the—"

She narrowed her eyes, jerking away fast. "Jack McCain, are you trying to sway me with flattery?"

."Well . . . no, I mean, I was—"

"Do you think I'm some empty-headed schoolgirl who swoons when a handsome man says pretty words he doesn't even mean?"

"Aha!" he said.

"Aha, what?" she demanded, fists on her hips.

"You think I'm handsome."

"I most certainly do not."

"You just said so. Handsome man, you said. I heard it. You think I'm handsome."

She rolled her eyes, turning her back to him.

"And for your information, Emily McCain—"

"Stop calling me that."

"Why? It's your name. And for your information, *Mrs. Jack McCain,* I don't think you're empty-headed, and I *do* think you're beautiful. So there!"

She went stiff, not turning to face him. "You do?"

"Yeah. I do." He moved closer. She felt him, heard his steps, and then his hands closed on her shoulders from behind. "And if you don't know it, then maybe you ought to spend some quality time in front of a mirror. Because you are, Emily.'' Then he came still closer, and she felt the heat of his breath on her neck, and then the touch of his lips there. Softly, gently. A fire licked at her belly when his whiskers rasped over her sensitive skin, and she jumped. But he stopped, lifting his head away.

"Your dinner is on the table,'' she said. "And there's water heating for a bath. Clem . . . he always liked a hot bath after a day of plowing. It'll be ready by the time you finish eating.'' Her voice was trembling.

"Okay,'' he whispered close to her ear. "You sure do take good care of me, Emily. You're one hell of a woman. One hell of a wife.''

Jack strode past her, whistling softly as he headed back inside. But he paused just inside the door, and wondered just what the hell was happening to him. Because he really had meant it when he'd told her she was beautiful. And when his lips had brushed across her nape, and she'd trembled in his arms . . .

Well, hell, it was only natural. He was a red-blooded man. He ought to be worried if he *didn't* feel some kind of response.

And it had been that. *Some kind* of response.

He sat down at the table. A second later, a tiny, warm body had snuggled up in his lap. He glanced down, and Sarah Jane glanced up with eyes as big as all outdoors.

"Get down, Sarah, and let Jack eat his dinner,'' Matthew said in a big-brother tone.

"But Pa used to let me sit on his lap while he ate his dinner!''

"Well Pa's not here anymore, Sarah,'' Matthew said, his voice softer now.

Sarah looked up at Jack, and her eyes were damp now. "Sorry, Jack,'' she whispered, and started to climb down.

Jack's arms snagged her little body and hauled her

right back up again, almost on their own. "You sit right here, Sarah Jane," he heard himself say. "I don't mind a bit."

Her whole face lit up when she smiled. And then she leaned her head on his shoulder, and something went soft in Jack's chest. He really didn't mind. It was the oddest thing.

5

Emily wished to heaven she knew what Jack was up to. Part of her was afraid that when he left this morning he wasn't going to be coming back. Even now he was packing leftovers from last night's meal into a sack, as if he planned to be gone a while.

"Jack, won't you tell me how you plan to convince men to work for us when we don't have a dime to pay them?"

Jack only smiled. Lordy, he was handsome when he smiled. And when he bathed.

Emily tried to chase the shameful thought from her mind, but couldn't. She'd been unable to resist peeking in at him last night, after she'd tucked the children into bed. He'd been soaking in the big metal tub, head tipped back, so relaxed she'd thought he'd been sleeping at first. He was even more beautiful undressed. Lean and strong. And as she'd looked at him, a strange, wonderful feeling had taken hold of her body. A kind of a yearning she thought was considered sinful in a woman. But it hadn't *felt* sinful. Just . . . new. And exciting, somehow.

Shame on her.

"If it works," Jack was saying, "then I'll tell you."

"And if it doesn't?"

He shrugged. "Oh, I'm pretty sure it will. This sort of thing is my area of expertise, after all."

"But if it doesn't?" she asked again.

He studied her face for a moment. "Then I'll be back to finish that plowing." He watched her eyes, then frowned slightly. "I *am* coming back, Emily. That's it, isn't it? You're afraid I won't."

Averting her eyes, she whispered, "Of course not."

"Well you're sure worried about something. If it isn't that, then what?"

Shrugging, she turned away. "Nothing."

Jack moved forward, took her shoulders, and turned her around again. "Talk to me, Emily. Come on, what good is a husband if you can't tell him what's on your mind? Hmm?"

Her eyes burned, and that made her angry. And suddenly it all just came flooding out. "Fine. I'll talk. Yes, I'm worried. I'm worried you won't come back. I'm worried that field won't get plowed, and the crop won't get planted, and the mortgage won't get paid. I'm worried I'll lose the only home those two children have ever known, and to be honest, I'm worried that I might have made the biggest mistake of my life when I decided to depend on a man I don't even know to fix the mess my life is in right now." The tears spilled over, but she dashed them away.

When she looked at Jack again, he seemed stunned, and maybe a little bit confused as he searched her face. He swallowed hard, his Adam's apple swelling with the force of it. And he said, "Emily, I'm worried, too. About all those things, and a dozen others that you wouldn't believe if I told you." He shook his head, glancing at the porch, where the children sat on the front step watching their every move. Then he met her eyes again. "Let's take it one worry at a time, okay? I *am* coming back, and I'm gonna do my damnedest to fix the rest of this. I promise."

She stared up at him, and she knew that hope was in her eyes when she did.

"Now are you gonna disappoint young Matthew by not kissing your husband good-bye?"

She felt her eyes widen, but before she could reply, Jack's arms slid around her waist, and he pulled her close. So close her body pressed tight to his. And then he bent his head and kissed her. His mouth was soft, gentle, coaxing, and in a moment she felt the tension ease out of her with a sigh. Her hands rested on his shoulders, and he moved his mouth over hers in a caressing touch that sent liquid heat spilling through her whole body. Her mouth relaxed beneath the tender touch of his, and when he straightened away, he looked down at her, and licked his lips.

"I'll be back," he said, his voice slightly hoarse. And this time she believed him.

Something was wrong with the way this whole thing was going. Jack tried to be analytical about identifying the problem, but it wasn't the type that could be analyzed. His motives had changed. All of a sudden, getting Emily's crop planted and saving that farm for her and the kids was just as important as finding his way back to his own time. All of a sudden, he wasn't just conning her. He really wanted to help.

The change had started the previous night when he'd held little Sarah on his lap. She'd fallen asleep there, and Jack had had to carry her up the stairs and tuck her into bed. She'd looked like a little angel, sleeping there in her pretty room with her little doll beside her. He hated to think where she'd be sleeping if she lost her home. And then there was Matthew, trying so hard to be a man. He'd spent the entire dinner hour giving Jack a list of tips on farm work, and telling how his dad always did it, the pride clear in his voice. He'd loved his father, and lost him. What if he lost his home, too?

But it was that kiss this morning that had been the topper. He never should have kissed her. Damn. She tasted like honey, and he wanted more. A lot more.

He kept thinking about last night when she'd started washing the dirt away from him with her balled-up apron. Her touch had done things to him . . . things it usually took a knockout of cover-model quality, wearing a thong, to do. He liked his women lean and mean and gorgeous. He liked them hot and hungry and without an inhibition in their fluff-filled heads. He liked them young, and comfortable in the fast lane.

He had *never* liked them shy, or old-fashioned, or— God forbid—moral!

But he liked Emily. He liked her *a lot.* She was strong and smart and determined. She'd do anything for those kids, and that, for some reason, made his heart go soft. She was a grown-up. A woman who knew who she was.

Jack thought about all of that as he sat in the saloon sipping a strong, dark-colored beer, wearing Clem Hawkins's best Levi's and his black Stetson hat. This place was great. He couldn't get over it. Batwing doors and a scuffed-up, rough-cut bar top. Even a mirror behind the bar in case a riot should break out. Hey, every Western barroom brawl needed one, so some no-account scallywag could get thrown into it and smash it to bits. Old-fashioned bottles lined shelves beneath the mirror, and malodorous men smoked hand-rolled cigarettes and drank shots of red-eye.

"Hey, you," someone said, and Jack turned his head to see his pal the sheriff pushing through the batwing doors. He didn't quite have The Duke's saunter down, but he was close. "Shouldn't you be out at the Hawkins' place, manning a plow?"

Finally, the opening he'd been waiting for. "No hurry, Sheriff. I can outplow any man in this town."

Some of the talk in the saloon stopped, and several heads turned in Jack's direction.

"Oh, can you, now?" Sheriff Stonewall asked.

"Damn straight. Shoot, I've never *met* a man who could plow faster than me. I'm the best there is."

The sheriff looked around the room with a grin on his face. No doubt thinking he was about to stir up trouble for the new kid. "You all hear that? Jack here thinks he can outplow any man in town."

"Oughtta put his money where his mouth is," said one oversized brute in bib overalls.

"Well, I would, if I had any. Truth is, I'm pretty much busted. Had to trade my watch just to get this beer."

"Shame," the brute said. "So I guess all you got is big talk, then, huh?"

"Oh, hell no. I'm willing to back it up. If anyone here is man enough to take me up on it, that is?" He looked around the room.

"Now just how in Sam Hill are you gonna do that?"

Jack shrugged, scratched his head, and searched the ceiling as if for answers. Then he snapped his fingers. "I got it! A challenge! A contest!"

"Now hold on," the sheriff began.

"What sort of contest?" another man asked.

"Well now, let me think on this a minute," Jack said, pretending to mull it all over in his mind. "Suppose we stage a plowing contest out at Miss Emily's place, hmm? Then I can prove once and for all that I'm the best man in this town. I'll take on all comers. I'll—"

"Shoot, that ain't no good," the big guy interrupted. "You need a prize for any sort a contest, an' you already said you was flat busted."

"I don't see that it matters. I'm going to be the winner, and I already have the finest prize in Oklahoma."

"Oh, do you, now? And what would that be?"

Jack opened his sack on the bar and began extracting dishes of food from last night's dinner, including a hefty slice of that blueberry pie. "I married me the best cook in seven counties," he said, hoping he sounded authentic. "That woman could make a man's mouth water from a mile away. Just smell this." He lifted the pie, and several men leaned over to sniff at it as he moved it around. "Hey, I know!" he shouted as if he'd just thought of it. "My wife could cook a full-blown feast of a meal for the winner and his family. Including a blueberry pie. A man's wife would be mighty grateful to have a night off from cooking his dinner." The men around him looked at one another, considering it.

Almost had them. Jack shrugged, set the plate down on the table in front of him. "Not that it much matters, because I'll be the winner. There's not a man in this town who can man a plow like I can."

"You're on!" the burly one yelled.

"I'm in," said another.

"Whenever you're ready," said a third.

Jack smiled, and shrugged. "Well, the sun's shining and it's early in the day. How soon can you fellas meet me out at the farm?"

Men crowded around Jack, and there was so much noise he could barely hear himself think. He saw Sheriff Stonewall shaking his head. "I'd best come, too," the sheriff said, leaning close. "You'll be needin' a judge, and someone to keep order. I hope to hell you know what you're doing, son."

Jack knew *exactly* what he was doing. And it was working like a charm.

"I don't believe it," Emily said, as she stood on the front porch looking on in amazement. Men, a dozen of them at least, were lining up in her three fields, each with a set of plows and a horse, or a mule, or an ox. She took three steps forward, and stopped, as Jack came limping up the path, being helped by Marty Burleson, a local farmer who was as big as a tree. And suddenly her throat went dry, and she found herself running forward.

"What's wrong, what's happened?"

"Oh, now, Miz Emily, he'll be fine. Turned his ankle is all."

"I'm afraid I've ruined it for everyone," Jack said, looking depressed, shaking his head. Then he lifted his gaze. "But no. I made a deal and the deal stands. Guess I just won't get to show off for my wife . . . this time."

"I'd have beat you anyway, Jack. But we'll have to hash that out when the ankle's better. Right now I gotta get back there, before the sheriff fires the signal shot." Marty handed Jack off to Emily, then lumbered away at top speed.

Pulling Jack's arm around her shoulders, Emily began moving toward the house. But he stopped her, and sent her a grin. "Not that I mind your arms around me, Em, but uh, the ankle's fine."

She blinked, staring at him. "Suppose you tell me just what is going on here, Jack McCain?"

He looked so sheepish, so pleased with himself, it made her want to shake him. "Well, it's a contest. To see who's the best plowin' plantin' farmer in this whole dang town. Winner gets a home-cooked meal, courtesy of the talented Emily McCain."

Her hands went to her hips and she gaped at him. "Oh, does he, now?"

"Yeah. I realize I should have cleared that part of it with you first, but I didn't exactly have a lot of time. The marks . . . er . . . contestants were ready to bite. I had to move fast."

"I see."

He studied her face, his smile fading. "Look, Em, by suppertime the plowing will be done, and not just that north field, either, but all of it."

"You *tricked* those men. Didn't you, Jack?"

"Well . . . no. I . . . I just bragged a little about how good I was to get their dander up, and—"

"So you lied to them, too."

"It got results!"

"It's dishonest. Jack, I don't like this! Don't you think they'll realize they've been taken advantage of?"

"Not until the fields are plowed, I hope," he said. "And the only thing I took advantage of was their overblown egos."

She lowered her head, and slowly shook it. "Oh, Jack . . ."

"Look, there's no harm done. The fields are getting plowed in a single afternoon, and all for the price of one good meal." As he spoke the sheriff's gun went off, and the men and animals began moving. Soon there was such a dust being raised that Emily couldn't even see the men out there working.

All while Jack was headed for the house and a cool drink on his supposedly turned ankle. Emily followed, snapping at him. "This is wrong, Jack. It's . . . it's just wrong, and I don't like it."

"Well, it's kinda late for that now."

"I want no part of this!"

Jack mounted the bottom step, shook his head, and kept walking. "Well, I suppose you can refuse to cook the prize for the winner if you want to, but it's a prize he'll have earned. And I don't imagine he'll be too happy about not getting it."

"None of them will be too happy when they realize they've been played for fools!" She followed him into the house. "Jack, you can go your merry way when this is over, but the children and I have to *live* here."

Jack turned to face her, lifting his hands palms up, at his sides. "Dammit, Em, I don't see what you're getting so worked up about! I'm only trying to help you here!"

"I can do without that kind of help, *Mr*. McCain."

"Shoot, you need any kind of help you can get. *Mrs*. McCain."

"If you do anything like this again, I'll . . . I'll . . ."

"You'll what? Send me on up to prison?"

Inhaling deeply, she forced herself to be calm. "I wouldn't do that." She sighed. "I suppose you . . . you were only trying to help. In your way."

He was quiet for a moment. "Yeah. Well, I guess I should have cleared it with you first. Next time, I'll—"

"There won't be a next time, Jack. I'll save this farm by honest hard work, or I'll lose it. Either way, I intend to keep my honor and my pride intact."

"Honor and pride," he said, very softly. "Do they keep you warm on cold, lonely nights, Em? Are they what you hold onto instead of a man?"

She went stiff, her back to him. "They'll have to do until I find a man I can love . . . a man I can respect, Jack."

She knew those words stung him when he didn't reply. Drawing a fortifying breath, she squared her shoulders and lifted her chin. "I'd best get to cooking that meal."

6

Jack woke in the small bedroom he'd been assigned. The sun beamed down blindingly, and he had the feeling he should have been awake long before now.

Yesterday had gone perfectly. The fields had gotten plowed in a matter of a single afternoon, and by the time a winner was declared (the huge brute Emily called Marty) Emily had made a feast fit for a king and packed it all in a wicker basket for him to take home.

Perfect.

Except for her reaction to it all. She'd as much as told Jack that she didn't respect him. Must have been the turned ankle thing, he figured. He probably would have looked better to her if he'd been out there plowing with the rest of the men. But hell, he didn't know what he was doing, and only would have made a fool of himself.

Maybe that was what she wanted.

Nah.

He got up, washed up, dressed, and headed downstairs in search of breakfast. He found it just by following his nose. The oven was still warm, and a plate full of eggs and bacon and biscuits and home fries was tucked away inside, waiting just for him.

Only, nobody else was around.

Frowning, Jack headed outside and followed the sounds of voices to the north field, where he spotted the others. Emily, Sarah Jane, and Matthew were all running around with sacks of seed, iron rakes, and hoes. The children seemed to be having fun, but Emily was hard at work. Sweat already glistened on her skin. And no wonder. It must be eighty out there already, and she was wearing a long-sleeved blouse that buttoned tight at the wrists, and a dark-blue skirt that reached to her feet. For Pete's sake.

He hurried forward. "Hey, you shouldn't be doing this," he said.

She stopped what she was doing and lifted up her head to eye him. Straggles of damp auburn hair stuck to her face. "Somebody has to."

"Yeah, well, I think I can handle this, at least. It doesn't look as tough as plowing." She shrugged and kept raking.

Jack moved forward and took the rake from her hands. "You should have woke me, Em."

"Saw no need."

"No doubt you figured I wouldn't be much help anyway," he said, watching her face. Then he amended, "No, it's not that. It's that you're still mad at me for yesterday." He dropped the rake and gripped her shoulders, shaking his head as he examined her face. "You look ready to drop, Emily. Don't do this to yourself again, you hear me? I don't like it."

"I'll do just exactly what I . . ." She didn't finish. Her eyes sort of rolled back and her body went limp.

Jack caught her in his arms, his heart damn near stopping with fear as he scooped her up.

Sarah Jane began to shriek at the top of her lungs, and for a long moment it didn't seem like she'd stop. Jack shouted her name, loud and firmly, until she snapped out of it and focused on him, her eyes red, puffy, and terrified. She stared up at him as he cradled her beloved aunt in his arms. He knew what the little one was thinking. That her aunt had died just as her mother and her father had done. That she was alone. The poor thing was so traumatized, all he wanted to do was hug her, and he likely would have if it hadn't meant setting Emily down first.

"Sarah Jane," Jack said, firmly but gently. "Your Aunt Em has only fainted, is all. From the heat. She's gonna be okay, I promise."

Those big green eyes blinked up at him so trustingly that Jack felt his stomach turn over.

"He's right," Matthew said, although Jack had seen the fear in the boy's eyes as well. "She was up late cleanin' up from that dinner she had to make, and then long before dawn, milkin' the cow and makin' breakfast before she came out here. I don't even think she ate. And I heard Miss Brightwater say she wasn't taking care of herself and was gonna work till she dropped." He looked up at Jack. "Is that what she did?"

"That's what she did, but she won't be doing it again," Jack said. "She'll be fine."

"She's not gonna die like Pa and Ma did?" Sarah Jane whispered.

Jack's heart was rapidly melting into a big muddy puddle. "No, honey. I won't let that happen, I promise. Now c'mon, let's get her back to the house, where we can take proper care of her, hmm?"

The children nodded hard, and Jack hefted Emily a bit higher in his arms, realizing for the first time how slight she was. God, she ought to be heavier, a woman of her height. But she wasn't, and he suspected it was because she'd been working so damned hard for so damned long.

No more, he heard some heroic-sounding stranger whispering inside his head. And then he wondered who *that* was.

At the house, he settled Emily in her bed, then used

the basin of cool water and the cloth that Sarah brought in to bathe her face and neck. Her skin was hot and sticky and he knew she had to get cooled down fast.

"Listen, I need you two to go on back outside, okay? I want you to pick your Aunt Em a nice bunch of flowers for when she wakes up."

The two seemed relieved to have been given something to do, and turned, but then Jack said, "Wait a minute." He went to them and touched each small face. They seemed okay. "Listen, it's hot outside. Get a drink of water, and look for those flowers in a shady place, okay? You don't want to get too much sun like Aunt Em did."

Nodding, they rushed off immediately. Good. Jack drew a breath and settled himself on the edge of Emily's bed. Then he told himself to keep this quick and clinical, and he began to unbutton her blouse. As he spread it open, he saw that she wore a shift underneath. It was white, with pretty lace around the neckline. Sleeveless and simple. He unfastened the heavy skirt and dragged that off her as well. He took off her shoes, and then he reached underneath the shift to peel away the ridiculous stockings. God, no wonder she'd given way to the heat.

But as his hands brushed over her thighs, her eyes slowly blinked open and then they went very wide as she said, "What in heaven's name are you *doing*?" and began kicking with both feet so that he either had to back off or risk a broken bone.

"Ow! Calm down, woman! For crying out loud, I was just—"

"Just *what*?"

At least she'd stopped kicking. Jack sighed and shook his head. "Look, you were working too hard, you got overheated, and you passed out cold."

"I have never *passed out* in my life, Mr. McCain."

"You have now, honey. And it's no wonder. My God, you were wearing more layers than—"

"I'm wearing what's appropriate," she countered.

"Not for hard work under the hot sun, Em. Come on, you're still running hot. Now just lie there and be quiet, will you? That shift covers everything important. Besides, we're married."

She glared at him. He glared back, and went right on with what he was doing. He sat down on the edge of the bed again, and when she didn't kick him off, he dipped the cloth into the cool water and brought it to her neck, dabbing it there, then moving it over her shoulders. She was stiff at first, but then she closed her eyes and sighed.

"It does feel good," she whispered.

"Sure it does. Now how's your head?"

"Throbbing."

"Um-hmm. I figured as much." He shook his head. "I have it on good authority that you haven't been taking care of yourself, Em—not at all. That's gonna end right here, right now. You're gonna lie right there in that bed today, and you're gonna let me take care of everything else."

She rolled her eyes. "Right."

"Exactly right. Now I'm gonna bring you up that plate of breakfast, and I'm gonna sprinkle a little extra salt in it because it's good for what ails you. And I want you to drink water today. All you can hold. You're dehydrated."

She frowned. "De—"

"No water and too much sweating. When you work like that you need to drink like a fish, Em. Not that you're gonna be working like that anymore. And if you try to put those ridiculous clothes back on again, I'll burn them. It's hot outside. God, where I come from, women wear short skirts or cutoff Levi's and sleeveless blouses in this kind of weather."

Her eyes went very big. "They . . . bare their arms? Their *legs*?"

"Yes, and nobody thinks anything of it."

She shook her head. "Where do you come from, Jack? You've never told me."

He looked at her for a long moment. "It's . . . probably about time we . . . er . . . talked about that. Maybe . . . maybe it'll help explain why I'm so damned useless around here."

"Oh, Jack, you're not—"

"You said so yourself, Em. But there's a reason. Look . . ." He lowered his head and slowly shook it. "Here," he said finally, reaching into his pocket and pulling out his little planning calendar. "Take a look at this."

Tilting her head slightly and frowning, she reached out and took the small booklet from him. Then she flipped pages, reading the notes he'd scrawled. It took a full minute before her eyes went wide, and she stared up at him again. "This says 1999."

"That's right."

"Well . . . well that's just ridiculous, Jack."

He sighed deeply. "Look, I know how it sounds. Why do you think it's taken me so long to tell you? Emily, I was born in 1971."

"Oh, Jack . . ."

Great, now there was worry in her eyes. Like maybe she thought he was losing his crackers. "Wait a minute. I'll be right back." He got up and headed into his room down the hall. He rummaged through the box of stuff he'd stashed under the bed, and finally just picked up the whole thing and carried it back to the bedroom. "Here," he said. "There's enough proof in here to convince anybody. Look." He pulled out a ring. "My class ring. See that?" He showed her, and she read the engraving aloud.

"Hillcrest High School, Class of 1989."

She was still blinking in shock when he stuffed a handful of crumpled bills in her hand. Tens and twenties, a few singles. "Go on, check them. This is all the cash I had on me. Look at the dates. Does that look like the money you use? And here, here's my credit card, with the expiration date, and . . ." He stopped there because she'd gone completely still, and her eyes were wide. She didn't look worried anymore . . . she looked scared.

"How can this be, Jack? What are you doing here?"

"Aw, come on, Em, don't be afraid of me. I don't know how this happened or why."

"Tell me what you do know," she said. "You're living in my house, with my children, and I—"

"And you think I'm some kind of demon or something. I know. Look, I'll tell you everything I know." He closed his eyes, sighing. "I hardly know where to begin."

"At the beginning."

He opened his eyes and nodded. "Okay. I was born not far from here. My mother died young and my father left, so I was raised by my grandmother on a farm out near the spot where we first met. But I hated farm work. All I ever thought about was getting away from it, finding an easy way to make money. Grandma always said I'd pay for it one day. I just didn't listen."

He glanced at her to see if she was still listening. She seemed riveted. "I got out young, and started pulling con games on rich locals: selling shares in nonexistent co-ops and playing phony land deals and making big money. But the cops started hassling me, and to be honest, my conscience bothered me, too. So I decided to turn over a new leaf. From then on I only swindled criminals." He shook his head. "And I was *good at it*."

"Good? How can you call cheating people good?"

"I figured they deserved it. They didn't earn their money honestly anyway."

"So that justifies you not earning yours honestly?"

He averted his eyes from her big, probing ones. "I know. You're right, I know." He sighed. "Anyway, the day that I ended up here with you, the police had picked me up. They didn't intend to arrest me at all. They really didn't care what I did as long as I didn't ply my trade on honest citizens. But I'd been involved with a major criminal, one they'd been after for years, and they decided I might have information they could use against him. So they took me in, put me in handcuffs, and told me either to tell them everything I knew, or they'd arrest me.''

She tilted her head. ''Why didn't they simply ask you? Surely you'd have told them if you knew anything that might have helped them stop a dangerous criminal.'' She looked harder at him. ''You would have ... wouldn't you, Jack?''

He shook his head. ''I don't know. If I did, he'd have shot me at the first opportunity. But the chance to find out never came. The criminal and his goons had no intention of letting me get to police headquarters to make a statement. They ambushed us, shot both the cops. I ran for it, they gave chase, and I dove over what I thought was a stone wall for cover. Only it was actually a well, and, when I hit the bottom, I was here. A hundred and nine years in the past.''

Her eyes were so big, so pretty and wide and curious and amazed. He'd never seen her look this childlike. ''That's why you asked me about the old wishing well.''

''Yeah. It ... it's crazy, but it's the only thing I could think of. My grandmother said there was a stone on that well with an engraved verse.''

''Yes. ...'Make a wish upon this well, but wishes don't come free. Make a promise here as well, and your wish you will see,' '' Emily quoted. ''As you fell ... you ... you made a wish?''

''More like a prayer,'' he admitted. ''I swore I'd go straight, work harder than I ever had to earn an honest living, if I only survived.''

She sighed deeply. ''And once you've kept your end

of the bargain . . . you'll find the well again. And then you'll be able to go back.''

He blinked. "Well . . . I guess so.''

Emily sighed again. "I suppose I should tell you, should have told you before, when you first asked me. Jack, I . . . I saw that well once myself. Not all that long ago. But I could never find it again. For a while, I thought I must have dreamed the whole thing. But dream or not, I pitched in a penny, and made a wish of my own.''

He nodded. "You wished for a way to keep this place for the kids, right? For someone to come along and help with the work.''

She looked away. "Something like that.''

"The well fairies must be having a hell of a laugh at both of us, then,'' he said. "You got stuck with a guy who knows about as much about farming as you can fit in a thimble, and I kept my end of the bargain by pulling a con to get the work done.''

She smiled slightly and shook her head. "This is all so unbelievable.''

"Look, you did me a huge favor by keeping me out of prison, Em. And the least I can do to pay you back is take care of you, until I find out how the hell to get back to my own time.''

She looked up quickly when he said that, eyes wide, then shuddered. "How . . . long do you think that will be?''

"I have no way of knowing. But until then, you're gonna be taking a well-deserved vacation.''

"But Jack, I can't—''

He covered her hand with his and she went silent, staring down at his hand and not saying a word. "Give me a chance, huh? No one ever has. I want to try to do this. Maybe if I keep my promise, actually do some work for once in my life, I'll get back where I belong. Let me try, Em. Just let me try.''

Closing her eyes, she whispered, "Okay. All right."

He grinned. "Great. Now I'm bringing up that food, and then I'm going to go out and finish the planting, and I don't want any arguments."

She nodded.

The bedroom door burst open, and the kids came inside bearing fists full of weeds in full blossom.

"Ah, my little helpers are back," Jack said. "Sarah Jane, you're gonna take care of Aunt Em just like she takes care of you when you're sick. If she tries to get up or get dressed or do any work, I want you to come right out and get me, okay?"

Sarah Jane nodded hard. "I will!"

"Matt, I need you to show me just what the heck to do out there in the fields. And don't be afraid to say so if I'm doing it wrong or making stupid mistakes, okay?"

Matthew nodded. Jack clasped the boy's shoulder. Together they headed out the door.

Emily disliked this. Jack's attentiveness. His pampering. Because he seemed so sincere, and so concerned for her, and she could get used to that sort of thing. She was used to being the one doing the worrying. She was used to putting herself last. Now someone was putting her first for the first time in her life.

And he was going to disappear again just as soon as he could find a way.

She hadn't told him all of what she'd wished for out at that old wishing well, because it had been so personal and so frivolous and girlish. But she'd wished for a man to love her. To love her the way she'd always dreamed of being loved . . . the way she'd given up ever finding for herself.

But he wasn't that man. He wasn't her wish come true. He was working to fulfill his promise because it would get him away from her all the sooner. And for no other reason. She'd best remember that.

• • •

The big lug who won that supper was on his way up the trail to Emily's place when Matthew and Jack went out the front door. "What's the matter," Jack called. "You run out of food already?"

Marty shrugged and sent a glance toward little Matthew. "I wanted a word with you, Jack. If you have a minute."

"A minute's about all I have. Matt, why don't you fetch us a jug of water to take out to the field with us, hmm?"

Matt was off like a shot, and Jack turned to Marty. "Okay. We're alone, what is it?"

Marty drew a breath. "You don't know much about farmin', do you, Jack?"

Jack felt his hackles rise, but Marty rushed on. "Look, don't take it bad, okay? But I figured out what you were up to yesterday, and to tell you the truth, I was pretty impressed with the way you pulled it off."

Jack's head came up. "Wait a minute. You knew . . . and you went ahead and plowed that field anyway?"

"Sure. Hey, a man's got his pride, you know. The thing is, Jack, I'm not the smartest fellow in town. And if I caught on, it's a sure bet the others will, too. You're not gonna be able to keep pullin' tricks like that contest all summer, and you sure as all hell can't raise and harvest the crop on your own. And if you don't, Miss Emily's gonna lose this place."

Jack sighed. "You think I don't know that?"

"So what are you gonna do about it?"

Shaking his head, Jack stood straighter. "I'm gonna learn as I go, I guess. Hell, what else can I do?"

Marty eyed him. "You can swallow your pride and let me lend a hand."

Jack's brows went up. "You want to help me?"

"Not you. Miss Emily. I can teach you all you need to know about farming, and help you out. You can give me a hand at my place. It'll all even out in the end, and if we're lucky, Miss Emily will have a healthy harvest and be able to pay off that mortgage. What do you say?''

Jack swallowed hard and kept his eyes on the ground. ''There's a lot I don't know about besides just farming,'' he said. ''You might be taking on more than you know.''

''Hell, we'll go a day at a time. I'm willin' if you are.''

Drawing a breath, and hating like hell to admit he needed help from the big lug, Jack told himself to buck up and do what was necessary. He thrust out a hand, and Marty shook it. ''It's a deal,'' Jack said. ''And uh . . . thanks.''

Marty grinned, and when Matthew returned from the well with the water jug in hand, the three of them headed out. All day, Marty and Matthew instructed Jack in the intricacies of farm work. It was hard, hot, and exhausting. But there was something else, too. There was the way young Matthew looked up at him. The way the kid would stand just the way Jack was standing when they stopped for a break. Or if they sat down to take five in the shade, the way Matt would sit just as close beside Jack as he could manage. It touched something in Jack.

He figured that was par for the course. This whole damned family was managing to get to him, somehow. He was starting to think he'd miss them like crazy when he found his way back to his own time. All of them. Especially Emily.

7

The summer sun burned hot, but Jack didn't mind. He sat on a blanket munching fried chicken and watching the kids splash in the stream. Emily sat beside him, leaning back against the wide trunk of an old oak tree. Above her, nestled in the branches, was the tree house Jack and Matthew had started building. It wasn't going to make *Architectural Digest*, but Jack thought it was shaping up nicely. And the hours he and the kids had spent there working on it together were—and this was odd—some of the best times Jack had ever had.

Emily looked better. Jack had been taking on more and more of the chores around the place, and she had more color in her cheeks. He just wished the worry he saw whenever he looked into her eyes would ease up.

"The crop looks good," he said, wanting to draw her out of her thoughts, or else crawl into them with her. He'd been growing more and more intrigued by and drawn to Emily with every day that passed. But she was like a closed book to him. It was as if her skin were a hard shell that covered everything underneath. And though he'd tried, he hadn't been able to break through that barrier.

"You've outdone yourself, Jack." She looked at him,

finally, and shook her head. "I can hardly believe you're the same man who didn't even know how to plow a field a couple of months ago."

"It's true, I've learned a lot. You know what surprises me most?"

"What?" she asked. The wind toyed with a runaway wisp of red.

"I . . . I'm kinda starting to like it. Oh, not the work part. But seeing the results, you know? I look out there at that sorghum standing tall, and I feel . . . I don't know . . ."

"Pride," she said, nodding. "You should be proud, you know. It's a feeling you can take with you . . . when you go back."

When he went back. It seemed that every time they talked she found a way to bring that into the conversation. Like she was reminding him . . . or maybe reminding herself.

"You know if you went and checked, that old wishing well might be there waiting for you even now. You've certainly kept your promise to work harder than you ever have."

"I haven't done what I came here to do yet, Em. I don't want to see the well again before I'm finished."

She nodded, licking her lips. "Have you spoken to the children about that yet?" she asked.

"About what? My leaving?" She nodded, and Jack shrugged. "I don't see the point. I mean, who knows if I'll ever find a way to get back to my own time? Why worry them for nothing?"

She lifted her chin. "They're getting awfully fond of you, Jack. It's not fair to keep it from them. You're going to leave us . . . them, I mean . . . either way. It's not as if you plan to stay married to a woman you don't love even if you can't find your way back where you belong."

"Hell, Emily—"

"Well, it's true, isn't it?"

He looked into her eyes, and felt something deep in his belly, something that scared the hell out of him. "Do we have to talk about this now? You're always worrying about things that haven't even happened yet, Em. Why don't we just put this off and deal with it when the time comes?"

"Because they need to know, Jack. They can't go getting their hopes up only to have their hearts broken in the end."

"They need to know?" he said, suddenly seeing something he hadn't seen before in her eyes. "Or maybe it's that you need to know."

She looked away quickly.

"Emily . . . have you ever tried to stop worrying about the future and just enjoy the present?" She shook her head, still not facing him, but he took her chin in two fingers and turned her head toward him. "I'm here, right now, today. At this very moment, I'm your husband . . . and you're my wife."

"But . . . it's not real." She had that scared look again. That doe-in-the-headlights look that made him just want to wrap her up in his arms and hold her there until it went away.

"Then let's make it real," he said, and he leaned closer, sliding his hand to the back of her head and threading his fingers in her hair. He held her still for his kiss, and pressed his mouth to hers. And for just an instant, she let him. She relaxed her lips apart, and let him trace them with his tongue, let him kiss her deeply, thoroughly, let him taste her . . . and he thought it was like tasting heaven.

And then she flattened her hands to his chest and pushed him away.

"Damn," he said, and he was breathless, aroused, hungry for more of her. "Emily McCain, you're gonna wish you'd made the most of this when I'm gone." He touched her hair, then closed his eyes. "I know I sure as hell am."

She shook her head in denial, parted her lips to speak, then closed them again. And instead of blurting out whatever she'd been about to say, she said, very calmly, "There's no future for us, Jack. Anything we have now is temporary . . . it's a fantasy, and we both know it. I've never been the sort of woman who could exist on fantasies."

He licked his lips, tasting her on them. "It's no fantasy, Em. I want you. And I think you want me, too. That's solid reality, lady."

"It's fleeting reality," she said. "It's a dream that ends the minute we open our eyes."

"Haven't you ever heard of living in the moment?"

She faced him, and he almost gasped aloud when he saw the tears brimming in her eyes. Tears! But why? "I can't live in the moment, Jack. Not when I know that moment will end. I don't want to spend the rest of my life wishing I could go back and live it again. I can't live that way."

My God. Could she . . . could she actually be starting to . . . to *feel* something for him? She got to her feet, turning away, but Jack leaped up too, catching her arm and turning her back again. "So you think you're better off if you never know what you're missing?"

"If I never know it, I can't very well miss it, now can I?"

He shook his head, frustrated. " 'Tis better to have loved and lost, than never to have loved,' " he quoted.

"Pretty words, Jack. But the wrong words. Lust is what you're talking about, not love. And I'm too old a woman to confuse the two."

He blinked and stared at her. "Did you just admit to feeling lust? For me? The prim and proper Emily Hawkins McCain? I can't believe it."

Her eyes narrowed and she glared at him. "Proper I

may be, Jack McCain, but still a woman."

He tried to touch her hair, but she pulled away. "Hey, come on. I was just being sarcastic, Em." She turned her back to him, and . . . God, she was trembling. "Emily, I'm sorry," he said, and he slid his hands over her shoulders.

"I'm weak where you're concerned," she whispered, and the way she said it made it sound like some dark confession.

"You're supposed to be. We're *married*, Emily. There's no shame in what you're feeling. To tell you the truth it . . . it's kind of humbling."

She made a noise of disbelief. "I should think you'd be proud to have reduced me to such an admission."

"No," he said, very softly. "Not proud. Humbled, Emily. To think a woman like you could . . . could feel that way toward a man like me. When I know damn well I'm nowhere near good enough for you."

"You're right," she whispered. "You're not."

He said nothing. Let her beat up on him if it made her feel better.

"The man good enough for me . . ." she went on, her voice strained, her body still shaking. ". . . will be a man who's willing to stay. To make a life here on this farm, and to be a father, a *permanent* one, to Matthew and Sarah Jane." He thought she was crying, but couldn't see her face, and knew she wouldn't want him seeing her tears anyway.

"And what about passion, Emily?" he asked slowly. "What about desire?"

"Those things are unimportant."

"That's bull and you know it."

She turned, and he saw he'd been right. Her cheeks glistened with the kiss of her tears. "I've lived without those things for a long time, Jack. And I was perfectly happy to go on without them until . . ." She bit her lip to stop her words.

"Until I came along," he finished for her. She didn't answer, but just stood there facing him with strands of her burnished hair framing her face and dancing in the breeze. Her cheeks flushed with color and her eyes were gleaming and damp. Her dress hugged her little waistline, hiding everything else, making Jack want to take it off her. Maybe . . . maybe he didn't have to leave her. Maybe . . . he could be the kind of man she wanted.

"What if—"

"No," she said before he could complete the sentence. "Don't even say it, Jack."

He searched her pretty face, her luminous eyes. "Why not?"

"Because I know you're very good at making people believe what you want them to. And because if you make me believe . . . you'll destroy me, Jack."

He wouldn't . . . or maybe he would. Because he didn't know if he *could* be the kind of man she needed. The kind who would stay. He didn't know. . . .

But maybe it was high time he found out.

8

"You plannin' to take Miss Emily to the harvest dance, Jack?"

Jack glanced up at the oversized Marty as they worked a row apart with hoes, chopping down weeds. He sure had come full circle, hadn't he? Jack remembered once vowing he'd never pull another weed in his life. He almost smiled as he wiped his brow with the back of his hand, and leaned on the hoe handle.

"Harvest dance? Hell, Marty, we haven't even begun to harvest this stuff yet."

"Well, you got your crop planted a mite later than most."

"So everyone else is already bringing it in?"

"Yeah. Most are done already. The dance is Saturday night at the Perkins' barn."

Jack nodded, eyeing the tallish, reed-type crop he'd grown. He'd worked harder than he'd ever worked in his life since he'd come here. And damned if he didn't get out of bed every morning looking forward to it, and fall into bed at night satisfied with what he'd managed to accomplish that day. And with the respect he saw in Emily's eyes when she looked at him now. That meant more to him than he ever would have believed possible.

He slept better here, and ate better, too. God, the way Emily cooked, he'd half expected to develop a spare tire by the time this summer ended. Oh, he'd grown bigger, all right. But none of it was spare anything. When he took off his shirt and looked in the mirror, he liked what he saw. He liked it a lot.

He'd made every effort to give Emily a peek at his newly muscular chest and flat abs and washboard pecs. Okay, not quite washboard, but they were getting there. And at his hardened biceps and all that. In fact, he'd paraded past her several times, stripped bare from the waist up.

All she ever did was turn her head and politely ask him to put some clothes on.

Hell. The woman was . . . the woman was . . .

He glanced back toward the house. That was the fourth pail of water she'd carried in from the well outside. She was overdoing it again. And even now that the sun wasn't quite as brutal and the nights were cool, it was still too warm for her to be working so hard. The kids were out by the barn, playing some kind of game that involved hopping, jumping, and shouting with laughter.

A reluctant smile tugged at Jack's lips as he watched them.

"So?" Marty prodded. "About the dance?"

"Well, I can ask her, Marty," he said slowly, still sending worried gazes back toward the house every few moments. "But I don't know if she'll want to go with me." What was she doing with all that water? Scrubbing floors? Washing clothes?

"She ought to."

Something about the tone of Marty's voice made Jack look at him and pay attention. "Why's that?"

" 'Cause . . . Well, Jack, folks have been speculatin' about . . . about the two of you, and . . ."

"And . . . ?"

With a big sigh, Marty shook his head. "Most are of the opinion that you'll only be around long enough to harvest the crop. And that Miss Emily will be a free woman again before October."

"Oh, they are, are they?"

"Yeah. A lot of the single men are hopin' you'll be gone sooner. Like by Saturday night. They watch every day to see if you've started bringin' in the sorghum yet."

Jack went very still. "Are you saying they're all just waiting for me to leave so they can move in on my wife?"

Marty nodded solemnly. "Yup. That's exactly what I'm saying."

"Why those dirty, two-faced little..." His head came up. "Does she know about this?"

"Well, she's always known. I mean, there was no shortage of suitors at the door once ol' Clem was buried. But Miss Emily..." Marty shook his head and grinned crookedly. "She opined that they were only after this 'ere farm. Can you imagine?"

Oh, he could well imagine that. The woman had chosen him because she thought he'd never be interested in her. And hell, he'd been burning up for her ever since.

But to know that other men might be as well... well, now, that put things in a whole different light. What if she decided that one of them would make her a better husband than smilin' Jack McCain, con man extraordinaire? What if that was why she kept reminding him that he planned to leave as soon as the harvest was in?

Dammit, she didn't *want* any of them. She wanted *him*!

But she'd told him herself that desire was low on her list of priorities. What she needed was a dependable man, one who was in it for the long haul. A father for the kids. This thought drew his gaze their way again, and then made his throat close off. Sarah Jane's pigtails were crooked. He'd braided her hair for her this morning, insisting it was about time he learn how, and the little monster had giggled and wriggled the whole time. Emily had wanted to redo his handiwork when she'd seen the results, but Sarah Jane wouldn't let her. She said she liked her hair just the way Uncle Jack had fixed it, crooked or not.

A tear welled up in Jack's eye—a hot one that had no business being there. And all of a sudden he threw the hoe down to the ground and stomped toward the house.

"Jack?" Marty called. "What're you doin'?"

"I'll tell you what I'm *not* doing, Marty. I'm *not* stepping aside to let some other son-of-a-gun move in on my family!"

He thought he heard a deep chuckle as he marched from the field to the house, but he ignored it. He wasn't sure what he was feeling right now, and he didn't bother trying to analyze it. He was too stirred up to think straight. He just knew he had to tell her . . . tell her . . . *something*.

He'd surged through the door, scanned the kitchen, and headed up the stairs, still running on pure emotion. But when he burst into her bedroom, he forgot everything.

Everything.

Because she was sitting in that big metal tub, leaning back against it, head tilted up, eyes closed. The water was only up to her waist, and she was completely naked, and utterly . . . utterly . . .

"Beautiful," he whispered.

Her eyes blinked open. Then she looked up at him, and they widened. "Jack, get out!"

He stayed right where he was with his hat in his hands, and reached back to close the door behind him even as he shook his head from side to side. "I couldn't walk out of here now if I tried, Em."

Her arms were crossed over her breasts now, head lowered, cheeks hot. Jack moved closer to the tub. When she didn't scream bloody murder, as he half expected her to, he moved still closer, until he could kneel down beside it. Then he reached up to take her hands in his. Very gently, he moved them away and lowered them to her sides, so he could look at her. She was blushing all over, with her hair loose and tumbling in burnished curls over her shoulders, its ends damp and dragging in the water.

"My God, Emily, I've never seen anything so beautiful in my life. I mean . . . I mean all this time, I've been living under the same roof with you, and I knew you were beautiful, but . . . but I didn't know the half of it."

"Stop it," she whispered.

Her arms were so long and slender; her skin milky, untouched by the sun; her breasts perfect, plump, and soft. He'd never seen anything look more . . . more feminine. Woman. She was just the soul of woman. A goddess. An angel. A woman.

"Jesus, Em, if I could paint, I'd paint you just like this."

"Jack . . ."

"Look at you," he went on. "How could you ever think I wouldn't want you?" Finally he lifted his gaze to meet her eyes. "Hmm?" Then he trailed the backs of his fingers over her breasts. She caught her breath as his knuckles skimmed her nipples. "I'd die to have you in my arms right now," he said, staring hard at her.

She looked right back at him. Her gaze was probing and deep; her voice, raspy and hoarse. "Are you saying what you think I want to hear, Jack? So you can get what you want?"

He shook his head slowly. "I'm saying the truth, Emily. And it's what we both want. But I'll turn around and walk out of here right now if you tell me to."

She licked her lips and said nothing. So Jack got to

his feet, and unbuttoned his shirt, and then shrugged it off. She sat still, just staring at him. And she looked scared, but she also looked aroused. And in need.

"Jack . . . I've never . . . been with a man."

He was so hard he ached. "I won't hurt you, Emily. I swear to Christ, I won't."

She closed her eyes. "Yes, you will, Jack," she whispered. "But not today, at least. Not today." She rose to her feet very slowly.

Water ran in gentle rivulets down her skin. She held out a hand. Jack couldn't move for a long moment as his eyes devoured her. And when he could, he managed to get free of his jeans, boots, and socks almost all in one effort. And then he took the hands she offered, and he stepped into the tub with her.

9

$\mathcal{L}$ He was so tender, so careful with her. His touches, his kisses nearly brought tears to her eyes. Emily had never been so brazen. And yet she felt no shame in this. She was thirty-five years old, and married, and she'd spent her entire life taking care of other people. Her sister, and then Clem and the children. Just this once, she was going to take care of herself.

She'd wanted Jack all along. She knew that. Oh, she'd denied it for a time, even to herself, but the feeling had been there, burning inside her, growing stronger all the time. She couldn't keep fighting it. She didn't want to.

Even knowing it didn't mean anything. Even knowing he'd be gone long before winter set in, leaving her alone again.

He sank into the water, his hands at her waist, and he pulled her down with him, cradling her in his arms. He kissed her . . . first her lips, and then everywhere. He kissed her eyes, her neck, her breasts . . . and Emily felt the fire burn like none she'd ever imagined. His hands moved over her with a touch that made her heart pound, and her breaths came short and fast. He touched her most private places, and when she shied away he whispered gently to her, coaxing her and calming her, and touching her until she couldn't resist or refuse. Her mind seemed to have melted into a pool of utter longing. A need gnawed at her belly and made her ache for some foreign kind of fulfillment.

Finally he pulled her legs around his waist and settled her atop him, and very, very slowly, he pressed himself inside her. Filling her. Stretching her. She gasped, impatient now because this yearning was going to explode soon if he didn't . . . didn't do something. She moved herself lower, then cried out in a sudden sharp pain. "Jack!"

He went utterly still. "All right," he whispered. "All right. It's okay now. Easy, Em. Trust me, my beautiful Emily." He stroked her, one hand toying with her breast while the other moved between them to tease her at the spot where they were joined. His mouth found hers, and in seconds, that fire was spreading through her again. And Jack began to move with her, slowly at first, but then faster, and harder, driving her closer and closer to something she'd never felt.

And then it happened. The sky exploded, and she cried his name, and her entire body was seized in the grip of utter sensation, and release, and pleasure so intense it made her shudder all over.

He held her close, bent to kiss her neck, and then whispered, "My God, Emily, it's never been like this for me before. Never."

She lifted her head, met his eyes. Breathlessly, she whispered, "Are you . . . can we . . ."

"Again?" he asked with a tender smile.

Emily nodded. And Jack got out of the tub, and bent over it to scoop her into his arms. He carried her to the bed and they did it again. Emily thought her body would shatter with the sensations he brought to her. She thought her skin would melt from the heat. But there was more. There was the emotion that flooded her heart for this man. And that was when she realized that she'd made a terrible mistake.

She'd fallen in love with him. She loved Jack Mc-Cain, this stranger from another time. This man who had to leave her in the end. She loved him, and when he went away, it was going to break her heart.

Lordy, but her heart felt as if it were already breaking!

He held her gently when it was over, tight to his chest, his arms almost possessive. She kept her face low so he wouldn't see her tears. Her body was sated, flushed with satisfaction. She felt like a woman for the first time in her life. But her heart was left yearning for more. So much more.

"Em?" he asked. "Honey? Are you okay?"

She only nodded. "It was . . . it was wonderful, Jack."

She heard the breath sigh out of his hard chest in relief. "I thought it was pretty wonderful myself," he told her.

She said nothing, just snuggled closer to him. She didn't want this to end. But she knew it had to.

"We . . . we should talk," Jack said.

Of course he'd want to talk. He'd want to remind her that this little interlude didn't change anything. That he still had to go back to his own time. Back where he belonged. And she still had to stay here and make a life for the children. Nothing had changed.

"It's all right, Jack," she whispered. "You don't have to say anything. I know."

He stroked her hair. "Do you?"

"Of course. I'm not a child. I understand that men have . . . have needs. I realize that's all this was."

He seemed to stiffen beside her. "Is that what you think?"

"It's what I know."

"But, Emily, I—" he stopped then, because the sound of rattling wheels and the clip-clop steps of a horse and carriage came clearly through the slightly opened window.

"Lordy, someone's come calling!" Emily hurried out of bed, taking the sheet with her and gathering up her clothes as she went. She peeked outside. "Goodness, it's Mr. Sheldon!"

"Who?" Jack sat up and began to dress at a more leisurely pace. Too leisurely, she thought.

"The banker! He's determined to take this farm from me and has been from the start! Hurry up, Jack!"

"Oh," Jack sighed. He was unwilling to let Emily go one more minute with her mixed-up notions about what he was thinking and feeling, but figured he had no choice. He figured she'd die of embarrassment if the jerk outside caught them naked in bed. So he finished dressing and headed downstairs just in time for the banker to rap on the front door. When he opened it, he saw Marty hurrying up the steps, too, obviously curious about what the man wanted.

The fellow eyed Jack up and down, a look of disdain crossing his pinched face as he stepped inside. He quickly dismissed Jack and searched for Emily. "I need to speak with Miss Hawkins," he said.

"That's Mrs. McCain," Jack told him. "And she'll be with you in a minute. But since I'm here, why don't you tell me what it is you're here about?"

Sheldon offered a fake smile. "It's business. Private business between Emily and myself."

"Is that right?"

He nodded. "So if you don't mind, I'll wait for her."

"I'm right here."

Both men looked up to see Emily descending the stairs, her skirts in place and her hair pinned up. Only Jack could see that her eyes still sparkled and her cheeks still glowed with the aftereffects of lovemaking. God, he wanted her again already. But there was something else

in those green eyes, too. A certain heartache he was
beginning to think he understood.

"Good," Mr. Sheldon said. "Now if you *gentlemen*
will excuse us—"

"Mr. Sheldon, Jack is my husband. Any business you
have with me, you also have with him. Is that understood?"

The man's head pulled back a bit, and he stiffened as
if surprised. "Come now, Emily. Everyone in town
knows this farce is more a business arrangement than a
marriage. McCain's only interest in you and this farm is
that it's keeping him out of jail. And your only interest
in him is as a free hand."

Jack had picked up Sheldon by his starched lapels
before he knew he was going to move, and he lifted him
right off his feet. Marty quickly gripped Jack's shoulders
and pulled him back. Jack had the satisfaction of seeing
the guy's eyes bulge before he set him back on the floor
again. "State your business and leave, mister, before I
decide to use you for fertilizer."

Sheldon brushed at his shirtfront and smoothed his
jacket. "Well. It's obvious you haven't changed your
criminal ways, McCain."

"What do you want, Mr. Sheldon?" Emily asked
firmly.

The man sighed. "Fine, have it your way. I only came
to deliver a friendly bit of advice, Emily."

"That being?"

"The grain auction is being held this Saturday."

Emily literally staggered two steps backward, her face
paling so suddenly that Jack thought she was going to
pass out cold. He rushed to her side and eased her into
a chair. "I don't get it," he said. "What does that
mean?"

"We . . . we have a steady market for the crops we
grow. Every September the farmers gather in town to
meet the buyers, who come to negotiate a fair price for

the grain. They're mostly cattle ranchers from farther south—from certain counties in Texas and Arizona where there's too little rain to grow the quality of sorghum we can produce here. They pay cash and haul the grain back with them.''

Emily explained it all slowly and clearly, but even then Jack could see her lower lip trembling and her eyes darting around in what looked like panic before they finally landed on the banker again. ''But we never hold the grain auction until the end of September. They shouldn't be here for three weeks yet.''

''Well, I sent a few telegrams, letting them know that all the locals would have their harvest in by the day after tomorrow, and that the date had been moved up accordingly. I thought it rather nice to hold the auction on the same day as the harvest dance for a change.''

Emily's eyes narrowed and she rose to her feet. ''You did this deliberately. You *know* I can't possibly get this crop harvested by the day after tomorrow!''

He shrugged. ''Oh? You can't? Well, then I suppose you might as well deal with me now, as later.'' He reached into his coat and pulled out a folded paper. ''Sign this, Emily. The farm will belong to me, and your debt will be forgiven. I've been very generous, even put in a clause allowing you and the children to remain living in the house . . . providing you get rid of this so-called husband of yours. I won't house a convict.''

Emily looked up at Jack. Her eyes were watering. Jack saw those eyes. Big and round, and damp. And he reached out, took the papers from Sheldon's hand, and easily tore them in half, then in half again, and again, and then he tossed the pieces over the guy's head like confetti.

''The crop will be in on time. The debt will be paid in full. And this *convict* isn't going anywhere. You got that?''

Emily blinked, looking stunned and slightly unsure.

"If you don't agree to my terms now," Sheldon said, "then my generosity ends. I'll take the farm anyway, and toss you *and* those orphans out. Not a roof over their heads, Emily. Is that the way you want to raise them? Is that what you promised your sister on her deathbed?"

"That's it," Jack said, and he grabbed Sheldon by one arm, twisted it and tossed the jerk right over his shoulder. "You wanna get the door, Marty? I need to take out the trash."

Marty grinned and opened the door, and Jack stepped through it and hurled the sputtering, shouting banker right off the porch and onto the dusty ground. "Don't let me catch you on this property again, or I'll have the sheriff arrest you for trespassing."

The man got up, brushed at his clothes, and shouted threats all the way to his buckboard. Jack stood on the porch with his arms folded over his chest until Sheldon rattled out of sight. Then a soft voice made him turn.

"It's impossible," Emily whispered from beyond the screen door. "It's just impossible. Jack, we only have two days until the auction, and we haven't even begun. It would take a dozen men to harvest the crop in that short a time. There's just no way . . ."

Jack went to her, and saw Marty standing behind her shaking his head as if he agreed with every word. Jack put his hands on Emily's shoulders. "I'll find a way. Trust me, Emily. I swear, I'll make this work."

She closed her eyes and lowered her head. "I know you'll try," she said, then turned and walked back into the house.

Jack watched her go.

Marty came out and walked beside him, back out toward the fields. "She's right, you know," the big lug said. "Jack, the two of us working dawn to dusk might . . . *might* be able to harvest half the sorghum in this field on time. But there'd be another half to go, and then two other fields. There's no way we can do it. Not if we could work day and night nonstop from now till Saturday. There's just no way."

Jack stopped halfway between the house and the fields, and stood looking out at the crops. "You sure?"

"I been doing this all my life, Jack. Yeah. I'm sure."

"Okay, then. Okay. I guess there's only one way. And Emily's not going to like it . . . but I don't see as we have a choice."

Marty stared at him, frowning. Then the frown eased and his brows rose. "Not another contest? Jack, Miss Emily'd have liked to skin you alive the last time! And she said if you ever did anything like that again she'd—"

"I know. I know." He gripped Marty's arm and steered him past the field, and toward the road into town instead. "So what do you think for a prize this time, Marty? Another feast? Or maybe we could offer cash . . . you know, payable once we sell the crop."

Marty just lowered his head and shook it. "Miss Emily's gonna be madder than a wet hen when she finds out," he muttered.

It didn't go exactly the way Jack had planned it. Oh, he altered his approach a bit. This time he didn't use boasting or bragging to lure the local men into an ego-fest. He tried being humble for a change.

With his back to the bar and a beer in his hand, he said, "Guys, I have to swallow my pride here and admit that I can't get my grain harvested in time for that auction on Saturday. Not alone, anyway."

"Gee," someone said. "What a surprise."

"No, no surprise. I suppose I should have seen this coming. But you know, it wasn't exactly fair of Sheldon to move the date up like that."

A few men muttered in agreement to that point, at least.

"So what you gonna do, Jack," someone said. "Stage another contest?" Laughter built up around him.

"Yeah," said another. "Fool us into harvesting your crop for you for free while you nurse a twisted ankle again?"

"All for the chance to win a meal!" The third speaker shook his head as the laughter grew louder. "We ain't gonna fall for the same trick twice, McCain."

"It wasn't a trick," Jack denied, putting on his most innocent face. "Okay, I'll admit, I didn't know what I was doing. And I did need the plowing done, but it was an honest contest. The winner got exactly what he was promised. Didn't you, Marty?"

Marty nodded. "That meal of Miss Emily's was worth every minute of plowing I done," he said, nodding hard to emphasize every word.

"So what do you say, guys? You want to do it again? You all compete and the guy who harvests the most grain by Saturday gets a feast, prepared and delivered, the very next day?"

The men in the saloon muttered and shook their head. "We been harvestin' sorghum for weeks now, Jack," one called. "You're gonna have to do better than that."

Jack gnawed his lower lip. "All right," he said slowly. "How about cash? I'll give a cash prize as well, just as soon as we get paid for the crop."

Again there was muttering and shaking of heads. "No man here would take cash from Miss Emily," one said. "It'd be like takin' food from those little uns' mouths."

Frustrated, Jack slammed his glass down onto the bar. "Well, what then? Name it, guys. I'm in a desperate situation here."

Finally, one guy, young and lean and good looking, sauntered up to the bar. "Well, I can think of one thing that might entice some of these men to take you up on this harvest contest idea, Jack. The single ones, anyway."

Jack felt a tingle up his spine. "What are you getting at?"

"The harvest dance, Saturday night. The winner gets to escort Miss Emily to the dance."

Jack blinked, searched the room, and saw many smiles and nodding heads. His throat went dry. He searched his mind. Searched his heart, too, and knew what he had to do. And then he heard himself say, "You're on."

There was a soft gasp from just beyond those batwing doors, and when Jack looked up, he glimpsed Mary Brightwater looking in at him, shaking her ringlets in disapproval.

10

"You . . . you . . . you did *what*?" Emily stood on the front porch watching hordes of men assemble in her fields. She'd known the moment she'd seen them descending that Jack had pulled another trick on them, had conned them with some phony contest just like before.

But she'd never dreamed he would have promised *her* as the prize!

"Look, there's nothing to worry about."

"Nothing to worry about!" She stared up at him, so shocked . . . so . . . so *hurt* that she could feel her entire body trembling with rage. "How could you, Jack? You bartered me as if I were some light-skirted saloon girl! Or is that what you think of me now? Is it? Just because I gave myself to you do you think I'm . . ."

"No!" he denied. "No, Emily, it's nothing *like* that. I mean, I have a plan. Trust me."

"Trust you? Trust *you*?" She drew back her hand and slapped him so hard the impact nearly freed her shoulder from its socket.

Jack just looked at her as his face turned red.

"I will *never* forgive you for this, Jack. Never!" She felt the tears brimming, so she turned her back to him.

She heard his frustrated sigh. "I want to explain," he said to her back. "But I don't have time now. I have to go. Just know you're all wrong about this, Em. But you'll see that. You'll see." Then his booted feet stomped away, across the porch and down the steps.

Emily walked into the house, her feet dragging. But she had barely heard the door slam behind her when a cheerful voice called, "Isn't this the most romantic thing you've ever heard of?"

Emily stiffened and tried to remember that Mary Brightwater was a friend. It wasn't her fault that this insane idea of hers had backfired so miserably. She'd only been trying to help.

"Romantic?" Emily asked. "He's bartering with me as if I'm a prize heifer at a county fair!"

"Surely two dances with one of the local boys isn't too high a price to pay for getting your harvest in, Emily."

Emily turned, brows lifting. "Two dances?"

"Well, yes. It was one of the conditions Jack set. Didn't he tell you?"

Tipping her head to one side, Emily said, "No. He didn't."

Mary smiled and hurried into the kitchen, lifting the tin pot to check its weight, then nodding and pouring the still-warm brew into two cups. "Sit down, Emily. You really ought to know the details."

"Yes, I suppose I should. Since I *am* the prize in question."

Mary shrugged and set the cups on the table, taking a chair. Emily sat opposite her. "Jack only agreed to let the winner have two dances with you. Any two dances he wishes, except the waltz, and the last dance of the night."

Blinking in surprise, Emily sipped her coffee and refrained from commenting.

"Jack further said that he would bring you to the

dance himself, and that only he would be allowed to take you home. And he informed the men that he would be keeping a close eye on the one who wins those two dances. At the first sign of impropriety, the deal is off.''

"Really?" Emily asked, but her voice had become a croak by now.

"And then he informed them that it wasn't going to matter at any rate, because he intended to win this contest himself.''

Emily sniffed. "He told them the same thing last time, and then faked a twisted ankle to get out of having to live up to the claim.''

Mary glanced toward the front door, through which the fields were visible. "Not this time," she said with a nod.

Emily looked outside just as the sheriff fired a pistol shot into the air to signal the start of the contest. Jack was there, at the nearest end of the field, sickle in hand, and when that shot rang out, he sprang into motion. Emily blinked and shook her head. "I don't . . . I don't understand. Why would he bother? The crop will get harvested whether he participates in this madness or not.''

Mary stared at Emily with her jaw gaping. "I declare, Emily, why do you think *any* of them are bothering?''

Emily look down at the floor. "Men are a mystery to me. I suppose it's something to do with the male ego.''

"It's something to do with *you*. Emily, you're a beautiful, capable, intelligent woman. Every unmarried male in this town is enamored with you.''

"I'm a thirty-five-year-old widow with two children,'' Emily corrected her.

"You're a prize that men would fight for, and that crowd out in your field is proof of it." She sighed. "Look at them, Emily. Look at Jack. I vow, he's fighting harder than any of them!''

Emily swallowed the sudden dryness in her throat.

"Let's go out and watch," Mary said, jumping to her feet and snatching Emily's hand. And before Emily could argue she was being dragged through the house and across the lawn to the north field.

Jack worked like a man possessed. Emily watched as he swung the sickle again and again. In a short while, he had to pause to peel his shirt from his sweat-dampened skin, and then he dove right back into the grain again. Emily stood mesmerized, her eyes on him and him alone. The steady flex and release of his corded muscles. The way his hair stuck to his face as it grew damp with sweat. In no time at all he'd pulled far ahead of his competitors. And to think he was a man who'd admitted that he'd spent his life avoiding physical labor. A man she was convinced felt nothing for her beyond sexual desire.

What if she'd been wrong?

A hand on his shoulder made Jack pause in swinging the sickle, which had been getting heavier with every arc. He turned, irritated at the interruption. He'd been totally focused on the rhythm of his movements. But when he saw who stood there, his irritation fled. "Emily . . ."

"I . . . brought you a cool drink. Lemonade."

He saw the dewy glass in her hand and took it, gulped the contents gratefully, then swiped his mouth with the back of his hand. "Thanks. I needed that."

She nodded and took the glass back. "The others have stopped at least long enough to snatch a bite to eat."

"Good," he said. "That'll give me a better lead on them." He sent her a wink and started to turn away.

"At least have a biscuit, and another drink. You'll . . . you'll dehydrate if you don't." She was using his own word, but he didn't mind when she pulled the biscuit from her apron pocket and poured more lemonade into the glass from the tin pitcher she carried in her free hand.

He didn't argue. He wolfed the biscuit down so fast he barely bothered to chew, and then he gulped more liquid.

As he did, Emily said, "Jack . . . I judged you too quickly before. I . . . Mary explained the conditions you set, and I want you to know it's all right."

He swallowed, licked his lips, and stared at her. "It is?"

"Yes," she said. "I . . . I won't mind so much dancing with one of these men. I mean, it's only two dances, after all, and it's little enough to ask in return for getting the harvest in."

"Really." He said it flatly, watching her face.

"Yes, really. So you needn't kill yourself trying to win. I won't be angry with you."

He smiled very slightly. He was exhausted, and the day was only half over. And yet there remained a little cockiness in him. "You may not mind dancing with one of those rednecks, Em. But I'd mind it. I'd mind it a whole lot. So rest assured, it's not gonna happen."

"It's . . . not?"

"I want you all to myself Saturday night."

"You . . . do?"

"I wouldn't have pulled this scam if I thought there was any doubt I could win. Even though I knew it was the only way to get the crop in, Em, I wouldn't have done it. Not if I wasn't sure."

She looked so damned bewildered that it was clear she still wasn't getting it. So he jerked her into his arms, pulled her tight against him, and kissed her hard and deep.

But when he lifted his head, she still looked bewildered. And now she was blushing to boot.

"Honey," he said, "I don't know how you expect me to carry out my plan to win this thing with you out here distracting me this way.'' He smiled at her, and she seemed totally at a loss.

"Well . . . I'll . . . go then.''

"Pick out something pretty for Saturday night,'' he called as she turned and began hurrying away. '' 'Cause I plan to claim every single dance with you. That's a promise, Emily McCain.''

She looked back and her lips pulled into a tremulous, uncertain smile.

"Damn,'' Jack muttered when she finally turned away again. "What a woman.'' He shook his head and lifted his sickle.

"We have a winner!'' the sheriff called, and he held Jack's fisted hand up high above his head. They stood on a slight rise among a crowd of tired, dirty, sweaty men, silhouetted in the twilight of dusk. Around them the field lay flat, nothing standing beyond uneven stubble and an occasional missed stalk, bent or broken.

Jack was coated in sweat and dirt and bits of sorghum. His hair was wet, his chest was bare, and his knees were wobbly. He didn't look as if he could stand up much longer. But he was grinning crookedly, all the same.

Emily's entire crop had been harvested. She saw Mr. Sheldon from the corner of her eye as he slammed his hat onto his head and stomped away. He must realize he'd lost. It was over. He was beaten.

But she stopped thinking about that when Jack sank to his knees in the dust. The men around him dissipated, shaking their heads in begrudging admiration and muttering that maybe he wasn't such a tinhorn after all. Even the sheriff gave Jack a friendly slap on the shoulder.

Emily went to Jack and dragged one of his arms around her shoulders, helping him to his feet.

"I did it,'' he muttered, looking up at her as he limped toward the house. "I won.''

"Yes, you did. But if you don't get some rest you won't be capable of dancing with me on Saturday night."

He sighed blissfully. "No chance of that, Em. No chance at all." He managed to move his feet every now and then as she helped him into the house.

11

Jack opened his eyes. He was wet. Cool. Oh, yeah, he was soaking in a lukewarm bath in that big ol' tin tub. And he was languishing under the gentle touch of hands that were as strong and capable as they were soft and erotic.

"Emily," he muttered.

"Who else?" She rinsed the soap off his chest. "Think you can stand up long enough to get into bed?"

"Hey, didn't I just prove I'm the manliest man out here?"

She smiled at him, but there was a sadness behind her eyes, even now. "Come on then." She gripped his arm to help him, steadied him as he stepped out, buck naked, and then briskly began to towel him off. She drew him toward the bed and yanked the covers back. "In you go."

He gripped her arm. "Not alone, I'm not." When he fell into the bed he pulled her in with him, and in a heartbeat his arms locked around her waist and his mouth found hers. God, it felt good to kiss her. And this time he felt like he'd earned her kiss. Like maybe he was worthy of her after all.

But then, why was she pulling herself free?

He let go, and she got out of the bed fast, jerking the covers back up over him, and shaking her head. "I . . . can't, Jack."

"But—"

"No buts. This . . . this thing between us . . . well, it's gone as far as it can, we both know that."

"Wha—"

Her eyes bored into him as she quoted the verse he'd seen carved on that well: the words he'd heard his grandmother repeat in her singsong voice so many times he knew them by heart.

"Make a wish upon this well, but wishes don't come free.
Make a promise here as well, and your wish you will see.
A voyage will you take then, your promise to fulfill.
And when you've kept your vow, shall I appear here on this hill.
With one more wish to grant you, one more gift to bestow.
Any wish you care to make; to stay, perhaps, or go."

"Emily, that's—"

"It's what brought you here. And now . . . now, well, you've done what you came here to do, Jack. You saw the crop harvested and even loaded the wagons and put them in the barn for the night in case of rain. You've done what you promised and then some. So I have no doubt you'll find that well right where you last saw it. You'll be able to . . . to go back."

He lowered his head and shook it. He wasn't even sure why, but the thought made his heart ache.

"Go to sleep now, Jack," Em whispered. "Matthew volunteered to milk Bessie for you tonight, and Sarah Jane is feeding the hens. They're already out in the barn getting started, so you just rest, and in the morning, we'll go find that well.''

He drew a breath, lifted his chin, and saw something in her eyes. Heartache. Longing. And a dancing reflection of . . . light. Red light.

He turned fast, and then sprang from the bed when he saw the tongues of flame licking up from the barn. ''Fire! Oh, Jesus, the kids!'' He was on his feet and pulling on his pants before Emily got out of the room and raced after him.

Fire leaped from every opening in the rough-hewn, weathered boards. The shingles seemed to melt before his eyes. Jack raced around the building seeking a way in, realizing that the crop, the entire crop, was being destroyed right before his eyes, and that as hard as he'd worked for it, it didn't matter. Nothing mattered except those kids.

Something emerged from the burning building—a large form, flames dancing from its back. ''Marty!'' Jack yelled, and he plowed into the big man, knocking him down and rolling him in the dirt.

''The children!'' Marty cried. ''I didn't know . . . and then I heard them and I went back, but they . . .''

''I'll get them.''

Emily was on her feet, running toward the burning barn, but Jack caught her, turned her. ''I'll get them, Emily. I swear to Christ, I will. Please, stay out here, safe. Trust me.'' He leaned in, kissed her hard and fast, then turned and, covering his face with one arm, ran through the flames.

''I do trust you, Jack!'' she called after him.

Jack burst through a gap between walls of fire and into the darkness of the barn. He couldn't see. He couldn't breathe. Smoke filled the place, and the heat was so intense it was like a furnace. A roar filled his ears and he wasn't sure he could have heard the kids if they had shouted at him. But he had to try. He wasn't leaving this damned barn without them!

"Matt! Sarah!" He moved forward, knowing a search would prove useless. He was blind. So he simply moved toward where he thought they'd be. Near the cow. Matt had been milking, right?

As he drew closer, Bessie's thrashing and frantic bellowing overwhelmed the roar of fire in his ears, and Jack followed the sound, found her in the thick smoke, and untied her. "You're on your own, girl." He pointed her toward escape and slapped her rump hard. The bovine bolted, bellowing to the heavens.

Jack knelt and felt around, discovering the toppled milkpail and the spilled milk. The little stool was still there. A sob tore through his chest. Cupping his hands like a megaphone he yelled again. "Matthew! Answer me!"

A long, wailing word he thought might have been "help" came from farther inside, and Jack ran, banged into a post, shook himself, and ran again.

"I'm right here! Talk to me so I can find you," he repeated. "Talk to me!"

"R-right here! Jack!"

He followed the frightened little girl's voice, and wound up on the floor where she'd been crouching, terrified, in a corner. Small arms twisted so tight around his neck that he couldn't even breathe the smoke-laden air. And he didn't care. He held that tiny body close and tried to calm her trembling. "Where's your brother, Sarah? Where's Matt?"

"I-I-I think he's dead!" she cried, and then started coughing and sobbing alternately.

Jack knelt down and felt the boy's limp body. He leaned close and felt the touch of Matt's breath on his cheek. Then he gripped Sarah's shoulders. "He's not dead. Do you hear me, Sarah?"

Her arms snagged him around the neck in answer, and

tears smeared his shoulder as little Sarah buried her head there. She wouldn't let go, terror made her cling to him. And he couldn't ask her to let go. "Sarah, climb onto my back," he shouted over the ever-growing roar. "Wrap your legs around my waist, and your arms around my neck. That's it. Tighter now."

She did as he told her, and as soon as she clung in place, he knelt to scoop Matt up into his arms. "Hold on tight, Sarah," Jack called. "Don't let go." He felt her nod, but didn't hear her answer. Her face was pressed to the back of his shirt, and he figured that was just as well. Maybe it would filter some of the smoke the poor child was breathing. But not enough. God, she was coughing with every breath, and a few steps more and he was, as well.

Matthew wasn't, but Jack almost wished he would.

Finally, Jack felt air on his face and stumbled forward, through an opening, into the night, the burst of fresh, cool air hitting him full in the face.

"Jack! Matthew!" Emily cried. She rushed forward and took the boy from Jack's arms. Jack sank to his knees and felt a weight lifted from his back. Looking up, he saw Marty, his face sooty but soft as he eased little Sarah off Jack's back and set her on her feet.

Sarah's arms instantly clamped around Jack's neck again. "I knew you'd come!" she cried. "I knew it. I love you, Jack."

"I love you, too, Sarah," he heard himself whisper hoarsely, the words so natural and honest that he didn't even have to think about them before he said them.

He glanced up to see Emily kneeling, clutching Matthew, and sobbing. "Emily?" Jack got to his feet.

"He's . . . not breathing, Jack. God, please . . . he's not breathing . . ."

Tears streamed over Em's cheeks, glistening in the fireglow. Jack was there in an instant, easing Matt from her arms. "I can't lose him," he said, as if the child were his to lose. But it felt as if he were. He recalled Matt's miniature imitation of the man of the house. The way he was so protective of Sarah and Emily. The smile on his face when he hauled that fish out of the stream. The front tooth just about ready to fall out.

"No dammit, I can't lose him!" Jack stretched the still child on the ground, pinched his nose, and leaned close, covering Matt's mouth with his own. Breathing into tiny lungs, he paused, repeated it, paused, and counted. He didn't even realize he was counting out loud. When he got to fifteen, he straightened and positioned his hands over Matt's sternum, depressed, released, depressed again. Back to breathing.

"Jack? Jack, what are you . . . ?"

"He's putting Matthew's air back, Aunt Emily," Sarah said, interpreting what she was seeing as best she could. "Uncle Jack will make Matthew all right again. I know he will."

God, let me live up to her innocent faith. I don't want to let that angel down.

Breaths again, compressions again, and over and over, for how long, Jack didn't know. He only knew that he'd have likely gone on all night long, but for one thing.

Matthew coughed.

Emily cried out. Marty gasped aloud. Sarah crowded in to hug her brother.

"Easy, easy," Jack said to everyone, including himself, as he watched Matthew blink him into focus, saw the color returning to his face in the glow of the fire.

Emily sank to the ground and gathered both children close to her. Her skirts were like a safe nest, a haven to them, and the children huddled close. She held them, but her eyes, gleaming with tears, were on Jack. The picture that the three of them made there, together, safe, made his chest swell with something that felt a lot like pride. But he'd failed, all the same.

"We . . . lost the crop, Em. I'm sorry."

"I don't care. Jack, I don't care if we lose every shingle on this place and the place with them. You saved my babies. I have them. I have *them*." She closed her eyes. "You are a hero, Jack. Our hero."

Jack's throat swelled, and he moved closer, knelt down, and put his arms around the three of them. Matthew could barely talk. His voice was coarse, gravelly. "I saw someone, Jack. That man, Mr. Sheldon, from the bank."

Jack went still. "He was in the barn before the fire?"

Matthew nodded. "He didn't see me, though. I ducked," he rasped.

"I seen him, too," Marty said. Jack rose again, turning. He'd forgotten Marty was even here. "I was comin' over to see if you needed any help with chores tonight, seein' as how you about killed yourself winning that contest today. And I passed him on the road, goin' the other way, back toward town. Then I seen the smoke."

"So you rushed out here to try to fight the fire."

Marty shook his head. "To save the sorghum. If I'd known those two younguns was in there, I'd have let it burn, but I didn't hear 'em yellin' until after I'd pulled the wagons out. I went back in, but . . ."

"Wait a minute," Jack said. "You pulled the wagons out?"

Marty nodded, then lifted a beefy arm and pointed. Off in the distance, five wagons heaped with freshly cut sorghum stood in a crooked row, perfectly safe from the fire. Bessie the cow, her rump singed in places, was nibbling a bit of the harvested crop.

Jack looked at Emily. She stared back at him and slowly, her face lit up in a smile.

Emily's happy mood dissipated Saturday morning. Oh, it had lasted through the bidding, and the collecting of a lovely price for her crop. And it had lasted through her visit with Sheriff Stonewall, and the pleasure of watching Mr. Sheldon be arrested and put in a jail cell to await the circuit judge's next visit. It lasted through the picnic lunch by the stream when Jack took Matthew and Sarah fishing, swimming, and tree-climbing.

It should have lasted all day. Because she had her farm, minus one replacable barn. And she had her precious angels, safe and happy, all thanks to Jack.

But now, as they sat watching the children play by the water's edge, Jack said the words that eliminated her good mood . . . maybe forever.

"Let's go up the hill and see if that well's decided to make itself visible to me yet."

Emily's throat went dry. Her heart seemed to shatter. She'd thought . . . well, that he'd at least stay with her until after the harvest dance tonight. He'd said . . .

Oh, but what did it matter? He'd saved her children and her farm, and the least she could do in return was let him go. Without guilt or repercussions or tears. But it was hard to be noble. Because she loved him. She loved him so incredibly much.

But she only said, "All right," and called to the children, "Take the picnic basket back to the house for me, darlings. Uncle Jack and I will be . . . I mean . . . I'll be there in a few minutes, all right?"

Sarah nodded and smiled. Matthew tilted his head, as if detecting something wrong with her voice or her words, but not quite able to figure out what. He hefted the basket, and the two ran off toward the house.

She turned, and when Jack offered his arm, she took it. They walked together around the bend in the river, to the narrow, dusty road beyond it, and along that road for a good distance. Then they veered off it, went up the slight hill, and parted some brush in the spot where the well was supposed to have been.

And it stood there, solid and real, as if it had been there all along. The words were still chiseled into its stone. And Jack drew a breath and sighed. "So I guess

I should do this by the traditional method, huh?'' he asked, and he fished a coin from his pocket.

"I guess so.'' Emily averted her face to hide her tears, bit her lip, and vowed not to cry until he was gone. "I'll . . . I'll explain to the children. I'll make them understand.''

He only nodded. "Would uh . . . I be out of line if I asked for a kiss? For luck?''

Her smile, she knew, was shaky, but she shook her head, and stood on tiptoe and pressed her lips to his. He kissed her, then kissed her again. And then he swept her into his arms and bent her backward and kissed her as if his very life depended on it.

And finally, he straightened away. "Well," he said. "Here goes nothing.''

Emily braced herself, wondering how it would happen. Would he simply vanish? Dissolve into some kind of magic mist and evaporate? It didn't matter. He'd be gone, out of her life forever.

"I'll never forget you, Jack,'' she whispered.

"Well, I should hope not,'' he replied, and then he tossed his coin into the well and cleared his throat, and held her hand tight. "I wish with all my heart that Emily Hawkins McCain would let me be her husband.'' She looked up fast, and he took both her hands and stared deeply into her eyes. "Her *real* husband,'' he said. "And a father to Matthew and Sarah. And I wish that she could love me. Because if she could, then I'd never have need to wish for anything else, ever again.''

Emily just stood there, blinking at him, her heart swelling until she thought it would burst as his words sank in. "Jack?'' she whispered.

"I love you, Emily,'' he told her. "I swear I do. I don't want to go back to the future. I want to stay here, with you and the kids. If . . . if you'll have me.''

Her lips trembling, she smiled. "If I tell you no . . . then I'll have no escort to the harvest dance tonight,'' she managed to blurt out, feeling giddy and silly and insanely, madly in love. Like a young girl! "So I guess I have no choice."

"Guess not," he said, but he still looked a bit uncertain.

"I love you too, Jack. I tried not to. I was afraid to let myself feel this . . . because I didn't think you'd ever feel it, too. And I thought you'd leave me in the end, and I didn't want my heart broken. But all my fighting didn't stop it. I love you, and I think I have from the second I saw you in your silly twentieth-century clothes in that crowd of convicts."

"Oh yeah?"

She nodded. Jack's smile faded slowly, and he pulled her close. "I want to spend the rest of my life making you happy, Emily. And we'll start tonight, at that dance. I . . . er, don't suppose you know the Macarena?"

She gave him a frown, then shook her head and snuggled close to his chest, relishing the embrace of his strong arms around her, knowing this was where she belonged, where they both belonged. They stood like that for a long moment, surrounded by brambles, caressed by the breeze, and cradled by the hillside. And behind them the old well shimmered for just a moment, and then faded away.

A Bride Most Common
Common

Angie Ray

1

Lucy Taylor had learned early in life that when you are five foot nothing, it isn't easy to get people to take you seriously. Especially when you are also blond and blue-eyed and overly curvy in the bust and hips.

She'd found this to be true all through her school years, and, when she quit college at age twenty to go to work full time after her parents' death in a plane crash, she'd discovered it to be true in many companies as well.

"I don't think you're qualified," the pimpled, eighteen-year-old John Parish had said during her interview with him and his uncle for the position of technical writer.

"I assure you, I'm quite capable," she responded, trying not to bristle at his teenage male arrogance.

"Now, John," Bill Branigan said. "Let's not be hasty. Let's see what she can do."

John did not look happy, but since the elderly Branigan was the owner and founder of Branigan Electronics Company, he couldn't really object.

Bill Branigan had given Lucy an assembly manual and asked her to see if she could find any mistakes.

Determined to do the best job possible, she pored over

the manual and found several glaring errors, as well as multiple less obvious ones.

Bill Branigan was delighted and hired her on the spot. Unfortunately, as she found out later, John was the one who had written the original manual. Four years later, he still resented her.

Which was why Lucy wasn't too thrilled when Stella, the spike-haired, ghoul-makeuped bookkeeper for the company, told her one afternoon that Branigan and his nephew wanted to see her in the laboratory—pronto.

"Is anything wrong?" Lucy pressed the save button on her keyboard, wondering what John could have found to complain about now.

"Definitely." Stella leaned her black leather-clad hip against Lucy's desk and waggled her gold-ringed eyebrow. "I haven't seen Cousin Bill so worked up since he caught Greg Mitchell trying to steal the schematics of the new radio project."

"Uh-oh. That's not a good sign," Lucy said. Usually the kindest and most trusting of men, Branigan had gone completely berserk when he found Greg Mitchell trying to take some blueprints home to work on. Branigan had accused Greg of trying to steal his work. In spite of Greg's emphatic denials, Branigan had fired him. "What set him off?" Lucy asked.

Stella shrugged. "I have no idea. You'll find out soon enough." She strolled back to her own cubicle.

Slowly, Lucy stood up and headed for the elevator. It was probably nothing. She'd given John her nearly completed manual to proofread—theoretically, they were supposed to be working together—and he'd probably found something to complain about. He was always complaining about something—that her manuals were too complicated, her editing sloppy, her turnaround time too slow.

It's probably nothing, she told herself again as she rode the elevator down to the basement. But still, it wasn't pleasant to have to constantly defend herself and her work against a little weasel like John. If she didn't like Branigan so much, she would have left long ago.

The elevator stopped, and when she stepped out her gaze immediately fell on John, sitting on a high stool at a long table littered with circuit boards, wires, a computer, pencils, slide rulers, notes, and other assorted junk. He straightened when he saw her and glared at her through his thick glasses.

"Here she is, Uncle Bill," he said rudely.

Automatically, Lucy looked over to the purple-and-green plaid couch resting against one wall. Sure enough, there sat Branigan, his rapt gaze fixed on the TV opposite. An owl of some sort soared across the screen.

"Uncle Bill!" John spoke loudly so he could be heard over the swelling orchestral music of the wildlife video. "Lucy Taylor is here!"

"Ah, Lucy!" Tearing his gaze away from the TV, Branigan rose to his feet and beamed at her. "How are you, my dear? And how is the new radio manual coming along?"

"Fine, Mr. Branigan," she said, some of her tension easing. Branigan looked like a white-haired, roly-poly cherub. He'd always treated her kindly, and he always listened to her and believed her when John made one of his complaints. There was no reason for her to be so worried. "The manual is almost finished."

"Any difficulties?"

"No, not really. Although using vacuum tubes instead of circuits caused a few complications." She saw John's ears perk up and added hastily, "But I'm sure the manual will be understandable to anyone trying to build an antique radio from scratch."

"Excellent, excellent." He was distracted for a moment by the TV—the owl was sitting on a branch now, eating a dead mouse. Branigan turned back to Lucy.

"Now, I suppose you're wondering why I decided to build an antique radio."

"Um, yes. A little." Although he was always coming up with some weird new project, this one mystified Lucy. She couldn't imagine that there was much of a market for manuals on how to build an antique radio from scratch.

"The fact of the matter is I have no intention of trying to sell this manual. I only wanted *you* to learn how to build an antique radio."

"Oh?" Lucy was confused. "Why?"

"Because—"

"Uncle Bill!" John burst out, rising to his feet. His face was pale, his hands clenched into fists. Steam fogged his glasses. "Think about what you're doing! Remember what happened last time you trusted someone outside the family!"

He must be referring to Greg Mitchell, Lucy thought, her curiosity growing. Everyone else in the small company was related to Branigan somehow—except for her.

"Yes," Branigan retorted. "And look what happened when I trusted someone *inside* the family."

John flushed. "I told you—it wasn't my fault!"

Lucy looked from John's red face to Branigan's stern one. What on earth were they talking about?

"My dear," Branigan said, taking her arm and leading her to sit down on the couch. He glanced at the TV again. A fluffy white baby owl with a crest of bluish feathers and huge orange eyes stared unblinkingly at the camera. Branigan quickly picked up the remote control and paused the image before turning back to Lucy. "I need to discuss my new, top-secret project with you. I'm trusting you not to reveal anything you are about to hear."

"Of course," Lucy said automatically. Although she thought he was a little paranoid about his "top-secret" projects, she would never dream of breaking his trust.

"You remember that government contract we got a year ago?" he continued.

"Yes," she said. "To detail the history of the radio."

"That's what I told everyone," Branigan agreed. "But actually, the government wanted me to document history in a much more accurate way—through time travel."

"Through time travel?" Lucy repeated blankly. "Um . . . does the government really believe people can travel through time?"

"Yes—because it *is* possible. I've found a way to do it."

Lucy stared at him. He was almost seventy, but he'd never shown any signs of senility. Until now. . . .

As if reading her thoughts, Branigan smiled a little. "I know it's hard to believe, but it's true. A year ago, I discovered a way to transport a person's consciousness through time using radio waves. Greg Mitchell volunteered to test it. He time travelled on ten occasions, each time to different eras and different bodies."

"Different bodies?" she repeated hesitantly. "Didn't the people whose bodies he took over object?"

"Not at all. We only transfer to dead bodies."

Lucy recoiled. "You transfer people's consciousnesses into maggoty old corpses?" She stared at the sweet old man she'd thought she knew so well, an image rising in her mind of a half-rotted mummy digging its way out of a grave. "I think I'm going to be sick."

"No, no, no. We only use fresh bodies," Branigan assured her. "That is to say, we've found that if we transfer the consciousness into the body right at the moment of death, immediately after the original soul departs, it causes an adrenaline surge that revives the body. In certain cases the body will live on for a long period of time. When the consciousness returns to the future, the body in the past dies a natural-seeming death. No fuss, no muss.''

A trifle dazed, Lucy glanced at John. In spite of his sullen expression, he wasn't disputing anything his uncle said. Time travel—could it really be possible? ''What happens to the body in the future?'' she asked after a long pause.

''We keep it hooked up to a life-support system. Greg said that when he returned, he felt like he'd just had a good night's sleep. There are no side effects whatsoever.''

In spite of Branigan's disclaimer, Lucy thought the whole thing sounded extremely dangerous. And not just to the person doing the time travelling. ''What if the time traveller changes history?''

''That was, of course, a major concern. Therefore, I had Greg perform several experiments. What we discovered is that time is extremely resistant to change. No matter what a time traveller does, history has a way of correcting itself. To make certain of this, I always keep a computer disk of history in a time-proof safe every time I send someone back.''

''A time-proof safe?''

''Another invention of mine. The area inside it has some of the properties of a black hole. Normal time and space don't affect anything inside it. When the time-traveller returns, I take the disk from the safe and check it against a new one. Until last week there were no discrepancies.''

''What happened last week?'' Lucy asked.

''After I fired Greg, I had to find a new volunteer to go back in time.'' Branigan glanced at John.

John stared sullenly at the floor.

Branigan sighed. ''John was very keen to go, and I finally agreed. Unfortunately, an anomaly occurred during the transport.''

''What kind of anomaly?''

"I don't know, exactly. I've tried to identify it, but I can't. It might have something to do with the fact that when he was transported into the body of Jack Planchard in the London of 1808, John panicked."

"I didn't panic!" John whined. "I was startled. Anyone would have been. There was blood all over me."

Branigan nodded. "Jack Planchard had just been shot. It was a frightening experience for John. When I transported him back here five minutes later, he was blubbering like a newborn calf—"

"I was *not* blubbering," John interrupted. "I was a little disoriented, that's all."

Branigan looked surprised. "If you say so, John. Although the way you were crying and carrying on, I would call that blubbering—"

"Uncle Bill, could you just get to the point?"

"Oh. Yes, well, the point is that John changed history."

"It wasn't my fault," John muttered. "I'm sure I could fix it if you would just let me try—"

"It would be too complicated to send you back again when you're already there," Branigan said. "Lucy will do fine, I'm sure."

Lucy gasped. "*Me?* You want *me* to go back in time?"

"There—she doesn't want to go," John said to his uncle. "I told you she wouldn't. Now you'll have to send me—"

"I didn't say I wouldn't go," Lucy automatically contradicted John. Although in fact, she *was* thinking that no way would she let herself be the guinea pig for one of Branigan's experiments. "I just need more information to make an informed decision. Whose body would I be going into?"

"A woman named Cynthia Randall," Branigan said. "She died of an overdose of laudanum."

"Sounds like a real winner," Lucy muttered.

"I'm sure it was an accident." Branigan rubbed his hands enthusiastically. "I couldn't ask for a better trans-feree. The adrenaline rush should help clear the body of the laudanum. You may be a bit woozy at first, but you'll have a perfectly sound body to inhabit."

"Once inhabiting this perfectly sound body, what would I have to do?" Lucy asked.

"Nothing too difficult. Just build a radio so we can communicate, and make sure some information gets passed on to the right party."

"Sounds easy enough," Lucy said. She pretended to consider the matter. From the corner of her eye, she could see John biting his nails. Wanting him to suffer for as long as possible, she waited a minute more before shaking her head. "I'm really sorry, but—"

"Lucy, don't say no," Branigan interrupted. "Not yet. Not until you hear what's happened."

"I don't think it will make any difference—"

"Just hear me out. When John went back into Jack Planchard's body, he failed to pass on some important information. This little mishap affected a battle during the Napoleonic Wars. Although the battle itself was not critical and didn't affect the outcome of the war between England and France, several nasty side effects have oc-curred. Pollution is much worse."

"It is? I haven't noticed it," she said.

"It may not seem like it, but it is. According to the computer disks, the pollution levels before John's trans-port were half of what they are now." He nodded toward the TV screen. "The increased lead and ozone in the air caused the last blue-tufted owl to die a few months ago."

Involuntarily, Lucy glanced at the screen where the baby owl was freeze-framed. Its big orange eyes stared at her helplessly, reproachfully. A pang shot through her. The poor little thing. . . .

"Why me?" she asked, trying to harden her heart

against the innocent-looking bird. "Why not Stella?"

"Stella might be a little out of place in nineteenth-century England—"

"Whereas you'll fit right in," John inserted.

"We need someone who knows how to build a radio," Branigan said, with a frown at John. "Someone intelligent, someone we can trust—"

"Someone that no one will miss if anything goes wrong."

"John! That was completely uncalled for! And untrue, too! I, for one, would miss Lucy terribly."

Lucy barely heard Branigan. John's words had hit her like a blow to the chest, making it difficult to breathe for a moment.

Because the fact of the matter was, what John had said was true.

"Lucy . . . Lucy? Are you okay?"

She looked up into Branigan's kind, anxious eyes. After her parents' deaths four years ago, she'd been completely alone. She had an apartment, but she'd felt homeless. No one had cared about her at all—until Branigan had offered her a job. He'd treated her like one of his family, something she'd needed desperately during that terrible year. Now he needed her help desperately. The blue-tufted owl needed her help. The *world* needed her help.

How could she say no?

"Lucy?"

She straightened her spine and took a deep breath.

"I've changed my mind," she said. "I'll go."

Two hours later, as Branigan and John strapped her into the equipment, Lucy was having second thoughts about her heroic impulse.

"When you said this was urgent, I didn't realize it was *this* urgent," she protested, trying not to panic as

John tightened the straps around her ankles. "Can't we at least wait until tomorrow?"

"There's no time." Branigan attached electrodes to her temples; wires now connected her to an elephant-sized radio. "Everything must be corrected as soon as possible."

"You're sure I'll be able to get back okay?" she asked anxiously. "This machine won't dissolve my molecules or turn me into salt crystals, will it?"

"It's perfectly safe," Branigan assured her. "You know how careful I am."

"Uh . . . yeah." She tried not to think of the explosion in the lab last year and the resulting fire that had burned the building to the ground. "But I wanted to do a little more research. I don't know anything about nineteenth-century England."

"I told you everything you need to know," John said.

Lucy frowned. He'd told her almost nothing about the nineteenth century in her hour-long "training session." The more she questioned him, the less he said. About all she'd been able to get out of him was that Cynthia Randall was a housekeeper in the home of a sweet old man named Kieran Walcott. He'd also told her that she should speak with an English accent.

"But I don't know how to speak with an English accent," she'd protested.

"Use a bunch of long words and you'll be fine," was his brilliant advice. "Oh, and one more thing . . . Cynthia was *meek* and *mild.*"

"She would be," Lucy muttered.

"Just go along, and don't ask too many questions," John said. "You can't let anyone suspect that you're from the future."

"Why not?" she asked. "It might be easier if I just told them."

"Then they would put you in an insane asylum." With unnecessary relish, John added, "Did I tell you that in the nineteenth century, it was common for people to visit the asylums to see the lunatics?''

Lucy shuddered.

''Now, Lucy,'' Branigan said, distracting her from her reverie. ''You'll have a month to build the radio and find the information about the arms shipment that Walcott's firm is sending to the British army. Make sure to give the info to Jack Planchard and make sure he passes it on. It's that simple.''

''Yeah . . . so don't screw up,'' John said with his usual helpfulness.

''She won't screw up,'' Branigan said. ''Will you, Lucy?''

''I'll try not to,'' she managed to say. ''How long did you say I would be there?''

''A month. Remember, you may experience some wooziness from the laudanum immediately after the transport. Don't worry if you do—it's perfectly normal.''

''A month?'' she repeated.

''Yes.'' Branigan checked her pulse. ''You should pass on the information to Jack Planchard in Walcott's garden at 1:05 A.M. on May sixteenth. We'll bring you back the same morning at 10:00 A.M. Contact us first to make certain everything's okay.''

Lucy's stomach knotted. ''I'm going to be living in this Kieran Walcott's house for a month?''

Branigan must have seen the panic on her face, because he sat down next to her and took her hand in his. ''We appreciate the sacrifice you're making, Lucy. But also, this trip will be good for you. You've buried yourself in your work for too long. I know it will be awkward for you with Kieran, but—''

''But we're sure you can handle him,'' John interrupted. ''If worse comes to worst, close your eyes and think of the blue-tufted owl. Uncle Bill, hadn't we better start the transporting process?''

Branigan nodded. John immediately went over to a machine and started fiddling with several knobs.

Lucy frowned after him. "What did he mean, close my eyes and think of the blue-tufted owl?"

"Don't worry. I'm sure it won't come to that. Kieran Walcott is probably an honorable man. . . ."

John flipped a switch.

A noise hummed in Lucy's ears. It grew louder and louder. Cold, arthritic fingers with wrinkled skin squeezed her hand. She glanced up to see Branigan's mouth moving, but she couldn't hear what he was saying. She stared at his mouth, trying to make out the words.

Don't . . . worry . . . Lucy . . .

The room began to spin. She closed her eyes, but the spinning continued, faster and faster and faster. She felt a pulling sensation as though she were a piece of taffy candy being stretched; the humming vibrated through her as if she were a human tuning fork. The sound grew louder and more intense, until it was almost painful.

Don't panic, she told herself, clutching Branigan's frail hand tightly. *Don't panic, don't panic, don't—*

The humming stopped.

Through a vast pink haze, she slowly became aware of two things.

She was freezing cold.

And the hand holding hers was no longer cold, wrinkled, and arthritic.

A warm, strong hand grasped hers. Cautiously, Lucy opened her eyes and stared up into the face of a stranger. Harsh, lines drew his coal-black eyebrows together as his dark brown eyes watched her. Why was he frowning so? she wondered hazily. She lifted her hand—her incredibly heavy hand—and touched one of the lines bracketing his frowning lips. Something flickered in those eyes—surprise?—before her hand fell to her side and she closed her eyes again.

Dimly, through her excruciating headache, she became aware of more sensations. She was lying flat on her back, with a hard, cold floor beneath her. Voices exclaimed and gasped and buzzed in her ears. She shivered violently, a small moan of pain escaping her. Something encased her rib cage, making it almost impossible for her to breathe.

The hand holding hers tightened.

Suddenly, the sharp odor of ammonia filled her nostrils. Gagging, she turned her head away, but the smell followed her persistently. Reluctantly, she opened her eyes again.

"Are you injured?" the frowning man asked. "Perhaps we should continue some other day—"

"Nonsense!" a shrill voice interrupted. Woozily, Lucy turned her head away from the man's intense dark eyes to see a thin woman in a long purple dress pushing her way through the crowd of people. "There's no reason to delay, is there, Cynthia?" the woman demanded.

"No . . . no, I'm fine," Lucy said. She'd traveled back in time, she realized. She was Cynthia Randoll, a housekeeper, and she couldn't let anyone suspect otherwise. "I'm perfectly able to continue."

But she still felt cold—except for her warm fingers. She glanced down at the large, masculine hand completely enveloping her own. Her blurry gaze traveled from the hand, up a long arm encased in the dark blue sleeve of an old-fashioned jacket to the man's face again. He was studying her face closely.

He pulled her to her feet. She was vaguely aware that he was only three or four inches taller than her before she swayed and nearly fell. She caught his arm and held on for dear life.

"Dear me, dear me!" said a little old man in front of

them. "Are you certain, Lady Cynthia? Your voice sounds a bit . . . odd."

Lady Cynthia? "Yes, I'm sure," Lucy said, closing her eyes halfway. A bright light behind the old man sent a stabbing pain through her head if she tried to look at him. "Let's continue."

"Very well," he said. "You were about to give your response."

"I was? Oh, yes, I was. Um, what was the question again?"

"Honestly, Cynthia," the thin, purple-clad woman shrilled. "Just say you will."

"Oh. Yes. I will."

Some of the tension eased out of the arm that supported her. She glanced up, the pink fog in her brain clearing a little. The man next to her was about ten years older than she was—about thirty-four. Who was he? And why did he look so serious? What was this place, and why was she here? It seemed like a ceremony of some kind. . . .

Before she could complete the thought, the old man in front of her spoke.

"I now pronounce you man and wife. Kieran Walcott, you may kiss the bride."

2

She was married.

Riding along in the old-fashioned carriage with Kieran Walcott, Lucy still couldn't quite believe it. *Married.* To a complete and utter stranger! It seemed like a nightmare. A nightmare authored by John Parish.

Her lips tightened. Why had he lied to her? Out of spite? She wouldn't put it past him. But she suspected he had another reason—he was hoping she would fail. He'd always been jealous of Branigan's respect for her. Nothing would make him happier, she was certain, than if she botched her mission.

Well, she wouldn't, she thought. She would accomplish what she'd come here to do no matter how many lies John had told her. No matter how many obstacles he threw in her path. No matter how many complete strangers she had to marry. . . .

From beneath her eyelashes, she studied the man seated across from her. In his dark blue jacket and white, high-collared shirt, with his hair cut into casual curls and long, narrow sideburns, he seemed very alien to her.

But then, in the hour or so that she'd been here, everything had seemed alien—the people, the language, the clothes, even her body. It felt heavy and tightly con-

stricted by what must be a corset. She hadn't thought
about corsets when she'd agreed to do this. The contraption didn't allow her to bend her back at all. She
wished she could see what her figure looked like, but
her dress—long, narrow, high-waisted with lots of ruffles—concealed just about everything.

Even the sounds and smells seemed strange to her.
The horns didn't honk—they blew, like trumpets. Tires
didn't screech—hooves clip-clopped. Instead of gasoline
and ozone, she smelled manure and burning coal. She
could also smell a rather heavy rose scent, as if Cynthia
had doused herself with perfume. It tickled her nose and
made her want to sneeze.

She looked at Kieran again. Actually, he wasn't all
that bad-looking—but what had carved those lines in his
face? They made him look stern and forbidding. He obviously wasn't the outgoing type. He'd barely said two
words to her after he'd given her that peck on the cheek
at the ceremony. Obviously not the passionate type, either. But that was probably the English way—everyone
knew how cold and reserved *they* were. . . .

The carriage jerked violently, jolting Lucy from her
thoughts and throwing her across the carriage.

"Oh!" she exclaimed, as she suddenly found herself
on her knees between Kieran's legs, her stomach pressed
against his crotch, her hands on his thighs, her face
smashed against his chest. The scents of soap, linen,
tobacco, and a slight tinge of musk enveloped her.

Strong, firm hands encircled her waist, steadying her
as she quickly leaned back. She glanced up to see his
black eyebrows arching.

"I didn't realize you were so eager, wife," he said.
"I'm afraid you'll have to contain your impatience until
we arrive at my home."

Lucy scrambled back to her seat, her cheeks burning.
"I'm not impatient!" she blurted out.

"You're not?" His brows rose even higher. "Then

perhaps it would be wise of you to hold onto the carriage strap so that I will not misinterpret your actions and be overcome with passion. I would not like to disgust you.''

Lucy grabbed the leather strap hanging from the ceiling. Realizing that she hadn't sounded very bridelike, she tried to correct her mistake. ''You don't disgust me. I just don't want . . . I mean . . . I'm a bit nervous, that's all.''

''That's perfectly natural,'' he said kindly. ''But do not fear—I will be gentle.''

Gentle? Oh, dear heaven! He expected her to go to *bed* with him tonight! No way was she going to allow that. But how was she going to prevent him? The backward men in this time period probably never heard the word ''no'' from their wives. What on earth was she going to do?

She groaned.

''Are you feeling ill, my dear?''

''No . . . I mean, yes!'' she said, an idea occurring to her. ''I feel carsick. I mean, carriagesick.'' She wasn't completely lying. The thought of what she'd gotten herself into did make her feel ill.

Kieran leaned back in his seat and glanced out the window. ''It's fortunate, then, that we will arrive at our destination in less than five minutes.''

''Even short trips make me sick,'' she said firmly. ''I often vomit after I travel anywhere.''

He turned from the window to stare at her. ''How unpleasant,'' he finally said.

''Yes,'' she said. ''It's *very* unpleasant. Sometimes I throw up all night long. Over and over again. The smell is terrible. Which makes me feel even sicker and I throw up even more. Most people can't even stand to be in the same room with me—''

''Try not to think about it.''

Lucy shook her head. ''I try not to, but then the carriage sways and bumps and my stomach sways and bumps with it. Oh, dear. I do hope I don't start throwing up in the carriage. I'm sure you would find it terribly repulsive if I did. It might even make you sick. It might even make you—"

"Perhaps you should try to rest until we arrive," he suggested gently.

"That sounds like a good idea." She tried to make her smile as pitiful as possible. "But I doubt I'll be able to. I'm having my period."

"Your what?"

"My, um, menstrual cycle. I get cramps. Bad ones. Terrible ones. So terrible that they make me vomit—"

He was staring at her with an odd expression in his eyes. "Between your cramps and your carriage sickness, it will be a miracle if you survive this night."

She nodded solemnly, but before she could continue her litany of horrors, the carriage stopped.

"We've arrived," Kieran said.

It was dark. As Lucy descended from the carriage, she could see by the light of streetlamps a tall, narrow townhouse with a black, wrought-iron fence.

A flurry of activity greeted them. The oversized door opened and several people rushed out, bowing and curtsying.

"Good evening, sir, my lady," a stiff little man in a green coat and powdered wig greeted them. "On behalf of the staff and myself, may I express our felicitations on your nuptials?"

"Thank you, Denton." Kieran removed his hat and gloves and handed them to the man.

A woman wearing a black dress and severe bun stepped forward. "Cook has prepared a light supper for you. Shall I serve it in the parlor?"

"That will be fine, Mrs. Rogers."

The mention of food made Lucy's stomach growl—she felt as empty as if she'd been on a diet for a week. But she was supposed to be sick, she remembered in dismay. Valiantly, she ignored the demands of her stomach. "Food will only make me become sicker. I think I'd better go straight to bed."

Kieran bowed. "As you wish." Mrs. Rogers led her up to a second-story bedroom.

Had he gotten the hint? Lucy wondered. His expression was hard to read. But even if he had, she worried that he would still probably expect at least to share a bed with her.

Only a few candles illuminated the darkened room. Lucy saw a mobcapped girl using a bellows at a fireplace, a large four-poster bed, and several other pieces of shadowed furniture. And a door in one wall.

"Where does that door lead?" she asked.

"To Mr. Walcott's bedchamber," the housekeeper said.

He had a separate room! He wouldn't need to share her bed! Weak with relief, Lucy smiled brilliantly as the housekeeper introduced the girl.

"This is Polly," Mrs. Rogers said, gesturing to the girl with the bellows. "If it pleases you, my lady, she will serve as your maid. Is there anything else I can get for you, my lady?"

Lucy hesitated. She was starving. If she didn't have some food soon, she might start gnawing on the bedposts.

"Perhaps you could bring me some fruit and some bread? That will settle my stomach," she added hastily, to keep up the pretense of being sick.

Mrs. Rogers nodded and within a few minutes, Lucy was devouring the contents of a heavily laden tray—ham, two slices of bread and butter, an apple, and a cream tart. When she was finished, she stifled a small burp, and smiled a little sheepishly at the housekeeper. "Thank you, Mrs. Rogers. I was hungrier than I thought."

"You're welcome, my lady. Would you like Polly to help you prepare for bed now?"

Lucy stifled an instinctive refusal. Obviously, this was something Lady Cynthia would expect. Besides, she wasn't sure she could get the dress off without help—there appeared to be no buttons or zippers. "Yes, thank you."

This isn't even your body, she told herself firmly a moment later as the girl untied the dress, petticoat, and corset. There was no reason to be embarrassed. Although, sheesh, couldn't Lady Cynthia even take off her own stockings and drawers?

Lucy was relieved when she had a nightgown on and Polly finally left. Now that she was alone, she wanted to find out exactly what Lady Cynthia looked like. She went over to the dressing table and bent down to look in the small mirror.

She inhaled sharply.

She hadn't realized now strange it would be to look in a mirror and see someone else's face. Slowly, she traced Cynthia's features with her finger on the glass. Blond hair, pale skin, light blue eyes—all several shades lighter than her own—and a baby-doll mouth.

As her shock faded, disappointment took its place. If she had to get transported into a different body, why couldn't it at least be a gorgeous one? She looked positively anemic.

But what did the rest of her look like? The mirror was too small to see anything below the neck. She glanced around and caught sight of a full-length mirror in one shadowy corner. She went over and looked into it, then gasped.

She was tall. And *thin.*

She hesitated a moment, then stripped off her nightgown. Milky-white skin greeted her stare—not so much as a freckle marred its smoothness. She had narrow hips and a flat stomach—so flat that she could see the jut of her hipbones and the definition of her ribs.

After a lifetime of being short, plump, and over-endowed, the image before her was like a dream come true. She raised her hands to her breasts. They were small, too. She hardly even needed a bra. Oh, if only she could take this body home with her. She could tolerate the pasty face—she could tolerate anything to be so tall and slender—

"How charming."

Lucy jumped. She whirled around and saw Kieran standing in the open doorway that led to his room. A blush enveloped her entire—and very naked—body. She snatched up the nightgown and desperately tried to cover herself.

"What are you doing here?" she squeaked.

Kieran raised an eyebrow. "What a peculiar question to ask your husband on your wedding night."

Lucy gripped the nightgown more tightly. Dressed in a silk robe of green, blue, and purple silk embroidered with gold thread, he should have looked effeminate—or at least ridiculous. But he didn't. He only looked big and broad and intensely, unmistakably masculine.

Don't panic, she told herself. "The carriage sickness . . ."

Her voice came out sounding more quavery than she had intended.

"Yes, I know." His voice wasn't quavery at all; it was smooth and silky-soft. "Mrs. Rogers told me that you'd eaten and were much recovered."

"Oh. Well, actually, the truth is . . . I'm still feeling a little queasy—"

"Don't worry, sweetness." He started walking toward her. "I know how to make you feel better."

"But . . . but . . . I'm tired. Very tired. Extremely tired!"

Amusement filled his face. He was still moving toward her. "I know how to awaken you."

Panic welled up in her. "I . . . I'm having my period!"

"I don't mind."

"Well, I do!" She stuck her arm out, putting her hand on his chest to prevent his coming any closer.

His eyes glinted down at her. "You told me you would do your duty."

"I did? Oh, yes, I did. I will. Just not right now."

He covered her hand with his. Lucy tried to retreat, but the full-length mirror was behind her. The cold, hard glass pressed against her heated skin from shoulder to buttocks to thigh.

He stepped closer, until barely an inch separated them.

"I'm afraid I cannot wait any longer," he whispered.

His hand grasped the hair at the nape of her neck, holding her still as his mouth covered hers, bruising the softness, forcing her head back until she was half bent over his arm.

She struggled, thinking frantically of that self-defense course she'd always intended to take.

He ignored her struggling. He pressed harder against her lips, until she parted them helplessly.

And then, suddenly, everything changed.

His tongue slipped in, sweetly cajoling. Sensation flowed downward and outward; then it raced back to concentrate in her breasts and belly and between her thighs.

He broke off the kiss, leaving her bewildered, wanting. He rained gentle kisses on her face, his fingers playing gently with the hair at her nape, while his hand at her waist caressed her bare skin, soothing and exacerbating the trembling she couldn't seem to control.

The tension inside her increased. His mouth and fingers seemed to know exactly where to touch—the side of her neck; the knob of her chin; the curve of her belly and rib cage; the erect nipples of her breasts. . . .

With a gasp, she tore herself away.

Stepping back, he stared down at her. She stared back. He was breathing hard, his color high, his eyes almost completely black as his gaze travelled over her face, then downward.

Realizing she'd dropped her nightgown, she gasped again and quickly snatched it up from the floor. Her tall, thin body was transmitting thousands of sensations, the force of them too intense for her to think straight.

Her chest heaved as she stared at him. Her brain whirled as fractions of sentences whirled through her head.

Go along ... don't screw it up ... be meek and mild ...

Kieran yanked the nightgown from her grasp. "Do not be shy, sweetheart." He reached out toward her breasts again. "I am your husband. . . ."

Instinctively, with all the strength she could muster, she slapped his hand.

The sound of it rang through the suddenly silent room.

3

Kieran entered the Earl of Barstow's office late the next afternoon. Barstow rose to his feet, reaching across his desk to shake hands, then gestured for Kieran to sit down. Kieran did so, his gaze fixed on the earl.

Barstow, a plump, genial man in his fifties with a taste for bright yellow waistcoats and high-point collars, was a special aide in the Treasury Department, and directed much of the commissariat for the army fighting Napoleon.

Right now, his lordship appeared upset.

Barstow shuffled some papers on his desk, then set them aside and met Kieran's gaze. "As you are probably aware, we were delighted to accept the offer you made a few months ago to provide supplies to the army. Your reputation for delivering, no matter what the circumstances, is excellent."

Kieran inclined his head. Over the years, he'd built up a complicated network of trade routes all over Europe; these had proven very useful to a government trying to circumvent Bonaparte's efforts to block British commerce.

"But now *another* of your shipments has been intercepted," Barstow continued. "This makes a total of three shipments lost."

Kieran frowned. He had heard the news about the lost shipment a few days ago, and he had not been pleased—to put it mildly. "I am taking steps to ensure that it doesn't happen again," he said.

"What steps?" Barstow asked. "It's plain you have a spy working for you."

"I checked all of my employees after the first shipment was taken and again after the second. None of them seems a likely suspect. They have all worked for me for years. Perhaps the leak is within your organization."

Barstow stiffened. "Everyone working for me is beyond reproach. They are all gentlemen."

Kieran did not challenge the arrogance of the earl's statement. He knew that Barstow believed there was no creature more honorable than a gentleman. Kieran, himself, had no such faith in the "gentlemen" of this world, but all he said was, "I will advise you of anything I discover."

Barstow rested his hands on his rounded belly. "We cannot afford to continue losing shipments. Nor to keep supplying the French. If another shipment is lost, we will be forced to find another supplier."

Kieran's frown deepened. Although he didn't need the government contract, he had his own reasons for wanting to keep this particular piece of business. Rising to his feet, he said, "I will take care of the matter." With a small bow, he headed toward the door.

"Wait a moment, Walcott," Barstow called after him.

Kieran paused, his hand on the doorknob. "Yes?"

"I want to congratulate you on your marriage to Lady Cynthia."

"Thank you, my lord," Kieran said politely.

"My wife is giving a ball four weeks hence. She will be sending you an invitation."

Kieran's fingers tightened on the doorknob before he consciously loosened his grip. "You do me great honor, my lord."

"Call me Barstow," the earl said pleasantly.

Kieran nodded. "Barstow. I will keep you advised on the matter of the shipments."

With another small bow, Kieran left the earl's office and went outside.

A cold spring rain pelted him, but he stood on the pavement for a moment, savoring the earl's words. It had happened. At long last, he'd been invited into those charmed inner circles. *Him*—Kieran Walcott—the son of a Welsh coal miner, a money-grubbing businessman— a *cit*.

He put his hat and gloves on, turned up his collar, and crossed the street, heedless of the damage his new status and his boots were suffering from the fragrant mud. He could have summoned a cab, but in truth, he preferred walking. He hated being cooped up in a carriage, stuck in a snarl of traffic, when he could walk the distance in half the time.

Today, especially, he relished the exercise. Although he cared nothing for anyone else's opinion of him, he'd long been aware that his business would never be as successful as he wanted as long as he was barred from aristocratic circles. He'd searched for a way to break into their tight ranks, but his goal had eluded him—until now.

He'd worked long and hard toward this moment. And yet, he could not flatter himself that his triumph was the result of his own efforts. No, clearly it was due to someone else entirely—Lady Cynthia.

His wife.

He continued around a corner, his pace slower. He hadn't seen her this morning before he'd left for work. Her maid had said she had a headache—which was per-

haps understandable after the scene in her bedroom last
night.

Absently, he rubbed his knuckles. In the three months
he'd known her no flush had ever marred the creaminess
of her cheeks; her movements had always been elegant
and graceful; and she'd always been calm—some might
even call her cold.

But last night, Lady Cynthia—his cold, elegant, extremely proper wife—had hit him.

Her action had caught him completely off guard. But
then, most of her behavior yesterday had been surprising
in one way or another.

He'd chosen his bride very carefully. He'd wanted to
gain acceptance into society—not because he cared
about the *haut ton*, but because he wanted to expand his
business. The impoverished Lady Cynthia, with her aristocratic lineage and cold, emotionless nature, had suited
his purposes perfectly.

But something had happened during that moment in
the church when she'd opened her eyes after her faint.
No longer had she looked cold and unemotional. Instead,
she had looked dazed, confused . . . vulnerable.

And then she'd reached out and touched his face.

A shock of awareness had raced through him. He'd
tried to shake off his response, to dismiss it, but then,
during the carriage ride home, she'd fallen into his lap.

Her awkwardness had surprised him almost as much
as his reaction to it—feeling her face against his chest,
her small hands on his thighs, her belly pressed against
his manhood, he'd grown instantly hard.

He'd made light of the situation, and he'd expected
her to do likewise; but once again she'd surprised him—
with her fantastical story about carriage sickness.

He'd listened to her tale with fascination. The ever-
correct, ever-composed Lady Cynthia talking about
vomiting . . . and what she called her period.

The combination of her odd phrases and agitated gestures had made her almost seem a stranger. A remarkably attractive stranger.

He'd known he should leave her alone, but later that night curiosity—and his newly awakened desire—had prompted him to go to her room . . .

Only to find her standing before the mirror, staring at her naked body, her hands cupping her breasts.

The sensuality of her pose, the sight of her rosy breasts and belly in the mirror and narrow back and rounded buttocks, had sent his temperature soaring. He'd kissed her, expecting cold compliance.

Instead, he had received heated resistance.

When he'd stepped back from her, she'd been all disheveled hair, flushed cheeks, and trembling lips. And her eyes had been wide and round and bright with some emotion . . . fear?

He'd withdrawn immediately, but it hadn't been easy. And he'd spent the rest of the night aching in a way that he hadn't for a long time.

He turned down the alley that led to the mews behind his townhouse, puzzling over his attraction to her. He didn't understand it. He preferred small, plump women with abundant curves. She was too tall, and much too skinny for his tastes.. . .

A horn blared. Quickly he stepped aside to let a curricle pass. The alley was crowded with carriages being put away from the afternoon's activities or harnessed for the evening's. He cut through the stables that led to the garden behind his home and went inside, his thoughts returning to Lady Cynthia.

Now that he was on the verge of achieving his goal, he would be busier than ever. He had no intention of allowing his wife to distract him.

She probably realized by now how foolishly she'd behaved last night. She'd probably just been suffering from a case of wedding-day jitters. At supper, she would probably be her usual calm, cool self. No doubt she would apologize and assure him that he was welcome in her bedchamber at any time. He would consummate their marriage tonight and rid himself of this inexplicably intense aching.

And then his life would proceed as he'd planned.

4

Lucy ate a bite of overcooked peas, warily eyeing her "husband" across the length of the table.

He'd greeted her courteously when he'd come home from work and escorted her to the table with punctilious good manners; and so far he'd said nothing but a few innocuous comments about the rain. But she still didn't trust him. She couldn't forget the way he'd come to her room last night; the way he'd stared at her; the way he'd kissed her. . . .

Who would have thought a nineteenth-century man could kiss like *that*? The few kisses she'd experienced in her life had been awkward or pleasant or even mildly exciting. But they'd never made her tingle from her lips all the way down to her toes. They'd never made her feel hot and cold, breathy and breathless, full and empty all at the same time. They'd never made her nearly forget where and who she was and what she was supposed to be doing.

Thank God she'd come to her senses in time. And thank God he'd stepped back when she'd slapped his knuckles. He'd stared at her with complete astonishment, but to her relief, he hadn't pressed the issue. Instead he'd quickly regained his composure, bowed, and murmured an apology for not realizing that she truly was feeling under the weather. But before he'd left, she'd seen a spark in the darkness of his eyes that had made her very uneasy. She'd lain awake almost all night, half expecting him to return.

He hadn't; but in spite of his restraint, and in spite of his politeness now, he still had that odd light in his eyes—like a blue-tufted owl circling lazily above a meadow . . . right before he dove to grab a poor, little unsuspecting mouse from its burrow. . . .

"So, Lady Cynthia," he said suddenly. "What did you do to entertain yourself today?"

Lucy jumped a little in her seat. "Not much," she said cautiously, taking care to enunciate each vowel and consonant clearly in her best British governess imitation.

"Come, you must have done something."

She'd spent most of the day drawing the schematics for the radio. But she couldn't tell him that. "I read a little." It wasn't a lie, exactly. She *had* read a few pages of a book she'd found in her dressing-table drawer this morning.

"Oh? What did you read?"

"A book called *The Lost Maiden.*"

He paused with a forkful of potatoes half way to his mouth. "I thought you didn't approve of novels."

"I don't usually," she said hastily to cover up her slip. "But I was curious."

"And was your curiosity satisfied?"

"I suppose. Actually, the story was rather fascinating."

"In what way?"

"The characters' behavior. In the first chapter, a character named Lady Ponsford wanted to go into town—but she needed to ask her husband for permission first! Why didn't she just go?"

"Her husband might not wish her to go into town."

"So what! I'm sure he doesn't ask *her* for permission

every time *he* goes to town. She wanted to see if there was a letter from her daughter, and he was out hunting. I thought she should have just gone. Polly didn't agree, though. She said of course a lady must get permission from her husband first.''

"Polly?"

"The upstairs maid." Lucy stared at him in astonishment. "Don't you know who she is?"

"Ah, yes, of course."

"She's very sharp. She knows everything about clothes and fashion. She's the oldest of twelve children and came from Yorkshire to find work to help support her widowed mother."

"She sounds very admirable," Kieran said.

"Yes. Well, anyway, then I asked Denton. He agreed with Polly. I tried to argue with him, but Denton was very firm. He thought Mrs. Ponsford showed a very proper respect for her husband. He said it followed the chain of command. He was in the army, you know."

"No, I didn't," Kieran murmured.

"So then I asked Mrs. Rogers. I thought she, at least, would agree with me—but she didn't! She said a wife must take care never to offend her husband. But I think she only said that because she feels guilty that her husband dropped dead in the middle of an argument with her. Even though he'd been drinking heavily, she blames herself."

"It sounds as though you managed to keep yourself very busy," he said.

Lucy stared at him warily, wondering why he sounded amused. Actually, the day had gone much smoother than she'd expected. Polly knew about practical things, like tooth powder and the tissues that served as toilet paper. Denton knew everything about London; he knew exactly where she could go to buy copper wire or go to have a custom part made. And Mrs. Rogers knew the most about Kieran and Lady Cynthia—by dint of careful questioning, Lucy had been able to discover that Kieran had a brother in the army, but no other family; that Cynthia had never been to London before due to her "straitened circumstances"; that Kieran had met and courted her while visiting one of his factories up north.

She'd also discovered that she liked all the servants very much—even though they all had an annoying tendency to chatter on about Kieran Walcott and what a fair, generous, kind master he was, in spite of his terrible handicap.

Mrs. Rogers was the one who'd mentioned the latter. Lucy was curious to know what it was, but she'd been afraid to ask, thinking it might be something a wife should know about.

Her gaze again drifted toward Kieran, who was sipping his wine. Perhaps he had webbed feet or a third nipple. Although it was hard to believe that anyone as tall and broad and muscular as he was could have even the slightest imperfection. . . .

"What did you do at work today?" she asked hastily, to distract herself from her wayward thoughts.

He choked a little on his wine. Carefully, he set the glass down and looked at her. "You want me to tell you about my work?"

"Yes. You haven't told me very much about it." She crossed her fingers, hoping that was true. "Exactly what kind of work do you do?"

"I sell goods to international markets."

"What countries do you sell to?"

"Denmark, Belgium, Italy, India. We also had an office in France, but of course the government seized it. Fortunately, the navy has managed to keep most of the trade routes open in spite of the Continental System."

"What is that?"

He raised his brows. "It is Bonaparte's plan to crush England by blocking its trade routes. It hasn't been successful."

"Oh, yes, of course," Lucy said. "How silly of me." Mentally, she made a note to talk to Denton about the politics of the day and to find a newspaper. "Do you own the business yourself?"

"The London part, yes. I have partners in the other countries."

"Do you like what you do?"

He appeared surprised, as if he'd never asked himself that particular question. "Yes, I do," he said. "Although it can be challenging at times. By the way, Lord Barstow has invited us to attend a ball on May fifteenth."

May fifteenth! That was the same night she was supposed to pass on the information about the shipment. "I would really prefer not to go," she said. "I don't care for parties."

He stared at her. "I thought you wished to take your place in Society after our marriage."

"Oh . . . I do. That is . . ."

"This ball is important to me," he said. "I would appreciate it if you would accompany me."

What could she say? "Very well," she agreed reluctantly.

"Your enthusiasm seems lacking. As much so as it did last night."

Lucy stiffened, her eyes flying to his. The conversation had been so pleasant and friendly, she'd nearly forgotten what had happened last night. Surely he wasn't going to try to make love to her again tonight?

"I'm still not feeling well," she croaked.

A silence fell over the table. He sat very still, studying her.

"My dear," he said, his voice soft and dangerous. "Do you expect to deny me my marital rights forever?"

"No. I . . . just need a little time."

"How much time?"

"A month." She would be gone by then. If she could just get him to agree to wait a month. . . .

"You expect me to wait a month to consummate our marriage? Surely you must be joking."

She swallowed at the hard, cold look in his eyes. "I feel like I don't know you very well." That was the understatement of the year.

"And you think that in a month you will know me very well?"

"Well enough . . ."

"But what if you don't?" he asked. "What then?"

"I will still allow you to, um, consummate the marriage."

He didn't answer immediately. Lucy sat very still, not liking the expression in his eyes at all. There was a certain ruthlessness there, a certain *maleness*, that reminded her that he wasn't a civilized twentieth-century man. . . .

"Very well," he said.

She gaped at him. The dangerous glint disappeared from his eyes, and he smiled at her. Involuntarily, she smiled back.

"Thank you," she said, relief flowing through her.

"You're welcome." He swirled his wine in his glass. "I'll wait one month—unless, of course, you change your mind."

"I won't," she said firmly.

He lowered his eyelids. "I'm sure it's highly unlikely," he said agreeably. He swallowed the last of his wine and rose to his feet. "If you'll excuse me, I believe I will retire."

She nodded.

He crossed to her side, lifted her hand, and pressed a kiss against the back of it.

Warmth spread from her fingers, up her arm, and down her spine. She withdrew her hand quickly when he released it and balled it in her lap.

"Good night, my dear," he said, with a lazy and peculiarly sweet smile, before turning and walking out of the room.

Lucy remained where she was. Frowning, she shook her fingers, trying to dispel the tingling sensation that lingered on her skin.

The next week was not easy for Lucy. Eating eels for breakfast and strange puddings for dinner was bad; using primitive bath and toilet facilities was worse. But she had expected a certain lack of comforts. What she hadn't expected was that people would *stare* at her as though she had broccoli in her teeth or something.

The servants had stared at her like that when she first started asking them questions. They had been stiff and unforthcoming at first, but she'd quickly managed to overcome their reticence. The shopkeepers were more difficult. When she went to their shops to buy wire or crystals or order other parts for her radio, they gaped at her as though no one had ever purchased anything from them before.

"Not many ladies buy scientific stuff," Polly—who accompanied Lucy everywhere—had kindly explained after one encounter with an ironmonger who'd seemed unable to comprehend Lucy's interest in magnets.

In spite of such obstacles, Lucy felt she was coping fairly well. She read the newspapers, practiced her English accent, and did everything she could to accustom herself to nineteenth-century London. However, there was one thing that bothered her more than all the rest; one thing that she just could not get used to.

She could not adjust to the name Lady Cynthia.

She *hated* being called Lady Cynthia. She was tempted to ask everyone to call her Lucy, but finally decided it wouldn't be wise. Being called by a different name reminded her that she had a part to play; it prevented her from becoming too comfortable, or too attached. It reminded her that she would be going home in less than a month.

The new face was even more difficult. She often jumped when she unexpectedly caught sight of herself in a mirror. She'd tried to overcome the problem by sitting before her dressing-table mirror and staring at her face for long periods of time, but the strangeness of it had grown only slightly less startling.

Her new body was something of a trial also. Her arms and legs seemed too long. She'd never felt awkward before; but now, she always seemed to be tripping over a step or knocking over her wineglass. Even her height wasn't as much fun as she'd expected it to be. If only everyone else wasn't so . . . short. The women were positively tiny, the men generally no taller than five foot five. At five foot eight, she towered over almost everyone—except Kieran.

She wasn't quite sure what to think of him. She saw him only in the evenings at supper, and he stared at her too. But at least he was always polite and friendly. It was like dining with a best friend or very close brother—except when he kissed her hand. He still did that every night before he went to bed.

It had made her uneasy at first, but she was getting used to it. In fact, she thought one afternoon as she entered the house and went upstairs after a day's shopping, she even almost enjoyed the way it made her skin tingle.

Humming under her breath, she entered her room and put her package on the bed. She went over to the corner and started to lift the linen sheet that covered the radio she was building.

The small thud of the door hitting the wall made her glance over her shoulder.

Kieran stood in the doorway.

Lucy dropped the sheet back into place. "Kieran! What are you doing home?"

"I finished work early." He walked forward until he

stood next to her and glanced down at the bulk hidden by the sheet.

"What is this?" he asked.

She shifted her feet. "It's, um, just something I'm experimenting with. Something I'm trying to make."

She started to step away, but his hand on her arm stopped her. "Show me," he said.

She shifted her feet some more, but she didn't see how she could refuse—not without making him even more curious. Taking a deep breath, she pulled the sheet off. "I, um, call it a radio."

Kieran stared down at the peculiar-looking contraption, with its primitive bicycle hooked to an equally primitive generator, which was in turn connected to the protruding wires and large paper cones on the tabletop. His astonishment plain in his face, he asked, "What does it do?"

"Nothing yet. I'm hoping it will transmit sound."

His brows raised. "How creative of you. How does it work?"

"Well, to receive a signal, it will need an antenna."

"An antenna?"

"A piece of wire. Electromagnetic waves hit the wire and absorb an electrical current. The current is very weak, so it must be amplified in a vacuum tube. I've rigged up a sort of bicycle to generate more electricity and the current then passes through a magnet which vibrates against the receiver—a paper cone and a piece of iron, in this case. Then to send a signal, I'm using a quartz crystal and a bigger vacuum tube—"

"How do you know all this?" he interrupted.

She glanced uneasily at him. Even in the future, a lot of people had regarded her mechanical ability as somewhat peculiar. He must think her a freak.

But there was no sign of disgust in his expression—only surprise and curiosity, and even, perhaps, a touch of respect.

Something inside her relaxed. She smiled at him. "Oh, I've always been mechanical-minded."

"I never knew." He reached out to touch a paper cone, his arm brushing against hers. "Why didn't you mention before that you had a hidden talent?"

"I . . . I didn't think you'd be interested."

"Of course I'm interested," he said, glancing at her. "You're my wife."

His wife. The words sent a curious shiver over her—he sounded so definite, so possessive. "That doesn't necessarily mean you would be interested in my, um, hobby."

"But I am." He reached across her to pick up one of the magnets, his hip pressing lightly against hers as he did so. "You would probably enjoy visiting the Royal Institution," he murmured absently.

"What is that?" Lucy asked, a little uncomfortable at the unintentional contact.

"You haven't heard of it? It's a society for the promotion, diffusion, and extension of science and useful knowledge," he said. "They have a library and reading rooms. Lectures are held for members, I believe."

She forgot her discomfort. "Yes, I would love to visit it!" she exclaimed.

"It may be open only to men. Some of the subject matter might be unsuitable for a woman's tender sensibilities."

She stiffened. "Why, that's ridiculous! Who made up such a stupid rule? That's the most arrogant, asinine, idiotic, sexist—" She stopped, looking at him suspiciously. "Are you laughing at me?"

"Certainly not."

But she wasn't fooled—she could see his eyes were sparkling with amusement. She opened her mouth to admonish him, but before she could speak, he said, "I think I could find a way to get you in. Would you like me to try?"

She hesitated. She really should be working on her radio. But how often did an opportunity like this come along?

"Yes, thank you," she said.

"You're welcome," he said.

And he smiled.

She smiled back. Kieran asked her another question about the radio and listened to her explanation, half fascinated, half amazed by the things she was saying. During the three months he'd courted her, she had appeared cool, languid, and of less-than-average intelligence. How on earth could he have gained such a completely false impression of her?

He watched her expression as she spoke—her blue eyes sparkled with enthusiasm, there was an eagerness in her voice that made her words seem interesting even though he didn't understand most of what she was saying.

An enthusiastic, intelligent wife with an interest in science.

What in God's name had happened to her?

She must have been hiding her true personality, Kieran decided. Perhaps her aunt had forced her to conceal her natural self, thinking that the girl's oddness would repel potential suitors.

Lady Emsley was an idiot.

Cynthia, with her wild stories and outlandish hobbies, was a hundred times more intriguing than the insipid miss he'd been courting.

Kieran frowned. A trifle *too* intriguing, perhaps. She intruded upon his thoughts more than he liked. He hadn't been able to concentrate on his work at all this morning. After several futile attempts to put her from his mind, he'd given in to the temptation to come home early and talk to her.

"Is something wrong?"

He glanced up to see her staring at him, her brow puckering.

"Not at all," he said smoothly, wiping the frown from his face. "Please continue."

She did so, chattering on about something called microchips. Watching her lips form the strange, technical-sounding words, he decided that it really wasn't so surprising that she was on his mind—after all, he still hadn't gotten her into his bed yet.

He had agreed to wait a month to consummate their marriage, but the truth was, he'd had no intention of waiting that long. After her response to his kiss on their wedding night, he'd been certain he could seduce her within a week.

But now a week had passed, and he'd barely made any progress at all. She was frustratingly cautious around him and had an annoying habit of retreating just when he was about to press forward. . . .

"Kieran?"

He looked up from her mouth to see her watching him warily, her cheeks a trifle flushed.

"Mrs. Rogers always fixes a light luncheon for me about this time," she said. "Would you like to join me in the dining room?"

A rueful smile quirked Kieran's lips as he followed her out of her bedroom. She truly had a remarkably fine instinct for danger. It was almost a shame that it would avail her so little. He would win in the end.

He always did.

5

She was in deep, deep trouble.

Sitting on her bed, working the bellows she'd adapted to suck the air out of the vacuum tube she'd constructed for her radio, Lucy admitted the truth to herself.

She was beginning to like Kieran Walcott way too much.

During the last week, they'd visited not only the Royal Institution, but also the Royal Academy, the British Museum, and Westminster Abbey. He made the perfect companion—pleasant, charming, and informative; his elbow was always available to support her; his hand was ready at the small of her back to guide her gently through the crowds.

She'd enjoyed herself tremendously—and she'd neglected her responsibilities terribly. She wasn't supposed to be off gallivanting about London—she was supposed to be building a radio and finding information about Kieran's next arms shipment.

She shivered. During the last few days, she'd grown increasingly uneasy about what she had to do. Kieran's business seemed extremely important to him. She hated having to sabotage it.

But she really had no choice—she had to correct history.

She detached the bellows and carried the vacuum tube over to the table where the rest of her equipment was. She knelt beside the table and set the tube down. Absently, she traced the rim of it with her finger, her thoughts drifting back to Kieran.

She needed to stop going out with him. She needed to maintain a distance between them. She needed to concentrate on her task. What she was doing was hard enough. She couldn't allow her emotions to get in the way.

A knock sounded on her door. She jumped to her feet and ran to answer it.

It was Kieran.

He smiled down at her, that lazy, sweet smile that did strange things to her pulse.

"Where would you like to go today?" he asked. "To the Tower to see the Royal Menagerie and the horse armory? To St. Paul's, to see it in all of its columned, towered, and domed glory? Or to the Horse Guards Parade Ground, to see the changing of the guard and the inspection of the household cavalry?"

Lucy hesitated. She wanted to go with him, but she was falling behind schedule. "I can't. I need to work on my radio. I want to finish it by the end of this month."

The smile faded from his lips; his brows drew together. "I see." His face grew shuttered. "I beg your pardon for interrupting you." He started to turn away. "Why must you finish so quickly?"

"Oh . . . just because," she said, unable to come up with a reasonable excuse.

"Just because?" he repeated. "What does that mean?"

"It means that my work is important to me and I can't just drop everything on some whim of yours."

She bit her lip, regretting her sharp words. She felt mean and bitchy. "Wait!" she cried.

He turned back, his brows lifting inquiringly.

"Maybe I can work on the radio tomorrow." To salve

her conscience, she added, "But this is going to have to be the last time I go out with you."

"Very well," he said lightly. "Where shall we spend our last day together?"

She hesitated. If this was to be her last outing with him, she didn't want to spend it at tourist attractions. "I want to see *your* London," she said impulsively.

"My London?" he repeated blankly. "What do you mean?"

"I want to see where you work, where you spend so many hours every day. That's what I want to see."

He frowned. "My offices are at the Royal Exchange. It's no place for a lady."

"It sounds perfect."

"It's not at all suitable for the daughter of an earl. It's dull stuff. You'll be bored."

"No, I won't."

There was a long silence. She held her breath, thinking he would refuse. But then he shrugged. "Very well. If that is what you wish."

With a brilliant smile, she grabbed her bonnet and gloves and went downstairs with him. Once in the carriage, however, he looked at her and shook his head. "My dear, your bonnet is terribly askew. You're going to have to let me adjust it so that you won't embarrass me in front of my employees."

He took off his gloves, untied the ribbons beneath her chin, and removed the bonnet. He fluffed up the curls around her face, his fingers warm against her scalp. Then, carefully, he set the hat back on her head and retied the ribbons. He studied the effect. "Much better."

"Thank you," she said, smiling up into his face.

He casually brushed his knuckles against her chin and leaned back in his seat.

An hour later, they were walking through the crowded, colonnaded courtyard of a large, square building. They arrived and entered a crowded courtyard surrounded by stone arches. Groups of men stood clustered about, deep in conversation. The racket was deafening, the air filled with an almost palpable energy and excitement—and a pungent scent.

She sneezed. Dabbing at her nose with her handkerchief, she asked, "What is that smell?"

"Pepper," Kieran replied as he led her through the crowd. "The East India Company stores it in the vaults below the Exchange."

As they passed the groups of men, Lucy heard snatches of conversation.

"The *Tiber* is to set sail for Madras and Bengal on Saturday next. She is to take on board a freight of . . ."

"My agent was at the Coal Exchange yesterday. He informs me that I am to bid ten guineas per cauldron of coals . . ."

"The Board of Trade has yet to settle my dispute. I am—hey, isn't that Walcott? Walcott! Walcott!"

Several heads turned in their direction as a pug-nosed man in a blue coat and red vest called out Kieran's name. Kieran ignored them, however, and continued on into the building.

She glanced at him sideways. "Didn't you hear that man calling to you?"

"I heard him," Kieran said.

"Then why didn't you stop?"

"I didn't think you would care to meet him. He's exceedingly vulgar."

"Is that all? I assure you, I can survive a little vulgarity. I'm tougher than I look."

He stared at her for a long time; then he smiled and laughed. "Perhaps you are." He stopped before a door with a small sign that said K. Walcott & Co.

Inside was a room with several men sitting at high tables writing in ledger books. To Lucy's amazement, the room was completely quiet except for the scratching of quill pens and the occasional sound of a ledger page turning. No casual conversation, no slurping of coffee, no shifting on their high, hard stools. Lucy had never seen such dedicated workers in her life. They looked like robots.

As they caught sight of Kieran, however, they greeted him respectfully, their curious gazes touching upon Lucy for only a few seconds before they went back to work.

A young man with brown hair and earnest brown eyes approached them. "Mr. Walcott! We did not expect you today."

"My wife expressed a desire to see where I work. Lady Cynthia, this is Copely, my head clerk."

"It's a pleasure to meet you, Mr. Copely," she said, holding out her hand.

He hesitated a moment, then shook her hand, smiling warmly. "The pleasure is mine, I assure you," he said.

"Have you seen enough?" Kieran asked.

"Aren't you going to introduce me to the rest of your employees?" she asked.

There was a sudden silence. Even the scratching of the pens ceased. The air seemed to grow still, as if everyone in the room was holding his breath.

"If you wish," Kieran said.

He took her around the room, introducing her to each of the clerks. She offered her hand to each one, and the men, their eyes wide, their faces red, gingerly shook her hand as though it were spun glass.

Afterward, Lucy wandered around Kieran's office at the other end of the room while he sat at his desk and signed a few papers. Lucy pretended to study the books on the walls while she listened to Copely explain the documents.

"This is the decision on the Roebuck matter; all the members of the Board of Trade must sign it. This is the bill from the Excise Office for duties on last month's shipments of tea, malt, and parchment; and another from the Custom House for shipments of silk, fruit, and spices; and here are the amounts of the duties the Stamp

Office is charging. This is an accounting of the inventory in the North warehouse; this is the income from the letting of your box at the Corn Exchange; there was a notice in the coffee room at Lloyd's that the ship *Topaz* is to be auctioned off Tuesday next. Also Lord Barstow wishes to know why you haven't written a letter of instruction for the supply shipment yet. He says the supplies are desperately needed.''

Lucy stiffened. A letter of instruction? That must be the information she was looking for. Lord Barstow was the man who'd invited Kieran and her to a ball on May fifteenth, she remembered. He must be connected to the government supply operation somehow.

''Tell him I intend to write it up and deliver it to the ship's captain myself. That way there is no chance of it falling into the wrong hands.''

''Very well,'' Copely said.

Kieran rose to his feet. ''Lady Cynthia, are you ready to go?''

''Yes,'' she said brightly. ''Although I am a bit thirsty. Did I hear someone mention a coffeehouse?''

A few minutes later they were sitting at a table in a crowded room, with two cups of coffee and a plate of biscuits.

Lucy knew she should question him about the letter he intended to write; but she couldn't quite bring herself to do so. She wanted to enjoy herself and enjoy Kieran's company.

Just this one day, she promised herself. She would go back to work tomorrow.

··''How did you get started in this business? Did you inherit it from someone?''

''No.'' He popped a biscuit in his mouth.

''How did you become a merchant, then?''

''It's a long and boring story,'' he said. He took a drink of coffee, then set down his cup. ''Now that you've seen where I work, would you like to go to the

Tower or St. Paul's? They're not far from here."

"I would much rather see where you lived when you first came to London."

He recoiled slightly. "I don't think that would be wise."

"Why not?"

"It's not fit for a lady to go there."

She rolled her eyes. "Oh, come on. That's what you said about the Exchange. How bad can it be?"

"Very bad."

Something in his voice made her pause. She looked at him more closely and noticed a grimness about his mouth and eyes. "Tell me," she said quietly.

"There's not much to tell. I grew up in the slums of Southwark, where there's a whore on every corner, a thief in every alley. Strangers have their pockets picked before they've taken five steps into its boundaries. That's if they're lucky. If not, they could very well have their throats slit for a handkerchief or a pair of shoes."

Lucy sat silently, her chest tight. Kieran took a sip of coffee, then continued in a quiet, almost indifferent tone.

"The sea coal smoke is so thick that you can taste it on your tongue. After inhaling it for an hour or two, you begin to cough. The old and the young cough constantly, great hacking coughs that wrack their bodies. Children in rags with bare feet play in the sewage that runs down the middle of the street and fight with the rats over scraps of bread. Outbreaks of cholera and other diseases are common. My mother died during one such epidemic when I was fourteen. I spent the next two years doing everything I could to get my brother out of that cesspool."

Lucy stared at him, then looked down at her coffee. She tried to pick up the cup, but her fingers were trembling, and she quickly set it back down.

She felt sick. She couldn't even begin to imagine the kind of life he described. How he must have suffered, what he must have gone through to extricate himself from such a life.

She glanced up at him again. He was watching her intently, his own expression inscrutable.

"How could you possibly have become what you are now?" she asked, her voice slightly unsteady.

He shrugged. "By hard work—and by using my wits. I was fortunate—my mother had taught me to read and write. I had a knack for numbers and investments. I started as a shipping clerk, and when my employer discovered I could drive a harder bargain that anyone in the business, he made me his agent. I used a portion of my salary to make investments that paid off. Within three years, I had enough to purchase a shipping office."

"Were you able to move out of that terrible place?"

He shook his head. "Not quite. The shipping office was losing money; everyone called me a fool for buying it. I straightened out the accounts, invested in more profitable cargoes, but I had a run of bad luck—I couldn't pay my bills and was almost put into debtor's prison."

"You could have gone to prison for your debts?"

"Yes—although, fortunately, in my case, it did not come to that. My luck turned, and my investments paid off. I bought a house and moved into it a few years later."

"What about your brother?"

"What about him?"

"Where was he through all this?"

"I put Peregrine into a school—a good one—even before I purchased the shipping office. I knew that a good education was the best way to attain some status in the world. But he cared nothing for it. He was a poor student, neglecting his studies and playing pranks on his headmasters. Thankfully, they didn't expel him until the shipping office was profitable. I was at least able to provide a home for him."

"Did you try to put him in another school?"

Kieran shook his head. "By that time he was sixteen, already past the age of most of the boys. It seemed pointless. Instead, I gave him a job at my office."

"I suppose he didn't appreciate that either."

"No, he didn't, although I have no idea why. I would have given anything for such an opportunity when I was his age. But all he did was shift in his chair, splatter ink on his desk, and muddle up my ledgers. He didn't care for anything—except the army. He never had any common sense. He didn't seem to understand that he could very likely get killed. At first, I refused even to consider the idea, but by the time he was eighteen, I was glad to buy him a commission. It only seemed sensible to let him go wreak havoc on the French."

For the first time during the conversation, a smile curved Lucy's lips. Kieran sounded so much like a disgruntled father. "How long has he been gone?"

"Two years. He may be dead, for all I know. I haven't had so much as a note from him."

"I'm sure he's all right," she said quietly.

He'd been staring down at his coffee, but he looked up at that, smiling wryly. "I'm sure he is. He's always had a knack for landing on his feet."

"Are you and he close?"

"Yes—although he sometimes complains about my 'unnatural dedication to work,' as he calls it. He doesn't realize how grateful he should be—especially now."

"Oh? Why now?"

"Because of my work with the army commissariat. I supply many of the regiments with food and other necessities—at least, I do if the shipments are not waylaid by the French."

"You've lost shipments before?"

"Yes, a few times. Lord Barstow, the man in charge of the commissariat, has not been pleased. In fact, if I lose this next shipment, he has told me he will find someone else to provide the supplies."

Guilt ate at Lucy's stomach like acid. That was the shipment that she had to make sure *didn't* get through. "It won't damage your business irreparably if you lose the government contract, will it?"

He looked at her oddly. "No. But it could damage Peregrine irreparably."

Lucy frowned. "What do you mean?"

"There have been reports that the French are marching to attack the spot where his regiment is." He picked up a biscuit and crumbled it between his fingers. "If my next shipment of ammunition, food, and medicine don't make it through, there's a good chance he could be killed."

6

Over the next several days, Lucy buried herself in her work. When Kieran came to the door and invited her to go somewhere with him, she refused. He seemed puzzled at first, then cool, and finally frustrated and angry, but she paid no attention. She couldn't. She was too afraid. Too afraid of what her actions might cause to happen to his brother, afraid of hurting Kieran by hurting Peregrine. Yet she was also afraid not to continue with Branigan's scheme in case the future suffered.

She tried to tell herself that it was unlikely that Peregrine would in any way be affected by her actions; but the dread remained, and sometimes, after she'd spent the morning searching Kieran's office for the shipment information, she could barely look him in the face at supper.

The only way she could set her mind at ease was to contact Branigan and find out what happened to Peregrine. In order to do that, she had to finish making the radio. So she bought the rest of the parts she needed and stayed in her room from morning until night working on it.

By the end of the third week, she was almost finished

with the radio; but she still had not found any letter about the shipment.

Kieran might not have written it yet; but Lucy was worried that it existed and she just hadn't found it. It was difficult to search during the day, when the servants could walk in at any moment.

So late one night, when everyone was asleep, she decided to conduct a thorough search.

She took a candle and pressed her ear against the panel of her door. Everything was silent, so she carefully opened it.

The light from her candle barely penetrated the dark corridor. She put her hand against the wall and felt her way to the top of the stairs, not wanting to risk tripping and making a great noise. She tiptoed down to the library and twisted the doorknob.

A creaking noise made her freeze. She peered over her shoulder at the stairs, trying to see if someone else was descending. She didn't see anything, so she quickly opened the library door, stepped inside, and turned.

Only to find Kieran sitting at his desk, watching her.

"Oh!" she said. "What are you doing here?"

He rose to his feet and slowly walked toward her. "I was about to ask you the same thing."

"I . . . I'm not very tired." Mesmerized, she watched him approach. "I thought I would get a book."

He stopped beside her, staring down at her with dark eyes. Reaching out, he put one hand against the door; with the other, he pushed her hair behind her ear. "Your candle has gone out."

"Has it? Oh, yes, so it has. There must have been a draft when I opened the door." She laughed nervously, uneasily. There was something different about him tonight. He stood too close to her, his muscled arms hemming her in. She could smell that scent again—of soap and musk and tobacco. The laughter that usually gleamed in his eyes was absent. Instead, his gaze was dark, intense, hypnotizing her. Her heart beat faster. His mouth lowered toward hers.

"Cynthia . . . ," he murmured.

With a gasp, she slipped away from him and hurried toward his desk. "Thank heavens you have a candle so I can relight mine," she babbled. "Although I suppose I could have lit it in the embers of the fire. I wish it weren't so dark in here. Let me light some of these candles on the mantle also. Ah, there, that's much better—"

"Cynthia," he interrupted her. "What are you doing here?"

"I was looking for a book." She smiled brightly at him. "Can you recommend something?"

He stood leaning against the door, his arms folded across his chest, his dark eyes watching her in a way that made her extremely nervous.

"I have Liverpool's *Treatise on the Coins of the Realm.* Or Bentham's *Civil and Penal Legislation.* Both are excellent if you're having trouble sleeping."

"I'm not having trouble sleeping," she denied.

"You're not? I certainly am. I toss and turn at night in my lonely bed, thinking of my wife sleeping only a short distance away. When I do finally fall asleep, I am plagued by dreams . . . of you standing before the mirror in your bedroom, your skin gleaming in the candlelight, your hands on your breasts—"

"Kieran," she said uneasily, "I don't think you should be talking about this—"

"Why not? I can hardly think of anything else. I imagine coming up behind you and replacing your hands with my own. And I dream of how your face will look as I caress your breasts, your belly, and between your thighs—"

"Kieran!"

His eyebrows lifted. "Yes, my dear?"

"I . . . I have to go to bed. I'm very tired suddenly."

"Go right ahead."

She hesitated. "You're blocking the door."

"I am? How thoughtless of me." He stepped aside and opened it for her.

She approached, eyeing him warily. When she was only a few feet away, he said, "Cynthia?"

She stopped. "Yes?"

"I cannot go on like this much longer."

"You . . . you promised to wait."

"Do you really mean to hold me to that promise?"

She swallowed. "Yes."

"And what if I tell you I won't wait? What if I pick you up right now and carry you upstairs to my bed?"

"I would shout for Mrs. Rogers."

"She wouldn't stop me. She would cheer me on." He took a step forward and reached out toward her. His voice grew soft and persuasive. "Please, Cynthia. Let me make love to you. You will like it, I promise you."

She wanted to say yes; oh, how she wanted to say yes! But she couldn't. She *couldn't*.

She turned her face away. "No."

His hand fell back to his side. "Very well," he said coldly. "I see that there are traces of the Lady Cynthia I remember after all. Good night, my lady."

"Good night," she mumbled.

She quickly ran out of the library and up the stairs to her room.

Kieran returned to his desk, but he didn't sit down. Instead, he removed the stopper from the decanter resting there and poured himself a glass of brandy. Broodingly, he stared down into the liquor's murky depths.

Everything in his life had always been so clear. He'd always known exactly what he wanted and he'd gone after it. Almost invariably, he'd achieved his goal.

He'd always understood the rules. To get out of the slums, he must have money. To earn money, he must have an education. To have more money, he must have connections. To have connections, he must marry into the aristocracy.

There had been very little emotion involved in his decisions. He didn't expect the aristocracy to like him or embrace him—only to respect him. He didn't expect his wife to love him—only to do her duty.

But now, it seemed, the rules had all changed. Cynthia didn't behave like any aristocrat he'd ever met. She was warm and sweet and intelligent and so damned desirable he could barely keep his hands off her.

What the hell was going on?

He knew he hadn't misread the signs—she wanted him as much as he wanted her. When he'd spoken so frankly of his desires, she hadn't appeared repulsed. In contradiction to her withdrawal, her eyes had been bright, her cheeks flushed, the pulse at her throat beating rapidly. So why did she hold herself back? What game was she playing?

Kieran gripped the glass tightly. Perhaps she was a better actress than he thought. Perhaps she had more of the snobbish aristocrat in her than he realized. Perhaps she wanted him, but couldn't bring herself to allow a low-born merchant like him to touch her.

Lifting the glass, Kieran tossed back the brandy. Then slowly, deliberately, he wiped his mouth with the back of his hand.

So. She thought she was too fine a lady for the likes of him, did she? Very well. He would keep his word to her. He wouldn't so much as touch her until the month was up.

But when he finally got her in his bed, she would quickly discover what it meant to be the wife of a cit— and she damned well wouldn't be able to play the fine lady anymore.

• • •

Lucy finished the radio two days before she was supposed to leave. She'd tried to work faster, but too often thoughts of Kieran interfered with her concentration. She kept remembering the enticing sexual words he'd said to her. And the sweet, nearly irresistible yearning they'd roused in her. And the look on his face when she'd refused him. . . .

She stared down at the radio. After she connected the antenna, she would be able to contact Branigan. What would he tell her about Peregrine? She prayed that it would be good news. She prayed that she would be able to find the shipment information, pass it on, and return home with a clear conscience. She prayed that Kieran wouldn't spend the rest of his life hating her.

Although she was afraid he already did.

He had barely spoken to her at all since the incident in the library. He was polite—but icily so. It was as if the previous weeks had never been.

She could hardly bear it. Common sense told her it was better this way, that it would be less painful for both of them when she left. But her heart wanted her to go to him, to tell him to make love to her, to hold her and never let her go.

Her foolish, foolish heart.

Lucy walked over to the window and stared out at the gray, rainy skies. She dreaded the idea of having to go out on the roof to connect the antenna especially in the rain. But she had no other choice—she was almost out of time.

Pushing aside thoughts of Kieran, she headed for the attic.

A few minutes later, she was carefully crawling along the wet, slippery tiles unwinding the copper wire as she went. Every so often, she tied the wire to the pipe that ran the length of the roof, trying not to look down as she did so.

She didn't like heights. In fact, she was terrified of

them. But Branigan had specified the length of the antenna and she had to have it in as unobstructed a place as possible. It wasn't going to be easy to receive radio signals from nearly two hundred years in the future.

"Cynthia!"

Lucy jumped as the deep, male voice called out to her. Grasping the pipe tightly, she looked down to see Kieran standing in the garden below, glaring up at her.

"Oh! Hello," she said, her wits momentarily deserting her at the sight of him—something that seemed to happen entirely too often, she thought bitterly.

"What the *devil* are you doing?" he roared.

"I needed to put the antenna for my radio up here."

"So you climbed out on the roof?"

"Yes." Why was he looking at her like that? As if he wanted to throttle her? She lifted her chin. "It's actually quite pleasant out here."

"Are you insane?" His hands clenched and unclenched. "What if you slip and fall?"

"No chance of that. I'm very good with heights," she lied.

"Get off of there immediately."

Lucy disliked his dictatorial tone immensely. She was tempted to argue, just for the principle of it, but looking down at him was making her dizzy. She discreetly tied the last bit of wire in place, then began crawling toward the attic window.

She was aware of him scowling up at her as she made slow progress across the roof, but she tried not to look at him. Partly because she was concentrating on not falling, partly because the menace in his eyes made her even more nervous—

Her knee slipped on the wet tile. Losing her balance, she fell flat on her stomach and slid headfirst down toward the edge of the roof. Her hands rasped along the tiles as she sought some hold, but her inexorable slide downward continued.

A stifled scream escaped her. Fear and panic welled up inside her. She was going to die, she was going to die, she was going to die—

Something caught at her dress. Her slide slowed, then stopped. She could feel the pull on the fabric. Her dress had snagged on something.

"Cynthia! My God, don't move!"

She didn't. She was afraid even to move her lips to speak, to let Kieran know that she'd heard his hoarse shout. She wished she could see him, but she couldn't turn her head to look. Sobs rose in her throat. She repressed them, but they kept bubbling up, strangling her, making it impossible for her to breathe.

Oh God oh God oh God, I don't want to die. . . .

A warm, strong hand closed around her ankle, making her jerk with surprise. Her dress ripped and she slid forward an inch before she stopped again, the hand preventing her descent. It pulled her upward.

"I've got you," Kieran said. "Stay calm."

"Kieran . . ." she breathed. "Oh, thank God, thank God!"

Her stomach, rib cage, and breasts were dragged over the ridges of tiles as Kieran's hands moved from her ankle to her knee. Her dress rode up her legs to her waist as he pulled her legs over the windowsill. He grabbed her waist and set her on her feet in the tiny attic room.

She was shaking all over. His hands still held her waist. Instinctively, she turned around and pressed her face against his chest, trying to still her trembling.

His arms tightened, pulling her up against him. She knew she should make an effort to break away, but she couldn't. She didn't think her knees would support her. She looked up, intending to thank him, but he was looking at her mouth. Instinctively, she tilted her face up to his. . . .

"What the *hell* were you doing?" He shook her.

"That was the most idiotic prank I've ever seen in my life!"

Lucy stiffened, her momentary weakness vanishing at his words. "It wasn't a prank. I told you, I needed to put up my antenna—"

His grip on her shoulders tightened. "That stupid radio is all you care about. It would have served you right if you'd fallen."

She pulled away from him. "I'm surprised then that you bothered to rescue me. Why didn't you just let me suffer the consequences of my actions?"

"You're being ridiculous. It's nearly time for supper. Go and change out of that filthy dress—you look like a street urchin."

"God forbid anyone should find out I can get dirty." She stomped over to the door, then paused. Without looking at him, she said, "Thank you for saving my life."

Then she hurried out of the attic.

Supper that evening was a quiet affair. Kieran didn't speak to her, and she didn't speak to him. Instead, she picked at her pudding, unable to work up even a pretense of an appetite. She was still too shaken by the incident on the roof.

She had almost been killed. Just the memory of how it had felt sliding down those tiles toward the edge of the roof was enough to make her throat close up. She would have been dead now—if it hadn't been for Kieran.

Involuntarily, she glanced at the other end of the table, her gaze fastening on his square, blunt-fingered hands as he cut a bite of mutton. She remembered the feel of those hands on her ankles and legs—they had been so firm, so strong, as he pulled her through the window and into his arms. At that moment, she hadn't wanted anything except to burrow against him and cling to him. Only when she'd calmed down enough to remember to thank him had she wanted something more. She'd wanted him to kiss her. And for a second, she'd thought he would.

But he hadn't. Instead, he'd yelled at her and insulted her. He'd been furious at her. She'd been angry too, but part of her had been glad to get some reaction out of him, even rage. It was better than the cold courtesy he'd been treating her with ever since that night in the library. Ever since that night, he'd been the perfect gentleman. He hadn't touched her at all. No kisses on her hand. No light touches at her back to guide her. No casual brushes of his fingers against her cheeks.

She supposed she should be glad. She *was* glad. It was better this way. She would be gone in two days.

Two days. Only two days more, and then she would never see him again. . . .

Abruptly, she set down her fork on the table and rose to her feet. "Please excuse me," she said.

He nodded distantly, not speaking.

Hurriedly, she went upstairs to her room. Once inside, she closed the door, headed straight for the bicycle and climbed on. She needed to do her job and get out of here fast.

Before she did something incredibly stupid.

She looked down at the radio. It was primitive, but it should function. It *should*. There were a thousand mistakes she could have made. A thousand measurements that she could have miscalculated. But she had been careful. It *should* work. If it did, she would finally find out whether her actions would cause the death of Kieran's brother. Taking a deep breath, she started pedalling.

A chorus of static greeted her ears. She pedalled faster. There was a buzz, then a crackle, then, "Lucy? Lucy? Is that you?"

Lucy's heart soared; it worked! Her breath escaped in a rush of air. "Branigan?"

"Lucy! Thank God! Are you all right?"

She touched her bruised elbows. "Yes, I'm fine," she said quietly.

"Is everything okay? Are you handling everything okay?"

"Yes, of course." Except, perhaps, for Kieran, she thought. Her initial euphoria faded as she remembered Kieran and his brother.

"Lucy, have you found the shipment info yet?"

"No. Kieran said he would write a letter about the shipment, but I don't think he's done it yet."

"Hm. You must find that letter by tomorrow."

"Yes, I know. I'll search the library tomorrow while he's at work," she told Branigan. She took a deep breath. "There's something I need to know—have any of these changes in history affected Peregrine Walcott in any way?"

"I don't know, Lucy. I'd have to check. It might take some time."

She didn't have any time, she thought in dismay. She had to find the information and give it to Jack Planchard tomorrow night. "How much time?"

"A day, maybe. Before midnight tomorrow."

That was cutting it awfully close, but she knew there was nothing she could do. "Okay," she said reluctantly. "But contact me if you find out anything sooner."

"Okay. Anything else?"

She hesitated a moment. "Actually, there is something I want to ask you . . ."

"Yes?"

"Just for curiosity's sake . . . would it be possible for me to stay here if I wanted to?"

She heard a choking sound, as if Branigan had swallowed his coffee the wrong way.

"What are you talking about? You can't want to stay there."

"No. Of course not. But is it possible?"

"No, Lucy. Too many things could go wrong. I'm transporting you home at 10:00 A.M. the day after tomorrow. Sooner if you keep talking like that."

"It was just a question," she said, an odd pang squeezing her heart. She didn't really want to stay here, she told herself. She didn't like the food or the chamberpots. She hated being Lady Cynthia.

But sometimes, she almost thought she could endure all that, if she could just be with Kieran. . . .

Oh, how silly. She couldn't stay here just because of Kieran. After everything that had passed between them, she doubted Kieran wanted her to stay.

She never should have come here in the first place. She wouldn't have if she'd known she would have to pretend to be Kieran's wife. If John hadn't lied to her, she wouldn't be hurting so badly inside now. "Is John there? I'd like to talk to him."

In the background, she heard the weasel's voice. "I can't come to the radio right now, Uncle Bill—I'm busy."

The coward. "I'll talk to him when I get back," she told Branigan. "Tell him I have something I want to say to him."

"I'll tell him."

"Thanks, Mr. Branigan."

"You're welcome, Lucy. See you in a few days."

She stopped pedalling the bike, and the radio went dead.

7

A thousand candles lit up the ballroom.

Lucy watched the flickering light they cast over the dancers below, wondering how big of a fire hazard all those candles were.

But no one else seemed concerned, so she turned her attention back to the circle of women she was standing with. Lady Emsley, aka "Aunt Roberta"—the woman with the shrill voice who had attended her wedding—was speaking.

"And then she seated Lady Powick below the viscountess, even though the Barony of Powick goes back to the Conquest and clearly had precedence!"

"No!" gasped the other women.

"Yes. Lady Powick was so offended that she snubbed Mrs. Gilroy at Michaelmas, and now Mrs. Gilroy has no one to sponsor her daughter!"

Lucy's attention wandered again. She was not enjoying the ball. Kieran had barely spoken to her on the way there, and once they'd arrived, he'd murmured some excuse and disappeared into some antechamber, leaving her to Lady Emsley's tender mercies. Unpleasant thoughts had plagued Lucy ever since.

She was going home tomorrow. And before she left, she would betray Kieran.

That very morning, she'd gone downstairs and found Kieran in the library just as he was putting a piece of paper in a drawer in his desk.

"Yes?" he'd asked coolly.

She tore her gaze away from the drawer. "I'm not feeling well. I may not be able to go to the ball tonight," she said, planning to investigate the drawer while he went to the party.

"Then we will forego the ball," he said, to Lucy's dismay.

"You don't need to stay home on my account," she assured him.

But he'd insisted, and in the end, she'd decided it would be easier to go to the ball and try to sneak away early.

He'd stared at her for a long moment when she came downstairs later in her silver-spangled ballgown. Her hair, thanks to Polly's efforts, was piled high on her head, and thin silk gloves encased her arms.

"You look beautiful," he'd said quietly.

She hadn't felt beautiful. She'd felt ugly. Ugly, because of the terrible thing she must do.

Lucy glanced toward the ballroom entrance, wondering if she could slip away yet. Lord and Lady Barstow were still standing there, greeting guests.

She turned her attention back to the conversation. It had moved on from Mrs. Gilroy's faux pas—which Lucy could not quite comprehend—to some gossip about a woman and her daughter who had been denied admittance to Almack's—a club of some sort, from what Lucy could tell.

She glanced toward the entrance again, and this time, the crowd there had dispersed. Relieved, she whispered to Lady Emsley, "I need to visit the cloakroom."

Lady Emsley, deeply engrossed in a discussion of the

merits and deficiencies of the various guests' attire, nodded absently. Lucy stepped away and walked casually
toward the ballroom doors. A footman in full livery
stood there at stiff attention.

"Pardon me," she said tentatively. "Could you summon my carriage for me?"

The footman opened his mouth to respond, but before
he could do so, a deep voice spoke behind her.

"And just where are you planning on going, Cynthia?"

Her heart beating rapidly, she turned to see Kieran.
He looked incredibly elegant in his severe black-and-
white evening clothes. A lump rose in her throat. Why
did he have to be so handsome?

"I'm not feeling well," she croaked. "I didn't want
to disturb you, so I thought I'd go home and send the
carriage back."

"I cannot allow you to go home unescorted," he said.
"Sit here while I summon the carriage and make our
excuses to our hosts."

She sat on a chair near the wall and watched him
stride away. She swallowed convulsively. What could
she do now?

"Cynthia!" a shrill voice interrupted her thoughts.
She looked up to see Lady Emsley approaching, an overly bright smile on her face.

"There you are! You must come at once! There is a
particular someone who urgently wishes to speak to you!
Come along, quickly." Lady Emsley tugged at her elbow, and Lucy followed, thinking for a confused moment that it must be Kieran who wanted to talk to her.

But when she stepped through a pair of French doors
at the opposite end of the ballroom, there was no sign
of Kieran. Instead, a pale, rather chinless young man
with a long face and even longer nose stepped from the
shadows.

"Lady Cynthia!" he said in vibrating accents.

Lucy stopped, staring at the stranger in consternation.

"Lord Timothy begged me to allow you to speak to him," Lady Emsley said coyly. "And I knew I could not stand in the path of true love. I will leave you two alone."

True love? What on earth was the older woman talking about? Who was this man?

Lady Emsley whisked inside before Lucy could ask her.

Taking a step toward the door, Lucy smiled uncertainly at the man. "Um, I don't think this is such a good idea, Lord, um, Timothy."

He grasped her hands tightly, preventing her backward retreat. "Do not try to be brave, my darling. I want to support you through your darkest hours."

Although she wasn't sure what Lord Timothy was commiserating with her about, Lucy tried to look appropriately sad. Had someone died recently?

"I am desolate," Lord Timothy continued. " 'Tis an outrage what one must endure nowadays. In my father's day, such a man wouldn't have been allowed within a hundred feet of a lady. Someone like him would have been whipped for his impudence if he'd dared approach a gentleman's daughter."

Lucy stiffened. Could Lord Timothy possibly be talking about her marriage to Kieran?

"I have spoken to my mother," he said. "And she has assured me that she will stand by you. You need not fear that she or my sisters will cut your acquaintance. Although they will not be able to acknowledge your husband, of course. I am sorry, my darling, that you must be burdened with a man possessed of such a terrible handicap."

Handicap. That was the word that Mrs. Rogers had used. "What handicap?"

Lord Timothy looked surprised; then he laughed lightly. "Why, his low birth, of course. The son of a

Welsh coal miner. And look what he's become—a common merchant.''

''You are mistaken.''

Lord Timothy arched his brows at the steely edge in her voice. ''He isn't a merchant?''

''He *is* a merchant. But not a common one. In fact, my husband is quite extraordinary.''

He tittered. ''Extraordinary?''

Lucy's hands tightened into fists as she fought an urge to slap Lord Timothy silly. ''Yes, indeed. He started with nothing—and look what he's accomplished. How many people could have done so much with so little?''

Lord Timothy's titters faded and he frowned. ''My dear, I'm surprised at you. I thought your aunt reared you better—to know what is important.''

''Oh?'' Lucy was so angry, she could barely formulate the words. ''And what is important?''

''Breeding, of course.''

''Like horses, you mean?''

He flushed bright red. ''Really, Lady Cynthia . . .''

Lucy ignored his shock. ''Now that you mention it, I *have* noticed that most of the aristocracy have a rather horsey look—''

''Cynthia!'' he exclaimed. ''Your irreverence is most unbecoming!''

''I beg your pardon,'' Lucy said. ''But judging by some of the specimens I've seen here tonight, I think your breeding program has failed.''

He gaped, but Lucy wasn't quite finished. Looking him straight in the eye, she smiled sweetly and said, ''I'll take a studmuffin like my husband any day.''

She probably shouldn't have said what she had, Lucy thought an hour later as she drove home with Kieran in the carriage. But how could she have remained silent? She couldn't believe anyone could be so snobbish—and so stupid. How could anyone value bloodlines over intelligence, grit, and accomplishments?

She knew it was stupid to get angry over anything a moron like Lord Timothy said. But she couldn't help herself. She hated to think of the people here looking down their noses at Kieran.

Remembering what he'd told her about his childhood, thinking of what he must have gone through, she felt her throat tighten. And even now, after he'd accomplished more than any human could expect, he still wasn't accepted. Did everyone treat him like that? Lucy wondered. Did he know that they all looked at him with disdain? She wasn't sure. When she'd reentered through the French doors, she returned to the ballroom entrance, only to find no sign of Kieran. She'd searched until she found him by one of the pillars lining the room; he'd been talking to a red-faced man who was gesturing angrily. Upon seeing her, Kieran had excused himself and approached her.

"The carriage is waiting," he'd said, studying her face. "Are you ready to go?"

He hadn't said anything since; nor had she. She was too upset.

The carriage stopped. Kieran got out and helped her down. He led her inside and up the stairs.

At her bedroom door, she turned to face him. "Good night," she said.

"Good night." He bowed and walked down the corridor to the next room. She watched him go inside.

She went into her own room and shut the door, and suddenly felt like crying. She would never see him again. She wished they could have parted on better terms. She wished she could tell him how much she'd enjoyed this month with him. She wished she could tell him . . .

A faint noise made her turn.

Kieran stood in the doorway.

Her heart seemed to expand inside her chest. She took a hasty step toward him; then remembering, she stopped, and the joy inside her faded.

"Haven't you ever heard of knocking?" she asked, trying to cover up her slip.

His gaze roamed over her. "You're my wife."

Her skin tingled wherever his gaze touched. "Does that mean you can forget your manners?"

"Sorry. It must have something to do with my lack of breeding."

Her gaze flew to his. A faint mockery lurked in his eyes.

"Oh." She bit her lip. "You heard about that, huh?"

"When I returned to tell you the carriage was ready, the footman said you'd gone out on the balcony. I followed and overheard part of your conversation with Lord Timothy." He studied her a moment. "I don't care what Lord Timothy and his friends say about me."

She twisted a fold of her skirt between her fingers. "Why do you go to those stupid parties, then?"

"For business, of course. I expect to increase my profits fourfold from the contacts I make at such occasions. As little as the aristocracy likes commoners, they do have a healthy respect for anyone who can make money for them."

"What a bunch of hypocrites!"

He laughed. "Of course. Just before we left, Lord Timothy's father informed me that he was cancelling our contract—he refused to do business with anyone who insulted his son. You cost me a pretty penny tonight."

"I'm sorry. I didn't realize—"

"Don't worry. In truth, I was touched by your wifely defense."

She scowled at him, hearing the mockery in his voice. "You should be. I don't know why I bothered."

"Nor do I." He gazed directly at her. "Why did you?"

"I wasn't going to let that little twerp insult you. He looked like a product of hundreds of years of inbreeding. I don't know what he thinks he has to brag about. I don't know how you can stand those people—" She stopped abruptly.

"Those are *your* people."

"Yes, well...um...I don't know. Somehow I never saw them very clearly before."

"Their horsiness."

"Yes."

"I'm honored to know you consider me a 'studmuffin.' I'm assuming that it's a compliment. Is it?"

Blushing, she nodded. "It's just an old slang term I heard somewhere. No one even uses it anymore. It seemed appropriate for the discussion."

"So you find me attractive, do you?"

"I only said that to shock Lord Timothy—"

"Are you saying you *don't* find me attractive?"

"Well . . . I suppose you're . . . well enough."

He stepped closer to her. "I find *you* very attractive. It's very odd. I used to prefer short, plump women. But after I married you, my tastes changed."

"Really?" she squeaked.

"Yes, really." He stepped forward again, which brought him to her side. He drew a finger around the low collar of her dress. "I want to go to bed with you."

He couldn't. *She* couldn't allow him. It was wrong. She was going to have to leave in a few hours; it was hard enough to leave him already. She didn't think she could bear it if they made love.

His lips feathered across her brow and down to her mouth. He kissed her, lightly at first, then more deeply.

And then, suddenly, she knew she couldn't bear it if they *didn't* make love.

She wanted to know him, fully and completely, in every way there was to know a man. And she wanted him to know her. She wanted them to share the deepest, most intense intimacy possible. Since she could have nothing else, she wanted this one moment in time to take back with her to the cold and lonely future. . . .

She put her arms around his neck and kissed him back.

A deep sigh seemed to escape him; his arms tightened around her, then he swung her up and laid her on the bed. He lay down beside her and kissed her again, his fingers untying her dress and pushing aside her petticoat so he could stroke her breasts.

His fingers were gentle—but fire raced along her skin. Need built up inside her like nothing she'd ever experienced.

He kissed her breasts, his tongue teasing her nipples. She arched up against him, feeling as though she were on the verge of finding something she'd been seeking her whole life. . . .

"My God," he whispered. "Dear heaven, how sweet you are . . . lift your hips, sweetheart. Let me get this gown off of you."

She obeyed and then raised her arms so he could pull off her petticoat, too.

She looked up at his face—dark and shadowed in the dim light. She wanted this—she wanted *him*—more than she'd ever wanted anything in her life.

He moved over, his hands stroking over her bare skin as he whispered in her ear. "I've wanted you ever since you woke up from your faint at our wedding and looked up at me. I don't know what it was . . . but at that moment, something changed. At that moment, I knew that somehow we were meant to be together."

She couldn't breathe. Her heart pounded against her chest. He had *known*. Somehow, he had known. And she had known, too. As much as she'd tried to deny it, this was where she belonged. . . .

He came inside her.

The world disappeared. There was nothing in the uni-

verse expect him . . . and her . . . and the music of their
two bodies.

Kieran lay in bed with his wife curled up against his
side, a peace and sense of well-being filling him in a
way that he'd never experienced before.

He thought of the conversation he'd overheard between her and Lord Timothy—listening to Lord Timothy, he'd felt nothing but amused contempt. However,
he'd expected her to agree with the petty lord.

Instead, she had defended Kieran with a heat that had
astonished him. Listening to her excoriate Lord Timothy, he had realized that he'd misjudged her—she wasn't
holding back from him because of snobbery. He didn't
know why she was holding back, but at that moment he
hadn't cared. All he'd cared about was knowing that his
wife cared enough about *him* to defend him. Somehow,
that meant more to him than he would have thought
possible.

He'd always been aware that he would never fit into
one of Society's rigid pigeonholes. He'd been aware of
the isolation of his position, even as he embraced it. But
now, suddenly, he was no longer alone.

He thought of the wife he'd believed he was marrying—a cold, unfeeling statue that he would set up in his
home. And he thought of the wife he'd gotten instead—
the warm, sweet, vulnerable, living breathing woman.

Dear God. Dear God, how he loved her. . . .

She moved, gently slipping away from his side.

Instinctively, he tightened his arm around her. She
grew still; but then a few minutes later, she moved again.
Realizing she likely needed to use the chamber pot, he
kept his arm lax, letting her go.

But instead of the clink of china, he heard her moving
quietly around the room, and then the rustle of cloth. He
frowned. She was dressing. Why?

He heard a whirring sound and then a strange, rough,

scratchy noise. She whispered, "Branigan?"

"Lucy? Lucy? Is that you?"

Kieran tensed, all his senses growing alert.

There was a strange man in his wife's bedroom.

8

"Ssshhh!" Lucy hissed into the microphone. She glanced over her shoulder to see if Kieran had been wakened by Branigan's booming voice.

She couldn't detect any motion in the dim light of the fire. She waited a second to see if he spoke, but all was quiet. With a silent sigh of relief, she turned back to the microphone.

"Yes, it's me," she whispered. "Did you find out that information I asked you for?"

"About Peregrine Walcott? Yes. I wrote it down. He did fight in that battle. Let me see . . . after the change, he lived until April twentieth, 1868. Before the change . . ."

Lucy held her breath. A sense of dread stole over her.

"Before the change he lived until April twenty-first, 1868. He lost a day."

"A day?" Lucy exhaled, almost giddy with relief. "That's it?"

"Yes. Kieran, however, isn't so lucky."

Lucy froze, her chest suddenly hurting as though she were breathing shards of ice into her lungs. "What do you mean?"

"After the change, he lived a remarkably long life. Before, he died May sixteenth, 1808."

"May sixteenth?" She glanced toward the clock on her mantel. A spark from the fireplace illuminated the face for a split second. The hands pointed to just a few minutes after midnight. "But . . . but that's *today*! Are you saying that he is going to die sometime in the next twenty-four hours?"

"If everything goes correctly. I'm sorry, Lucy. I should have checked this before. I hope you haven't grown too attached to him."

She closed her eyes. Dear God. Oh, dear God.

"Lucy? Are you still there?"

"Yes," she whispered.

"What's wrong? You sound funny."

"Branigan, I can't do this."

All the kindliness disappeared from his voice. "What the *hell* are you talking about?"

She bit her lip, not responding.

"Lucy," he said in a harsher voice than she'd ever heard him use, "this is no time for games. The situation here is growing worse. The blue-tufted owl was one of the few natural enemies of the cypress tree rat. Without the owl, the rat population has quadrupled. Rodents are decimating the crops. Farmers are going out of business, and the economy is taking a nosedive. People are saying capitalism is dead. The communists might win the next election. War is imminent. Thousands—no probably *millions* will be killed. You *must* do what we planned. You hear me, Lucy?"

"Yes, I hear you," she whispered.

"You must give the shipment information to Jack Planchard. Do it now, Lucy."

Slowly, she got off the bike and walked with halting steps to the door. She went downstairs and into the library. She lit a candle in the fireplace, then opened the drawer and stared down at the sealed envelope Kieran had placed within. A pistol lay beside it. Slowly, she reached out and took the envelope. At 1:05 A.M., in the garden, she must give this letter to Jack Planchard. Then she must contact Branigan to make sure his history had been corrected before he transported her back to the future. She left the library and went out the rear door.

The moon provided a pale, intermittent light as cool, misty air flowed around her. She trembled. She sat down on the steps leading to the garden, and buried her face against her knees, thinking of the man she'd left sleeping upstairs.

She was still tingling all over from Kieran's lovemaking. She'd never known it could be like that. She'd never known that a connection between two bodies could be so intense, that it could reach down to the corners of her soul and wipe away all the loneliness.

She loved him.

She loved everything about him. She loved his kindness, the way he talked to her, the way he'd worked so hard to make something of himself. She loved the way he made her feel.

But now she must leave him.

Tears stung her eyes. She knew what it was like to lose people you love. She *knew*. So why hadn't she been more careful? Why hadn't she prevented this from happening?

She'd tried. Honestly, she had—

A noise made her look up. She saw a dark shadow gliding toward her through the fog. Jack Planchard? John? Or someone else?

Filled with dread, she waited for him to draw near. What should she do? What *could* she do? She had no choice. . . .

The figure stopped when he saw her. He hesitated a moment, glancing furtively around. Then he smiled, revealing black, rotted teeth.

"Well, well, well. And wot's a pretty lady like yerself doing out on a night like this?"

He certainly didn't sound like John. "Are you Jack Planchard?" she asked.

His small, mean eyes widened, then narrowed. "And wot if I am?"

Obviously, he *was* Jack Planchard; but she didn't like the way he was looking at her. She wished she'd taken the pistol from Kieran's drawer . . .

Swallowing, she rose to her feet and stepped backwards up the stairs. "There's something I want to give you. If you'll wait here a moment, I'll get it and come right back—"

"Hold on just a minute, yer ladyship." He took a pistol from the waistband of his pants and pointed it straight at her. "You wouldn't be thinking of telling someone inside about me, would you?"

"No, of course not. . . ."

"I'd prefer not to take any chances. You come right on down here. My, ain't you a pretty one." He put his arm around her waist and leaned close, sniffing her. "And you smell good, too—"

"Release her," a hard cold voice ordered.

Relief flooded through Lucy. She turned to see a tall, shadowed figure standing in the open doorway. Kieran!

Jack stiffened; then suddenly, he whipped around, his pistol swinging toward Kieran.

Fire and smoke erupted from a shadow at Kieran's side; a shot rang out. Lucy froze, not sure exactly what had happened.

She looked from Kieran to Jack, then gasped as she saw the dark, wet stain spreading over Jack's chest. He released her arm, tottered a few steps, then fell to the ground.

She stared at the limp figure, surprise, shock, and queasiness roiling through her.

"You should choose your friends more carefully, *Lucy.*"

Startled, Lucy turned her gaze back to Kieran. He

stepped forward, out of the shadows, and she saw the gun in his hand—the one that had been in the drawer in his desk.

Her eyes flew to his. Even in the moonlight, she could see the coldness in them. She began to tremble. "I—"

Before she could say any more, she saw a flash of motion from the corner of her eye. She turned.

Jack Planchard jackknifed to an upright position.

"Where am I?" he asked, his voice sounding very different—and very familiar.

She swallowed the lump in her throat, knowing she couldn't explain to Kieran right now—she had to deal with the matter at hand. "John?" she asked, trying to control her trembling.

He looked up, his face panicked. "Who are you?" he asked in a high, shrill voice.

"It's me, Lucy Taylor." Even though she didn't look at him, she was acutely aware of Kieran standing on the doorstep listening to what she was saying. "Branigan sent me."

"I don't believe you! You're lying!"

"How else would I know who you are? You certainly don't look like yourself."

John glanced down. "Oh, my God!" he shrieked. "I've been shot! Oh, my God! Oh, my—"

His hysteria helped her regain her own self-control.

"For heaven's sake, get a hold of yourself, John, or I'll slap you!"

He abruptly stopped wailing and stared at her. "You *sound* like Lucy."

"Well, I told you I am, you idiot," she said.

He glared at her. "I'm not an idiot. Why should I believe you? You're not supposed to be here."

"I'm here because you didn't pass on some information and you changed history."

"I don't know what you're talking about," John said. "I don't have any information."

"I know you don't." Again, she was keenly aware of Kieran standing quietly behind her, listening to the exchange. She swallowed. "I have it."

"And I'll take it," a new voice suddenly intruded.

Lucy turned to see a figure emerge from behind a tree—Lord Timothy!

He was holding a double-barreled pistol, and he was smiling. "Lady Cynthia, what a surprise. When I heard Lord Barstow mention that Walcott was writing a letter of instruction at home, I thought I would need a thief to find it. I certainly didn't expect you to be so obliging as to save me the expense. The letter, if you please."

Lucy hesitated. She looked at Kieran, seeing the anger in his face; but underlying it she sensed something else—the deep pain of disillusionment. How could she do this to him? It seemed so wrong. But what would happen in the future if she didn't? Could she bear to be responsible for the deaths of so many people?

Suddenly she remembered something else—Kieran was supposed to die today. Within the next few minutes Lord Timothy would very likely shoot him.

Her breath caught in her throat. Every instinct inside her shouted that this was all wrong. It was wrong that Kieran should die because people in the future couldn't figure out how to take care of their natural resources. Why should he pay the price for the stupidity of people living two hundred years from now?

"Lady Cynthia, please hurry." Lord Timothy beckoned imperiously. "This night air is not good for my lungs. Give me the letter now."

"No." The word escaped her throat in a harsh whisper without conscious thought—but once she'd said it, she felt as though a dark burden had been lifted from her. "No," she said again, more strongly this time.

Lord Timothy's eyes narrowed. "Lady Cynthia, I hate

to be ungentlemanly, but if you don't give me that letter, I will shoot you."

"Go ahead," she said defiantly.

"Wait!" Kieran said. He turned to her. "Give him the letter."

She gaped at him. "You can't be serious!"

His face was hard. "Do as I tell you."

If she did, Lord Timothy would shoot him, she knew it. "No," she said again.

Kieran's eyes darkened. He grabbed her shoulders and held her while he searched her body for the letter.

She struggled furiously. "Stop that!" she yelled as he passed his hands over her breasts.

He ignored her. Angry tears gathered in her eyes as he pulled the letter from her sleeve. "Don't give it to him," she begged. "You don't know what will happen—"

"Yes, I do." His mouth brushed her hair. "I can't let him shoot you."

"But he'll shoot you." She had to squeeze the words past the painful lump in her throat.

"I know. My dear—"

"What are you two whispering about?" Lord Timothy suddenly demanded. "Walcott, throw the letter down."

Kieran tensed. He stepped away from Lucy. Moonlight glinted off the hard angles of his face. "No. You'll have to come and get it."

"So you can attack me?" Lord Timothy sneered. "I'm not that stupid. Never mind. I have no regrets about shooting a common merchant like you—"

Lucy saw his finger tighten on the trigger.

"No!" she screamed. She heard the gun fire as she launched herself at Kieran, knocking him back onto the steps.

She squeezed her eyes shut, waiting to feel the pain of the bullet entering her.

But there was nothing. Had Lord Timothy missed?

She opened her eyes to see Kieran's pale face below her. His eyes were closed.

No. Oh, dear God, no. "Oh, no. Oh, no. Oh, no," she whispered. She dropped her head against his chest, tears pouring down her face. "No, you can't die, you can't. Wake up. Wake up! Wake—"

"I'm awake," a wry voice said.

Lucy grew still. She looked at Kieran. His eyes were open and he was staring at her.

"You're alive," she said, rather stupidly.

"Er, yes. I just hit my head on the steps when you knocked me over."

"Oh. I'm sorry."

"Never mind." He smiled at her—a slow, sweet smile.

Automatically, she smiled back. Her shock faded, and happiness began to trickle into her veins. He was alive!

But . . . how?

She felt him tense, and instinctively, she stiffened also. Was Lord Timothy standing behind her, waiting to shoot again?

Cautiously, she turned her head and saw Lord Timothy lying on the ground, blood seeping from the wound in his shoulder. Shocked, she turned her gaze to where John lay, a pistol in his hand, his head sagging against his chest.

As if feeling her gaze, he looked up. "I shot him," he said.

"*You* shot him?" She disentangled herself from Kieran and stood up. Slowly, Kieran followed suit.

John gasped for air. "Yes. Lucy . . . I'm sorry about what I did. I'm sorry for everything. I'm sorry I was jealous of your mechanical expertise."

"I forgive you." She moved to his side and knelt beside him. She took his hand in her hers. "Thank you, John."

His lips curved in a faint smile; then suddenly, the

light in his eyes vanished. Jack Planchard's body sagged against the ground.

Slowly, she rose to her feet.

Kieran was staring at her. "He sounded as if he loved you."

"John? No. He didn't."

Before Kieran could respond, the door opened. Denton, dressed in a long nightshirt and woolen nightcap, stood in the aperture, a shotgun in his hands. He looked from Lucy and Kieran to the two bodies lying on the gravel.

"Shall I summon the night watchman to take care of the bodies, sir?" The butler spoke with his usual calm demeanor.

"Please do," Kieran said. He took Lucy by the elbow and half led, half dragged her inside and up the stairs to his bedroom. Once there, he released her and stepped back, folding his arms across his chest.

"I think you owe me an explanation," he said grimly.

She told him everything; he listened quietly, only interrupting her occasionally to ask a question. She spoke quickly, unsure whether he would believe her or not, afraid that he would think her insane.

When she finished, he was silent for a long time.

"Do you believe me?" she asked half hopefully, half anxiously.

"I don't know," he said slowly. "It's such a wild tale . . . what happened to Cynthia?"

"She died of an overdose of laudanum."

He frowned. "I see."

He was quiet for another long moment. Then he asked, "Why would you leave your home to come to the past for the sake of a bird?"

"I did it more for Branigan," she said. She paused a moment, then shook her head. "No, maybe that's not true. I think I did it for myself. I had buried myself at work since my parents' deaths. I never went anywhere, I never took any risks. This was something important, something that I could do to help others.'' She gave him a strained smile. ''Only I guess I didn't do that great a job.''

''If you failed to change history back the way it was, what will happen to the future?''

She bit her lip. ''I don't know. It will probably be terrible. Branigan said the world is on the verge of war.'' She swallowed. ''I guess I'll find out when I return.''

''You could stay here. With me.''

Her throat felt tight. ''I have to go home. I don't have any choice. Branigan said I can't stay. He's transporting me back in a few hours.'' She looked at his dark hair and eyes and the frowning lines in his face. ''I'll miss you.''

''God, Lucy, is that all you can say?'' he asked harshly.

She tried to swallow back the lump in her throat, but she couldn't. ''What do you want me to say?'' she whispered.

''I want you to tell me to take you to bed and make love to you. I want you to tell me to hold you tightly and never let you go.'' His voice lowered to a gruff whisper. ''I want you to tell me that you love me.''

She tried to smile but she couldn't. ''Take me to bed and make love to me. Hold me in your arms and never let me go.''

He swept her up and carried her to the bed.

''I love you, Lucy,'' he murmured in her ear.

She kissed him, her face wet with tears. ''I love you, too, Kieran.''

Lucy kissed Kieran. He didn't move, although she knew he wasn't asleep. Quietly, she slipped out of the bed. Pulling on her petticoat, she walked into her own room and climbed on the bicycle.

She sat there for a long moment. She wanted to stay; dear heaven, how she wanted to. But she knew she couldn't. She had to go home and face the consequences of her actions.

She wondered if war had broken out. She wondered if anyone had been killed. Even though she still believed that Kieran shouldn't be the sacrifice for the future's stupidity, she knew she would always carry a burden of guilt for what she had done.

She took a deep breath and started pedalling. Static filled the room.

"Branigan?" she said. "Are you there?"

"I'm here." Branigan's voice floated through the air. "Lucy, what the heck did you do?"

She bowed her head. "I'm sorry. I know I failed—"

"Failed?" Branigan's excited voice interrupted her. "What are you talking about? Everything has worked out beautifully! The pollution is gone and blue-tufted owls are everywhere! The cypress tree rat is under control and the farmers all have bumper crops!"

"But . . . but what about the battle Kieran's brother fought in?"

"The English won the battle and the war, nothing's really changed with regards to that. But other things *have* changed. It's fantastic, Lucy! You wouldn't believe how clear the skies are! And how cute the blue-tufted owls are—there's a nest right outside the basement window with three of the little fellas!"

"I don't understand," she said. "How can that be?"

"It's because of *you*, Lucy. *You* fixed history—*and* the anomaly."

"*I* did?"

"Yes. Your children and grandchildren and great-great-great-grandchildren are instrumental in solving many of our environmental problems. One of your descendents invents a solar engine that's more powerful than the combustion engine. Another is instrumental in passing laws to protect wildlife. And another—''

''Wait a second! What are you talking about? I don't have any children.''

''You will. In fact, your first one will be born exactly nine months from today.''

Lucy sat back, her hands flying instinctively to her stomach. ''Are you saying I'm *pregnant*?''

''Um, well, yes. I take it''—he paused delicately— ''that you and Kieran have been busy the last few hours?''

''That's none of your damned business,'' she said, but her voice lacked any sharpness. *Pregnant.* With Kieran's child. She couldn't believe it.

''Lucy . . .'' Branigan's voice sounded suddenly serious. ''You know what this means, don't you?''

Still reeling from the shock of discovering that she was pregnant, Lucy stared blankly at the paper cone in front of her. ''What are you talking about?''

''I'm talking about the fact that you can't come home. You're going to have to stay there in the past.''

''I am?''

''Yes. And Lucy, you're going to have to destroy the radio. It's too dangerous to keep it when it doesn't belong in that time.''

''I see.''

''Lucy, I'm really sorry about this. I didn't know this was going to happen. I hope you will forgive me—''

''There's nothing to forgive,'' she said. ''I want to stay here. I think this is where I belong—with Kieran.''

''Do you love him, Lucy?''

''I—''

Before, she could finish her sentence, the radio spluttered and went dead. She fiddled with wires and magnet but to no avail. Finally, her hand trembling slightly, she disassembled all the parts and put them in the wastebasket—the dustbin, she corrected herself—severing her last link to the future.

Then she went back into Kieran's room.

He was lying on his back, his arms folded behind his head. He was staring up at the canopy above him with a bleakness in his eyes that made her throat ache. She stepped forward.

He turned his head sharply. He stared at her.

"Lucy?"

She nodded, a smile trembling on her lips.

"You don't have to go?"

In answer, she crossed the room and climbed into bed with him. His arms closed so tightly around her that for a moment, she couldn't breathe.

He buried his face in her hair. "I love you, Lucy."

Tears of happiness filled her eyes. "I love you, too."

She cuddled up beside him; then, a smile curving her lips, she closed her eyes and went to sleep.

9

Bill Branigan reconfigured a wire, then leaned back in his chair, staring at the contraption before him. After deciding that it was just too dangerous to send people back in time, he'd destroyed his radio time-travel device. But he hadn't been able to stop thinking about time travel—and about Lucy. When he'd come up with this new idea, he'd poured all his time and energy into building it.

With a trembling hand, he reached out and turned on his time-travelling TV.

Images of a horde of Huns filled the screen.

It worked! He could see the Huns attacking, he could see every detail of their filthy clothes.

He moved onto the purple-and-green plaid couch and picked up the remote control—a necessary element, he'd decided when designing the prototype—and flipped through the channels. This was fantastic—the past at his fingertips. He didn't have to worry about changing history—he could watch it all from the comfort of his living room sofa. This was better than soap operas.

Click. Click. Click—

"Uncle Bill, what are you. . . . *stop!*"

Surprised, Branigan glanced over to see his nephew

had entered the room. John was staring at the screen as if he'd seen a ghost.

Branigan glanced back at the screen. He didn't recognize the woman, although there was something vaguely familiar about her. He stared, trying to place her. It wasn't really the features of the woman that seemed familiar so much as something about her smile. . . .

Good God! Branigan straightened in his seat. *"Lucy?"*

Nodding, John sat down next to him on the purple-and-green plaid sofa.

Branigan barely noticed; he was staring at the screen. Lucy! A different Lucy, tall and thin, with unfamiliar features, but Lucy all the same. She was about twenty years older than when he had known her, her face softened with smile lines and a sprinkling of silver in her hair. She was holding a baby in her arms and smiling up at a young woman standing next to a handsome youth.

"She looks just like you, Jane," Lucy said.

"Does she, Mama?" the girl named Jane asked.

A trio of boys, ranging in age from about six to sixteen, gathered around and looked down at the baby. "Why is she bald?" the youngest one asked.

Jane scowled and opened her mouth, but before she could speak, another man moved into the picture—an older man with a liberal sprinkling of gray in his hair. "Babies are always bald, Ian."

Ian shrugged, but Bill Branigan paid little attention to the boy. He was watching Lucy—and the way her face lit up at the sight of the man.

"Kieran," she said. "When did you return?"

"Only a few minutes ago, my love." He grasped her hand.

Branigan watched a few minutes more, studying each of Lucy's children, and her new grandchild. He watched the way she and Kieran held hands and exchanged glances, their eyes smiling as they did so.

A sigh distracted Branigan from the TV. He glanced over at John.

John met his gaze. "She looks happy."

Branigan nodded and smiled.

Lucy had finally found her home.

CONYN'S BRIDE

Ingrid Weaver

1

"But it's your last night of freedom, Alanna! I can't believe you're going to spend it working."

Alanna Moore carefully set the twenty-three-hundred-year-old gold bracelet on top of its nest of bubble wrap, then shifted the telephone to her other ear, and tipped back her chair. "There are things I need to do before the honeymoon, Fleur. It's bad enough that I'll be taking two weeks off at the museum's busiest time of year. I really should finish cataloguing this new shipment, so thanks for the invitation, but—"

"There'll be men," Fleur persisted.

Alanna's laughter echoed merrily off the steel shelves and cement walls that lined her office. She swiveled her chair around, her gaze going to the storeroom beyond the doorway. The last of the three wooden crates that had arrived this morning was still resting in the center of the worktable awaiting her attention. "The only men I'm interested in seeing tonight will be made of bronze and be a few millennia old."

"Ah, the ones I'm talking about will be hard, too, but they'll be young and naked."

"Fleur!" Alanna sputtered. "Shame on you!"

"Don't tell me the blushing bride is saving herself for her wedding night."

Her laughter faded as a knot of something Alanna didn't want to think about tightened her stomach. It wasn't fear. It was. . . . anticipation. Of course that's what it was. She *wanted* to get married. She really did. Despite the fact that every one of her friends had been trying to talk her out of it from the moment she had announced her engagement. "Well . . ."

"Come on, what's the harm in watching a few male strippers? All of us are going."

"Again, thanks for the invitation, but I'm sure Reginald wouldn't like the idea. I don't want to hurt his feelings."

"Do you honestly think your hubby-to-be is moping around by himself tonight?"

Alanna hesitated just a beat. No, Reginald Ainsworth III wouldn't be alone on the eve of his wedding. Besides, he never moped. He was far too elegant to mope. She turned back to her desk and picked up the bracelet again, rubbing her thumb over the delicate design that had been worked into the gold. "He said his cousin is taking him out to a concert. Reginald loves Vivaldi."

"Is that the name of the girl who'll jump out of the cake?"

"Fleur, Reginald isn't like that."

"Scratch away the civilized veneer and all men are barbarians under the surface. You've been living in that basement too long, Alanna."

"I don't live down here," she said automatically.

A hissing noise came through the receiver. At first Alanna thought it was Fleur's reply, but then she realized the noise was coming from the line itself. She glanced at the telephone. The buttons along the side were all dark.

"Fleur?" she tried. "Hello?"

The hissing ended with a sharp crackle and the line went dead.

This was the second time in a week the telephone had gone out on her. The renovating crew on the first floor had probably cut through the wires again. She was surprised that they were working this late in the evening, but then she was still here, wasn't she? Well, whatever the cause of the dead phone, at least it was one way to end the discussion.

With a sigh of relief—and a quick feeling of guilt over the fact that she was relieved—Alanna dropped the receiver back into its cradle. She didn't want to argue with her friend. And she was tired of having to make excuses for preferring the peace and solitude of the museum to the excitement of a strip bar on the night before her wedding.

Sure, she had plenty to do here, what with the new exhibit of Celtic artifacts scheduled to open next month. She truly enjoyed handling these objects from the past. And while the basement of the Royal Ontario Museum might seem bleak to most people, it was her favorite place to be.

Besides, as long as she could immerse herself in her work, she wouldn't have to dwell on the fact that she was about to marry a man she didn't love.

Then again, Reginald didn't love her, either. They were two mature, sensible adults who enjoyed each other's company and had decided they had reached a point in their lives when they would like the comfort and security of a permanent relationship. Actually, they had discussed the matter of love quite openly and they both agreed that love was a myth, an illusion, a convenient rationalization to justify the natural urge to find a life mate.

No, not a mate. Reginald Ainsworth III couldn't be described as anything so. . . . primitive. He would be her spouse.

And that was what she wanted. Yes, indeed. She had outgrown her romantic dreams long ago. She had thought it all through carefully, and it was far too late to have doubts now. She'd lose her deposits on the caterer, the florist, and the photographer. Her wedding dress was already paid for, and Reginald's mother would be arriving in Toronto tomorrow for the ceremony, and. . . .

So much for not thinking about it. Maybe she should have accepted Fleur's invitation after all.

Blowing out her breath in exasperation, Alanna turned her attention back to the bracelet she still held. It had been in the first crate she'd unpacked, but somehow she hadn't yet gotten around to checking it off on the inventory. The gold had grown warm where she'd been holding it, sending an odd tingle along her fingertips. She rubbed her thumb across the design again, tilting it toward the light to get a better look.

The workmanship was exquisite. The metal had been shaped into two smoothly twining strands that ended in a pair of delicate knobs. A stag with whimsically swirling antlers danced at the base of one knob while a doe tilted her head coyly to watch him from the other.

Alanna's lips curved in pleasure. The professional in her noted the traditional Celtic fondness for nature imagery and the Greek influence in the realistic detail and the high-quality workmanship. Yet the woman in her wondered at the person who had owned this piece of jewelry. Had she found it beautiful? Had she been proud to wear it? And how had she felt about the man who had given it to her?

Alanna thought of the flashy diamond engagement ring that she kept locked in a box in her desk drawer. It wasn't practical to wear it while she was working—the large stone tended to catch on everything she brushed against. Naturally, the diamond was of the highest quality, but it was meant more as an investment than as a token of love. It had none of the vitality of this age's old gold.

And yet once she finished documenting all of these artifacts, this bracelet would be locked away, too, placed in a glass display case. What a shame if it wasn't worn for another twenty-three hundred years. She held the bracelet against her arm, imagining the way it must have looked. No one was here to see her. What harm would there be if she. . . .

Seized by a crazy impulse, Alanna slid the bracelet over her wrist.

The odd tingle she'd felt in her fingertips earlier now spread to her arm, as if tiny electric shocks were travelling over her skin from the place where the bracelet rested. Puzzled, she tipped her head to take a closer look.

The fluorescent light that hung from the ceiling flickered. Thunder rumbled beyond the thick walls of the museum, setting up a vibration that rattled the metal shelves and sent a tingle through the soles of Alanna's feet.

Maybe it hadn't been the workmen who had cut off the phone line. Maybe it was a storm—the weather had been hotter than usual for June this past week, so it would be a relief to get some rain. That might explain the electricity in the air. She rubbed her arm, surprised to feel the tiny hairs standing on end. Her fingertips grazed the bracelet. . . . and the gold appeared to glow.

"Maybe Fleur's right," Alanna murmured, shaking her head. "I've been down in this basement too long." She started to slip the bracelet off, but it wouldn't go past her wrist. That was odd, she thought. She hadn't had any trouble getting it on. She tugged harder and had just managed to wedge it over the base of her thumb when a sudden draft curled past her ankles, as if someone had opened a door in the storeroom outside her office.

She jumped out of her chair and turned to face the

doorway, thrusting her hand guiltily behind her back. It was probably only Gilbert, the security guard. Just her luck that he had decided to come down here—he seldom strayed far from his little TV set during baseball season. She'd be in trouble if word got out that she was starting to wear the exhibits. "Hello?" she called.

Another rumble of thunder shook the shelves. This time she felt it all the way through her bones to her teeth. The draft that swept through the office doorway strengthened as the lights flickered and dimmed.

"Gilbert?" Alanna called once more. "I hope you have your flashlight with you because it looks as if the power—"

With a muted tick, the light winked out and the basement was plunged into blackness.

"—might go out," she finished weakly.

There was a sudden crash, accompanied by the ominous sound of splintering wood.

"Don't move!" Alanna ordered, fumbling her way toward the door. "The contents of that crate are priceless."

A low, masculine groan came from the darkness.

Alanna didn't even think to be worried about who might be out there. All she was concerned about were the treasures that had been left in her care. Holding her hands out in front of her, she moved as quickly as she dared toward the direction of the sound. Her shin struck the metal support of the worktable and she swallowed a cry of pain. Leaning down to rub her leg, she paused to call out. "Hello? Where are you?"

Something scraped across the cement floor to her left.

Pivoting in that direction, she moved forward more cautiously, stopping when her toe nudged a loose object. She bent down, groping in front of her until she felt a piece of rough wood. "Great," she muttered, picturing the damage that could have been done when this crate had cracked open. She got down on her hands and knees, feeling along the floor in front of her so that she wouldn't step on some artifact by mistake. Wonderful. If she wasn't fired for wearing the inventory, she'd be fired for letting the Celtic exhibit get ruined. "Gilbert, I told you we need emergency lighting down in this end of the basement. If one of these pieces gets damaged—oh!"

Her fingers encountered warm, rough-woven cloth. She moved her hand, her fingertips tracing along the contour of what felt like a shoulder. . . . a very broad, very hard shoulder. . . . that led to a smooth expanse of taut skin that stretched over a very hard muscle—

"Oh, excuse me!" she exclaimed, yanking her arm back.

Another moan, this time from right in front of her.

Alanna sat back on her heels. "Uh, Gilbert?" she tried, although she knew it couldn't be the elderly security guard, not with biceps like that.

There was a silence. Then without warning, a hand clamped over her knee.

She shrieked and scrambled backward.

"Alanna? 'Tis you?"

At her name, she paused. The voice wasn't Gilbert's raspy drawl, that was for sure. No, this voice was deep and rich, like the rolling green of the valley that stretched beyond the village to the mountains—

Good heavens. Where had that thought come from? "Who's there?" she demanded.

"Sweet stars, 'tis the voice of my dreams. Alanna, my love. I have found you."

She would have remembered a voice like that. Any woman would have. It was so. . . . male. It was sending shivers and tingles over her skin just like the thunder. "Listen, whoever you are, you have to be very careful not to move because the floor could be covered with delicate artifacts."

There was a whisper of movement, then the hiss of an indrawn breath.

Belatedly, Alanna remembered the moans. "Are you hurt?" she asked.

"How could I suffer when I am reunited with you at last?"

The incredible voice was getting closer. The words carried the hint of an accent she couldn't identify, something like a cross between the strong tones of German and the musical lilt of Irish. And over the typical basement scents of dust and stale air she caught a teasing hint of. . . . pine. And sunshine. Freshness and freedom and endless horizons. . . .

Okay, so he was wearing fantastic cologne. That was no reason to sit here and let him grab her again. She inched backward, her knees sliding over the cold cement as her dress hem dragged across the floor. She bumped into another fragment of splintered wood and she set it to one side. "That packing crate was heavy," she said. "Do you remember hitting your head when you knocked it over?"

"Nay, but why do you choose to be in such darkness? What is this place where there is no glimpse of moon or stars to guide me to your side?"

Oh, yeah. He must have hit his head, all right. He'd have a killer of a headache when his brains unscrambled. "We're in the storeroom. And until we get some light in here, I'd really prefer it if you didn't come any closer."

"Sweet Alanna, why do you flee from me when I have journeyed so far to find you?"

"It would probably be best if you don't move," she said, continuing to retreat. It couldn't be much farther to the doorway of her office. If she could just reach her telephone, she could call for an ambulance or maybe some men in white coats with big nets. . . .

But her phone had gone dead, she remembered.

"My love." His voice echoed softly through the cavernous room and settled around her like a gentle caress. "Alanna."

She couldn't understand it. Logically, she should be starting to get worried right about now, and not only because of the possible damage to the material for the new exhibit. Whoever this stranger was, he seemed to have decided that he . . . well . . . had a thing for her. And he was between her and the only way out of the basement. No one would hear her if she screamed since the walls of this old building were several feet thick, which the workmen had been grumbling about for the past week. . . .

Aha! The workmen. This stranger was probably one of the men who were working on the renovations. That would explain the broad shoulders and the muscles. And it would also explain what he was doing in the museum after hours, and how he would know her name. He'd probably been responsible for cutting her phone line after all, and he had been on his way to let her know when the power had gone off and he'd stumbled over that crate and hit his head and become delusional.

Good. Fine. She had a logical explanation for not feeling as alarmed by her situation as she should have been feeling.

"Hold on," she said, reaching behind her. Her elbow hit the side of the office doorframe. Wincing, she hung onto the doorframe and pulled herself back to her feet, then waved her arm through the blackness until she felt the edge of a shelf. She didn't have a flashlight, but the last time Reginald had visited here he'd left one of those disposable lighters in one of his cigarette packs. She'd given the cigarettes to Gilbert—Reginald had promised to quit once they were married—but she'd kept the lighter. If only she could remember where she'd put it.

"I would dearly love to hold on, Alanna, as long as I could hold you."

For a construction worker with a serious knock on the head, she couldn't deny that he had a certain . . . charm. She twisted around to fumble through the items on the shelf. "I meant, stay put. I don't want you to break anything."

"The only thing in danger of breaking is my heart, my love, until I can hold you once more."

Her lips twitched into a smile at his over-the-top romantic language. Again, she probably should be feeling some misgivings by now, but those words, and his deep, resonant voice . . . and the fresh tang of his scent . . . all of it was stirring something inside her—

Hmm. Maybe Fleur was right and she *had* been spending too much time down in this basement. "Here it is," she said, feeling an edge of smooth plastic underneath the knapsack that held her spare sweater.

"My heart?"

"The lighter." She flicked her thumb over the wheel. With a grating click, a small flame sprang upward. Holding the metal tab down with her thumb, she extended her arm and turned back to the doorway.

The blackness of the storeroom was too deep for her wavering light to penetrate. She took a step forward, moving the lighter in an arc so that she could see the floor. There were scattered pieces of broken wood everywhere, but no gleam of bubble wrap or glint of gold or bronze . . . unless she counted the gleam of bronzed skin less than an arm's length away.

The stranger was standing in front of her. She hadn't heard him approach. Her pulse thumped as she raised her gaze from the sculpted ridges of his washboard stomach to the broad expanse of his bare chest. A loop of metal chain joined twin brooches that were fastened to the sides of a cloak. . . .

A *cloak*?

She lifted her gaze further. A heavy gold necklace glinted beneath the upper edge of the cloak, its knobbed ends resting in the hollow of the man's throat. The man was tall, at least two inches over six feet. His jaw was square, his cheekbones high, and his nose bold and slightly crooked, as if it had been broken at some time in the past. It was impossible to tell the exact color of his hair, but she could see that it was dark and brushed straight back from his forehead. Deep lines bracketed his lips, which were curved into a smile that softened the otherwise unrelenting masculinity of his face.

Her gaze finally met his. And the smile that played around his lips crinkled into tiny laugh lines at the corners of his eyes. Incredible eyes. Shadowed by arching black brows, surrounded by thick dark lashes, his gaze was as blue and clear as the river that flowed past his grandmother's hut. . . .

She blinked hard, trying to dispel yet another one of those weird images. She had to get a hold of herself. All right, he was without a doubt the most spectacularly handsome man she had ever seen. That fact alone would be enough to rattle any woman's thought processes, but add to it this power failure and his unconventional clothing and the way he sounded and the way he smelled and was it any wonder her mind was playing tricks on her?

"Alanna, my love. You're more beautiful than I remember in my dreams."

Even though he was looking straight at her, he still seemed to believe that they knew each other. But she had never seen him before in her life. She was certain of that. Because any living, breathing woman would remember this man if she'd met him before.

Wouldn't she?

Her hand shook. "You're not one of the renovators, are you," she said.

His smile dimmed. "Alanna, have I changed so much that you do not know me?"

"Mister—"

"Look at me," he said urgently, flinging out his arms.

His cloak flapped behind him dramatically, revealing even more bronzed skin and rippling muscle. "It is I. Conyn."

Her mouth went dry, her palms went damp. She wiped her hand on her skirt and tightened her grip on the lighter. Think, don't ogle, she ordered herself. But he *had* invited her to look at him, right? Her gaze moved over him once more. This time she noticed the sheen of leather trousers, very tight leather, that molded thighs as impressive as his arms. More leather crisscrossed his shins, binding what appeared to be boots made of animal hide. Metal glinted from the shadows at his side, looking suspiciously like some kind of sword. . . .

The details of his clothing finally registered. Hide boots, leather pants, coarsely woven cloak, the twin brooches, the necklace that looked like an antique torque . . . the *sword* . . .

He wasn't dressed like any construction worker. He looked more like a character out of one of the early Schwarzenegger movies about barbarians. "Oh, this is too much. Did you say your name is . . . *Conan*?"

"Conyn ap Rhys."

Something niggled deep in the recesses of her mind at the sound of his name. No mystery there. She'd probably heard it on some late-night movie. "All right, Conyn ap Rhys. Why are you really here?"

"I have come for you, Alanna."

"You're an actor, right?"

"I am a warrior," he said, his hands dropping back to his sides. "It grieves me that you do not remember. I did not intend to be gone from you so long."

Of course, he had to be an actor, she thought, glancing at the muscles that bulged on his impressive body. With pecs and biceps like that, he could probably earn a good living as a male stripper—

"Oh, my God," Alanna murmured, shaking her head. "Fleur put you up to this, didn't she?"

"Who?"

"What was this supposed to be, one of those singing, stripping telegrams?"

His smile disappeared. "Singing? I am no bard, I am a warrior. I have fought Epaminondas and the Boeotians. I have travelled over the mountains to the land of the southern sea."

"It's okay, you can cut the act now," she said. "Let me see if I can find some candles and I'll show you the way out. I don't know how you got in here in the first place. Is Gilbert in on this, too?"

"I do not know of this person."

"Well, while your performance didn't go as planned, I did find it entertaining, so—"

Her words cut off on a startled squeak. He moved so swiftly, she didn't have a chance to step back before his hand clamped around her wrist.

"Please, do not send me away, Alanna."

She could feel restrained strength humming in his grasp. His hand was so large, his fingers easily spanned her wrist. He could snap her bones with one squeeze.

She should probably be starting to get really, *really* worried right about now.

And yet beneath the undeniable strength of his grip, she felt something else. Awareness and a spark of . . . familiarity. It was as if his touch were telling her things her brain couldn't quite accept, as if something were bypassing her logic functions to suppress her fear and stir up a response on another level altogether.

His thumb moved tenderly over her skin, stroking the underside of her wrist in a way that sent tremors up her arm. "Please, Alanna. Let me help you remember our love."

Love. How many times had he said that word in the past few minutes? Probably more times than she'd ever heard it. But he was an actor. That kind of romantic language would come easily to him. Because love was

a myth, an illusion, just a word that he could use like
the costume he wore.

But God, the things he was doing to her just by moving the tip of his thumb. She straightened up, realizing
that she'd been swaying toward him. "Excuse me, Mr.
ap Rhys, but I have work to do. I'm really very busy."

"The bracelet!" he exclaimed suddenly. He caught
her hand and brought it closer to the flame of the lighter.

With a start, she noticed the circle of gold on her
wrist. She'd forgotten that she still wore it. "Uh, I was
about to take it off when the lights—Oh!"

He bent over and brushed his lips across the back of
her hand. "Does it please you?"

The sensation of his mouth on her skin stole her
breath. Surprise, that was all. "What?"

He lifted his head, stepping closer. "I thought of you
wearing it. The goldsmith struck a hard bargain. He demanded two pounds of salt and the harnesses from my
team, but I knew it belonged on your arm, Alanna."

Well, she had to give him credit for sticking to the
role he'd decided on. "Are you claiming that you
bought this bracelet, Mr. ap Rhys?"

"Aye. 'Tis no spoil of war. I did not wish to bring
you goods that had been looted."

"How . . . upstanding of you."

"The stag and his mate reminded me of us. Two
halves of one whole." He enclosed her hand within his.
"Joined for all time."

Once again, her breath caught with surprise. He
couldn't possibly have made out the detail of that engraving. And how could he have known about it beforehand? She'd just unpacked the ornament herself this
afternoon. Had it been a lucky guess?

Well, what else could it be? It wasn't as if he could
be telling her the truth, was it? "As I said, you can cut
the act now. Nice try, Conyn, or whatever your real

name is, but I know for a fact that you didn't buy this bracelet."

"I do not understand."

"This piece comes from a collection that spent the past fifty years on display in the Bern Museum until it was shipped here as part of an exhibition. The estimated age of this particular artifact is twenty-three hundred years, give or take a few centuries."

"Nay. It is not so. I watched the goldsmith complete it myself."

"That would have been impossible." She paused. "Unless, of course, you happen to be twenty-three centuries old," she said wryly.

A tremor went through his body. For a moment, he stared at her without speaking, his blue gaze burning with intensity.

She could see that her statement had jarred him. Perhaps she shouldn't have been so direct about popping the fantasy he'd tried to construct.

"The woman did not lie," he said finally, his voice hoarse.

"What woman? Do you mean Fleur?"

"The old woman who sent me said I would cross a great distance to find you. I had not known she meant a distance of time."

"Time? What on earth are you talking about?"

He closed his eyes briefly, his chest heaving with an unsteady breath. Then he lifted her hand to his mouth and pressed his lips to the back of her knuckles. "Oh, my love. I have indeed travelled a long way to claim my bride."

2

His bride? Alanna thought, lighting one of the fat white emergency candles she'd found. He had come forward in time twenty-three centuries to claim his bride? Well, for an act, it was certainly original. Fleur had probably told him about the upcoming wedding, so like any good actor, he'd decided to improvise.

And he was more than good. He was fabulous. The amount of background research he must have done for this role was mind-boggling. And he'd taken such pains to make sure his costume was authentic. How many strippers—no, they probably preferred being called male exotic dancers—happened to have a routine that necessitated dressing up as an ancient Celtic warrior?

That must be why Fleur had decided to hire this particular man, Alanna thought. Her friend had known about the Celtic exhibit, and how wrapped up in her work Alanna was. As a matter of fact, the history of the Celts had intrigued her even before she'd come to work at the museum. They were a fascinating people. They had populated much of Europe and coexisted with the Greek and then the Roman Empires, establishing their own distinct culture despite their wanderings and their fierce individualism.

"Forgive me if I seem impatient, my love, but I have waited for this day so long. I do not wish to wait another moment to marry you."

She tilted the candle, using the drops of melted wax to fix it upright on the lid of a jar. The sensible thing to do would be to escort this . . . this warrior out of the basement and up the stairs to the main reception area, then wake up Gilbert, who was undoubtedly either snoozing at his desk or wrapped up in the ball game, and have him unlock the door to let the man out in time for his next show.

But if Fleur had paid for Conyn's time, why not let him finish his act? What harm could there be in that? He seemed determined to give her her money's worth.

Oddly enough, Alanna still didn't feel even the slightest inkling of alarm over being alone with this strange man. It was more than his astounding good looks. It was his manner. In spite of his size and his obvious strength, there was a gentleness about him. It was in his movements, and his smile, and his scent of pine and sunshine.

And the simple truth of it was, Alanna was enjoying herself. Very much.

"Sorry, Conyn," she said, setting the candle on the center of her desk. She brushed the dust from the front of her dress before she sat down in her chair and swiveled to face him. "But I have no plans to get married today."

"You still do not remember me."

The disappointment on his face looked so genuine, she felt her heart turn over. "It must have been the time lapse," she said, playing along.

"I understand. You wish to be wooed anew before we pledge to each other."

Wooed? Reginald had never wooed her. They were both far too sensible for any of that romantic nonsense. "Uh, Conyn, let's not get carried away."

"I will help you remember, Alanna. I will give you this night, but tomorrow, before the sun sets, you will be my bride."

If everything went ahead as planned, she would be married before the sun set tomorrow all right, but not to him.

Pulling the spare chair close to her desk, Conyn reversed it so that he could straddle the seat. The tip of his sword sheath clunked against the floor. "I always loved watching you in the firelight, Alanna. Your hair gleams like the breast of a raven."

She lifted her hand and tucked a curl behind her ear self-consciously. "Thank you."

"You have cut it since I last saw you. Your tresses once fell to your knees." He studied her for a moment. "I had not believed it possible, but you are even more beautiful like this. Your short curls have the innocence of a child's but the sensuous depth of a woman's."

"Thank you again."

"Without the long strands to become tangled around my fingers, perhaps even this clumsy warrior would not cause you pain when I thrust my fingers into your hair."

"Uh . . ."

"Did you like the mirror?" he asked, his voice dropping.

"Mirror?"

"It was not as fine as the bracelet, but I wanted to think of the polished surface caressing your image when I could not be there to touch your beloved face myself."

Oh, he was good, she thought, feeling a warmth steal into her cheeks at his continued flattery. "Sorry, I must have misplaced the mirror. Which reminds me," she said, tugging at the bracelet. "I'd better take this off before—"

"Nay, Alanna. 'Tis meant for you, an adornment for a woman more precious than gold."

As before, the bracelet wouldn't go past her wrist. She

hesitated, not wanting to pull any harder and risk damaging the artifact. She'd have to try soap later. "About this bracelet, I'd appreciate it if you don't, uh, tell anyone that I, well, tried it on."

"But it is yours."

"We'll keep that between the two of us. My museum board of directors frowns on the staff playing with the inventory."

He smiled. "Your wish is my command, my sweet."

Her pulse did another quick thump. Why did he need to wear a sword when he had a smile that deadly?

He'd been attractive enough before, by the flickering flame of the lighter, but here in the cozy shadows of her office, with his face bathed in the intimate glow of candlelight, he was downright gorgeous. She could see now that his hair was dark auburn, pulled into a no-nonsense queue at the nape of his neck with a strip of leather. The laugh lines around his eyes were echoed by twin dimples that she could glimpse at the corners of his mouth. And there was an intriguing hint of a cleft in his chin that she itched to explore with her fingertips.

But he was gorgeous because he was a professional performer. It was all an act, she reminded herself, meant for her entertainment. "So, Conyn," she said, clearing her throat. "Tell me more about how you happened to come forward in time."

He folded his arms across the back of the chair and leaned toward her. "I do not know what method of magic the old woman used, Alanna. All I remember is walking into the circle of standing stones on the eve of the summer solstice and fixing my mind on the woman who holds my heart."

Circle of standing stones? Well, there were people who believed places like Stonehenge had some kind of mystical powers related to the calendar. Furthermore, the equinoxes and summer and winter solstices were considered important days to the ancient Celts, and today was the first day of summer, so his story wasn't all that bad, in a vague, New Age kind of way. "All right, I'll give you points on that one. What about the language problem?"

"Language?"

"If you're really a Celt from the third century B.C., then why do you understand English?"

"English?"

"It's the language we're speaking."

"In my travels, I learned many new tongues, but not this one. 'Tis strange indeed." He paused as if to consider it. "Perhaps the gift of this new language was part of the old woman's magic so there would be no further gulf between us when finally we were reunited."

"Mmm. You're going to have to work on that one. It's not as good as the time-travel answer."

He quirked one eyebrow. "I hear in your voice that you are not ready to trust my word, Alanna."

"No offense, Conyn, but—"

"I would expect no less of you, my sweet. You were always one who wanted to understand the workings of the world."

"Oh, really?"

"When we were young, you were forever searching through the stones near the riverbank to find the bones that were trapped in the rocks. Although others might have mocked your belief in those ancient creatures, your thirst for knowledge was a source of great pride to me." He reached into the leather pouch that hung by his waist. Loose change jingled under his fingers before he pulled out a small stone. "See, my love? I still carry the tiny animal you gave me in my sixteenth summer."

Curious, she stretched out her arm to take the stone from his hand. Even in the candlelight, she could see the pale outline on the rock. "Why, this is a fossilized trilobite," she exclaimed. She looked up quickly. "How did you know I used to collect fossils when I was a kid? Did Fleur tell you?''

He tilted his head, a wistful smile curving his mouth. "Nay. I saw for myself."

"But—"

"Many is the time I would return home to my grandmother with wet leggings because I had followed you into the water in pursuit of your rock creatures. She would scold me and pour her vile onion broth down my throat."

Yes, his grandmother's hut was beside the river near the shallow bend with the best rocks. Granny Ula grew onions in her garden and brewed a tonic from them every autumn, convinced it would ward off colds. Conyn stayed there in the summer months to help her with the sheep. . . .

Alanna shook her head to dispel the unexpected image. Not counting the thin explanations for the time travel and the language thing, he truly was a phenomenal actor. He must be, since he was even getting her to share his fantasy. She handed back the fossil. "Very clever, but this doesn't prove anything."

Shrugging his massive shoulders, he tucked the stone back into his pouch. "I am a warrior, not a philosopher. I could never match wits with you, Alanna. Your mind is as swift as the fox and as nimble as the swallow. During all my travels I never met man or woman who could be your equal."

She swallowed a sigh. Too bad this was only an act—a woman could get accustomed to hearing compliments like that. A barbarian who was proud of her "thirst for knowledge" and believed in the intellectual equality of females? This was some fantasy he was weaving.

"I did not intend to be gone so long, my love," he continued, his voice growing deeper. "When I arrived in the village to find you gone, I thought my life had ended. How could I exist without my Alanna? For ten years, the thought of returning to your arms gave me the strength I needed to survive every battle. The memory of the taste of your lips sustained me through the winters when many others perished. The hope of holding you at my side when I slept gave me the will to arise each morning.''

She swallowed again, although this time it was because of the sudden lump that had come to her throat. He sounded so sincere, it must be more than an act. Had he lost someone he had loved? Was he drawing on his own remembered pain in order to play this role?

He looked at her in silence for a moment, his gaze stark. Then he reached across the space between them and tenderly stroked her cheek. ''I wager you will remember me if I kiss you.''

Oh, yes. Any woman who had been kissed by this man would remember the experience, she thought, her gaze dropping to his lips. Kissing Conyn might even make a woman start believing in other fantasies, like love and romance and happily ever after.

Only, she didn't believe. Any of it.

Once, long ago, she had. With each new set of foster parents she'd been transferred to, she'd hoped to find love that would ease her loneliness. While the succession of temporary homes had provided her with the necessities of life, from the time she'd been old enough to understand what ''foundling'' meant, she'd longed for a place to belong. Not just a physical home, but an emotional one.

That was probably why she'd been haunted by a feeling of incompleteness when she'd become an adult. But she'd learned to cope. She knew nothing of her own history before the moment she'd been found abandoned on the steps of Trinity Church, so she channeled her desire to know about the past into her work with antiquities at the museum. She had reasoned that since she would never know the security of a real family, she would compensate by marrying Reginald and becoming part of his.

Right. Reginald. Her fiancé. She'd thought it all through, she reminded herself. Marrying Reginald was the sensible, logical thing to do. She didn't believe in love. Her childhood had taught her that yearning for what she couldn't have invariably led to pain and disappointment.

So she had no business whatsoever yearning for the feel of Conyn's lips on hers.

But oh, his face looked so handsome in the candlelight, with his eyes sparkling and the taut skin over his cheekbones gleaming and his mouth curved with a smile that hinted at sensual pleasures the likes of which she'd only known in her most secret dreams. . . .

Abruptly she pulled back her head, breaking the contact with his hand. "I've kept you here long enough. You can take one of the candles and find your way out."

"I will not leave without you, Alanna."

The words had the ring of a vow, and that should have worried her. Dammit, this whole situation should have sent her screaming for help by now. But for some crazy reason, the determination in his voice caused a twinge of . . . satisfaction.

He wouldn't leave her.

But he'd abandoned her before, when he'd gone to seek his fortune as a mercenary. Just as she had been abandoned on the doorstep of that church—

Whoa. This story of his was really messing with her head. She rubbed the gold that warmed her wrist. It seemed to be an evening for craziness, and it had all started when she'd slipped on this bracelet. "Conyn, I think this has gone far enough. It's not that I don't appreciate the entertainment, it's just that it's time for you—"

Her words were cut off on a startled cry when the lights suddenly came on. After the semidarkness, the fluorescent bulbs in the ceiling fixture seemed painfully bright. She squinted and shaded her eyes just in time to see Conyn leap off his chair. Metal whispered over metal as in one smooth movement, he slid his sword from its sheath.

"Do not fear, my love," he said. Before she could utter a protest, he slipped his free arm around her waist and lifted her from her chair. Holding her back to his chest, he raised his sword and pivoted so that his body shielded her from the humming overhead light.

"Conyn, what—"

"Whatever manner of sorcery this is, I will not let it harm you, Alanna."

"Conyn!" She grabbed the arm he had clamped around her waist, trying to loosen his grip, but his muscles were like steel. She kicked her feet, which dangled several inches off the floor, but only managed to tangle her legs in the folds of his cloak. "Put me down!"

He was taller than he'd appeared in the candlelight. With his sword arm extended, the tip of his weapon could easily reach the light fixture.

And for a theatrical prop, that sword looked disconcertingly real. The iron blade was broad and heavy, the edges honed to what had to be a razor's sharpness and tapering to a deadly point. A design of finely etched intertwining curves ran from the center of the blade to the T-shaped hilt that fit Conyn's large hand as if it had been custom-made for him.

No, it had been forged in the village for his father, Alanna thought. Conyn had inherited it when he'd still been a boy and had scarcely had the strength to lift it that day his uncle had brought it home for him. Arms trembling, he'd rested it on his shoulder as he'd bravely blinked back the tears of loss and had vowed to become a warrior as great as the father he'd so admired. . . .

Alanna's breath hissed through her teeth as she increased her efforts to break free of Conyn's hold. Must be lack of oxygen to the brain that was making her imagination act up like this. "All right," she gasped. "The joke's over. Put down that sword before you electrocute both of us."

Muscles ridged like coiled rope down his arm from the effort of holding the iron weapon aloft, but the tip of the sword never wavered. One step at a time, he worked his way around the light until they were at the doorway. He lowered his head so that his lips brushed her ear. "The instant I release you," he whispered, "seek shelter in the far chamber. I will defend you with my life."

"But—"

"Go, my love." He set her feet on the floor and spun away. "Now!"

In disbelief, she saw him step back to the center of the room and raise his sword over his head, as if he meant to slice the bank of fluorescent lightbulbs in half.

Flinging out her arm, she hit the light switch.

"Stand and fight, you demon!" he challenged into the darkness.

"Conyn—"

"Alanna, you must hide yourself. It could return."

"What? You mean the light?" she asked, flipping the switch back on.

He kept his sword pointed at the bulbs, moving his head only enough to glance at her over his shoulder. His eyes narrowed in a wary frown.

Alanna turned the light on and off a few more times. Conyn's gaze darted between her hand and the glowing, humming bulbs, and gradually his frown turned to an expression of bewilderment. Backing toward her, he reached out to flick the light switch himself. "By the stars," he murmured. "What marvel is this?"

"A pair of hundred-watt lightbulbs."

"Where is the flame? How do you light the lamp's wick from this distance? And why is it so bright?"

She pressed her hand over her stomach and took a few deep breaths. "I've heard of method acting, but you're really into this Celtic warrior gig, aren't you?"

"I *am* a warrior."

She stared at him, torn between laughter and awe. His reaction to the power being restored was completely in keeping with the character he was portraying. "Well, you can put down your sword. The light won't hurt anyone. It's just one of our modern conveniences called electricity."

Conyn flipped the switch half a dozen more times, then slowly lowered his sword, his eyes round with wonder. "Much has changed in the world."

"Oh, yeah. Electricity, internal combustion engines, space shuttles, computers, pollution. We've come a long way in twenty-three centuries."

He looked at the light again, then at his sword. And gradually, a dull flush crept into his cheeks. "You must think me a fool."

"No, you acted very convincingly when you, uh, grabbed me," she said.

One corner of his mouth lifted in a lopsided smile. "I might regret behaving like a fool before you, but I cannot regret finally having you in my arms, however it came about."

If she was honest, she'd have to admit that the sensation of being held so securely against his taut, muscular body was far from unpleasant—tingles of awareness were awakening in the places where he'd touched her. Just as her passion had awakened the first time she had gone to him and they had lain together in the meadow with the wildflowers dancing in the sunshine and Conyn's embrace so warm and tight around her. . . .

Alanna clenched her hands, pushing the image away and concentrating on what was real.

Yet reality was no less disturbing than her imagination. In the unforgiving harshness of the fluorescent light, Conyn looked more impressive than ever, from his broad shoulders to his six-pack abs to his perfectly shaped leather-clad legs. She focused more carefully. His muscles were too lean and rangy to be the product of some narcissistic health club. No, he'd come by that build the honest, old-fashioned way, through years of hard work.

What had he done before he'd become an actor? And why would someone who was such an exceptional actor be working as a stripper? Maybe she was wrong about the stripper part. So far he hadn't made a move to take off any of his clothes. But she had to admit, she wasn't sure she would protest all that much if he did.

She bit her lip, her gaze going to a jagged white slash that snaked down his sword arm. More scars crisscrossed his chest, some of them recent enough to bear the pink of healing skin. Stage makeup? Would an actor go to that much trouble to appear like a genuine warrior?

Without pausing to think, she lifted her hand and touched her fingertips to a long, thin scar that curved down the side of his neck.

This was no stage makeup. It was real. If he was an actor, wouldn't he have sought plastic surgery to eliminate this?

But if he wasn't an actor, then what was he?

"Time has brought changes to my appearance," he said. "I apologize if it no longer pleases you."

"What? Oh, no," she said, snatching her hand back. "There's nothing wrong with your appearance." And that had to be the understatement of the millennium.

"Do not move away, my love. Your touch is dew to parched earth. A taste of bliss, leaving me longing for more." He placed his hands on her hips, drawing her nearer. "Perhaps if you touch me again the veil will lift from your mind."

It wasn't her mind that concerned her right now; it

was her body. His hold on her hips was light, more of a caress than a grasp, but for the life of her, she couldn't move away now any more than she could have freed herself before.

His fingers curled, tracing the shape of her buttocks through the folds of her cotton dress. "Ah, my love," he murmured. "If your touch is the dew, then your scent is the very air I breathe." His nostrils flared as he inhaled slowly. "No perfumed oil of the East could compare to my sweet Alanna."

"Uh, Conyn . . ."

"Many was the night when cold stone was my pillow that I warmed myself with the memory of your scent. You are like the flowers in the meadow and the forest after a rain." He dipped his head, rubbing his cheek against her hair. A low, masculine sound of pleasure rumbled from his throat.

She brought her hands between their bodies, intending to push him away. But then she touched the bare skin of his chest and instead of drawing back, she swayed closer.

Oh, but his chest was magnificent, scars and all. She splayed her fingers, absorbing the smooth warmth of his skin, feeling the teasing softness of his whorls of dark hair. Beneath her palm she felt the steady rhythm of his heart, and her own heart skipped a beat.

"Do you feel my blood pound for you, Alanna?" He nuzzled aside her hair to brush a kiss over her ear. " 'Tis like the time when the autumn snow caught us far from shelter and we thought to warm each other. Remember how our hearts near burst with love?"

She slipped her fingers under the edge of his cloak. The scent of pine and sunshine rose from the homespun fabric and she closed her eyes, helpless to stop the image it evoked.

There were two young lovers, huddled together in a shallow cave while they watched a blanket of white muffle the world outside. He took the cloak from his shoulders and spread it over the bough-strewn floor, then smiled and took her hand to draw her down with him. The pine needles rustled under their weight, tiny twigs crackling when Conyn moved, but he laughed at the sounds and pulled the cloak around them both. His laughter became a yelp of surprise when Alanna placed her icy hands on his back. He cupped her cold fingers with his and breathed on them until they warmed, then grinned and placed them beneath the waistband of his breeches. And then neither of them felt the cold. . . .

Her eyes flew open. She gulped in a few short, rapid breaths. No cave. No lovers. She was in her office.

But the image had seemed so real, she could almost remember the sleek skin and crisp curls under Conyn's tight leather breeches. . . .

With a choked cry, she jumped back.

Conyn dropped his hands to his sides. "What is wrong, my love?"

What could she tell him? That she was fantasizing about putting her hands down his pants? Was that *wrong* enough for him? Was she losing her mind? "Hypnosis. That's what you're using, right?"

"I do not understand that word. Is that another one of your modern conveniences?"

She rubbed her eyes. Maybe she should have taken the evening off after all. "Conyn, I think it would be best if you leave now."

"What have I done to displease you?"

"It's not you. I'm just under stress. Yes, that's it. I'm stressed and I'm not thinking very clearly."

"Alanna . . . ," he began, moving toward her.

"I really have a lot of work to do." She backed out of the office to the storeroom, then hurried to the electrical panel on the wall and flipped every one of the switches until the room blazed with light. "And I have to check the damage that was done when you knocked that crate ... over ..." She stared, her words trailing off.

The last remaining crate of Celtic artifacts was still in the center of the worktable where she had left it. It was completely undamaged. Except it was missing its lid.

Her gaze went to the floor. There were pieces of wood everywhere, ranging from splinters to a few large chunks. On the largest, there was still a remnant of the pink shipping label she'd signed that morning.

Evidently, those pieces of wood were all that was left of the lid.

How had Conyn managed to cause that kind of damage to the lid while leaving the rest of the crate intact and in place? Not by knocking it over. Not by prying the lid off, either. No, if she didn't know better, it looked as if the lid had exploded outward, as if something that had been inside the crate had burst out.

She rubbed her eyes again. Stress. Yes. That's all it could be. Nothing had burst from the inside. The crate could have fallen on Conyn and the lid could have cracked and then he could have put the crate back on the table while she'd gone to find the lighter.

Conyn's cloak billowed behind him as he strode across the floor. His hand went to the hilt of his sword and his steps slowed briefly as he glanced at the overhead lights, but then he set his jaw and continued toward her. "Tell me what troubles you."

The gold bracelet felt heavy on her wrist. She grasped it and tried once more to tug it off, but it seemed more solidly fixed than ever. Could the gold have contracted somehow? Or her wrist swelled? "I, uh, really have to get to work."

"Then I will share your task to ease your burden. What is it you must do?"

This was getting really crazy. How could she be carrying on a conversation with a virtual stranger, especially considering his outlandish costume, and her even more outlandish fantasies? She gave up trying to pry loose the bracelet and waved her arm at the table. "I have to inventory those artifacts before I leave. Thanks for the offer of help, but unless you happen to be an antiquities expert—"

"By the stars, you didn't misplace it," Conyn said, reaching into the crate.

She lunged forward to stop him, but she was too late. He had already withdrawn his hand. "Conyn, you'd better let me—"

" 'Tis yours."

"What?"

"As I promised." He offered her the object he held, his face stretching into a pleased grin. "For you, my love."

She took the object from him carefully. It was made of bronze, the handle curving gracefully into a flat circular surface that was about seven inches across and smooth enough to hold a reflection if it was polished. . . .

Her fingers tightened over the handle, the bronze slippery on her palm. She swallowed hard. "It's a mirror."

He nodded, looking immensely pleased with himself. "Your mirror, Alanna."

She stared at him. Back when she'd first seen him, he'd asked if she'd liked the mirror. She hadn't paid much attention then. She'd assumed it was more of his actor patter. How had he known about this, and how had he known about the design on the bracelet? Coincidence? Another lucky guess?

Her gaze moved back to the twenty-three-centuries-old artifact that she held. And for an instant, she caught the flash of a familiar face in the metal surface. A woman, with green eyes and a pointed chin and raven-black hair that fell to her knees.

A bubble of something that could have been hysteria rose in Alanna's throat. Of course she recognized that face. It was her own. Who else's face did she expect to see when she looked in a mirror? As for the hair, well, the edges of the metal were tarnished, so it only appeared as if her hair were long.

"And look, Alanna. Here is the dagger given to me by the Spartan general after we defeated Epaminondas."

Biting her lip, she looked back at Conyn. He was continuing to delve into the crate, pulling objects from their wrappings and setting them on the long table. He handled the millennia-old artifacts as casually as if they were ordinary items, as if he saw this kind of treasure every day.

"Now, how did these old halter studs get in here?" he muttered, tossing a pair of metal disks aside.

Alanna came out of her stupor and fumbled to catch them an instant before they would have hit the floor. "Conyn!"

He straightened up, a happy smile still dimpling his cheeks. "Yes, my love?"

Moving very, very carefully, she put the metal disks and the mirror down on an empty spot on the table. Then she tucked her hair—her short hair—behind her ears, straightened her shoulders, crossed her arms, and lifted her chin. "All right," she said. "Who *are* you? Really."

3

Well, ask a stupid question . . .

Who was he? He was Conyn ap Rhys, of course. He insisted that was his name, although evidently he didn't carry any ID along with the loose change and trilobite fossil he kept in that leather pouch that hung from his belt. And there was no sign of the outline of a wallet in those tight pants of his. And it seemed that he had left home without even his American Express card.

The real question wasn't who he was but *what* he was. Alanna was pretty certain now that he wasn't an actor or an exotic dancer, although with his phenomenal looks and his flair for drama, he could probably make a good living as either one. No, despite his physique, he had to be some kind of scholar who had extensive training in archeology. His expertise in the area of Celtic artifacts was genuine and quite possibly surpassed her own.

Yet for some reason known only to him, he was determined to stick to his insane story about a time-traveling groom.

Sighing, Alanna set her clipboard down on the worktable and propped her chin on her hand. Was he insane? She didn't want to think so. She clearly remembered the crash and the sound of his moans when the lights had gone out, so his confusion was probably the result of a knock on the head, that's all.

She moved her gaze to the other end of the table where Conyn was inspecting a stone figurine. He'd followed through on his offer to help her with her work. Between the two of them, they had unpacked the crate and sorted through the contents in no time. As a matter of fact, the kind of ease he'd displayed with those objects could only have come from years of experience, perhaps in a position similar to hers at some other museum. . . .

"Aha!" she said, struck by a sudden thought. "You work at the Bern Museum, right? *That's* how you know so many details about these particular artifacts. You're really their antiquities expert."

Conyn set the figurine down and walked over to where she was sitting. "Why are you so determined to believe I am something other than what you see?"

Was she imagining the trace of hurt in his tone? "No offense, Conyn, but—"

"I know you did not approve when I chose to follow a warrior's path like my father, yet it was my destiny to do so, Alanna," he said, kneeling by her chair to bring his face level with hers. He took her hands and folded them within his. "Just as it was our destiny to find each other through time. Once more, I apologize for being gone from you for so long, my love. But do not fear I will hire my sword to anyone again. My days of war are over. I wish only for peace and a long life with you as my bride."

She really should yank her hands away—she was getting far too accustomed to feeling his touch. "Did the museum send you here to supervise the unpacking? Or was it your idea?"

"I came through the standing stones."

"You would have read the shipping invoice, so that's how you would know my name," she continued. The more she thought about it, the more sense this explanation made. "That's why in your confusion you'd think these things were for me."

"I chose these gifts for my bride. And your name has been echoing in my soul from the day we met, my love."

"I knew ap Rhys sounded familiar. I probably read it on one of the forms."

He inhaled slowly, as if striving for patience. "I will be whatever you want me to be, Alanna. A farmer, a carpenter, a smith, it matters not, as long as it does not take me from your side again. If it would make you happy for me to be this expert of antiquities," he said, pronouncing the word carefully, as if it were unfamiliar to him, "then that is what I will be."

She tried to withdraw her hand, but he didn't release it. Yet she still felt no reason to be alarmed, especially now that she was finally starting to figure things out.

Of course, he must be connected with the museum in Switzerland. That would explain his accent. And he might have come by those scars in a . . . a mountain-climbing accident or something. As for his outfit, well, wasn't she still wearing the bracelet that had been part of the exhibit? Wasn't it possible that Conyn was a tad eccentric and had done something similar, only on a larger scale?

All right, so her explanations still had a few holes in them, but at least they were more plausible than his. He was going to be terribly embarrassed when his concussion-induced delusion finally wore off. She wasn't sure whether she should continue to confront him—perhaps the kindest course of action would be to humor him until he came to his senses. "Well, Conyn, I think we're making progress."

"Good." He straightened up smoothly, drawing her to her feet. "Is your work here completed now?"

She glanced at her clipboard. With a start of surprise,

she realized it was. "Yes. Thank you for your help."

"It was my pleasure, Alanna. And now that you have finished your task, let us leave this place."

Leave with him? Well, why not? Maybe fresh air would do him good. Actually, it might do them both good, considering those strange images her oxygen-starved brain had been producing. And maybe once she got him away from the isolation of this museum basement and insisted on behaving normally, his delusion would fade. It was the least she could do for a colleague and a fellow history buff.

"All right," she said, walking back to her office to retrieve her purse. She flipped off all but one of the light switches and returned to where Conyn was standing. "I haven't had dinner yet, so we could stop at a restaurant." She hesitated, glancing at his costume. "Or we could get takeout. I'm sure you'll feel better if you eat something."

"Then we are near a village?"

"I'd say two and a half million people more than qualifies as a village."

"Million . . ." He shook his head. "It matters not as long as we can find a priest."

"A . . . priest? Why?"

"To perform the wedding," he said. And with that, he bent over, swept her into his arms, and started for the door.

Had she thought they were making progress? "Conyn, what are you doing? For heaven's sake, put me down."

"Why? Does my sword cause you discomfort?"

"No, but you can't keep grabbing me and carrying me around like this. It's just not done in my world."

He halted when he reached the storeroom doorway and very demonstratively peered up and down the corridor. "I wish to protect you from the evil demon in those lamps."

"The what? Conyn, you're not going to start trying to fight the lights again, are you?"

"Fear not, Alanna. Whether I am a warrior or this antiquities expert you want me to be, I will let no harm come to you."

"But—"

"Hold tight to me, my love," he murmured, settling her more securely against his chest. "And give me a kiss for strength."

She braced her hands on his shoulders and tipped back her head to see his face. Although his muscles were tensed as if he as prepared to do battle, and his jaw was set and his eyebrows lowered fiercely, the effect was spoiled by the twinkle in his eyes.

And Alanna suddenly realized that he was joking. "You're not serious, are you," she stated.

In reply, he lifted one shoulder. An adorable, lopsided smile was twitching around the corners of his mouth.

"Conyn . . ."

"Ignorance of your ways served me well for an excuse to hold you before."

"Conyn . . ."

"Who knows what perils of your modern world await us beyond that doorway. Would you have me face them without the taste of you on my lips?"

She felt her own mouth curve in response to his teasing. It was hard to resist a man who could laugh at himself.

"Just one kiss," he coaxed, his smile spreading to his dimples.

Oh, she was tempted. More than tempted. But when he started to lower his head, she retained enough sanity to press her fingertips to his lips. "Nice try, Conyn, but I think you can manage to get from here to the subway without encountering any demons."

"Subway?" he mumbled, catching her index finger gently between his teeth.

The sensation of his teeth on her skin sent a shudder through her body. Reflexively, she curled her other hand around his neck. "It's a public transit system."

He flicked her captive fingertip with his tongue.

"You, uh, board this underground train and it takes you . . ." She drew in an unsteady breath. "Mmm."

Closing his lips around her finger, he sucked on it hard.

"Mmm," she repeated. That's all she seemed to be able to say. What was the matter with her? She had a bachelor's degree in history, a master's degree in medieval architecture, and a doctorate in anthropology, and yet her brain couldn't come up with anything better than a throaty mumble.

He shifted her higher in his arms, and her dress slid upward, baring her knees. He released her finger to turn his head. "These garments you wear, are they more of your modern wonders?"

"Uh . . ."

"The weave of the cloth is so fine, it slides over your skin like thistledown." He moved the arm that supported her legs so that he could slip his hand under the hem of her skirt. His fingertips rubbed warmly over her thigh. "Your tunic is the color of new ferns, yet it cannot compare to the springtime beauty of your eyes, my love."

Oh, he must be quite the man when his mind was clear if he was this romantic when he was deluded. "Um . . ."

"We can find the priest tomorrow," he murmured. He lowered her feet, letting her slide down the length of his body as he backed her against the corridor wall. With his hand still under her skirt, he braced his legs and cupped her bottom, fitting her boldly against him. "I will try to be gentle in my wooing, but it has been so long since we loved."

Shock—it had to be shock—at their intimate position knocked the air from her lungs. She gripped his shoulders, her fingers digging into the rough wool of his cloak.

And she thought about how much softer the mantle of fox pelts had felt under her fingers when Conyn had laid her down on the floor of his hunting tent. The fur had tickled and teased her, turning her skin so sensitive that the merest whisper of his breath had made her quiver. The heavy warmth of Conyn's body on top of her, the luxurious fur sliding beneath her, the crackle of the wood fire, the distant calling of the owl . . .

"My love," he murmured. "Ah, how I've missed you."

She tried to blink the fantasy from her mind, but it persisted. The embers in the fire pit glowed, casting dancing shadows over Conyn's bronzed skin. Alanna tossed her head, moaning her pleasure as he picked up a scrap of fur and used it to stroke her from her forehead to her toes. Trembling, she wriggled out from beneath him and reversed their positions, straddling his legs as she took up the fur herself and returned the torment, building their need to a fever pitch . . .

"Hey, Miss Moore! Everything okay down there?"

At the sound of the voice, reality snapped back into place in a sobering rush. Alanna gulped in a deep breath. Her pulse was racing, her body throbbing, and a bead of perspiration trickled down the side of her temple.

God God, what had come over her?

Conyn stepped away from her and spun around, his sword already in his hand.

"No, Conyn," Alanna gasped, making a grab for his arm. "Put the weapon away."

Footsteps shuffled slowly from the direction of the stairwell. "Miss Moore?"

"It's only Gilbert," she whispered. She pushed her hair off her forehead and gulped again. "He's the museum's security guard."

"He guards this place?" Conyn asked, lowering his sword.

"Yes. Please, put that thing away or you'll give him a heart attack."

"Miss Moore?"

"Everything's fine, Gilbert," she called, giving Conyn's arm a jerk.

"It's getting pretty late. The ball game's already over." A short, white-haired man moved into view at the corner of the corridor. "Hey, I didn't know you had someone down here with you."

"This is your guard?" Conyn muttered disdainfully, resheathing his sword. "He does not look fit to guard a crop from the crows."

Gilbert paused, squinting toward them. "Hey, are they shootin' a movie here again?"

"Something like that," Alanna said. "Has the rain stopped yet?"

"Rain? What rain?"

"There was a storm earlier. It knocked out the power and the phones."

"I never noticed nothin.' "

He had probably been asleep, she told herself, tucking her hand into the crook of Conyn's elbow and tugging him forward. She endeavored to smile normally as she said good night to Gilbert and headed for the stairs. But then the side of her breast brushed Conyn's arm, and a quiver as gentle as the teasing brush of fox fur snuck over her skin.

Had she thought she was in need of fresh air? What she really needed was a long, very cold shower.

Naturally, she knew he would stop traffic.

Yet although people stared, no one dared to approach them on the short walk—on an oddly dry, puddle-free sidewalk—from the museum to the subway. Alanna suspected many people assumed the same thing Gilbert had, that Conyn was involved with some movie shoot. And compared to the other colorful downtown characters with their spiked green hair or pierced body parts, Conyn's appearance wasn't all that wild.

Still, it wasn't only his outfit that attracted attention. With his looks and his bearing, he would cause a stir in a three-piece suit. He walked with the relaxed, easy stride of a predator, his entire body moving in well-honed harmony. His blue eyes were alert with interest and glowing with intelligence as he took in his surroundings. Overall, he projected the innate confidence of a man who was completely secure about his masculinity, and that confidence would be recognized in any culture . . . or any era.

Contrary to what Alanna had hoped, his delusion showed no signs of fading. Yet somehow she found the way he approached each new modern "wonder" very . . . endearing. The glass windows of the subway car fascinated him, as did the plastic seats and the tile floors. His wariness when the train began to move changed to sheer delight as the car picked up speed. And when they finally emerged from the tunnel and boarded a streetcar, he pressed his face to the window and demanded to know the names of each type of vehicle that passed them.

He seemed particularly impressed by the cherry-red Corvette and the black Jeep, but when he spotted the motorcycle, Alanna had to swallow her laughter at his expression of awe. Evidently, antiquities experts who believed they were Celtic warriors were partial to Harleys.

"How about a pizza?" she asked. They had gotten off the streetcar a few blocks from her apartment. She was trying to steer him toward a nearby restaurant but he'd spotted a television set in the window of an electronics store and wasn't budging.

"Pizza?" he asked, tilting his head to one side to

watch the soaring plane on an airline commercial.

"Or if you'd rather have chicken, there's a place on the next block. What would you like?"

"How does the metal bird fly within that box, Alanna?"

"That's just a picture, Conyn. A television station sends a signal through the air to that box, and it projects what you see on the screen."

He glanced at her sideways. "You jest."

"And that thing flying is another passenger vehicle."

He returned his gaze to the screen, his mouth moving into a wide smile. "It is truly a world of miracles."

"Most of these things we take for granted."

"I have much to learn here."

"You're doing all right so far."

He shook his head, his smile dimming. "The world has changed so much, there would be no need for the skills of a warrior. Or for a farmer or a smith."

"Oh, we still have all those occupations, in one form or another."

"But you wish me to work in a place you call a museum," he said, turning to face her. "So that is what I will do."

Had she ever met a man who was so open with his emotions? she wondered. He smiled readily, but he made no attempt to hide his other feelings from her, even when he was embarrassed or puzzled or uncertain, as he seemed now.

That couldn't be a product of his delusion, she thought. His honesty must be part of his basic character. It went along with the confidence he projected, the underlying strength that she had felt from the start. He wasn't afraid to admit his ignorance. He didn't seem to feel the least bit threatened by her knowledge. He respected her intelligence, even when he was trying to coax her into giving him a kiss.

And, Alanna realized, she liked him. She felt comfortable with him, as if she'd known him for years instead of only hours.

Then again, the rapport she felt with him probably stemmed from their similar professions and their shared interest in the past. And her unwillingness to leave him alone to fend for himself was simply professional courtesy, right?

But like her explanations for everything else that had happened tonight, she didn't want to delve into that one too deeply, either.

They ended up getting a pepperoni pizza, a bucket of fried chicken, and the number three dinner special from the Dragon Moon Cafe. Grinning like a kid in a candy store, Conyn carried everything into Alanna's apartment and arranged their feast on her living-room coffee table. He tossed the pillows from her easy chair on the floor and sat down cross-legged, waiting until she took the pillow beside him before he started to eat. And for a Swiss scholar, he displayed a healthy appetite, alternating between wolfing his food down like a barbarian and savoring each new morsel, as if he truly hadn't tasted it before.

Throughout their meal, he continued to ask her about her world, but Alanna soon found herself out of her depth as his questions grew more and more technical. So she decided to change the subject.

"Conyn, tell me about your home."

He swallowed the last piece of fried chicken and was about to wipe his hands on his pants when he stopped himself and picked up one of the paper napkins she had used. He studied the paper as he cleaned his fingers. "How is this woven? These fibers are so fine, why do they not break?"

"I'm going to have to get you an encyclopedia."

"Is that another device for cleansing?"

"No," she said, smiling as she remembered his enthusiasm at his first sight of her bathroom. "It's a record of information. But it's my turn to ask the questions. Where are you from?"

He sighed and pushed the coffee table away, then unfastened the twin brooches at the neck of his cloak and let the garment fall to the floor behind him. "You still do not remember?"

She tried to keep her gaze on his face. Apart from the gold neck torque, he was naked from the waist up. Yet he seemed perfectly at ease. And unlike most good-looking men, he seemed completely oblivious to the effect of his appearance. She probably should have offered to take his cloak before this, but what was the usual etiquette when entertaining a scholar-barbarian? "Is it in Bern? Somewhere nearby?"

"Our village is beside the lake where the river flows from the mountains, Alanna."

The river. The same one where she hunted fossils near Granny Ula's hut. . . .

She drew her knees to her chest, tucking her skirt around her ankles. Mountains. Sounded like Switzerland. "What's your place like?" she asked, hoping to trigger a more specific memory. "Is it an apartment? A house?"

"I have no place there now," he said quietly. "My grandmother's home was swept away in the spring flood the year after I left. My uncle's cabin was burned the next winter when he and his family died of the spotted fever. I have no family left there, either."

"I'm sorry, Conyn."

"I knew I would be gone many years when I chose the path of a warrior."

"You mentioned that your father was in the military?"

"Yes. I vowed when I first picked up his sword that I would someday follow him. It was because of you that I delayed as long as I did." He stretched out his legs and leaned back on his elbows, turning his head to look up at her. "And it was because of you that I finally chose to go."

"Me? Why?"

"It was the only way to gain the wealth I needed."

"Needed?"

"To make you my wife. Your parents would not agree to a match with a poor man."

"My parents," she said. "Conyn, I never knew my parents."

He shook his head. "Your family was the most powerful in our village. They called you a princess and would not permit anyone with callused hands or earth beneath his nails to aspire to touch you. To them, their position of power was all that mattered. They did not believe in love."

Neither did she, Alanna thought. It was just a myth. It led to nothing but heartache.

"I loved you from the first moment I saw you, Alanna," he went on. "Yet I was content to be your friend until your body had blossomed with the curves of womanhood and you stole out to the meadow to meet me."

Meadow? Hadn't she remembered something about lying with him in a meadow in the sunshine?

No, not remembered. Fantasized.

"Oh, how we loved," he murmured, reaching out to stroke her leg. "It mattered not where we made our bed, our passion put the stars that burned in the night sky to shame."

Fox fur. Pine boughs in a cave. Sunshine in a meadow of wildflowers. . . .

She cleared her throat. She should really think about fixing some coffee to clear her head.

"But stolen moments were not enough for me, Alanna. I wanted to love you in the light of day, to declare to the world that we belonged together. I wanted to have you by my hearth each night and see you nurse our babe and someday watch you hold our grandchild on your knees.''

His words touched a chord inside her. She understood the need for security, the desire to belong, to have a family. Conyn spoke with such feeling, she knew he must have wanted exactly the same things that she used to long for.

"We were destined for each other, Alanna," he said. "Because your parents demanded wealth, then I would give them wealth. For ten years I earned my way with my sword and my wits so that I could gather the gifts that would give me the right to claim you as my bride." He moved his hand to her wrist. "Many was the time my courage faltered, but thoughts of our future led me through each hardship. And each treasure brought me one step closer to you."

She sighed, knowing she probably shouldn't encourage him to expand on his delusion, but right now, she couldn't pull herself away from the romantic tale he was weaving.

Suddenly, he sat up to kneel in front of her, twining his fingers with hers. "I vowed to come back to you, Alanna. But when I arrived in our village, you were already gone."

"What?"

"I tried to be in time, I swear it."

"But—"

"My horse went lame before I reached the pass through the mountains, but I took up my packs and walked three days without rest to reach you."

"What happened?"

He bowed his head. A lock of auburn hair that had pulled loose from his queue brushed across her hand. "Your father had lied. He never meant to give you to me. He had promised you to the son of a noble in the next village."

"And I . . . married him?" she asked, caught up in the story.

"Nay, Alanna," he said. "Your love for me was too strong. You waited for my return for ten long years, refusing to wed another. When your father learned I was one day's travel from the valley, he knew his plans would come to naught unless he sent you away."

"And that's why I was gone when you got home?"

His grip on her fingers tightened. "Nay. You would not agree to leave, so your father told you I was dead."

"No," she breathed.

"They said you would not believe him and ran into the night to find me."

She waited for him to finish, but he remained silent. "And then?"

He met her gaze, his eyes shining with moisture. "Oh, my love. It matters not now that I have found you again."

"Conyn, tell me."

His jaw flexed. He paused to swallow before he could go on. "The same storm that delayed my journey through the mountain pass made the river overflow its banks. You tried to cross it to reach the mountains when the old wooden bridge gave way beneath your feet."

A cold draft swirled across the floor. She shivered. "What do you mean?"

"By the time I reached you and pulled you from the water, you were already gone."

"Gone?" she repeated. "You mean . . . drowned? *Dead?*"

He nodded. A tear brimmed over his lower lid and traced a jagged path down his cheek. "I wanted to die myself. There was no reason to keep living without my Alanna."

The torment in his voice made her own eyes sting. The love he described was the stuff of legend. Of classic literature and timeless tragedies. "Oh, Conyn."

"The wealth I had gathered for a decade meant nothing. I was preparing to cast it all into the river when the old woman came to me with her bargain."

"Old woman?"

"The one who lives by the willow grove and practices the rituals of the ancients. She said she would reunite me with my Alanna in exchange for all my treasures."

She lifted her hand to his face, touching her fingertips to the tracks of his tears. Raw emotion shone from his eyes. There was no doubt whatsoever in Alanna's mind that Conyn's heartache was real. He had lost someone he loved. Love might only be a myth for some people, but not for him. His belief was so deep and unshakable, it was pushing aside barriers and surging past defenses that she'd spent her entire life building.

But love meant pain and disappointment. He should know that. Just as she did.

"I have indeed travelled far to claim my bride," he said, echoing the words he had said when he'd first seen her. He pressed a fervent kiss to her palm. "It was well worth the price."

Alanna's breath hitched on a sob. How could anyone just sit here and listen to this story without being moved? It was the most beautiful tale of true love she'd ever heard. So what else could she do? She pulled Conyn into her arms.

4

At first he didn't move, his body trembling with the same emotion that still shone in his eyes. Alanna shifted closer, smiling tentatively in an offer of comfort.

Conyn's shoulders heaved on an unsteady breath. Then he wrapped his arms around her and crushed her to his chest so tightly her head spun.

"My love," he murmured, his voice hoarse. He dipped his head, pressing his face to the crook of her neck. "My Alanna."

She slid her hands up his back, her fingers splaying over his bare skin. "I'm sorry, Conyn. So sorry."

"I have no regrets now that you are in my embrace once more."

"You must have loved her so much."

He rubbed his cheek against hers, spreading the last of his tears on her skin. "You," he said. "I love you."

She should stop him now. She should set him straight once and for all. But hearing those three words did something strange to her sensible, logical heart.

No one had ever said that they loved her. Oh, they had complimented her on her dependability, or they had appreciated her usefulness, or they had admired her knowledge, but no one had ever simply loved *her*.

So maybe she would hold him, and let him hold her, for just a little longer. What could be the harm in that?

Conyn dragged his lips along the edge of her jaw, his breath hot and rapid. "I love you, Alanna," he whispered. "I always have. I always will."

The feel of his lips on her skin scattered her thoughts. How could any living, breathing woman resist this man? she wondered, her head falling back as he kissed his way downward, his tongue moistening the hollow at the base of her throat.

He opened his mouth over her collarbone, his teeth grazing the delicate skin in desperate passion as he grasped the neckline of her dress and yanked it aside to bare her shoulder. "To taste you again," he said. "To draw your sweet scent into my lungs. How I have longed for this."

She shuddered, her hands going to the strip of leather that held back his hair. She pulled the knot free and tossed the leather aside, then closed her eyes and sighed with pleasure as his long, silky locks slid over her fingers. "Mmm."

She had always loved the feel of his hair. Even as a young man his body had been hard with muscle, but the sensuous softness of his hair had been an unexpected delight. She was glad he hadn't bleached it like so many other warriors. The dark auburn color reminded her of the autumn, when the nights grew longer and the fires grew brighter and Conyn wrapped her in furs after they loved. . . .

No, wait. That was only part of his story, right?

With one arm around the small of her back, Conyn guided her down to the floor. He rolled on top of her, his hand closing over her breast.

Alanna's eyes flew open. "Conyn."

"Let me taste you, love," he murmured. "I want to feel the way you swell and ripen on my tongue."

Her heart thumped with a sudden, mindless surge of desire. "Uh . . ."

He kissed his way to the edge of her neckline, then gave a quick, teasing lick beneath. He tugged at her dress again, but the fabric had stretched as far as it would go. Making a low sound of frustration, he lowered his head and closed his lips over the layers of fabric that covered her nipple.

"Ahh . . ." Alanna arched upward, her nails digging into his shoulders. "Conyn."

With a decisive tug, he drew the nipple into his mouth.

Her vision blurred with another image. And somehow she was looking down, watching the way Conyn's dark hair slid across the pale skin of her naked breast. He turned his head to look up at her, a dimple flashing at the corner of his mouth, but he wouldn't release his hold. It was late, and she had to start home soon, but Conyn had promised to show her the stars. He swirled his tongue in a lazy circle as he slipped his hand between her thighs. And the stars burst across the meadow just as he had promised. . . .

Alanna blinked. It was starting again. The memories. What was happening?

Conyn grasped the hem of her dress and pushed it upward. Warm, supple leather glided over her skin as he slipped his leg between her thighs. "I ache for you, Alanna," he said. "I burn."

The passion in his voice sent a shiver of response all the way to her toes. "Conyn . . ."

"Join with me now, and the years we have been apart will be but a memory."

She struggled to think. No, it wasn't a memory. It was a fantasy. A delusion.

"We were meant to be together. Always."

The feel of his fingers at the apex of her legs jolted through her like lightening. This was no fantasy. This was as real as it got. Gritting her teeth, she pushed at his shoulders. "Conyn, wait!"

He braced his arms on either side of her and lifted his head. His eyes were dark with hunger, his nostrils flared. His hair was wild and loose, brushing over the stiffened tendons of his neck where his pulse throbbed hard against the ancient gold torque.

And he looked exactly like a barbarian warrior. A very desirable, very aroused warrior. A man who could snap her bones with a twist of his wrist. A man she had known only a few hours. A man whose tears were drying on her cheek.

Oh, God. What was she doing? Was this how she gave comfort? "Conyn, I, uh, we . . ."

His mouth thinned. A muscle in his cheek twitched.

"Oh, Conyn, I'm sorry. I never meant . . ."

His eyebrows lowered.

"I only meant to hug you," she finished weakly.

"Alanna."

That's all he said. Just her name. But there was so much pent-up longing in his voice that it brought a lump to her throat.

But it wasn't longing for *her*. "This is wrong," she said.

"Nay, it is destiny."

"We shouldn't . . . we can't . . ." She bit her lip. "It's wrong. You don't really love me. You love some woman from your past and you're confusing me with her."

His frown eased. "Alanna, I am not confused."

"Yes, you are. And it would be completely wrong for me to take advantage of you."

He stared at her, his nostrils quivering as he took a deep breath. "Go ahead. Take advantage of me." A sheen of moisture dampened his forehead. The muscles in his arms shook with restraint. "Please."

"Conyn, I'm sorry for your loss," she said softly. "I really am."

"Then kiss me, Alanna."

Her gaze dropped to his mouth. And she shuddered again as she thought about how he'd used it on her body. "You're going to be so embarrassed when you come to your senses. I can't let this go any further."

"It is you, not I, whose mind is hazy. Kiss me and the fog will clear."

"Conyn, I want to, but it would be wrong."

"Why?"

"Because I don't know you."

He clenched his jaw and tipped back his head, his lower body pressing into hers for one sizzling, breath-stealing moment before he dropped his head on her breasts.

"I'm sorry, Conyn. Really, I am. I'm just not that kind of woman."

A minute went by as he lay without moving, the tension slowly easing from his muscles. Then his shoulders began to tremble.

"Conyn, are you all right?" she asked.

His shoulders shook again. A muffled snort escaped his lips.

"Conyn?"

He rolled to his back, flinging his arm across his eyes. His chest heaved with laughter. "By the stars, Alanna," he gasped. "In twenty-three centuries you have not changed."

She pushed herself up, straightening her dress as best she could. "I can't understand what you find funny about—"

"Indeed." He snorted again. "My uncle always counseled me to marry a stupid woman. But no, I chose to love the one woman in the whole valley who demands to understand how the sun rises in the morning before she will open her eyes."

"What?"

"You will not kiss me until you remember. And you

will not remember until you kiss me. 'Tis enough to send a philosopher to the horse trough to soak his head.''

"Conyn . . .''

"I have waited ten years and traveled twenty-three hundred more,'' he said. "I can wait one more night.''

"But—"

"But tomorrow we wed,'' he stated, his voice firm despite the lingering trace of humor. He sat up, raking his hair back from his face in a quick, impatient movement. "I can see now that I must convince your mind before your body remembers. What will persuade you that I tell you the truth, Alanna?''

She hesitated. "I believe that you did love someone, Conyn. And that you lost her tragically. That probably has a lot to do with this delusion—"

"It was you, Alanna. Your lips I tasted. Your thighs I lay between.'' He ran his fingers through his hair again and narrowed his eyes. "It was your mark in the shape of a crescent moon that I kissed.''

"My . . . my what? How did you . . . I mean, who told you—"

"It is the color of a ripe apple and the width of my thumbnail and it lies there,'' he said, touching his index finger to the side of her left hip.

She jumped. He had pinpointed the exact location of her crescent-shaped dark red birthmark. "How . . . no, you must have seen it when you pushed up my skirt.''

"And here is the place where you fell on your mother's spindle when you were a babe,'' he went on, moving his finger to her right arm.

She looked down. The short sleeve of her dress hid the small white pockmark. Its origin had always puzzled her. She had assumed it had happened when she'd been very young, and the knowledge of what had caused it had been lost when she'd been transferred from one foster home to another. How could he . . .

"Lucky guess,'' she croaked.

"Your skin swells with small red spots when you eat strawberries. You sing when you bathe. You cross your arms and drum your fingers when you are angry and you bite your lip when you are uncertain. And you like to sleep on your stomach with your left knee bent," he added, dropping his hand to her thigh.

Somehow she couldn't seem to catch her breath. Everything he had said was true. But how could an antiquities expert from Bern know all of those personal things?

"You *are* my Alanna," he said, cradling her chin in his hand and turning her to face him. "It is you I love. You."

"But . . ."

"Our love was too strong for fate to keep us apart." He looked at the bracelet that she hadn't been able to get off her wrist. "Even my gifts were destined to find you."

What he said was impossible. It was ridiculous. Insane. There had to be a logical explanation for everything, right? *Right?* Like the way the packing crate had burst open . . . and the way there had been thunder with no storm . . . and the way the lights and the phone had gone out only in the basement and the way this gold bracelet refused to leave her wrist. . . . "This is too much," she said, her voice breaking. "I don't understand it."

"Then do not try," he said, scooping her into his arms. He rose to his feet and walked over to the couch, then sank down on the cushions with her on his lap. "Just feel. What does your heart tell you?"

Her heart? She couldn't listen to that, because it was screaming about love. And she didn't believe in love any more than she believed in time travel or reincarnation or destiny.

But where had she come from? Who were her parents? How had she ended up on the steps of that church?

Why had she always yearned for a place to belong, and why had she been so certain when she grew older that love only brought pain? And then there was the way she had chosen a profession that dealt with the past, and the way she had felt such intense interest in the history of the Celts. Was it because she was . . . remembering?

Or was it because she was so incredibly attracted to this man that she was willing to consider this bizarre theory in order to excuse her behavior?

Conyn's arms were warm and strong around her, his heartbeat steady beneath her ear. "Do not be afraid, my love. We are together now. As we were meant to be."

She turned her face to his chest. "You are an eccentric scholar from Bern," she said unsteadily. "You hit your head when the lights went out. You're a . . . a . . . lucky guesser."

"I am the man who loves you."

If she were a different woman, she would want to believe him, she thought, closing her eyes as she drew in his scent, that mixture of pine and sunshine and an underlying sweet musk that was purely Conyn.

But love *hurt*. She didn't want to love. She had cried for days after he'd left. She had walked the path from her father's house to the bridge each night to watch the trail from the mountains, hoping against hope that Conyn would change his mind and come back to her. . . .

"I love you, Alanna," he whispered, his broad, callused hand achingly gentle as he stroked her hair.

Oh, yes, how she had wanted to believe.

Alanna awoke gradually, rubbing her cheek against the pillow and slowly straightening her left leg. Something tickled the sole of her foot. Yawning widely, she rolled to her back and rubbed her foot against the mattress.

What a dream she'd had last night. It had been so vivid. A Celtic warrior, star-crossed lovers, hearts that were destined to find one another again. . . .

Mmm. It was so romantic. Especially the part when the man had held her and vowed his love.

She sighed, lifting her arms over her head in a luxurious stretch. Nonsense, pure nonsense, but that was why dreams were so fascinating. They bypassed the reasoning process and went straight through the layers of the subconscious to uncover things that the mind otherwise preferred to keep hidden.

It wasn't like her to fantasize about anything, especially heroic warriors and undying love. She was far too rational and sensible. Yet dealing with her aversion to that emotion through her dreams must have been therapeutic. Instead of feeling disturbed by it, she felt . . . good. Different. Her entire body was suffused with a sense of well-being, as if she had slept for much longer than one night, as if on some deep, previously unacknowledged level she were waking up completely for the first time.

She yawned again. Something brushed lightly across the tip of her nose. She turned her head, rubbing her face with her hand. A faint, slightly peppery smell like petunias drifted through the air.

"Alanna."

That voice. It was the one from her dream. She opened one eye warily.

There was a purple petunia just inches from her nose. It looked suspiciously like one of the blooms from the planter on her neighbor's balcony.

The mattress dipped. "You have not changed, my love. I see you still prefer to wait until many hours after the sun crests the horizon before you rise."

She opened the other eye and turned her head.

Conyn was sitting on the bed beside her, one of her lilac-colored towels wrapped loosely around his hips. Rosy sunlight slanted over his damp skin and gleamed on his wet hair. Evidently, he'd figured out how to work the shower.

Alanna's eyes widened. It hadn't been a dream. Not all of it. Conyn. He was real. He was here.

"Oh, my God," she mumbled, clutching the sheet to her chest as she scrambled back against the headboard. She bit her lip, glancing quickly around the room. Her head was so muddled with sleep, she almost expected to see a fire pit and a fur blanket and rough wooden walls, but this was her bedroom. These were her flowered sheets. That was her chest of drawers. There was the green dress she'd been wearing last night. She lifted the sheet to glance underneath, relieved to see that she was still wearing her underwear, for all the modesty that provided. "What happened?" she asked, looking around again. "How did I get here?"

"You fell asleep in my arms," Conyn answered, retrieving the flower. He brushed the petunia across her fingers where she was gripping the sheet. "I carried you here and made you comfortable so that you would rest."

She'd fallen asleep in his arms? Something niggled at her memory, a fragment of a dream just on the edge of her consciousness. She strained to reach for it. It was something significant about love and pain and being left behind, and she knew she would understand if only she could remember. . . .

"What manner of fastening holds that fern-colored tunic together so smoothly?"

The dream fragment slipped out of reach. "What?"

"It was unfamiliar to me, and took much time before I understood the workings."

"A zipper," she said, pulling the sheet to her chin. "It's called a zipper."

"Ah. Another modern wonder. And those small clothes you wear underneath are unfamiliar as well, but I wager I would have no trouble ridding you of them if you wished. The fabric is no more substantial than the morning mist."

She probably should have been uncomfortable having

a strange man undress her while she slept. Actually, if there ever was a time to get really, really worried, it was now. After all, she had known this man for less than twelve hours—or more than twenty-three centuries, depending on which story she believed.

Yet it wasn't panic that made her pulse accelerate. It was pleasure. He hadn't left her. He was still here, just as he'd promised.

He brushed her hair back from her face and tucked the flower behind her ear. "These modern garments are enticing, yet it matters not how you clothe yourself, Alanna. You will always be beautiful in my eyes."

His smile was far too appealing. As a matter of fact, everything about him looked way too good. A drop of water fell from his hair to his shoulder, tracking a sinuous path downward over the rigid contours of his biceps to the jagged white scar that curled over his forearm. That was his sword arm. He would have received that injury in battle. . . .

She strained to jog her brain into gear. No. The scar was from a . . . mountain-climbing accident, or something else perfectly ordinary. This was Conyn ap Rhys, the Swiss scholar and antiquities expert who happened to be suffering from a strange delusion. . . .

No, he was the proud, courageous warrior who had been her best friend and her only lover. . . .

And he'd laughed with delight at the speed of a train and had smiled with wonder at a lightbulb and had wept as he'd told the story of his lost love.

He braced his arms on either side of her and leaned down, his hair swinging forward to frame his face. "Forgive me for waking you so soon, Alanna. After so many years apart, I do not wish to waste a single moment of our time together." He dipped his head and nibbled lightly at her earlobe, then got lithely to his feet. "Do not move," he said, pointing his finger at her in mock sternness. "I have prepared a surprise for you."

He strode out of the bedroom, all rippling muscle and lilac towel. There was some clunking from the direction of the kitchen before he returned a few minutes later. He'd pulled his hair back into its queue and donned his pants, but the rest of him was still gloriously bare. And if the sight of Conyn's chest wasn't enough to make her mouth water, the aromas of the food on the tray he carried would have done it for sure.

There were jars of jam and honey beside a loaf of French bread, a bowl filled with grapes and peeled oranges, a pot of tea, and a foil pan full of brownies. And scattered around the plates, bowls, and mugs, there were at least a dozen more purloined petunias.

Alanna wrapped herself in the sheet and moved over to make room for him on the mattress. "Breakfast in bed," she murmured. "A woman could get used to this, Conyn."

He grinned, placing the tray between them. "The variety of food in your larder is truly wondrous. What do you call this flavor?" he asked, scooping a fingertip of icing off the brownies.

"Chocolate."

His eyes rolled in pleasure as he licked his finger. "Wars have been waged over less."

"Mmm," she said, popping a grape into her mouth.

He poured some tea into a mug and passed it to her. "The flavor of these herbs is strange, too, but pleasing. That device with the fire in the rings, is it more electricity?"

"The stove? Yes."

"I could not find how to get the picture into that box on the wall, although I tried every switch."

It took her a moment to figure it out. "Ah. You mean the microwave. That's not a TV, it's a type of oven."

"I have much to learn," he said, breaking off a chunk of brownie and holding it up to her lips.

She hesitated. She knew she shouldn't be having this

kind of high-calorie treat for breakfast. But Conyn looked so endearingly pleased about offering it to her that she opened her mouth and took a bite anyway.

Then, of course, she had to return the favor by prying off a section of orange and offering it to him. Breakfast turned into a teasing game as they fed bits of food to each other. The appetite that Conyn displayed was as impressive as it had been the previous night, although he took care to ensure that she'd eaten all she wanted before he finished the rest.

He didn't look like a man who was suffering from a head injury, she thought, watching as he moved the tray aside. His gaze was clear and honest and intensely . . . lucid. "I forgot those paper cloths," he said, reaching up to wipe the corner of her mouth with his thumb.

"It doesn't matter. I can't remember when I've enjoyed a meal more."

"I can." He lifted one eyebrow, his dimples deepening. "There was the morning we went to gather honey and we decided to explore how it tasted on each other."

"Oh."

"And once at the harvest feast you spilled ale on your tunic. We wrung out the tunic and I licked the rest from your skin." His lips curved in a lopsided smile. "I did not want to waste good ale."

She laughed.

Shifting closer, he picked up her hand and brought it to his mouth. "I see some juice from the orange remains here," he murmured, kissing her fingers. He straightened her arm, moving his mouth to the inside of her elbow. "And here." He kissed the tiny white pockmark on her upper arm. "And here, too."

She placed her hand on his shoulder, her laughter fading. "Uh, Conyn . . ."

He tugged loose the end of the sheet that she'd tucked under her arms and drew his fingertip along the upper edge of her bra. "One wayward drop has found its way here as well."

The sheet fell to her waist. "Conyn . . ."

"I find I am still hungry, Alanna." He traced his way over the lace to the hooks at the front closure. "But I fear my clumsy warrior's fingers might rend this fabric before I can peel the cover from this luscious fruit."

"There's nothing clumsy about your fingers," she murmured, leaning into his touch. "But we shouldn't be doing this. I already told you that last night."

"We have done it before, my love."

Only in her dreams, she thought, inhaling shakily as her heartbeat pounded in her ears. She knew there were plenty of reasons why she should stop him. And as soon as her brain was working again, she'd probably come up with a few. But the touch of his hands on her flesh felt *right*. Too right to question. And the sense of well-being she'd awakened with was deepening with every second that passed.

This was a man who would be all too easy to love.

The hooks gave way with a barely audible click. Conyn gave a low groan and cupped her breasts in his hands.

The pounding of her heart grew louder.

"Nay," he whispered. "Not now."

Alanna arched her back. Her pulse beat so hard, it sounded just like knuckles rapping against a door.

Conyn muttered a short, sharp word in a language that she didn't recognize, but she could tell by the tone that it was an oath. He lifted his head. "Is there a guard in this dwelling?"

"Mmm? No."

He frowned and glanced over his shoulder.

Another series of staccato raps sounded in her ears. And Alanna finally realized that it was more than her pulse. "Oh, no," she said. "Someone's at the door."

Conyn repeated the oath, then gave her breasts a gentle squeeze and slid from the bed. "Do not move," he said. "I will return." He bent down to pick something up from the floor. It was his sword.

"Conyn? What are you going to do?"

He slid the sword from its sheath. The iron blade glinted with deadly purpose in the morning sunlight. "You have no guard. I must check there is no enemy."

Alanna made a futile grab for him. "Conyn, wait."

"I have waited long enough to make a sane man mad, my love," he muttered, striding from the room.

"Conyn!" She wriggled off the bed, her feet tangling in the folds of the sheet. Grabbing one end, she wrapped it around herself toga-fashion and hurried after him. "It's probably only one of my neighbors," she called. "Or my friend Fleur."

"Then I will teach some manners to whoever dares interrupt us when we are in our bed." Holding his weapon level with his shoulder, Conyn grasped the doorknob and flung open the door.

Alanna skidded to a halt. "Oh, no," she breathed.

The man on the threshold looked from Conyn to his sword, his jaw going slack. His typically pale complexion turned waxen as he took a stumbling step backward. "I say!"

"State your business or be gone," Conyn growled, bracing his legs apart as he drew himself up to his full height.

"I . . . I . . ." The other man swallowed hard, his Adam's apple bobbing against his tightly buttoned collar. His hand rose to the knot of his tie. "I must have the wrong apartment. I was looking for Alanna Moore."

Conyn didn't move. "She does not wish to be disturbed."

Disturbed? Alanna thought wildly, pulling the sheet more tightly across her breasts as she moved closer to Conyn. However one defined the word, it definitely applied to her already.

Her visitor took another step back, peering around Conyn's bulk. "Alanna?" His gaze darted to the sword again. "Er, is everything all right?"

She had a crazy desire to laugh. All right? Oh, sure. Things couldn't be better. She was dressed in little more than a sheet while a stranger who claimed to be a time-travelling warrior was threatening her fiancé with a three-foot length of razor-sharp antique iron. . . .

Her whirling thoughts came to a stop with a sickening lurch. Grasping Conyn's arm for balance, she leaned to the side and stared at the man on her doorstep.

Her fiancé.

Reginald Ainsworth III.

The man she had promised to marry. Today.

5

How could she have forgotten? Alanna asked herself. The wedding had been planned for months. She'd thought it all through logically. It was a sensible decision. It was what she wanted to do. The church was booked, her dress was paid for, the caterer was probably icing the cake at this very moment.

Oh, God. What was she going to do? She had completely forgotten about Reginald.

And according to Conyn, she had completely forgotten about him, too.

She seemed to have a serious problem keeping track of her fiancés lately.

"What is your business here?" Conyn demanded, the tip of his sword aimed at Reginald's silver tie clip.

It didn't seem possible, but Reginald turned even paler. He glanced toward the elevators and started to inch sideways. "Excuse me, perhaps I should be going."

"Conyn, please," Alanna said, tugging on his sword arm. "You can't go around threatening people with that thing or you'll end up in jail." She waited until he had lowered the weapon, then summoned up what she hoped

was a reassuring smile. "Reginald, come in. We were
. . . having breakfast."

"I really can't stay, Alanna," he said, continuing to
inch away. "Mother's flight is due to arrive in fifteen
minutes and you know how she hates to be kept waiting."

Alanna rubbed her eyes. Reginald's mother. Mrs. Reginald Ainsworth II. Yes, they had planned to meet her
at the airport together. "Uh, I don't think that it would
be convenient for me to come with you," she said.

"I see." Reginald brushed at the front of his suit.
"Alanna, are you sure everything is all right? You don't
seem quite yourself today."

"I, uh . . ."

He looked from her to Conyn, then stared pointedly
at her slipping sheet. "I'm aware you are still technically
a single woman, Alanna, but I hope you won't embarrass
us this way in the future."

She hadn't expected Reginald to fly into a jealous rage
at the sight of his fiancée in a compromising situation.
After all, they had both admitted that they didn't love
each other. But his lack of passion was somehow too
. . . civilized. "Uh . . ."

"You will get rid of this person before the wedding,
won't you? Mother wouldn't approve of his sort."

"Wedding?" Conyn asked, glancing sideways at her.
"How does he know we are to wed today?"

"Um . . ."

"I've heard steroids damage the brain," Reginald
said, regaining his courage now that he considered himself out of Conyn's reach. "So I understand why he
might be confused. Alanna, you did tell your, er, friend
here that you're engaged to be married, didn't you?"

"There is naught amiss with my brain," Conyn said,
turning back to Reginald. "I care not for the tone you
use when you address my bride."

"*Your* bride?" Reginald gave his head a slight shake.

Not one of his perfectly moussed and styled hairs moved out of place. "My dear sir, Alanna is *my* fiancée. We will be married this afternoon at Trinity Church."

Conyn reacted immediately. Seizing Reginald by his shirtfront, he lifted him up and slammed him against the corridor wall. "You lie," he said. "She is my bride. We are destined for each other."

Alanna grabbed Conyn's arm and tried in vain to loosen his hold, but as she'd already discovered, his muscles were as inflexible as steel. "Conyn! Don't hurt him."

"I know not what mischief this pale worm of a man hopes to stir," Conyn said. "But nothing will stop our wedding this time."

"Help!" Reginald gasped, clawing at Conyn's hand. Up and down the corridor, the doors to several other apartments were beginning to crack open. "Someone, please help me!"

"Conyn, please!" Alanna urged. "Please, put him down."

"First he must retract the lie."

"But he's not lying," she said. "Reginald and I *are* engaged."

Conyn's fist tightened on Reginald's shirt until his knuckles were white. A button popped off and bounced to the floor. "Nay, Alanna," he said hoarsely. "Tell me it is not so."

"It's true. Oh, Conyn. I'm sorry. I never meant to hurt your feelings. I just . . . forgot."

Still holding Reginald up with one hand, Conyn moved his gaze to Alanna. "Nay," he whispered.

Her eyes stung as she met his gaze. Conyn had never tried to hide his feelings from her, and what he felt now was mercilessly clear. His eyes snapped with a mixture of anger and betrayal, his lips were thinned into a tight line, as if he struggled to hold back a cry of pain. Every muscle was quivering with tension in his battle to control his emotions. And despite the strength that was so evident in his body, he looked fragile enough to shatter.

"Oh, Conyn," she murmured, pressing her face against his chest. "I'm sorry. I'm so sorry."

His ribs rose as he inhaled unsteadily. "Why, Alanna? Why did you not wait for me?"

What could she say? That she hadn't known he was coming? That she hadn't believed in love in the first place? That she figured it would be better to marry a man she didn't love rather than spend the rest of her life alone? Hadn't she wanted the security of marriage and a family to belong to at any price?

The Ainsworths were rich. To them, wealth and position were what mattered the most. She and Reginald got along well, but she knew he didn't have tender feelings for her; he only wanted an appropriate wife, someone who wouldn't embarrass him, someone who would enhance his social standing.

She swallowed a sob. Conyn had told her that her parents were rich, and they hadn't cared about her feelings. Wealth and position had mattered the most to them.

Was she seeking out the same kind of family she had grown up in? Was her fear of love and all its pain driving her to accept the fate she'd refused before?

No, that was all just a story. Right? *Right?*

The murmur of voices in the hallway finally penetrated her thoughts. Alanna looked around. Her neighbors were watching with interest from their doorways. She tugged up her drooping sheet. "Conyn, we need to talk."

"First I must kill this worm."

"No! Conyn, no!"

"Then you care for him?"

"Yes, but that's not the point. You have to let him go."

Conyn slowly eased Reginald down until his feet touched the floor, then sheathed his sword and contemptuously turned his back on him. "Do you prefer a man like that, Alanna? Have you changed so much?"

"I haven't changed, Conyn. I'm still me. Alanna Moore. I'm a reasonable, independent, modern woman with a responsible job and a briefcase full of degrees. I'm not this person you remember from your past." She reached up to touch Conyn's tightly clenched jaw. "Give me a chance to explain. Things have happened so fast."

"Nay, it is not fast. Our lives have been linked together for twenty-three centuries."

She dropped her hand, distressed by the hardness in his voice. "Conyn . . ."

"I gave up my world for you. My wealth. My future. I gave up my time because I cared not what happened to me if I could not see my Alanna again. I crossed a distance unimaginable to make you my bride." His throat worked as he swallowed. "And now I find you wish to give yourself to another."

"But I was already engaged before I met you."

He flicked his hand toward the spot where Reginald was cringing against the wall. "I said I would be whatever you wish me to be, Alanna. But do not ask me to be a man like the sniveling grub you have chosen."

"Conyn, please," she repeated helplessly. "I feel differently about things today. If we could talk it over . . ."

"You said that you did not know me, my love. Perhaps it is I who do not know you."

"But—"

Without warning, he caught her in a hard embrace, burying his face against her hair. His tall frame shook as he held her against him. They remained like that for a timeless moment. Then he set her back on her feet and reached up to unfasten the gold torque from his neck. He placed the artifact in her hand. "I did not give everything to the old woman. This I kept for you. It is your wedding gift."

She closed her fingers over the gold, feeling the heat from his body. Tingles shot over her skin, raising the fine hairs on her arm. A cool breeze swept through the doorway of her apartment, and in the distance there was a rumble like thunder. She staggered back. "Conyn?"

He took his cloak from her closet, flung it over his shoulders, and turned away.

"*Conyn!*"

Without a backward glance, he walked out her door, strode to the end of the corridor, and went down the stairs.

Alanna stood where she was. Too many images were clamoring in her brain. Fragments of dreams, pieces of fantasies, bits of memory—everything was tumbling together in total confusion until one thought burned through the rest. He was leaving her.

Again.

"Conyn, no!" Alanna cried, gathering up the sheet to run after him. "Conyn, come back!"

She reached the stairwell, her blood pumping painfully in her lungs. There was no sound from below. But he always walked quickly. Just as he had when he'd crossed the bridge and taken the path to the mountains. . . .

"No, Conyn," she called. Her voice echoed hollowly down the stairs. "Conyn!"

But she knew he was gone. She sensed his absence like a shadow in her heart. She blinked hard, feeling the heat of tears on her cheeks. "Conyn," she breathed, the strength gone from her voice. She sank down to her knees, leaning her forehead against the cold metal railing. Tears splashed on her hands and on the gold neck torque she held. She lifted it to her face.

And that's when she saw the whimsical design that had been etched at the base of the twin knobs.

A stag and a doe. Two halves of one whole. Joined for all time.

Choking back a sob, she grasped the matching brace-let. For twelve hours, she hadn't been able to get this off, no matter how hard she had tried. But now it slid effortlessly over her wrist. And the loss that stabbed through her knocked the air from her lungs.

Our love was too strong for fate to keep us apart. Even my gifts were destined to find you.

But it had only been a story and mixed-up pieces of dreams. How could she be feeling this much pain over a man she'd known less than a day?

Holding Conyn's gifts to her breasts, she keeled over and wept.

It was amazingly easy to cancel a wedding. Who would have thought that an event that had taken months to plan could be stopped with no more than a few phone calls?

Alanna shifted the ice bag over her eyes and stretched out on the couch. Another tear trickled from beneath her swollen lids and she wiped it away impatiently. She would have thought that her tears would have dried up by now. It had been five hours. And yet they showed no sign of slowing down.

Her friends had been right to try to talk her out of marrying Reginald. The whole idea had been a mistake from the start. She'd be crazy to marry a man she didn't love merely to find some kind of home. What was a home without love to fill it? What was a family without love to bind it together?

Thank God she'd figured that out in time. And it was all because of Conyn. He had made her believe in love again. He'd shown her that love could give a person strength and purpose and that anything was possible. . . .

She wiped her cheeks again and tossed the ice bag on the floor. Anything? Including time travel?

The telephone rang suddenly and Alanna groaned. Hadn't she already spoken with everyone that she knew?

Pushing herself up, she leaned her elbows on her knees and stared at the phone.

There was only one person she wanted to talk to, and she wasn't sure if he knew how to use a telephone.

But why should Conyn want to talk to her, anyway? Delusion or not, she had broken his heart. How would *she* feel if she believed she'd given up everything she'd known and had been transported a few millennia ahead in time only to find out that her one true love had promised to marry someone else?

She sniffed, rubbing her wet cheeks with her knuckles. With a resigned sigh, she reached out and picked up the phone.

"Alanna, are you all right? I just got back from the hairdresser's when I found your message on my machine."

"Hello, Fleur," she said, slumping back on the couch.

"Is it true? The wedding's off?"

"Yes, it's true."

There was a pause. "I don't know what to say. Would you be offended if I let loose with a few yee-hahs?"

Alanna's lips trembled into a watery smile. "No, I wouldn't be offended. You're a good friend. I should have listened to you months ago."

"Back to my first question—are you all right? I mean, really. I can be there in ten minutes."

"Thanks, Fleur, but I'm fine. I didn't love Reginald. You only get hurt if you love someone," she said, thinking of the expression she'd last seen on Conyn's face. She sniffed again.

"Do you need any help with the fallout? There must be a million details to handle."

"No, it wasn't that hard. Reginald was a big help."

"Reginald?"

"We had a . . . discussion this morning and we both decided that we weren't what the other was looking for. He and his mother both agreed the marriage was ill-considered. Mrs. Reginald Ainsworth the second was only too happy to notify the guests.''

"Excuse me for saying this, but I've been holding it in for a long time. Reginald's a worm.''

Alanna hiccupped. "That's what Conyn called him.''

"Who?''

She licked away a tear that had trickled down to the corner of her mouth. "Fleur, you didn't by any chance arrange a surprise visitor for me last night, did you?''

"What do you mean?''

"Someone from that strip club you had invited me to?''

"Heck, no! But I wish I'd thought of it. Why? What happened?''

"It's a long story,'' Alanna said. "Tell me, Fleur, how long do you think it takes to fall in love?''

"Hey, you're talking to a dyed-in-the-wool romantic here. I'd say it can be anything from years to days to minutes. Why? You're not thinking of giving Reginald another chance, are you?''

"No.''

"Well, I believe true love is worth holding out for, Alanna. At the risk of sounding like the lyrics to some corny song, it's what makes the world go round.''

"And if you met a man who had been deeply in love with a woman who had died, do you think he might be able to love again?''

"Depends on the man. Now you've really got me curious. What's going on?''

"I think I've fallen in love, Fleur.''

"When? Who?''

"I don't know when. And I'm not sure who he is. But he's a sensitive, smart, passionate man who for some reason is convinced that he loves me.''

"Alanna, if I didn't know you better, I'd be worried that you're suffering from some kind of delusion.''

"I know exactly what you mean, Fleur. There's a lot of that going around."

She hung up the phone then groped for a box of tissues and pulled out a handful to dry her face.

And she remembered how hot and wet Conyn's tears had felt when he'd dried them on her cheek.

Would he be able to love again? Once he came to his senses and realized that the woman he'd confused her with was really gone, would he be willing to risk giving his heart so completely once more? She hoped so. Even in the short time they'd spent together, she could see that he was intelligent, honest, open, courageous, and considerate, and he deserved to find some happiness.

So had she fallen in love with Conyn? Probably. It was more than his looks or his spectacular body. It was the way his dimples softened the harsh lines of his face when he smiled and how his eyes twinkled when he joked. It was his uninhibited enjoyment of life. It was the way his touch felt so right . . . as if they'd been made for each other.

Two halves of one whole.

But he was gone, and she had no idea how to find him again. When she had returned to her apartment, it had taken almost twenty minutes to calm Reginald down and convince her neighbors that there was no need to call the police. By the time she had finally pulled on some clothes so she could go outside to look for Conyn, he was nowhere in sight. She had searched the area around her building for an hour, checking all the stores and restaurants, every alley and bus shelter—but to no avail.

How could a six-foot-two long-haired leanly muscled half-naked man in leather pants and hide boots simply disappear? Unless there happened to be a circle of standing stones in the park that she hadn't known about. . . .

No. He was an eccentric antiquities scholar who was observant and intuitive and was a phenomenal guesser.

There was no such thing as time travel, right?

Just as there was no such thing as love?

But he'd handled that sword as if he'd done it every day of his life. And he'd effortlessly picked Reginald up with one hand. And his appetite for food was as genuine and primitive as his appetite for her.

Wadding the tissues into a ball, she dabbed her eyes and took a bracing breath. She had been through this before. Her mind might have been fuzzy yesterday from those stray fantasy images, and her reasoning might have been impaired by the incredibly strong attraction she felt toward Conyn, but it was high time she stopped avoiding the issue of what was and wasn't and discover the truth.

She picked up her purse, looking through it until she found her copy of the packing slip from the shipment of artifacts that had arrived at the museum. She carefully pressed out the creases, then squinting at the number on the return address, picked up the phone and dialed.

The phone rang nine times before it was answered by a gruff-sounding man who said something unintelligible.

Alanna checked the number on the slip, then cleared her throat. "Excuse me, I'm looking for the Bern Museum."

"We are closed," the man said in heavily accented English.

Grimacing, Alanna looked at her watch. Of course, with the time difference, it would be late evening in Switzerland. "I'm sorry. I'm trying to get in touch with someone from the antiquities department."

"Pardon?"

"It's concerning a shipment of Celtic artifacts. I'm calling from Toronto."

"Ah. You want exhibit director."

"Fine. Could you give me his number?"

"Her. She is Gerta Mueller."

"Thank you. Could I possibly have her number?"

"She is still here."

"Oh. May I speak with her?"

"I put you through," he said. There was a series of clicks, then the phone started to ring again. Alanna tried not to think about what the overseas connection was costing her. She should have done this before now. Perhaps if she'd checked out her theory about Conyn's identity earlier, things might not have gone so far. Instead of playing into his fantasy, she could have gotten him the medical help he needed.

A woman came on the line. "Mueller."

"Hello, Miss Mueller," Alanna said. "I'm Alanna Moore calling from Toronto."

"Ah, Miss Moore," the woman said immediately. Her accent was almost imperceptible, a slight hardening of the consonants. "Did the shipment arrive without trouble?"

"Yes, it arrived yesterday, thanks."

"Good. I stayed late to supervise the packing myself."

"The pieces in the exhibit are exceptional. They all came through in perfect condition."

"Very good." She paused. "Is there something I can help you with?"

"Well, actually I'm hoping to get some information."

"There was complete documentation with each item, wasn't there?"

"Yes, but I'm curious about the people who worked on it. Would you have a man named Conyn ap Rhys on your staff? I believe he works in your museum, most likely as an antiquities expert. Or perhaps he might have been employed there recently."

"I have been in charge of the museum's antiquities department for twenty-three years, and I am sure that we have never had anyone on staff named ap Rhys."

Alanna frowned. Maybe it wasn't his real name. "Perhaps you'll recognize him if I describe him. He appears to be in his mid-thirties and is about six foot two, very muscular, has blue eyes and long, auburn hair and a series of thin scars on his chest.''

There was a short silence. ''Is this a joke?''

''No, not at all, Ms. Mueller. Do you know who he is?''

''If I had such a man working here, Miss Moore, I would have noticed.'' She laughed. ''And if you have one to spare, please send him over.''

She thought quickly. ''Perhaps he's a local historian. Would you know if anyone was particularly interested in that exhibit?''

More laughter. ''Do you have any historians in Toronto who look like that?''

''Um, not that I know of.''

''As I said, I have been here for twenty-three years, and if anyone had expressed interest in those Celtic artifacts, I would have been the person he would have spoken with, as several pieces remained in our storeroom because of lack of appropriate display space.''

If not all of the pieces were on display, then how could Conyn have such detailed knowledge about every one of them? Alanna chewed her lip briefly. ''Were the gold neck torque and the matching bracelet on display?''

''Pardon?''

''The neck torque. It has the engraving of the stag on one knob and the doe on the other, like the bracelet.''

Another silence. ''Miss Moore, there were no pieces like that in the shipment which I packed.''

Shaken, Alanna terminated the call and dropped her head into her hands. All right. Conyn wasn't a stripper that Fleur had sent. He hadn't worked in the museum in Bern, either. And the gold artifacts he'd left with her weren't part of the collection.

There had to be a logical explanation. There had to be. And as soon as she thought of one, she'd . . .

She'd what? What did she think would change when she found out the truth? Conyn would still be the same man. And whoever he was, she wanted to see him. No, she wanted a lot more than that. She wanted to run to him and throw herself into his arms and hold him as if she'd never let him go and tell him that he could love again and beg him to give her the chance to show him.

Why did she need a logical explanation, anyway? Why did she have to think? Her decision to marry Reginald had been the result of careful, logical thinking, and it had been a huge mistake. Reason didn't apply when it came to matters of the heart.

What does your heart tell you?

Her heart? She hadn't wanted to listen to it last night, because she didn't want to believe in love.

But Conyn had made her believe.

And her heart was telling her to find him.

But she had looked before, and there hadn't been any trace of him.

Yes, well, then she'd better look again. If he believed he had journeyed across twenty-three centuries to find her, couldn't she at least cross the city?

Alanna walked up the church steps, her shoes gritting over the worn stone where thirty-two years ago the official records of her life had begun. She pushed open the heavy door. The creak echoed loudly from the vaulted ceiling and she paused to let her eyes adjust to the gloom.

Thankfully, Reginald's mother had obviously been true to her word about spreading the message that the wedding was cancelled. The pews were empty. It must have been too late to stop the florist, though—sprays of flowers decorated the ends of each pew and two enormous bouquets rested at the front of the church. The sweet scent of roses and the tang of greenery wafted through the hushed air.

Alanna lifted her hand to touch the knobbed ends of the gold torque that circled her neck, then rubbed her fingers over her bracelet. It no longer caused the tingling reaction it did before. Nor was it stuck—since she had stopped fighting it, the gold sat passively against her skin, as if it belonged there.

Now that she knew these pieces weren't part of the museum's exhibit, she had no intention of parting with them. How Conyn had managed to get the bracelet into that crate before he'd arrived was yet another of those inexplicable things. And there were a lot of inexplicable things that had been happening lately. And there were so many inexplicable things. But Alanna was willing to accept them, because she was beginning to listen to her heart.

During the hours she had spent searching for Conyn, she had come to terms with her feelings. There was no longer any doubt in her mind that she loved him. As sudden as it seemed, it didn't cause her any distress. Instead, the feeling of . . . rightness that she had awakened with this morning continued to strengthen.

Whatever problems he might have, they would deal with them together. Alanna was so sure of this, she wouldn't care if his crazy story turned out to be true.

But first, she had to find him.

She moved up the aisle and slid into the first pew. Slanting rays from the setting sun probed weakly through the stained-glass windows. It would be dark soon. Where would Conyn spend the night? He had no money and no identification, and he wasn't familiar with the city. She hoped he would be all right.

Of course he would, she told herself. He was intelligent and resourceful. He'd find some way to get by. Simply because she hadn't been able to find him yet meant that she wasn't looking in the right places, that's all. She had checked the museum. She had checked the hospitals and the police stations and even the university. Yet she wasn't about to give up. And as soon as she had the opportunity to catch her breath, she'd start over again.

The door at the back of the church creaked open.

Alanna turned around and saw a tall man silhouetted in the doorway. She only had a glimpse of close-cropped hair, a neat suit, and a pale shirt before the door swung shut behind him. Solid footsteps echoed from the floor as he started to walk forward.

"I'm sorry," she said, getting to her feet. "You must be here for the wedding. I guess you didn't get the message."

He continued to approach, his footsteps getting nearer. He passed through a finger of sunlight as he walked by a window, his short hair gleaming like the leaves in October.

Alanna's heart thumped. The light must have picked up the tint of the stained glass. There was only one man she'd ever known who had hair that color. She moved into the aisle. "Conyn?" she whispered.

His stride was swift but relaxed, like the easy grace of a stalking predator. Even in the tailored suit, he projected an air of confidence that would be recognized in any culture or era. . . .

"Conyn!" she cried, breaking into a run.

He stopped and opened his arms. "Alanna, my love."

The flower-draped pews blurred as she raced past. All she could see was the smile of the man who stood waiting for her. She would know him anywhere, anytime, no matter how he was dressed. Laughing tearfully, she flung herself into his embrace.

Conyn lifted her from her feet and crushed her against him. "I made the merchants hasten and told the driver to go like the wind but I feared I would be too late again."

"Too late?"

"I came to stop the wedding. Where is the pale worm?"

"I don't know and I don't care," she said happily. "Oh, Conyn, I've been looking all over for you. I thought you'd left."

"I would never leave you, Alanna."

"Then where have you been?"

"You said you were a modern woman, so I thought to become a modern man for you."

"What?" She clasped her hands behind his neck and leaned back in his arms to get a better look at him.

The first thing she noticed was his hair. The ponytail was gone. His long, auburn locks had been cut to within an inch of his head. She hadn't believed it was possible, but the haircut made his chiseled features look more strikingly masculine than ever.

She dropped her gaze. Tailored gray pinstriped wool stretched over his broad shoulders. A crisp white shirt covered his chest, and a navy-blue silk tie was knotted at his throat. His clothes were tasteful, expensive, and extremely civilized.

Yet like his haircut, his clothes couldn't conceal the appealing warrior within.

"Does it not please you?" he asked. "The shopkeeper vowed it was what men wore in your world."

"You look wonderful, Conyn," she said, rubbing her fingers over his hair. "But you looked great before, too. How did you manage all of this? I thought you didn't have any money."

"I exchanged the gold coins in my pouch for paper."

"Gold . . ." She stared at him. "You had *gold* coins? That was your loose change?"

"Most were minted in Sparta, but your moneylender was eager to take them."

"Sparta . . ." She shook her head. "I'm not even going to ask. I don't care. All that matters is that I found you. Oh, Conyn, there's so much I want to say."

"And I, too." He eased her away from him, settling his hands on her waist. "Alanna, it matters not to me if you never remember our past love. In my joy over seeing you once more, I lacked patience. I beg you to let me woo you anew, as if we truly are meeting now for the first time." He smiled. "I wager I will make you love me again."

"Oh, Conyn," she said. "I already do."

"You . . ." The knot of his tie bobbed as he swallowed hard. "Alanna?"

"I love you, Conyn." Framing his face with her hands, she rose up on her toes and kissed him.

The scent of pine and sunshine rose around her. A low rumble vibrated through the floor and something flashed just on the border of her vision. A familiar sweet taste stole over her tongue. . . .

And she remembered the last time she had kissed him. They had stood on the bridge over the river. She had begged him to stay, but he had been immovable. He had told her that only by being apart now could they hope to be together later. And she'd known he was right. Earning the wealth her father demanded was the only hope for their future. If she had defied her parents' wishes and married Conyn then, she knew her father would never have harmed her because she was too valuable an asset to him; but he would have seen to it that the poor orphan she loved would disappear.

Yes, Conyn had been right, but she had thrown herself at him and hit him with her fists when he'd met her to say good-bye. He had waited until her weeping was spent, then he'd kissed her with a passion that had burned brighter than the stars in the heavens. They had clung to each other in desperate, heartbroken yearning. And he had sworn by the power of their love and the life in his veins that he would come back to her.

She gasped and pulled back her head. This wasn't a dream. It wasn't a fantasy. It was as real as the man who held her.

Conyn smiled and kissed her. Again.

And she remembered everything. The flowers in the meadows and the fossils on the riverbank and white-haired Granny Ula with her onions. A lifetime of images burst into her head, surging into every corner of her mind to fill her soul with the missing part of herself.

It was true. All of it. She knew who she was. She knew how she had died. And by some miracle, she had been given a second chance.

Tears filled her eyes. Only this time, they were tears of happiness.

Conyn lifted her up and spun her around, his lips moving over her face as he kissed everywhere he could reach. "Alanna, my love. I have waited an eternity to hear you say those words to me again."

"Then marry me, Conyn. Now. Here." She laughed as her tears fell on his cheeks. "The church is booked. The flowers are paid for. I even have a wedding dress in the back of my closet."

"Alanna, I love you."

"I love you, too, Conyn. I always have," she said against his lips. "And I always will."

If you enjoyed *Veils of Time*
you won't want to miss

IREBIRD

The stunning novel from *Janice Graham*

One

So far as we know, no modern poet has written of the Flint Hills, which is surprising since they are perfectly attuned to his lyre. In their physical characteristics they reflect want and despair. A line of low-flung hills stretching from the Osage Nation on the south to the Kaw River on the north, they present a pinched and frowning face to those who gaze on them. Their verbiage is scant. Jagged rocks rise everywhere to their surface. The Flint Hills never laugh. In the early spring, when the sparse grass first turns to green upon them, they smile saltily and sardonically. But as spring turns to summer, they grow sullen again and hopeless. Death is no stranger to them.

—JAY E. HOUSE
Philadelphia Public Ledger (1931)

ETHAN BROWN WAS in love with the Flint Hills. His father had been a railroad man, not a rancher, but you would have thought he had been born into a dynasty of men connected to this land, the way he loved it. He loved it the way certain peoples love their homeland, with a spiritual dimension, like the Jews love Jerusalem and the Irish their Emerald Isle. He had never loved a woman quite like this, but that was about to change.

He was, at this very moment, ruminating on the idea of marriage as he sat in the passenger seat of the sheriff's car, staring gloomily at the bloodied, mangled carcass of a calf lying in the headlights in the middle of the road. Ethan's long, muscular legs were thrust under the dashboard and his hat brushed the roof every time he turned his head, but Clay's car was a lot warmer than Ethan's truck, which took forever to heat up. Ethan poured a cup of coffee from a scratched metal thermos his father had carried on the Santa Fe line on cold October nights like this, and passed it to the sheriff.

"Thanks."

"You bet."

They looked over the dashboard at the calf; there was nowhere else to look.

"I had to shoot her. She was still breathin'," said Clay apologetically.

"You did the right thing."

"I don't like to put down other men's animals, but she was sufferin'."

Ethan tried to shake his head, but his hat caught. "Nobody's gonna blame you. Tom'll be grateful to you."

"I sure appreciate your comin' out here in the middle of the night. I can't leave this mess out here. Just beggin' for another accident."

"The guy wasn't hurt?"

"Naw. He was a little shook up, but he had a big four-wheeler, comin' back from a huntin' trip. Just a little fender damage."

She was a small calf, but it took the two men some mighty effort to heave her stiff carcass into the back of Ethan's truck. Then Clay picked up his markers and flares, and the two men headed home along the county road that wound through the prairie.

As Ethan drove along, his eyes fell on the bright pink hair clip on the dashboard. He had taken it out of Katie

Anne's hair the night before, when she had climbed on top of him. He remembered the way her hair had looked when it fell around her face, the way it smelled, the way it curled softly over her naked shoulders. He began thinking about her again and forgot about the dead animal in the bed of the truck behind him.

As he turned off on the road toward the Mackey ranch, Ethan noticed the sky was beginning to lighten. He had hoped he would be able to go back to bed, to draw his long, tired body up next to Katie Anne's, but there wouldn't be time now. He might as well stir up some eggs and make another pot of coffee because as soon as day broke he would have to be out on the range, looking for the downed fence. There was no way of telling where the calf had gotten loose; there were thousands of miles of fence. Thousands of miles.

ETHAN BROWN HAD met Katherine Anne Mackey when his father was dying of cancer, which was also the year he turned forty. Katie Anne was twenty-seven—old enough to keep him interested and young enough to keep him entertained. She was the kind of girl Ethan had always avoided when he was younger; she was certainly nothing like Paula, his first wife. Katie Anne got rowdy, told dirty jokes, and wore sexy underwear. She lived in the guest house on her father's ranch, a beautiful limestone structure with wood-burning fireplaces built against the south slope of one of the highest hills in western Chase County. Tom Mackey, her father, was a fifth-generation rancher whose ancestors had been among the first to raise cattle in the Flint Hills. Tom owned about half the Flint Hills, give or take a few hundred thousand acres, and, rumor had it, about half the state of Oklahoma, and he knew everything there was to know about cattle ranching.

Ethan had found himself drawn to Katie Anne's place; it was like a smaller version of the home he had always dreamed of building in the hills, and he would tear over there in his truck from his law office, his heart full and aching, and then Katie Anne would entertain him with her quick wit and her stock of cold beer and her soft, sexy body, and he would leave in the morning thinking how marvelous she was, with his heart still full and aching.

All that year Ethan had felt a terrible cloud over his head, a psychic weight that at times seemed tangible; he even quit wearing the cross and Saint Christopher's medal his mother had given him when he went away to college his freshman year, as though shedding the gold around his neck might lessen his spiritual burden. If Ethan had dared to examine his conscience honestly he might have eventually come to understand the nature of his malaise, but Katie Anne had come along, and the relief she brought enabled him to skim over the top of those painful months.

Once every two weeks he would visit his father in Abilene; always, on the drive back home, he felt that troubling sensation grow like the cancer that was consuming his father. On several occasions he tried to speak about it to Katie Anne; he ventured very tentatively into these intimate waters with her, for she seemed to dislike all talk about things sad and depressing. He yearned to confess his despair, to understand it and define it, and maybe ease a little the terrible anguish in his heart. But when he would broach the subject, when he would finally begin to say the things that meant something to him, Katie Anne would grow terribly distracted. In the middle of his sentence she would stand up and ask him if he wanted another beer. "I'm still listening," she would toss at him sweetly. Or she would decide to clear the table at that moment. Or set the alarm clock. Mostly, it was her eyes. Ethan was very good at reading eyes. He often wished he weren't. He noticed an immediate change in her eyes, the way they glazed over, pulled her just out of range of hearing as soon as he brought up the subject of his father.

Occasionally, when Ethan would come over straight from a visit to Abilene, she would politely ask about the old man, and Ethan would respond with a terse comment such as, "Well, he's pretty grumpy," or "He's feeling a little better." But she didn't want to hear any more than that, so after a while he quit trying to talk about it. Ethan didn't like Katie Anne very much when her eyes began to dance away from him, when she fidgeted and thought about other things and pretended to be listening, although her eyes didn't pretend very well. And Ethan wanted very much to like Katie Anne. There was so much about her he did like.

Katie Anne, like her father, was devoted to the animals and the prairie lands that sustained them. Her knowledge of ranching almost equaled his. The Mackeys were an intelligent, educated family, and occasionally, on a quiet evening in her parents' company when the talk turned to more controversial issues such as public access to the Flint Hills or environmentalism, she would surprise Ethan with her perspicacity. These occasional glimpses of a critical edge to her mind, albeit all too infrequent, led him to believe there was another side to her nature that could, with time and the right influence, be brought out and nurtured. Right away Ethan recognized her remarkable gift for remaining touchingly feminine and yet very much at ease around the crude, coarse men who populated her world. She was the first ranch hand he had ever watched castrate a young bull wearing pale pink nail polish.

So that summer, while his father lay dying, Ethan and Katie Anne talked about ranching, about the cattle, about the land; they talked about country music, about the new truck Ethan was going to buy. They drank a lot of beer and barbecued a lot of steaks with their friends, and Ethan even got used to watching her dance with other guys at the South Forty, where they spent a lot of time on weekends. Ethan hated to dance, but Katie Anne danced with a sexual energy he had never seen in a woman. She loved to be watched. And she was good. There wasn't a step she didn't know or a partner she couldn't keep up with. So Ethan would sit and drink with his buddies while Katie Anne danced, and the guys would talk about what a goddamn lucky son of a bitch he was.

Then his father died, and although Ethan was with him in those final hours, even though he'd held the old man's hand and cradled his mother's head against his strong chest while she grieved, there nevertheless lingered in Ethan's mind a sense of things unresolved, and Katie Anne, guilty by association, somehow figured into it all.

Three years had passed since then, and everyone just assumed they would be married. Several times Katie Anne had casually proposed dates to him, none of which Ethan had taken seriously. As of yet there was no formal engagement, but Ethan was making his plans. Assiduously, carefully, very cautiously, the way he proceeded in law, he was building the life he had always dreamed of. He had never moved from the rather inconvenient third-floor attic office in the old Salmon P. Chase House that he had leased upon his arrival in Cottonwood Falls, fresh on the heels of his divorce, but this was no indication of his success. His had grown to a shamefully lucrative practice. Chase Countians loved Ethan Brown, not only for his impressive academic credentials and his faultless knowledge of the law, but because he was a man of conscience. He was also a man's man, a strong man with callused hands and strong legs that gripped the flanks of a horse with authority.

Now, at last, his dreams were coming true. From the earnings of his law practice he had purchased his land and was building his house. In a few years he would be able to buy a small herd. It was time to get married.

Two

Ethan pulled the string of barbed wire tight and looped it around the stake he had just pounded back into the ground. It was a windy day and the loose end of wire whipped wildly in his hand. It smacked him across the cheek near his eye and he flinched. He caught the loose end with a a gloved hand and finished nailing it down, then he removed his glove and wiped away the warm blood that trickled down his face.

As he untied his horse and swung up into the saddle he thought he caught a whiff of fire. He lifted his head into the wind and sniffed the air, his nostrils twitching like sensitive radar seeking out an intruder. But he couldn't find the smell again. It was gone as quickly as it had come. Perhaps he had only imagined it.

He dug his heels into the horse's ribs and took off at a trot, following the fence as it curved over the hills. This was not the burning season, and yet the hills seemed to be aflame in their burnished October garb. The copper-colored grasses, short after a long summer's grazing, stood out sharply against the fiercely blue sky. They reminded Ethan of the short-cropped head of a red-haired boy on his first day back at school, all trim and clean and embarrassed.

From the other side of the fence, down the hill toward the highway, came a bleating sound. *Not another one*, he thought. It was past two in the afternoon, and he had a desk piled with work waiting for him in town, but he turned his horse around and rode her up to the top of the hill, where he could see down into the valley below.

He had forgotten all about Emma Fergusen's funeral until that moment when he looked down on the Old Cemetery, an outcropping of modest tombstones circumscribed by a rusty chain-link fence. It stood out in the middle of nowhere; the only access was a narrow black-top county road. But this afternoon the side of the road was lined with trucks and cars, and the old graves were obscured by mourners of the newly dead. The service was over. As he watched, the cemetery emptied, and within a few minutes there were only the black limousine from the mortuary and a little girl holding the hand of a woman in black who stood looking down into the open grave. Ethan had meant to attend the funeral. He was handling Emma Fergusen's estate and her will was sitting on top of a pile of folders in his office. But the dead calf had seized his attention. The loss, about $500, was Tom Mackey's, but it was all the same to Ethan. Tom Mackey was like a father to him.

Ethan shifted his gaze from the mourners and scanned the narrow stretch of bottomland. He saw the heifer standing in a little tree-shaded gully just below the cemetery. To reach her he would have to jump the fence or ride two miles to the next gate. He guided the mare back down the hill and stopped to study the ground to determine the best place to jump. The fence wasn't high, but the ground was treacherous. Hidden underneath the smooth russet-colored bed of grass lay rock outcroppings and potholes: burrows, dens, things that could splinter a horse's leg like a matchstick, all of them obscured by the deceptive harmony of waving grasses. Ethan found a spot that looked safe but he got down off his horse and walked the approach, just to make sure. He spread apart the barbed wire and slipped through to check out the other side. When he got back up on his horse he glanced down at the cemetery again. He had hoped the woman and child would be gone, but they were still standing by the grave. *That would be Emma's daughter*, he thought in passing. *And her granddaughter*. Ethan's heartbeat quickened but he didn't give himself time to fret. He settled his mind and whispered to his horse, then he kicked her flanks hard, and within a few seconds he felt her pull her forelegs underneath and with a mighty surge of strength from her powerful hind legs sail into the air.

T HE WOMAN LOOKED up just as the horse appeared in the sky and she gasped. It seemed frozen there in space for the longest time, a black, deep-chested horse outlined against the blue sky, and then hooves hit the ground with a thud, and the horse and rider thundered down the slope of the hill.

"*Maman!*" cried the child in awe. "*Tu as vu ça?*"

The woman was still staring, speechless, when she heard her father call from the limousine.

"Annette!"

She turned around.

"You can come back another time," her father called in a pinched voice.

Annette took one last look at her mother's grave and knew she would never come back. She held out her hand to her daughter and they walked together to the limousine.